CAGED TO KILL

LAWYER DAVID THOMPSON LEGAL THRILLERS SERIES BOOK 2

TOM SWYERS

HILLCREST HOUSE PUBLISHING

Hillcrest House Publishing

New York

ISBN: 978-1-941440-03-2

For those who have served or who are serving sentences in solitary confinement without remedy.

Please forgive us for torturing you.

EPIGRAPH

Any imposition of solitary confinement beyond 15 days constitutes torture.

—Juan E. Méndez, United Nations special rapporteur, August 5, 2011.

~

First thing you notice is that it's anything but quiet. You're immersed in a drone of garbled noise—other inmates' blaring TVs, distant conversations, shouted arguments, I couldn't make sense of any of it, and I was left feeling twitchy and paranoid, I kept waiting for the lights to turn off, to signal the end of the day. But the lights did not shut off. . . . I sat with my mind. How long would it take before Ad Seg [solitary] chipped that away? I don't know, but I'm confident that it would be a battle I would lose.

—Raemisch, Rick, Former Executive Director, Colorado Department of Corrections, "My Night in Solitary." *The New York Times*, February 20, 2014.

~

Senator Gustavo Rivera: "Do you know a gentleman by the name of Rick Raemisch? Rick Raemisch is the Corrections Commissioner for the State of Colorado."

Anthony Annucci: "Oh, yeah, yeah, yeah. I know, Colorado."

Senator Gustavo Rivera: "One thing that I would suggest as he did, he actually spent 24 hours at a SHU [solitary housing unit]."

Anthony Annucci: "Yes, I know that."

Senator Gustavo Rivera "And I would suggest that's one of the things maybe you should do as well . . . ."

Anthony Annucci: "It would probably be the best night's sleep I'd had in a long time."

(Laughter)

—*New York State Joint Budget Hearing on Public Protection* (January 30, 2018) (conversation between New York Senator, Gustavo Rivera, and the Acting New York State Commissioner of the Department of Corrections and Community Supervision, Anthony Annucci).

PRAISE FOR CAGED TO KILL & READER NOTES

"Tom Swyers has written not just a suspenseful and chilling work of fiction, but an important treatise on solitary confinement and mass incarceration in America. Anyone interested in criminal justice reform should be prepared to have their eyes opened after reading *Caged to Kill.*"

~**Gilbert King**, Pulitzer Prize winner and *New York Times* bestselling author of *Devil in the Grove* and *Beneath a Ruthless Sun*

IMPORTANT NOTE TO THE READER:

Before jumping to any conclusions about whether the events in this book did or did not happen, or could or could not happen, readers are invited to research the name "Ewen Cameron" and project "MK-Ultra" and to also research the circumstance surrounding the alleged August, 2019 suicide of Mr. Jeffrey Epstein in a New York prison.

CHAPTER 1

Death was about to make a house call.

Convicted murderer Phillip Dawkins wasn't in his cell at Kranston Maximum Security Prison that day. He was on the run. Freedom had called his name. Dawkins should have been long dead—should have been executed—for killing a cop back in 1985 when he was nineteen. That's what the newspapers said. That's what the district attorney said. That's what Dawkins' smirking face on television said.

After pronouncing the sentence, the judge added that he'd personally drive him down to Sing Sing and pull the switch to watch him fry as Old Sparky's 615th victim.

But New York State didn't have a death penalty back in the '80s and still doesn't today. Instead, Dawkins was sentenced to the maximum penalty allowed by law: life without the possibility of parole.

An hour south of Kranston, lawyer David Thompson had just sat down facing the TV in his upstate New York home, located in suburban Indigo Valley. The house was empty and quiet, just the way he liked it on the weekends. The front doorbell was disconnected because that's where all the salespeople, politicians, and other undesirables came to call. Anyone who mattered to David knew to come to the side door. They knew to ring that doorbell because it was wired to work. The people who went to the front door could press the bell until hell froze over for all he cared. He'd find their flyers and brochures days later attached to the door handle and would respectfully recycle them.

David sat in his living room watching a Yankees preseason show on ESPN. On the day before Easter, it still felt like winter in Indigo Valley. Temperatures in the high thirties with a brisk 20 mph wind brought to mind snow showers, not May flowers. Easter wasn't a big deal in the Thompson household. Opening day for baseball, on the other hand, was a huge deal. That was Monday and it marked the official first day of spring as far as David was concerned.

When he first heard a tapping sound, he ignored it. He figured it was the wind whipping the utility wires against the house. But after a couple more rounds of three taps and a pause, he figured it must be something else.

Stupid woodpeckers.

He jumped off the couch and looked for inspiration—something to take outside and throw at them. The peckers loved to drill holes in his cedar clapboard siding—not to nest—but just for the hell of it. They left a rash of perfectly round holes like someone had shot a high-velocity rifle at the house. It was a yearly event in a decades-old war. But while he debated between throwing either a football or tennis ball at the bird, David saw the family's two cats, Ritz and Oreo, sitting patiently, wagging their tails, glaring at the front door. From his living room, through one of the front door's sidelights, he saw the outline of someone standing on the stoop.

On this Holy Saturday afternoon in 2015, Phillip Dawkins stood on David Thompson's front steps, tapping on the door with his index finger, the same way he used to tap away the time with his prison-issued pen. For hours on end, he'd tap that ink-filled cocktail straw on his steel bedframe. Like a metronome, mechanically and methodically, he'd mark the passage of his life sentence one tap at a time.

The dark walnut door of David's home sounded very different from the prison bedframe. No ding but rather a soft, hollow thud. Phillip Dawkins hadn't touched wood in thirty years. His life had been all steel and concrete. The sound, touch, and smell of the wood fascinated him and scared the crap out of him at the same time.

David headed to the door, ticked off that someone had interrupted his down time. He wanted to be left alone after the long work week. But Phillip Dawkins wanted Thompson, right then and there. He planned to tap all day and night, if that's what it took. The lifer on the stoop had plenty of practice at both tapping and waiting.

David opened the door and stared out at Dawkins. His visitor sported a beige leisure suit, right out of the late 1970s. In the early spring wind, it flapped like a used car lot banner around a physique that was both tall and cadaverous. The bony body was wrapped in alabaster white skin, the kind that showed no melanin whatsoever. His chestnut brown hair looked like he shared the same barber as Moe from *The Three Stooges*.

Who is this joker?

One thing was for sure--he was a tall one. David could look directly into the visitor's gray eyes only because of his position one step up on the door threshold. He didn't recognize this man. He couldn't place him in the context of his suburban home turf. He only knew the man from the inside of a prison because that's where he had last seen him years ago, and that's where David had left him to rot.

"Can I help you?" David asked.

"Hell-o, Mis—ter Thomp---son," Dawkins said in a rusty singsong. He hadn't spoken more than a handful of sentences aloud over the past few months; he wasn't familiar with the sound of his own voice. Not much call for conversation in a solitary cell, unless you were talking to yourself, and he did that often enough. He called Thompson by his surname because that's the way the correction officers—COs for short—said to address civilians in prison. It was something he had done rarely; maybe once every few years, when a reporter or a human rights lawyer came to visit him.

"Do . . . you re-mem-ber me?" Dawkins asked.

David looked at him closely now. He didn't recognize the face and wondered if his middle-aged brain was having a senior moment. "I'm sorry, I don't . . . ." But then David saw one of the man's hands rise to sheepishly wipe his dripping nose and David's stomach nearly turned over. The visitor's hands were huge; disproportionately large compared to the rest of his body. David could feel his entire body erupt in perspiration, panic spurting from every pore, as he leaped back from the threshold and slammed the door shut.

He recognized the hands and that's all he needed to know. They were the same hands that could totally engulf a basketball when Dawkins was a point-guard prospect for Syracuse University's basketball program in high school. They were the same hands that strangled Officer Pete Carlson in an

LSD-crazed rage back in 1985 in Syracuse, New York. Now David feared those hands were coming for him.

"What are you doing here?" David screamed through the door while his sweating hands fumbled for the deadbolt. He was relieved that Annie, his wife, and Christy, his teenage son, weren't at home. They were off visiting family across town.

"I'm out," Dawkins said.

"I can see that. I can't believe you *broke* out."

"I did not break out . . . ."

"Oh, so they just let you out through the front gate then?"

"Yes."

David didn't believe him. The idea that a man could be sentenced to life without parole for murdering a cop only to be set free couldn't be true. He thought Dawkins was trying to con him—to get him to open the door so he could jump him. "I don't buy it, Phillip. I'm calling the police."

"But I need your help."

"The last time I checked, harboring a known fugitive was a crime."

"Don't you get the news . . . paper?"

"What? What does that have to do with anything?"

"The story about me was in the paper."

"I only get the Sunday paper."

"What's today?" Phillip asked.

"Saturday."

"Really?" Dawkins said, stroking his chin thoughtfully. He had trouble keeping track of the days. It hadn't mattered what day it was in his life for an eternity. Every day had been the same for him, at least up until yesterday. He couldn't believe David only got the Sunday paper. Then Phillip couldn't believe he could remember that newspapers were a big deal when he was a kid. He hadn't thought about his childhood for decades. But now he remembered that everyone got the daily paper back then. "I didn't break out of prison. You can look it up on one of them fan-cy phone things." Dawkins had heard about cell phones, had spied a few in magazines, but he had never seen one for real before arriving at the Greyhound station.

With his back braced against the door, David took his cell phone out of his rear pocket, Googled Dawkins's name and checked the news. There was an article from *The Post Standard* out of Syracuse about Dawkins being set free by the work of lawyers from the Innocence Project using new technology. Officer Carlson put up a fight in 1985. The Innocence Project attorneys filed a motion for DNA testing on skin cells collected at autopsy from underneath Carlson's fingernails, something that hadn't been done prior to trial. That skin cell DNA didn't match DNA that the Bureau of Prisons took from Dawkins. The prosecutors chose not to retry him and Carlson's family didn't protest. In a few days, Dawkins was out.

David couldn't believe his eyes. Dawkins had always proclaimed his innocence, for all the good it did him. *Oh my God, he was telling the truth.*

"Why are you here at my house?" David asked while he sifted through his memories of Dawkins—what he thought was truth had been lies. It was unsettling.

"Don't you re-mem-ber what you said to me?"

"Five years ago at Kranston?" That was when David visited him last. "Give me a break. I don't remember what I said yesterday."

"You said that if I ever get out, I should look you up."

David opened the door a crack but braced it with his foot. He looked at a man who was dressed like he had found his clothes in a time capsule. "You and I were joking," David said. "I think you offered to take me to dinner when you got out and I told you to look me up. But we both knew you weren't getting out."

Dawkins managed a weak smile. "Yet here I am."

David shook his head in disbelief. "When did you get out?"

"Yesterday."

"Where did you stay last night, then?"

"At the Albany bus terminal. I took a Greyhound bus from Kranston to get there."

"How did you find me?"

"I kept your letters. They had a return address." Years ago, David and Phillip had exchanged letters as part of New York's Offender Correspondence Program. Inmates could write to anyone outside of prison. Phillip had randomly chosen David's name from a lawyer directory and had written asking him to take his Civil Rights case for unconstitutional incarceration. Phillip wanted out of solitary confinement and a lawsuit in federal court was the only way. David declined the case because he didn't have the deep pockets to fund such a protracted lawsuit against the State in federal court, not counting the appeals the State would most certainly launch. That's the way the system worked.

"Why are you here?" David asked, knowing full well that Phillip didn't have any immediate family. Not that he would have wanted to see his Dad and his belt again. That brutal figure had departed this earth with a bottle in his hand; his mother faded away in a nursing home. His friends outside the clink moved on. They wanted to forget Phillip's life and live their own. He was easy to forget. Kranston was miles from his home base of Syracuse. It sat right in the middle of the Adirondack Park—the largest publicly protected park area in the continental United States. Phillip was put in a box in the middle of nowhere.

Now Phillip was beginning to find his voice. "The ex-con who was gonna pick me up didn't show. No shelter would take me. Some of them said they don't allow ex-cons. Others said they were all booked up. A guy at the bus station showed me where you lived on his cell phone map. I had the $2.00 for bus fare down and I walked the rest of the way. I got no place else to go."

David still spoke through a crack in the door but no longer braced it with his foot. Yeah, he realized Phillip was innocent. That's what the news-paper said. But he was still nervous. Dawson had spent his entire sentence in solitary confinement. The system had just dumped a man straight from thirty years in a 6' x 8' box onto his doorstep in a single day. Even Amazon couldn't match that shipping time. On top of it all, there was something else that worried David. "Are you mad at me?"

The sun came out from behind a cloud and hit Phillip's face. He jerked a hand upward and, like a small umbrella, it shielded his sensitive eyes. Sunlight at Kranston came in flickers, not in steady streams. "Why would I be mad at you?"

David's guilt was only surpassed by his terror of Phillip. He knew that the one thing Phillip could use to get him through his solitary confinement was correspondence via snail mail. That was the only contact Phillip had with people. There was no human contact allowed within prison walls for those in solitary. Confined to a concrete box twenty-three hours a day. An hour for recess in a cage for the other hour. Like a dog kennel for men. Except the COs did the barking when they shouted out orders. That's all the contact the system tolerated. What he couldn't find on the inside, Phillip tried to find on the outside via the few postage stamps he was allotted every month. It was the only loophole in the system.

"Because I stopped writing to you," David said, trying to meet Phillip's eyes.

After David declined to take Phillip's case, the two exchanged many letters. David even visited him once. But it became too much to sustain. Phillip would send him thirty-page letters neatly written in perfect cursive on lined notebook paper. One after another after another. They were written in pen with rarely even one mistake. The letters detailed his stay in solitary. They were heartbreaking to read. David thought they deserved an answer. Every last one of them. But responding to them was both painful and time consuming. And his responses just generated more letters from Phillip. The system was devouring Phillip and their pen-pal correspondence made David feel as if he was tagging along for the ride.

David finally decided there was nothing he could do to help Phillip. He had written letters to the editors of newspapers, to politicians, even to the prison itself. But nothing happened. It was as if he was banging his head against a wall. Nobody gave a rat's ass about a cop killer in solitary. He was getting what he deserved and could burn in hell. That's what the haters said on Facebook when David's Op-Ed articles were posted, right before they said Phillip should be fried to death.

All David could do to move on with his life was to stop writing to Phillip. It was easy enough to do. He asked the New York Bureau of Prisons to place his name on the negative correspondence list. The system informed Phillip that he couldn't write to David any longer. There was no messy breakup. Just block Phillip's mail and be done with it. Out of sight; out of mind.

Like everyone else, David tried to justify his thinking by telling himself that Phillip was a cop killer. *What about the cop's family? Maybe Phillip deserves solitary after all.* You lie to yourself sometimes when there's a problem that's way bigger than you. You lie to yourself so that you can move on.

"You weren't the only one who stopped writing," Phillip said. "There were others before you and after you."

"Really? I didn't know . . ."

"Well, that's because I didn't tell you. I didn't tell anyone about anyone else because nobody would write to me then if I did. They'd all figure, you know, I'd always have someone else to write to if they didn't want to anymore."

David stood there speechless as he took in Phillip's point of view. "I think I understand. I'm sorry I couldn't write you anymore. It's just—"

"Forget it. It's okay. I got used to people dropping out. It's kinda the way my life goes. Family drops dead. Friends on the outside fade. COs come and go. Other inmates move on or kill themselves. I just sit in my box."

They put the wrong man in a box for thirty years. The thought consumed David as the wind blew a cloud over the sun. It was chilly outside. Phillip was shivering. He didn't have a coat.

"Come in," David said, opening the door.

"Are you sure?" Phillip asked, stepping over the threshold.

"Yeah. Don't worry. Christy and Annie aren't home." But David knew they would be within the hour. He also knew that Phillip needed to leave before they came back. Otherwise, she'd ask him to stay for supper before he could talk to her privately. That was her nature. She didn't know Phillip by name. All she might recall was that years ago David had tried to help a prisoner. Cop killers or any bad guys having to do with David's law practice weren't Topic A at the dinner table.

"Do you want something to drink?" he asked just as Annie had trained him to do when company called.

Phillip's eyes lit up, one eyebrow higher than the other. David recognized that look. It was the same look he gave when David fetched a bag of Doritos for him from the prison vending machine in the visiting area.

"You know I'm not talking about alcohol, right Phillip?"

"Sure," Phillip said, eyes unchanged. "Do you have a Coke, by chance?"

"How about a Pepsi?"

"That'll be fine, thank you."

David closed the front door and walked past Phillip on the way to the kitchen. "Have a seat," David said, pointing to the dining room chairs.

As David reached for the refrigerator door, he looked into the dining room. Panic hit him like a wave. Phillip was not within his range of view. The visitor wasn't sitting in any of the chairs.

Where did he go?

David grabbed a Pepsi from the six-pack rings—the same type of rings that Phillip used from a beer pack to help strangle Officer Pete Carlson. Except that he didn't do it. *He's innocent, remember?*

But all of a sudden, it didn't matter that he was innocent anymore. In a heartbeat, David recalled how prison changes a man. He had spent time in the county jail himself when he was falsely accused of killing his friend and expert witness, Harold Salar. He recalled how quickly his mental state deteriorated in jail. He tried to be a badass inmate in his quest to survive. He had violent thoughts and was just one bad day away from acting on them. David knew if you weren't guilty of something before going into the slammer, you'd find yourself guilty of something inside of it. That's the way the system works you over. David had spent less than thirty days in jail and had become a basket case before his release. He couldn't imagine what he'd be like after thirty years. *Maybe a monster.*

When David re-entered the dining room, Phillip was stroking the mahogany credenza with his index fingers. The top drawer was slightly open. That's where Annie stored the holiday carving knives—the large decorative ones used to cut the big turkeys at Thanksgiving and Christmas. Those sat right next to the stainless steel poultry shears—so large and sharp that they could sever the joint of an adult. David didn't remember the drawer being ajar. *Gotta make sure he doesn't steal something or stab me with one of those things.*

"Here's your Pepsi," David said.

Phillip looked up over his shoulder. "This is a great piece of furniture you have here. Six dovetail joints in the drawer. I haven't seen one like this since . . . forever."

"Thank you," David said, not knowing what else to say. He handed the soda to Phillip. The face of the can disappeared as that huge right hand engulfed it.

"Sit down, Phillip," David said, while closing the drawer.

Phillip lowered himself into a padded wood armchair, one of the eight around the table. When his butt hit the seat, he grinned. "Comfortable." He hadn't sat in a chair in decades. His cell didn't have one. No furniture. Just a metal sheet that served as a bed frame and a skinny mattress. He'd throw the mattress on the floor. That would be his seat when he used the solid steel bed frame as a desk to write.

Phillip had chosen David's chair, the one with the arms, the more ornate one at the end of the table. It bothered David a bit. Everyone in the family knew not to sit in his chair. Everything else of David's was fair game. Just not the chair. But David told himself to shrug it off. *The guy deserves my chair. Thirty years in prison and innocent. Jesus.*

David sat down beside him facing the window. He could see the driveway from that chair. He could spot Annie's approach. He'd have to hide Phillip if he saw her. He just didn't know where. David could imagine Annie opening the coat closet door and finding Phillip standing there. *Oh, honey, don't worry. It's just Phillip. You know, the guy who murdered that cop who I tried to help years ago. No need to panic. He's innocent. They let him go. Why is he in the closet? Um, because he's used to small rooms.*

But David didn't want to bring Phillip into Annie and Christy's life. He didn't even know if he wanted him in his life or, if so, on what terms. Phillip's release was very much a shock to him. He needed time to sort it out.

David's eyes met Phillip's. "What are your plans?"

Phillip looked down at the bare mahogany dining room table. He touched the abstract outline of his face visible in his reflection on the polished surface. He circled it slowly with his index finger, round and round. His lips began to quiver as he tried to speak. Nothing came out.

David realized then that he'd asked a stupid question. *He hasn't planned a damn thing for thirty years. The COs told him what to do every second of every day. He doesn't know how to plan.*

"I'm not sure," Phillip said sheepishly, before bringing his index finger to his nose and inhaling. "What's that smell?"

"Lemon oil, I think." David had seen Annie polish the table with it the day before.

Phillip smiled. "That's what a real lemon smells like?"

"Yeah, sort of."

"It's nice."

David heard the faint electric hum of the Toyota Prius his wife drove. He looked up. Annie and Christy had just pulled into the driveway.

David bolted upright. "You need to leave," he blurted out. "You need to get out of here this minute!"

Phillip stood up. He knew those words. He had heard them yesterday at Kranston and then from some cop at the bus station. "What's wrong?"

"Annie and Christy are home. They can't see you here."

"Oh, okay," Phillip said, moving towards the front door.

"No! You can't go out that way. They'll see you. We'll go out the back door. Follow me." David felt awful for kicking Phillip out. It was frigid outside and the wind was howling in gusts. Phillip didn't have any money, didn't have a coat. Then it hit him. The storage shed way at the back of the yard would serve as temporary shelter. David opened the rear door. "Go hide in the shed back there. It's open. I'll come and get you later."

"Okay," Phillip said as he strolled out the door.

"You've got to hurry, Phillip."

Phillip tried to upgrade his shuffling step into a jog. He had some spring in his step, but not much stride. He hadn't run more than five yards in thirty years. There wasn't room in his exercise cage. Instead, he'd bounce around to get his heart racing, maybe do jumping jacks, try to keep his strength up, work to fight off the demons.

Later, under cover of darkness, David opened the shed door. He peered into the structure with an LED penlight in hand to find Phillip lying on some patio furniture cushions, covered with lawn tarps to keep warm.

"Phillip, wake up."

"I'm awake, just had my eyes closed."

"Let's go. We need to move you."

"Really?"

"Yeah, you'll freeze to death out here."

They walked around the dark side of the house over to David's waiting 1974 Mustang in the driveway and got in. David had told Annie and Christy that he was going to drop off a book at the library and then stop at Stewart's to pick up some milk and eggs. He had the car engine already running and had boosted the heater up to full blast. Phillip bathed in the warmth, putting his big hands up to the heater vents and rubbing them together. His lanky body twitched and shivered as he absorbed the luxury of the hot air and leather seats.

"Buckle up," David said.

They backed out and headed a few miles to Central Avenue in the town of Karner. It was the commercial road and a straight shot from Albany to Mohawk City for miles, punctuated by a stop light at every quarter-mile mark. Car dealerships, run-down diners, dollar stores, strip malls, mobile home parks, fast food joints, and flophouses lined either side in a more or less seedy continuum.

Food was the first order of business. After he got over the shock of seeing so much hot food and being able to select freely for the first time in decades, Phillip almost put the Golden Corral into bankruptcy by scarfing down everything he could at the all-you-can-eat buffet. Then they headed for the neon-lit Red Apple Motel sign. The motel served as a refuge for errant husbands who had been kicked out of the house and itinerant construction workers. David knew that it offered weekly and monthly rates. He paid a week's rent to the bored desk clerk. Phillip requested a small room. The clerk replied that all of the rooms were small.

Side by side, David and Phillip walked past room after room in the one-story brick motel that formed a "U" facing the four-lane road. The place reeked of cigarettes and stale beer, and other odors best left unmentioned. Each room had a picture window overlooking the littered parking lot. The debris of broken lives shifted in the wind around the cracked tarmac—wrappers from Burger King, shredded Price Chopper Supermarket flyers and half-crushed beer cans. In one room, they could see a balding over-weight man in a wife-beater T-shirt lying on his bed watching TV with a cheap cigar in one hand and a bottle of Thunderbird in the other.

David left Phillip at room 133 with fifty dollars in cash and a promise to return the next day. Phillip thanked him, closed the door, and dropped on the bed. He opened his leisure suit jacket with one hand and plunged the other hand down a hole in the jacket's interior lining to remove the sheathed carving knife he had taken from David's house. He whipped it out, held the razor edge up to his face, and smiled.

CHAPTER 2

Phillip drew the shabby curtains over his smudged picture window, barely dimming the racket of traffic on Central Avenue, and pushed a button to turn on the nightstand lamp. He clicked it off and on, over and over again. At Kranston, he had to ask a CO to turn off the lights. Half of the time they'd ignore him.

Next, he figured out how to turn on the heat to his room, with the knob on the rust-tinged vent under the window. He couldn't believe he had control of the room's temperature. Turning the wobbly knob as far as it would go, he cranked the heat all the way up—not only to take the chill out of the place, but also to make up for all the heat he'd missed out on over the years while he was laid out in cold storage.

Phillip went to the bathroom to get ready for bed. The toiletries were the same size as prison issue, but the soap smelled incredibly sweet, like fruit or candy. It wasn't harsh like the lye soap scraps he had been using for thirty years. In the shower, he waited for the CO to holler that his five minutes was up. The only noise he heard was the whoosh of jet streams of warm water pulsating off his back and circling down the drain with a gurgle. From force of habit, he hurried up anyway and dried off. He couldn't believe that he could shower every day—every second of every day —if he wanted. No more three times per week shower schedule. The terry cloth motel-grade towel felt as thick as shag carpet to him.

As he climbed into his lumpy double bed, he marveled at the thickness of the blanket and bedspread. He didn't notice that they were dated and worn. It didn't matter. They both beat out his thin, prison-issued blanket and the clammy gray sheets that came from the laundry in the joint every few weeks. The rumble of the room heater sounded like the engine of a car. He remembered sleeping in the back seat footwell on the floor of his parents' Plymouth station wagon. He used to curl up, rest his head on the drive-chain hump in the middle of the floor, and sleep to the sound of the car racing down the Thruway. The floor was always warm, just like his bed now. His motel pillow was way softer than that hump or anything the Bureau of Prisons issued. After a minute, he fell into a deep sleep.

He saw the white cinder block walls of Kranston again in his dream. All he saw outside of his bars were those white cinder block walls. Though stained with urine, feces, blood spatter, and the boot scuffs from the COs, they were the only bright thing about Kranston. Everything else in the place was the monotone color of dirt, steel, and rust.

It was Phillip's turn for an hour in the recreation cage.

"Garcia? Jose Garcia? I'm supposed to share my rec cage with him?" Phillip asked the CO as he backed into his meal slot to get cuffed for the trip from solitary to the rec cage.

"Yeah, he's your rec partner today. No more lip from you, Dawkins, or I'll write you up."

The system was brilliant in its design in those days. Cage the men to the point of insanity and then pair them off for a play date for an hour per day.

Another CO joined them to the rear, and all three of them rounded the corner of the long corridor and the rec cage came into view—a caged area about the size of a trailer unit attached to a big rig on the highway. Phillip was panic-stricken when he saw Garcia uncuffed in the cage doing pushups. He looked the CO directly in the eye.

"Sir, can I ask you a question?"

"What is it now, Dawkins?"

"Did you search him in his cell?"

"Of course we did."

"How about pat-frisking him before he went in the cage?"

"Sure. That's all standard procedure. You know that, Dawkins."

Phillip didn't say anything else. There was nothing else to be said. Though he didn't know Garcia, Phillip knew that he had attacked another prisoner with a piece of broken glass thirteen years ago, inflicting a cut on the prisoner's arm. But to refuse rec would be like calling the CO a liar. Refusing rec was like admitting you were a coward. And you don't want that rep in prison. But it would be the first time and the last time that Phillip would share rec with Garcia. Years later, each inmate would have a separate cage for rec periods.

The CO opened the rec cage and Phillip entered with his cuffs on. The door closed and locked behind him. Phillip backed into the door slot to get uncuffed when Garcia stood up from doing push-ups.

Before he could get uncuffed, Garcia gritted his teeth and made a bum rush at Phillip, shoving him to the ground. "Incoming missile, you son of a bitch," Garcia screamed.

A "missile" was prison slang for a contract hit. Some gang member had demanded that Garcia cut up Phillip or else. You could never avoid your enemies in prison. They'd use someone else to hunt you down.

Phillip fell on to his back and tried to keep Garcia away by thrashing his legs and feet.

"Get the hell away from me!"

With every kick from Garcia's foot, Phillip grunted and gasped for air. When the horror hit him that he couldn't protect his face, his eyes bulged; his face turned crimson red.

One CO yelled for Garcia to stand down while the other rolled his eyes and sighed while reaching for his radio to call for backup.

Fights during rec were not uncommon and the COs appreciated this aspect of the system. They would rather have the inmates beat the crap out of each other than beat on them.

As Phillip writhed wildly trying to keep Garcia in front of his feet, Garcia got around Phillip and stepped on his hair. Phillip could hardly move his head. Garcia whipped out a shank from the back of his shoe—a razor melted in a toothbrush handle.

Phillip screamed when he saw it. The same CO yelled at him again, ordering him to put it down. But Garcia knew the protocol. The two COs would not enter the cage without backup. Time was on his side.

Phillip saw the blade come at his face like Garcia was thrusting in slow motion. He turned to one side to protect his face; the razor severed his ear and cut his neck open. Phillip felt the warm blood on his skin. He knew he'd been slashed but didn't know where.

Terror and shock, a one-two punch, froze him for a second though it seemed like an eternity. He feared Garcia had severed a neck artery and that he'd bleed to death *in a few minutes. His eyes bulged as he faced his own mortality for the first time ever.*

Phillip saw a long hallway of light appear above Garcia's shoulder. It grew longer and larger.

"Put it down, Garcia! Put it down!" the CO screamed.

But he didn't look away from his prey. Garcia was spaced-out in his kill zone— a serial killer's favorite place.

Blood was gushing out of Phillip as Garcia raised his hand again. Phillip saw some figure standing in the light at the end of the hallway.

"Noooooooooooo!" Phillip pleaded.

The next slash found his cheek. The incision quickly faded in a pool of blood. Phillip felt like his face was on fire.

Phillip flipped his feet over his head to try and kick Garcia. But all he could do was graze his shoulder. Garcia grinned. A struggling victim was an extra rush.

The next slash took part of Phillip's nostril off and traveled across his left cheek. The blood was now pouring into his eye sockets. He couldn't see. It flowed into his mouth and nose. He felt as if he were drowning. One ear was filled with blood. Phillip could barely hear. What he did hear was the muffled laughter from Garcia.

Backup arrived, and a squad of COs in "hats and bats" slowly opened the cage door. Garcia stepped away and sat down with his back to the cage. He took a deep breath and looked at peace, while Phillip roiled in agony, still bound by his cuffs, unable to even press his hands against his face to stem the flow of blood which flowed over his chin and down his neck.

Phillip waited for his life to flash before his eyes, but there was nothing.

All of a sudden, Phillip shot up in bed and let out a loud screech. He was shaking like a rattle; his cotton shirt was drenched with sweat. His hands covered his face and he was breathing heavily. He realized immediately that the recurring nightmare had found him again. But something was different. The nightstand lamp he left on didn't shine on white cinder block walls. Instead, there was dark-stained paneling. He remembered now that he was in a motel room. He thought that David had put him there, but he wasn't sure if that was just another dream.

The carving knife lay before him on the nightstand. It told Phillip that David wasn't a dream. He picked it up and slid it from the leather sheath. The knife glistened under the lamp. Streams of reflected light shot out against the shiny paneling as he gently twirled it. He admired its genuine staghorn handle. Phillip read the manufacturing engraving: "Sheffield." He thought it was a well-balanced knife: twelve inches in overall length, a four-inch handle and an eight-inch blade. His breathing slowed and his eyelids grew heavier with each twirl. He eased the knife back into the sheath and cradled it, carefully laying the leather piece on the bedspread beside him. He rolled over on his side and fluffed up the pillow before resting his head there. His face, still hot from the nightmare, was cooled by the pillow. He recalled the agony of twenty-five years ago. After hundreds of stitches and a dozen operations and a year of sleeping in bandages, he couldn't sleep on a pillow because of the excruciating pain until years later. It all seemed like yesterday.

Never again.

As he drifted off to sleep, a voice in his head kept repeating one name. *David . . . David Thompson.*

CHAPTER 3

Over the next week, David tried to get Phillip a place to live through government agencies, non-profits, and some churches. But in his mind what they had to offer was worse than the Red Apple Motel. The few rooms or apartments they showed were all located in far off, crime-infested neighborhoods in Albany or Mohawk City. Phillip said he didn't care about the neighborhoods so long as the room or apartment was small and quiet, like the self-storage lockers along Central Avenue. David feared Phillip was going to live like a hermit wherever he ended up.

But David figured that Phillip would have to walk outdoors one day and all he could see in these neighborhoods were scenarios that would land Phillip right back in prison. There was no program in place to help convicts like Phillip make the transition from solitary to the streets. The Red Apple Motel was a ten-minute drive from David's house. He could easily keep an eye on Phillip there and quickly respond to any urgent calls.

When the Mustang pulled out of the motel the following Saturday, everything—including the man and woman panhandling in front of ALDI's Supermarket—was covered in a film of road salt. The white crusty coating was left over from an early April snow squall that had hit midweek. Phillip was hanging out the open passenger window like a dog when they passed U-Haul Moving and Storage. They passed it every time they cruised up and down Central Avenue. Today they were on their way to David's house to have lunch with the family.

"Phillip, do you mind rolling up your window? I know it's sunny out there, but it's barely above 50—"

"You know, come to think of it, I really think I could live in one of them storage units."

"I don't think it's allowed, Phillip."

"Nobody would know."

"Sooner or later, they'd find you out and we'd be right back where we are today—looking for a place for you to live."

"I could wash my clothes in the laundromat next door. I could use their bathroom there too. That ALDI's store is close by for food."

"Sure, and we could install a wood stove in the unit for heat."

"No, the vent for the wood stove would be a giveaway. You'd want a kerosene heater. It doesn't need a vent."

"Drop it, Phillip. If you're thinking of living there, you might as well call up the superintendent at Kranston and ask if your cell was still available."

Phillip sat back in his seat, rolled up the window, and became quiet. David's comment had hit too close to home. Phillip despised being in solitary from day one. But now he found himself afraid of freedom. He'd be a liar if he said he hadn't thought about retreating to his cell. Life was awful there, but at least it was predictable. Everything was new to him now; all his nerve endings were raw. He felt like he'd been ripped from the womb at age fifty.

The Mustang rumbled down the inner lane of Central Avenue toward Albany. There were two lanes headed in each direction, separated by a single turning median. David heard a siren wail in the distance; it was getting closer fast. He looked left and right at the intersection fast approaching, but he didn't see any sign of the source. No flashing lights directly in front of him either. He quickly checked his rearview. Nothing. He glanced over his right shoulder at the outer lane and saw it was jammed with traffic so he couldn't pull over.

Phillip was of no help. He didn't move and stared straight ahead like a statue. He wondered if the siren meant they were coming to take him back to Kranston.

David's turn to cross the intersection was imminent. If he missed it, he'd have to travel a full mile before he could turn around. So he rolled the dice and entered the turning median. The light was red and he came to a full stop to wait for the green arrow that would let him cross Central. Nobody was behind him. The siren screamed closer.

David looked at his rearview once again. "Oh, no!"

Phillip turned to David. The film of sweat on his forehead glistened in the sunlight. "What's wrong?" he croaked.

David pointed to his rearview. He spotted the siren's source. The broadside of an emergency vehicle dressed in flashing lights was making a turn in his direction into the median from the opposite side. "Paramedics," David blurted.

Traffic on the other side was backed up in both lanes. The only way for the paramedics to clear the intersection was through the turning median and David was smack dab in the middle of it.

David pulled the Mustang over to the right as far as he could to allow the paramedics to pass, but it took a good thirty seconds more for traffic to clear in the oncoming lanes so the vehicle could squeeze through.

When his turning arrow finally changed to green, he made a left. Now there was another siren. He checked his rearview with a sinking sensation. There was a dark sedan flashing a red and white strobe light riding his rear bumper. The high beams flashed. David understood. They wanted to pull him over.

"Police," David muttered as his stomach dropped to the floor. He knew if they ran his plates they'd stumble across his FBI rap sheet and it would be game on. Yeah, he hadn't been convicted of anything, but it did not matter. They'd still find it and it would raise a red flag because he was sure that the sheet didn't reflect the dismissal of charges against him. David had meant to take care of that. It was on his to-do list. But paying the feds eighteen dollars to correct their mistake, after all that they put him through, rubbed him the wrong way. So he had put it off and now it was going to bite him in his behind.

The matter of Phillip's rap sheet crossed David's mind, as well. He hoped to God it showed Phillip was released from Kranston and not still serving time there. The last thing he wanted was to be gunned down with Phillip for aiding his escape from prison.

Phillip looked over his shoulder, peering between the seats. Droplets of sweat began to form on his forehead. David could see the red veins in back of his eyeballs as he strained to make out the car. For thirty years, Phillip had worried about his own skin and that was it. That's all he *could* think about while he struggled to survive each day of solitary.

David pulled his car into the parking lot of Bruno's Pest Control and waited for the officer to approach.

"Well, this is a first," David grumbled.

"What do you mean, Mr. Thompson?"

"I told you to call me David. You're not in prison anymore."

"Sorry, it's a habit."

"No need to apologize," David sighed as he stared at his side-view mirror. A man in blue emerged from the driver's door of the dark blue sedan. "It's just that I've never been pulled over by the police."

"I see," said Phillip. "Turn off the engine and put your hands on the dash."

"On the dashboard?"

"Yes, so he can see your hands." Phillip laid his trembling hands flat on the dashboard above the glove compartment. The big, veined hands showed a multitude of scars from prison. David placed his hands on the dash but wondered if Phillip should put his in his pockets. They looked like battle-tested weapons.

The officer stood behind David and knocked on his window. David carefully removed his left hand from the dash and rolled the window down. He looked up to see a young officer dressed in a navy uniform, visor cap, and sunglasses. The sun's glare and his wraparound shades hid his facial features from David. The cop flipped open his wallet to show his brass badge and quickly closed it. "License and registration, please."

David leaned forward and slowly pulled his wallet out of his jeans back pocket. He eased it open to reveal his license tucked behind a clear plastic window.

In the passenger seat, Phillip rubbed his leg against the door. The subtle motion reassured him, as he felt the sheathed carving knife that was tucked in his sock and riding up the side of his calf.

"You can take it out," the officer said to David.

Phillip froze. For a second, he thought the cop was talking to him about his knife.

David removed his license and handed it to the officer.

"Registration?"

"It's in the glove compartment."

"Okay, go ahead and get it."

David glanced at his passenger before he leaned over and reached into the glove compartment. A drop of sweat ran down Phillip's face as he stared at David's open window with his mouth agape. His hands hadn't budged on the dashboard. David retrieved the registration and handed it to the officer.

"You know why I pulled you over, don't you?"

"No, officer, I don't."

"Oh come on, Mr. Thompson," the officer shot back.

"I'm sorry, but I don't know."

"New York Penal Law, Section 195 point 16: Obstructing emergency medical services."

"You mean back at the red light?"

"So you do know then," the officer snapped.

David banged the back of his head against the headrest. Phillip placed his left hand on David's shoulder. "Let it go," he whispered before removing his hand and setting it back on the dashboard. It was the first time that Phillip had touched someone for as long as he could remember. The human contact felt good.

"I'm sorry, officer," David said. "It's just that—"

"Never ruin an apology with an excuse, Mr. Thompson."

David shook his head in frustration. The source of the ambulance siren had become clear after it was too late. He didn't intentionally block the paramedics. There was no option to move his car anywhere else. He felt the officer was pushing his buttons; he wanted to give him a piece of his mind.

But before he could retort, Phillip bent down to catch his eye. David looked over to see Phillip silently mouth, "Let it go."

Phillip hated tickets. In prison, inmate misbehavior reports were also called tickets. The COs routinely wrote Phillip up tickets for misbehavior. A few times they were justified—Phillip even would admit that to himself—but most times they weren't. He had successfully appealed many of them. He could go for years without getting written up for a ticket, but when the solitary confinement committee reviewed his status every month, it didn't matter even if he hadn't had a ticket in five years. There was no reward for good behavior. The decision was always the same: "Continuation in solitary is recommended. There have been no significant events to warrant a change in segregation status."

Phillip's hands formed fists on top of the dash. He didn't want David to say anything to upset the officer because he knew he was a split second away from pulling out his knife and cutting up the man dressed in the all-too-familiar blue uniform. As his face turned crimson red, Phillip once more pleaded with David and silently mouthed, "Please let it go."

David nodded. He was leaning toward Phillip's suggestion the first time he asked him to let it go. David didn't want to escalate matters and put both of their rap sheets into play. Things could get ugly then.

But now the sight of Phillip trembling, sweating, making fists with his face all red, made him realize he *had* to listen to Phillip's plea. David had never seen this side of him before; it made him scared for both of them. Luckily, the officer never even glanced at Phillip.

"I apologize, officer," David said, mentally biting his tongue.

It seemed like an eternity passed before the officer said anything else. Phillip tried not to think about how he'd carve up the cop but he couldn't help himself. He figured he'd slash him just like Garcia had cut him up. He always thought the COs should have had time to remove his cuffs before Garcia attacked. And he believed it took the COs far too long to respond and intervene when he was trapped in the cage with Garcia. Phillip always wondered if COs had set him up for the attack. The COs said they searched Garcia twice before he entered the rec cage but didn't find his shank.

"Good," the officer finally said. "I'm going to let you both off with a warning this time. But I'm going to keep my eyes open for both of you. Same goes for my partners back there in the cruiser." David looked back in his rearview. Another man sat in the passenger seat, sporting sunglasses. The third guy leaned forward from the back seat, with his head poking out over the console. David thought he recognized the cop in the back seat before he sat back and his face disappeared from view. "When you guys make a move, we'll be there to take you down." With that the officer handed David his license and registration and walked back towards his police cruiser. The cops sped off with Phillip watching in the rearview, while David fumbled to slide his license back into his wallet.

"Now there's a cop with an attitude issue," David said as he dropped the registration back in the glove compartment.

"Ain't a cop," Phillip said, with a deep shuddering breath, slowly peeling his sweaty hands from the dash.

David started the car as Phillip spoke, but now he wasn't going anywhere. "What are you talking about?"

"For one thing, that Crown Vic had a red and white bubble-light suctioned to its roof."

"So, what of it?"

"Only emergency vehicles like fire engines and ambulances can use red and white lights in New York."

"How do you know that?"

"I read it in a law book. Vehicle and Traffic law, I think," Phillip said, wiping his brow.

"Really? I didn't know about the light law and I'm a lawyer."

"Let's just say I had plenty of time on my hands to read while doing my bid. It's not like the prison library had a great selection for me to choose from. You know, it takes more than a decade for a book to be approved for the prison library. Law books were allowed. I used to read them cover to cover to keep the demons away."

"Don't police cars use red and white lights too?"

"Yeah, they do. But they are allowed to use blue lights too."

"But they don't have to use blue, correct? I think I've seen some without blue."

"Right, that's another thing, though. In this town, I've seen all the marked and unmarked cars use blue. Some lady got run over crossing Central Avenue one night last week. I saw it out my window. All the cop cars—marked and unmarked—were using red, white, and blue lights. By the way, the car that pulled us over didn't have any markings."

"Maybe this was an older, unmarked car? A spare in the fleet?"

"It had a bubble light suctioned to the roof. This town doesn't have those on their cars—not the ones I've seen. They have these really bright array bars on top and in the windshield—even in the grille. This car didn't have anything close to that."

"You mean LED lighting?"

"Yeah, I think that's what they call them. Anyway, how many times have you seen three cops to a car?"

"Not very often, I guess."

"You bet. The cops I saw the other night were one to a car. When I was growing up, I think it was two to a car in my neck of the woods. But three?"

"I don't know. Maybe he was a trainee, or maybe a ride-along. You know, Phillip, you've been cooped up in a cell for a long time and the system may have taken its toll on you. Did anyone ever tell you that you might be a bit paranoid?"

Phillip thought for a second. "After what I've been through, I've got reason to be paranoid. I guess that kind of thinking is good for me. I'd say the choice I had in the box was to not think at all or to be paranoid. If my thinking is paranoid, it means that I still want to live. I think paranoia makes me stronger."

David couldn't believe his ears. But at the same time, Phillip's twisted point of view made sense to him.

There's one more thing though--about those supposed cops," Phillip said.

David sighed. "What's that Phillip?"

"I've seen that badge he flashed at you before. That's a Bureau of Prisons badge for COs in New York State."

David looked down, put his hand to his forehead and began to rub the growing ache between his eyebrows. "What are you saying, Phillip?"

"I'm saying that was a gang of COs looking to send us a message."

"Are you serious?"

"Dead serious."

"You think these three would put their careers at risk by impersonating police officers?"

"They are peace officers and what they did was legal. Trust me, I've learned a lot in prison about what COs can do, what they can't do, and what they can get away with. As peace officers, they can pull over cars if they witness a misdemeanor. Obstructing emergency medical services is probably a misdemeanor."

"Let me guess, you read it in a law book."

"Uh-huh."

"If that's true, I doubt the Bureau of Prisons would look too kindly upon COs pulling over civilians for traffic violations."

"Yeah, I suppose there may be a liability issue. But I call 'em as I see 'em," Phillip said matter-of-factly

"You sure do, Mr. Jailhouse Lawyer."

"Are you making fun of me?"

"I'm just joking around with you, Phillip. You need to learn to loosen up a bit."

David was trying to take his own advice by making light of the situation.

Taken one at a time, each of Phillip's points made sense to David, but his conclusion was hard to swallow.

David kept thinking about the man in the back seat who looked familiar. He kept trying to put a name to the face as he shoved the Mustang in gear and drove off down New Karner Road on the way to his house. COs or not, he was glad that it was over and that neither of them had ended up in jail.

Phillip stared out his window as he tried to process what had just happened. In the madness that reigned in the Kranston solitary confinement wing, there were moments when he could talk to his immediate neighbor—even though he couldn't see him. He could also share his thoughts with other inmates by writing notes and "fishing" them—that's what they called it—under the bottom cracks of cell doors by using long threads from his bed sheets. He missed these interactions.

Since his release, Phillip realized he had more in common with his cellies back in solitary than he ever would with anyone on the outside. He missed them, as he didn't really have anyone else to relate to—except maybe David, who had done a little time in protective custody while he was being held county jail. Phillip thought in the back of his mind that he'd like to go back and visit a few men in solitary. He knew they'd appreciate the company. It was always a big day when any of them had a visitor. And visiting them might even help him to ease his survivor's guilt.

But he wasn't going back now—not after his encounter with the rogue COs in the parking lot. He swore to himself that he'd never go back to Kranston or any prison either as a visitor or as an inmate.

Phillip hated the violent thoughts that surfaced when the COs pulled David over. If prison brought out the worst in him, he decided then and there that he wanted to stay away and live the rest of his life as a free man.

CHAPTER 4

"How do I look?" Phillip asked when they pulled into David's driveway. He wanted to make a good impression on Annie. He hadn't seen a woman up close, in the flesh, in years and hadn't had lunch with one since he could remember.

"You look fine," David said, wondering if Phillip's tan cargo pants and deep violet-blue turtleneck looked a bit dated. David had done the best he could in his role as Phillip's personal shopper. Modern clothing from Kohl's or Boscov's was rejected by Phillip in favor of clothing from SALs—the Salvation Army Thrift Store. David's efforts had at least moved Phillip up a decade in clothing style from what he wore when he showed up at the Thompson doorstep a week ago, but that wasn't for lack of trying on Phillip's part. Fortunately, SALs didn't have any '70s or '80s clothing that would fit him in stock that day.

Over the past week, Phillip had lamented to David that he couldn't find his "street legs." There was no way he would miss the screams of lost souls in Kranston's solitary wing, but he wasn't used to the quiet of his motel room either. He was afraid to venture outside into a world that offered no physical boundaries; he kept looking over his shoulder to see if there was anyone behind him. With nothing more than a sink-or-swim support system buoying him, David feared that Phillip was almost guaranteed a return ticket back to prison.

David had recently earned a big fee when he settled a personal injury case for his client, Ben Prior, so he thought he could afford to give back to someone in need like Phillip Dawkins. But it couldn't hurt to have some moral support from Annie and Christy to help the cause. Besides, he didn't want to handle Phillip in secrecy, behind his family's back. Not that this would be an easy thing to do when his law office sat in the basement of his home. Sooner or later one of them would find him out.

Concealing things from Annie and Christy was something David had done in the past to protect them both, as well as to make his own life easier. When David was fighting tooth-and-nail to save the town's baseball league, he didn't tell Annie about all the nasty things going on behind the scenes nor did he tell her about his crazy plan to physically defend the field from those who were determined to crush the league. He also didn't tell either her or Christy about how the law was trying to pin a murder rap on him in the death of his good friend and expert witness, Harold Salar.

Each time Annie learned about David's shenanigans after the fact, she didn't explode as he feared. She might have been disappointed, but she was always supportive in the end. David felt bad afterward and thought, perhaps, that he should trust his wife to be stronger and more understanding. Phillip was his test case for this new approach in his relationship with his Annie.

Annie was a very generous woman. As a child, she once decided to help her mom by rearranging her typewriter keys in alphabetical order. Recently, every charity in the country had gained a foothold in the Thompson's mailbox—and for good reason. With Annie, everyone who held out a hand palm upward was entitled to a check. Eventually, all the charities would become pen pals with the family and would invite themselves back on a regular basis, eagerly asking for more. The charities were also considerate enough to follow up with a telephone call—conveniently during dinner—just to make sure their most recent mailing arrived.

In established, well-oiled marriages, harmony comes from checks and balances that often operate behind the scenes. When David retrieved the mail from the box at the bottom of their sloping drive, he'd deposit all the charity solicitations into the large recycling can by the garage before they ever entered the house. The charities could send all the nickels, dimes, return address stickers, pens, pencils, notepads, and calendars they wanted because it all went directly into the green and yellow bin unopened. It wasn't that he was uncaring of the needy, he just knew that when Annie got the mail, she'd more than make up for his neglect. He simply offset his wife's incredible generosity without having to confront her about it and risk a fight. In his mind, what she didn't know wouldn't hurt her and would go a long way to ensure that a happy wife gave him a happy life.

But up until now, Annie's innate generosity started and stopped at the checkbook. She simply didn't have the time outside of her teaching job to volunteer to serve the needy directly. That's why she told David it's what she wanted to do when she retired.

David knew that Annie had never dealt with a charity case in person. She certainly had not been involved with an accused murderer fresh out of prison. David thought it would be a marketing tour de force to sell Phillip's cause to Annie and he was up to the challenge.

His strategy was to feint and distract. He would soften her up by addressing one of her longstanding concerns for David in their relationship at the same time as he slipped Phillip through the back door. David asked Annie if he could have a guy friend over to have lunch with her and Christy. He knew Annie would agree immediately. She always said David should have more friends, so long as they were *male* friends.

"Oh, I think that would be wonderful, David," she said, with the warmest of smiles when he told her about Phillip a few days ago.

A commitment right out of the gate from Annie was just the thing David expected. He knew that it would be much more difficult for her to back out now. Of course, David neglected to tell her Phillip was an accused murderer right up front. That was the last thing he mentioned *after* he had sold her on Phillip's virtues in contrast to his dire living situation.

"Murder?" she exclaimed, with her eyes going wide in dismay.

"Yes, honey, but he's *innocent*," David replied. Innocence was Phillip's saving grace. Without it, even David would not involve the convict in his life—let alone the lives of his beloved wife and son. David added, "They locked him up and threw away the key until thirty years later, when they discovered he was innocent."

"That's awful," Annie had said, throwing up her hands. "The poor, poor man!"

When Annie said this, David knew that he had tapped into her generous nature and the only thing left on his agenda was to schedule a meal. Today was the date and now was the time.

Phillip jumped when David slowly applied the parking brake to the Mustang in his steep driveway.

"It's just the emergency brake, Phillip—you know—to keep the car from rolling down the hill into the street." Once, David forgot to engage the parking brake and his beloved Mustang not only rolled into the street, but also across the way onto his neighbor's front yard. Thankfully, it made the trip without hitting anyone or anything.

"Oh, okay," Phillip said, thinking that the sound of the brake reminded him of his cell door closing at Kranston.

"Are you ready to meet the family?" David asked as he opened his car door.

"Okay, I guess."

Following his host through the winter-ravaged yard, Phillip entered through the side door of the red Cape Cod house. He stepped directly into the dining room, while David held the door behind him. The table was set and Phillip immediately was overcome by the wonderful aromas of a working family kitchen: fresh rolls baking in the oven, coffee brewing, and the lingering aura of bacon from breakfast.

"Hello," Annie called from the kitchen, when she heard the side door open.

"We're here," David replied.

Annie walked through the archway from the kitchen to the adjacent dining room. Her jeans, with their sequined back pockets, were barely tight enough to reveal her slightly bowed legs. It was something that she had grown self-conscious about after a catcaller at college hollered, "Bow-legged ladies make the best lovers." She wore a lavender sweater—pastels were always in season for her—that revealed the curves of her petite frame. Her shoulder length, sandy-blond hair wrapped around her face and set off her chocolate eyes like a pair of Brown-Eyed Susans.

"Annie, I'd like you to meet Phillip Dawkins," David said as the fragrance of her perfume permeated the room. David wondered if he should've asked Annie to tone it down a bit for Phillip. Kranston didn't have sweet scents like perfume. David was concerned that Phillip might have an allergic reaction.

Phillip stood at attention with his feet rooted into the oak floorboards. "Hello, ma'am," he said, bowing slightly.

"Please call me Annie."

"Yes, ma'am—I mean Annie."

Phillip shook his head and looked at the floor.

Annie and David shared a smile with one another.

"Whatever you do, don't call her Anne," David said

"Yes, that's what my mother calls me when she's angry with me," Annie giggled.

Christy walked in from the kitchen, wiping his hands with a dish towel. He was sixteen, already slightly taller than his dad with a slimmer frame.

"This is my son, Christy," David said.

Christy extended his hand. "It's nice to meet you, Mr. Dawkins."

Phillip gently grasped his hand and shook it slowly. "It's nice to meet you, too. Please call me Phillip."

"Okay," Christy said, pushing back his light brown hair with his free hand. It was the first time that any adult had asked Christy to interact with him on a first-name basis.

"It's so nice of you to come join us for lunch," Annie said. "You can sit over there by David if you'd like." Annie pointed to a chair on the side of the table.

"You can sit in the chair at the end here if you want," David said. He pointed to the more ornate captain's chair he always took as head of the family.

Phillip sat down at the end of the table and David claimed a seat at his side. The sporadic April sunshine, which seemed so chilly out on Central Avenue, pooled its warmth from the bay window in a halo around the spot Phillip picked.

Annie carried in a platter of deli meats and a selection of macaroni and potato salads from Gershon's Delicatessen. She positioned them at the center of the table on the neatly ironed white linen. Christy brought out a basket of fresh-baked sandwich rolls and filled the drink requests.

Phillip practically leered at the meal unfolding before him and marveled at the entire table setting. Annie had broken out the fine china; Phillip sure didn't miss the tired old routine of shoveling every meal from a Styrofoam tray that doubled as a dish. Annie had neatly folded cloth napkins beside each plate. The silverware glistened in the light cast by the brass chandelier overhead.

Phillip heaved a sigh of relief that each setting boasted a dinner knife. It meant that they wouldn't look for the carving knife he still had tucked in his sock beneath his cargo pants. Phillip knew that the zipper circling his knee on each pant leg would not only create cargo shorts but would also allow him to grab the knife handle in a second. That's why he selected this pair of pants at SALs.

Annie sat herself beside David, close to the kitchen so she could fetch any forgotten items. Christy pulled up a chair across from his parents in a long-established pattern.

"Did you want to say Grace, David?" Annie asked.

"Okay," David replied, extending one hand to grasp Annie's and the other to hold Phillip's huge paw. Christy reached out to take Phillip's hand and across the table to hold his mother's fingers.

For a moment, Phillip looked back and forth at David and Christy's hands, unsure of what he should do with them. Then he spotted Christy's arm extended across the table that let him hold his mother's hand. He took the hands that Christy and David offered. They were much smaller than his, and much warmer.

"Lord, thank You," David said, bowing his head, "for the food before us, the family and friends beside us and the love among us. Amen."

Unexpectedly, Phillip felt his eyes start to well up with tears, as he released their hands. He hadn't held someone else's hand for as long as he could remember—decades. It struck him that he was being included in a family gathering. He had forgotten what that felt like. He wondered if it was too late for him to have a family of his own.

"David tells me you're living on Central Avenue," Annie ventured. "Are you getting settled all right there?"

Phillip finished chewing the potato salad in his mouth and swallowed. The whipped mayonnaise dressing tasted so light and sweet, not institutional at all. "Yes, thanks to your husband."

"It's a crying shame what happened to you," Annie said, her voice cracking.

Phillip took a bite out of a half spear of sour pickle. He couldn't believe how it crunched in his ears when he bit into it and how the strong, clear flavor brought a pucker to his lips. Limp, soggy pickle chips were the order of the day at Kranston--when they even *had* pickles.

"I can't imagine what it was like for you," Annie added.

Phillip nodded while he chewed the precious pickle.

"Can I ask you how it feels to be free after all these years?" Annie asked.

David jumped in, "Maybe he doesn't want to talk about it."

Phillip swallowed. "It's okay."

Christy wiped his mouth with his napkin. His eyes were locked on Phillip. This was a totally foreign experience for Indigo Valley; not many convicts wandering around the 'burbs.

"It's a lot to process in such a short time," Phillip said, with both hands folded on his lap. Smiling, he added, "Maybe you should ask me that a few years from now?"

All of the Thompsons smiled back.

Christy joined the conversation, turning his body to face their guest. "Can I ask a question?"

"Sure," Phillip said.

"What did they allow you do to in your cell?"

"Reading, writing, drawing, and they gave you a pair of earphones."

"Earphones for what?" Christy asked.

"Well, they have a jack in the wall and they pump music into it, mainly rap. Maybe you'll hear a television station, but that's hard to follow without seeing what's on the screen. That's about it."

Annie asked, "Were there any educational programs made available to you?"

"No, there's nothing like that offered to inmates in solitary. They have a few in-cell study programs, but that's it."

"Really?" Annie shook her head. "How about job training opportunities?"

"No."

Annie rolled her eyes then bit her lower lip. "You mean they just threw you out on the streets after leaving you in a cage for years?"

"Yes," Phillip said matter-of-factly. He longed to get back to the luxury of his lunch. Intimate conversation was a rarity in his life. When his cellies peppered him with questions, he always felt like he was being set up. And he was usually right.

"Annie," David said, "it happens all the time in this country. Inmates do their time in solitary and then they're released straight into communities without anything to support them."

What David wanted to also say was that the worst inmate problems became a neighborhood problem in a flash. But he wasn't going to lob that verbal grenade with Phillip around.

David knew what Annie was driving at with her questions. It was her years of human resources work experience bubbling to the surface. She understood that Phillip's odds of making it on the outside weren't good without education or training.

Annie had pinpointed the issue and now her laser focus was on finding a solution. She looked at David. "What can Phillip do to support himself?"

"We've been talking about that," David said.

"I can be a barber," Phillip blurted out.

David sat there with his mouth wide open. Phillip and he had talked about job prospects, but barbering was never mentioned.

"Why a barber, Phillip?"

Phillip had been in a fog ever since his release from prison a week ago. His mind worked like a sputtering engine: trying to tie thoughts together, to think about concepts beyond his immediate survival needs, to revive long-lost memories. He had trained himself not to think while in the box. He knew if he thought too much about the hopelessness of his situation there, he'd bug out. The bugs were the solitary cons who'd scream all day and night—cries of desperation, rage, and loneliness—as their spirit was sucked out of their souls.

Not that Phillip didn't scream—because he did. He could scream with the best of them. But most of the time he'd scream at them to shut up or else he'd slice them up into pieces. Every night he'd cram those earphones deep into his ears—all the way to his brain—so he couldn't hear the men in agony anymore.

While in the box, he lost his memories of life before prison, one by one, like a vulture was picking at his brain. He struggled to keep the memories because, once they were gone, he felt as if he would never get them back. He tried to replay a continuous loop of all of his memories in his head. He panicked when one fell out of the loop, if only for a minute.

Still, while trying to clutch to his memories, he had lost so many links to the real world that at times he questioned his very existence. The line between reality and fantasy was breached daily, if not hourly, and Phillip would hear voices that he thought were real and see things that were not anything but hallucinations. He was reluctant to look in the mirror because he was afraid he wouldn't recognize himself.

But once he set his mind on the goal to never go back to prison—to live his life as a free man—in the face of the COs that pulled David over, he needed a plan to survive. The barbering memories floated to the surface and he latched on to them like a drowning man clutches a life preserver.

Phillip smiled—not so much at the memory—but at the satisfaction he felt in finding something he had lost decades ago. "When I was a teenager, my family didn't have enough money to get my hair cut. My mother would cut it using a bowl as a guide. The kids would make fun of me. My eyeglasses didn't help. All the cool kids got their hair styled—not just cut— by . . . by Manny . . . Manny Romano. In our neighborhood, Manny was a god."

"Where was this, Phillip?" David asked.

"Syracuse, the Northside. I remember begging for him to style my hair-- to layer it, to blow-dry it, to make me look normal. Finally, he said if I'd cut his lawn, he'd cut my hair. His lawn wasn't that big. He lived in a two-story house—the bottom was his shop and he lived on the second floor—and so I cut his lawn and he shampooed and styled my hair. I never looked so good before in my life. After school, I'd always stop by and see Manny to ask if I could do anything so he'd style my hair the next time I needed it. I was a pest . . . and he finally broke down and hired me as a shampoo boy at twenty bucks a week. I also cleaned the shop—swept up the hair, cleaned the bath- rooms. I was the coolest boy around—having a job at Manny's—with my perfect hair. I'd start shampooing a head when he gave me the signal. Then I'd pass them on to Manny for styling when his chair became free. It was just me and Manny . . . we were like a well-oiled machine."

"Did you ever cut any hair yourself?" Christy asked.

"Yeah, I started to train under Manny as an apprentice barber when I turned seventeen."

"Did you get your license?" David asked.

"I finished the two-year apprenticeship, but . . . you know . . . life got in the way . . ."

David's eyes met Annie's. He had told her and Christy that Phillip was convicted at age nineteen.

"That's something we'll have to look into, Phillip—if you want to be a barber."

Phillip grinned while he nodded. "I think I'd like doing that," he said. He had a vague memory of being happy cutting hair.

In prison, Phillip had been like a man locked in a septic tank. His nostrils had been filled with the smell of feces and urine—the two means of protest most readily available to everyone held in solitary. But he wasn't a participant in hurling his crap and piss at the COs; though he was tempted to some days.

He struggled to overcome the memory of that daily stench—to recall the sweet barbershop aromas: the combs soaking in the ocean-blue Barbicide, the talc, the hair tonic, the bay rum aftershave. These fragrant memories of barbering excited his senses. The thought of holding cool steel once again in his hands did too: the memory of his metallic combs, his thinning scissors, his sleek eight-and-a-half-inch pointed shears, and his long straight-edge razor—all made of polished stainless steel. They were all high-quality tools of the trade that could double as lethal weapons. It was the best of both worlds in Phillip's mind: he could earn a living and protect himself at the same time.

The thought of holding the straight-edge razor against the jugular vein of a helpless man leaning back for a shave in his barber chair put Phillip at ease. He would be in control. No con was going to cut him up. No screamer was going to throw crap at him. No CO was going to lodge a steel-toed boot into his ribs. He could finally run his own life now. He felt liberated at the prospect, but at the same time he never felt more scared in his life.

CHAPTER 5

A week later, David walked through the door of the Yellow Ribbon Diner on Central Avenue, midway between his home and Phillip's motel. Johnny McFadden was already ensconced on home turf, in *his* back-corner booth—the largest one in the place—chatting with his favorite waitress. It was where McFadden held court; it was where David had last seen him years ago.

The waitress departed as David wove through the tables and waiting patrons. The din of cutlery hitting china and the chatter of happy customers filled the place. Johnny's eyes locked on David's and they both grinned ear to ear. He stood up and the two embraced man-style, with a little back slap. In a second, Johnny lost his smile.

Johnny was a stocky man; average height but square bodied, with larger-than-life forearms. His brown hair, now graying a bit at the temples, was still combed from front to back perfectly, like a nor'easter had blow-dried it. He continued to sport a bristle-like mustache—nothing sloppy—just a brush that claimed his upper lip for the male gender. While his face now showed some crinkles and crevices of aging, he looked in great shape—more muscular than David remembered.

"It's great to see you, Johnny."

"Been too long."

"Yes."

"Sit down, David." Johnny raised his hand and the waitress returned as if attached by an invisible string. "You remember Suze?"

"Why, yes, I think I do. It's been a few years," David said.

Suze bent her firehouse red lips in a smile, as she chomped on her gum with her back molars. "What can I get you, hon?" You knew she didn't need the Ticonderoga pencil stub tucked behind her ear to track orders from Johnny's booth.

"Cup of decaf, black."

"High-test for me, babe," Johnny said.

When Suze was out of earshot, Johnny came clean, as if he couldn't wait to clear his conscience. "Yeah, that was me in the back seat of the car that pulled you over the other week. I figured that's why you texted me and wanted to meet."

Now David's smile evaporated. He thought the man might have been Johnny, but he couldn't quite make himself believe it. More than anything, the encounter reminded David that it was long since time to catch up with Johnny. "What the heck is going on with you?"

"I swear to God I didn't know it was you until afterwards—"

"What were you doing in the back of that car?"

"I became a corrections officer, a CO—"

"Were the other guys in the car COs too?"

"Yeah, but you didn't hear that from me and you can't say anything to anyone about it."

David rolled his eyes. Phillip was right after all. "Why not?"

"Because I'll lose my job."

"Really? How did you get involved in this line of work? The last time I saw you, you were selling meat door-to-door from the back of your truck."

"I couldn't compete with all these new grocery stores," Johnny said, pointing out the window toward ALDI. "Bills were piling up. I needed a job with security, benefits, and a future to support my family. You don't need a college degree to be a CO. So I sat for the Civil Service Exam for COs, passed it, and graduated from the Albany Training Academy. That's the short of it."

"Where are you working now?"

"Kranston Maximum Security Prison. I commute the one hour up and back every day from Albany."

"How long has this been going on?"

"Six months at Kranston. Like most COs starting out, I did time at Sing Sing and—"

"Oh yeah? What were you in for?" David asked, straight-faced.

"Funny guy, ha ha. Actually, the only real differences between us and the cons is that we serve our sentence in eight-hour stretches each day, get paid for it, and, if we hang around long enough, we'll also draw a pension."

Suze effortlessly slid two cups of coffee in front of the men, hardly breaking stride in her white Skechers, as the china mugs hit the Formica tabletop.

"So how did you end up at Kranston?"

"I put in a bid for a job there when I started working at Sing Sing, and I got lucky. I've put a bid in on a prison even closer to Albany. When I get a little more seniority, I'll get it."

"So why did you and your buddies pull me over the other day?"

"It wasn't me. I was just along for the ride. I swear I didn't know it was you until after the fact. You see, being a CO is like belonging to a fraternal organization—like Elks or the Moose—"

"You're pulling my leg—"

"Dead serious. We call each other brother or sister, you know, like they call me Brother McFadden."

David almost spat out his coffee as he choked in disbelief. "Not on the job?!"

"No, no, not on the job—when we meet as part of the New York Corrections Officers Union. We're a close-knit group. You know, there are generations of COs from the same family—it's like the son takes over the father's business. There's siblings, cousins, nieces and nephews all over the place. We're all part of an extended family in a way. You're not black, white, red, or yellow when you're a CO, there's only blue—the color of our unis."

"Yeah, I'm familiar with the union. They run ads on the TV all the time. I always wondered why they spend all that money on ads to tell us that they keep us safe. I mean, I don't see any other law enforcement unions spending money to tell us that they are doing their jobs."

"We have to look out for one another. There's so few of us when compared to the number of cons and we don't have any weapons except a baton, sometimes mace. We can't carry guns on our beat, 'cause we can't risk the cons getting their hands on them. I'll tell you, David, I got the biggest and hardest baton they'll let me use. It's freakin' dangerous in there."

"What does this have to do with pulling me over?"

"I'm getting there. They told me to get in the car—"

"Who told you?"

"The two other senior COs—"

"They got names?"

"I can't tell you. I shouldn't even be talking to you now."

"Why not?"

"It's against the code—the code of the brotherhood."

David glanced up from his cup of coffee. Johnny's eyes were drooping. He'd never seen that look on him before. "Geez, this is starting to sound like some kind of cult or something."

"I hear ya. I wonder every day if I made a mistake in becoming a CO. But I'm into it too deep. I went through two months of BS at the training academy. Then I really learned how to be a CO on the job at Sing Sing for a year. I lived in an RV outside the prison wall because the living costs around the prison were sky high—it being Westchester County and all. Froze my butt off in the winter. The cons were living better inside than I was on the other side of the wall. I only saw my family on the weekends. Then I finally got a transfer to Kranston. If I quit or lose my job as a CO, it would all be for nothing. The only thing I could get with my experience is some minimum wage job doing mall security. I don't want to be a rent-a-cop."

David cradled his rapidly cooling cup of joe and looked out the window at the traffic idling on Central Avenue. He remembered when Johnny used to own the street. He was his own man, selling meat. He could do anything and say anything he wanted—both on the job and off. He used to be fiercely independent and it was this quality that David admired most. Johnny used to do crazy, wonderful things with a sparkle in his eye and a grin on his face. Together, they saved baseball for thousands of sandlot players in the region. But now it seemed like the same system that owned Phillip had a hammerlock on Johnny.

"So, why was I targeted for this pull-over?"

"Promise me this conversation won't go any farther than this table and I'll spill."

"Well, tell me first if I can expect to be harassed by a goon-squad car in the future."

"All I can promise you is that I won't be riding in it. I know enough now to make sure that won't happen again."

David thought a second. He didn't like the idea that he might still be walking around with a bulls-eye taped to his back. He wondered if this put his family at risk, too. But what more could he really expect from Johnny? There was no harm, no foul from the pull-over. Not at this point. It also seemed like Johnny would help keep him in the loop, so long as he shut up about it. And if he learned one thing from working with Johnny to save baseball for kids, it was that you always want him on your side. "Fair enough. I promise."

"It was you and the company you keep."

"You mean Phillip Dawkins?"

"Who else?"

"What about him?"

"They say he's dangerous—a psychopath."

David didn't know if he was dangerous or not. He knew Phillip wasn't entirely with it. That was to be expected given his experiences. Still, he couldn't shake his memory of how Phillip almost lost it during the pull-over. "Who's they?"

"The senior COs I was riding with—the CO brotherhood."

"You know Dawkins was found innocent, right?"

"What difference does that make? I'm just telling you what I heard. I'm not sure what his deal is either. If I asked too many questions, they'd get suspicious. I don't need them riding my ass any more than they have already."

"If he's dangerous, it's what solitary confinement did to him over thirty years."

"Says you."

David got the sense Johnny was holding back. "What else do you know about him?"

"I think he's got enemies in high places. Many of the COs look up to him in a way. Not because he's innocent. All cons claim they're innocent and that's not our call to make. We just deal with what they send us. Some COs admire Dawkins because they couldn't break him. He never cracked in the box or at least he didn't show it. He didn't bug out. He didn't throw crap or urine at anyone. He'd fight the CO tickets and win more often than not. There were times when he was well-behaved for years at a time, before they could get a misbehavior ticket to stick. Some COs wondered why they wouldn't give him a chance in the regular population. Nobody could figure out what was going on." Johnny shrugged his shoulders. "But innocent or not, they say he's a killer. That's all I know about him."

"Do those COs you rode with know that you and I have a history?"

"No, I'd never say anything about that to anyone. That might come back and bite me in the ass as a newjack."

"Newjack?"

"Yeah, a newjack—a rookie CO."

"Okay, you said the COs had a beef about me too. Is that because I'm helping Dawkins out?"

"That's part of it."

"What's the rest of it, then?"

"It's what you've done publicly about solitary. They told me you wrote letters to everyone about The Mandela Rule passed by the UN. You know, the one that prohibits solitary beyond fifteen consecutive days."

"I know what The Mandela Rule is all about. You know, this United Nations rule was supported by the US government."

"Yeah, well, that doesn't matter."

"Well, I think it matters. They found that after fifteen days, you risk causing inmates irreversible psychological damage. They called it torture—pure and simple torture. That sounds like it's cruel and unusual punishment under the US Constitution to me."

"Jesus, you haven't changed. You did the same thing back in our baseball days. When you go legal, you just don't know when to shut up. Writing letters to editors, writing magazine articles, speaking at public functions—always going ballistic about the rights of these low-life cons who would kill us in a heartbeat."

Here we go. Shifting into typical us-versus-them mentality. "Did you ever think that his hostility is somehow related to being confined to a box 23-7?"

"They were put there for a good reason."

"Maybe so, but the goal should be to modify their behavior to get them back into the general population, if possible. They can get some training there, some education, a chance to make it on the inside, a chance to make it on the outside if they're ever released. You're too afraid to release them from solitary back into general population, but you have no problem setting them free into our neighborhoods."

"Dude, I got nothing to do with this! Even if I wanted to work in solitary, I couldn't. That's reserved for the senior-most guys."

David knew Johnny was right. Solitary was secure inside and from outsiders too. No accountability. Photographs of the cells or the inmates were never released, out of concern for prison security. "Sorry, I didn't mean 'you' personally. I meant 'you' as part of the system, 'The Blue Wall.'"

"None of this matters to what's going on with you. It's not so much what you did for the boxed cons. It's all about what you're doing to the COs."

"Huh? Come again?"

"You are threatening them—their livelihoods, their jobs. It takes more staff per inmate to oversee solitary and so you are threatening them that much more by attacking the box. Kranston, like a lot of other upstate towns, has lost its manufacturing jobs due to plant closures. They have become prison towns. That's the biggest and sometimes the only employer around and the union works hard to keep those jobs no matter what."

"That explains the union TV ads."

"I guess."

"So, what was the goal of the pull-over?"

"To send you two a message."

"What message is that?"

"You figure it out. I really don't know. I was a lackey on this run. It was like my initiation or something. Like I said, newjacks don't ask questions. The first lesson I learned at the academy was not to stand out from the crowd. I can't afford to rub these guys the wrong way. When there's three of us COs in the yard watching over hundreds of cons and we're armed with only a stick apiece and stupid can of mace, I need all the backup I can get— like the COs in the watchtower armed with rifles. If they want to screw me over, all they have to do is look the other way for a few seconds. The worst nightmare of any CO is being held hostage."

"The CO who shook me down said, 'When you guys make a move, we'll be there to take you down.' Do you have any idea what that means?"

"Nope," Johnny said, rubbing his face and eyes with his hands.

Johnny looked uneasy. It was a new expression for him. David never saw him behave like this before. He wondered if it meant he should be afraid of Phillip, too. But so far, Phillip had been nothing but cordial to him.

Still, this gave David a pang of regret for bringing Phillip into his life. He wasn't afraid for himself. He feared for his family. The last thing in the world he wanted to do was to put his loved ones in harm's way. Annie and

Christy had grown to like Phillip. They were spending time with him alone when David couldn't monitor his behavior.

It had been a week since the CO pull-over and nothing else had happened. He wondered if he were to distance himself from Phillip, then the COs would back off. But he didn't want to just abandon Phillip. That wouldn't be right. He'd go straight back to prison, for sure. David figured that he had a little time to figure out a way to extricate himself from the situation without feeling guilty.

David believed that any danger Phillip presented to him or his family was the direct result of him being in the hole for thirty years. He figured that the more time Phillip had to air out from the box, the less threat he was to anyone. It wasn't like the COs were parked across the street, calling his house phone, or following him around town. His plan was to help Phillip get started as a barber. Then the Thompsons could keep their distance from him, as he invested long hours to get his business off the ground.

"Johnny, please do me a favor."

"What's that?"

"Just give me a heads-up on anything you think I need to know."

"I'll do what I can, David. Be careful. COs are licensed to carry concealed weapons on the outside."

David exhaled as he raised the chipped china cup to his lips to finish it off. He watched Johnny peel back the aluminum cover to yet another vanilla creamer and stir it slowly into his coffee, watching the vortex form and grow. Like two men who served together in combat, David knew that he and Johnny would always have their baseball memories to bond them, even in this new chapter of their lives. But he also realized things had changed between them. Johnny was no longer the carefree, happy spirit eager to take on the world. The sparkle in his eyes had been replaced by a blank stare. His jagged features revealed no curiosity or passion, no disgust or delight—like a face chiseled out of the old slate quarries that ran along the Vermont border outside of Kranston.

David had seen that look before. It was the face that Phillip Dawkins brought to his doorstep the day after his release.

CHAPTER 6

Late one evening, Phillip was lying in his bed at the Red Apple Motel when he sensed the entire ceiling starting to crush him like a vise.

It had been a good day. David had taken him on a tour of the historic Old Cider Mill in Karner first thing in the morning, when it was quiet. That outing was part of David's tour plan to transition Phillip back into the American mainstream. They would go on regular day trips to new places like tourists from a foreign land. The idea was for the different experiences to give Phillip a comfort level with being free and taking care of himself.

Phillip took his nightly vitamin with a glass of tap water, then he stretched out on his lumpy mattress. After a few minutes, he visualized himself as a pile of apples plucked from cold storage at the mill and wrapped in cheesecloth—ready to be mashed under the cider press. He instinctively sat up. It was a reflex to try and block the ceiling from dropping any lower with his head. But when he felt the walls began to close in too, he knew he had to work everything back into place. He fell back on his coping mechanism, just like he did while he was trapped in the box. He stood up, flexed his shoulders and rotated his head to work the ceiling upwards. Next, he paced—four steps forward, four steps back—to work the walls outward, like he was doing a jig. He called it the Anti-Bug-Out Dance. After a few minutes focused on the back and forth movements, his perspective changed and suddenly everything snapped back into place.

When he felt the ceiling was going to stay put, he tried once again to fall asleep on his back. He didn't pull the covers or place the pillow over his head. The flimsy sheets and foam felt like the weight of the world on his face, trying to smother him alive. Phillip fought off the urge to strip down to bare skin to rid himself of the suffocating weight of his pajamas, too.

Inhale through your nose, hold it and count to four, then exhale through your mouth. Think positive thoughts.

Phillip opened the top drawer of the wobbly nightstand by his bed. He pushed the motel room copy of the Gideon Bible aside to grope for his red transistor radio and his earphones. He had discovered the radio in his leisure suit side pocket when he got to the Greyhound bus station on the day of his release. He figured someone from the prison knew he liked to listen to the radio through the prison audio system, so maybe it was a going-away present. Tonight, he tuned it in to WAMC—the public radio station in the Albany area—in the hope that some classical music would calm his brain. He still wasn't accustomed to the quiet of his motel room; the absence of sound made his ears ring.

At Kranston, every surface was metal, concrete, or brick. Nothing served to absorb the endless ricochet of sound except thin mattresses and the bodies of inmates. When the screams didn't echo down the hallways, there was a constant buzz of distant voices—sometimes whispers. The noise would ebb and flow like a constant aural tide, washed over now and then by the sound track of prison life—keys jingling, locks clicking, hinges creaking.

Now, in the absence of that sea of noise, he clung to his transistor radio like his life depended on it. Soon, the calm strains of Strauss and Debussy on the evening music show put Phillip into a deep sleep.

Initially, Phillip had hoped his nightmares would fade after he left prison. But he could not have been more mistaken. He could deal with the old, established ones because it was like watching reruns of a familiar horror show. Over time he had grown somewhat numb to them. But these new nightmares were vivid, intense, and vastly different. It was like his brain sprung a jailbreak, which made anything and everything—no matter how bizarre—fair game.

Phillip's dream took him back to Kranston. Court was now in session. He found himself back in the hearing room where he was months ago. He sat alone at the single table bolted to the floor, wearing a hunter green jumpsuit—a pair of prison flyers on his feet—decked out in full jewelry; a waist chain, ankle shackles, and handcuffs.

Unlike the hearings before the solitary confinement committee, Phillip could attend his disciplinary hearings. But, as a prisoner, he wasn't entitled to legal counsel. He was on his own. Advantage: the system.

A CO guarded the door from the inside. When the judge entered, the CO said, "All rise."

Leon Wolack entered the room dressed in a pair of wrinkled navy blue Dockers and an open collar, powder blue dress shirt worn white at the elbows. It wasn't a casual workday. His stomach covered his belt buckle. They officially called him a hearing officer because calling him a judge suggested he had a legal education and license to practice law. Leon Wolack had neither, but he required inmates to address him as "judge" or "your honor" in his room.

When there was an opening for the hearing officer job five years ago, Kranston's superintendent, Martin Kleinschmit, could appoint anyone he wanted to the position. When Leon's father, John—a twenty-five-year veteran CO at Kranston and an area sergeant—got wind of the opening, he made a call to Kleinschmit, his former bunkmate at the academy. John wanted a better deal for his son, who was a CO there at the time. Better for his son meant he would get away from the inmates and slide into some desk job. The old pals struck a deal. Leon could transfer from his CO job to the hearing officer position on the condition that he enroll in an online college degree program with a major in criminal justice from the State University of New York at Delhi. It irked Leon's father that some cons received college credits, even degrees, from behind bars at his expense as a taxpayer, while he personally had to foot his son's tuition bill.

"It's you again," Wolack said to Phillip.

Phillip wondered who else Wolack might expect to see since he held his case file. But he bit his tongue. "Yes, it's me, Judge Wolack."

"I would have thought you might have gotten the message by now."

Phillip knew Wolack was trying to yank his chain. Wolack wanted to get him riled up before he turned on his tape recorder. A stark raving mad Phillip giving recorded testimony would make his job easier. "I'm here to exhaust my administrative remedies, Judge Wolack." That's what the prison aid lawyer said to do, the last time she visited Phillip five years ago: exhaust his administrative remedies in the prison system so he could take his appeal to the courts.

Wolack nodded. He could sense that Phillip was focused today. It was the sixth time he had heard one of Phillip's misbehavior ticket appeals. Still, he needed to probe to see if he could get Phillip to bug out on the record. It was part of the game. "Suit yourself."

Leon Wolack pulled out his state-issued, standard cassette tape recorder—the same type of recorder used in disciplinary hearings ever since Phillip could remember. Wolack clicked the button to record and the faint hum of the recorder filled the room. The cassette clicked with each revolution of the tape.

"This is a tier three disciplinary hearing," Wolack said. New York has three tiers of hearing with the third tier reserved for the most serious allegations, subject to the most severe punishment. "My name is Mr. Leon Wolack and I have been directed and authorized by Superintendent Kleinschmit to conduct this hearing. State your name and department identification number for the record."

"Phillip Dawkins, 85C1015."

"Inmate Dawkins, you may call witnesses on your behalf at this hearing. Nothing said by you in response to the charge pertaining to this misbehavior report shall be used against you in any criminal procedure. You should present any oral and documentary evidence that you wish to be considered by me. Any procedural objections, claims, defenses should be made promptly during this hearing so that may be considered by me. Do you understand your rights and obligations?"

"Yes, sir. I do."

"The charge is a violation of rule 113.15 which covers unauthorized exchange between prisoners. I will now read the misbehavior report into the record. 'On the above date and approximate time, I was providing security coverage for the morning recreation run when I observed inmate Dawkins, 85C1015, pass an unknown object to inmate Jones, 98A5420, through the cage bars. Both inmates were pat frisked and metal scanned prior to entering their separate recreation cages. This indicates that inmate Dawkins must have secreted the object on his person before passing it to Jones. I reported it to my supervisor and continued my duties.' That's it. How do you plead to the charge of violating 113.15 by participating in an unauthorized exchange?"

"Not guilty."

"What do you have to say in your defense?"

"First off, I don't know the CO who wrote the ticket."

"You don't have to know him in order for it to be a valid ticket."

"I was presented with the ticket five days after the date of the alleged incident by another CO."

"So . . .."

"So, why wasn't I given the ticket the day after the alleged incident? That's the usual practice."

"Maybe because they were busy doing something else."

"In all my years in the system, I've never been given a ticket five days after it supposedly happened."

"It happens. Do you think at the time of the riot in Attica, the inmates got their tickets in a timely fashion?"

"Judge, I don't think Kranston had a prison riot that day. I think that time lapse suggests that it isn't a valid ticket."

"Anything else?"

"Yes, I'll tell you what really happened. I walked into the cage and Jonesy was in the cage next to me already."

"Inmate Jones or Officer Jones?"

"Inmate Jones. CO Jones wasn't on duty that day from what I can remember."

"Okay."

"I went into the cage, a CO uncuffed me, and Jonesy said to me, 'What's up?' I said, 'What's up?' He stuck two fingers—ring and index—through the bars and I walked over to tap them with my fingers. That's it. That's all I did. We've been tapping fingers like that forever. I do it with other inmates too. I don't recall the face of the CO who wrote me the ticket. Some other inmates told me he was new. Maybe he didn't know that's how we greet one another here."

"He said he saw you pass something."

"He said he frisked me before entering the cage. I took my sneakers and socks off and he checked them out. He passed a wand over me. How did I get it by him?"

"He didn't strip frisk you. Maybe you had it tucked between your butt cheeks or in your crotch?"

"Assuming that I did, though I didn't, why would I pass something to Jonesy in plain view of the CO? Why would I bring this ticket upon myself?"

"I don't know why cons do what they do. Motivation is irrelevant."

"I can't speak for any other inmate, but my motivation is very relevant to me. I've fought every ticket I've received over the past five years and won eventually in the courts, if the state doesn't fold first. My record is very important to me. A clean record is the only chance I have of getting out of the box back into the general population. So if that's my motivation, why would I do something so stupid in front of that CO?"

"The CO saw what he saw."

"Well, where is it then? Where is the thing I allegedly passed to Jonesy?"

"I don't know—"

"Exactly, because it didn't exist. The rules say that if there's a violation, the *exercise period will be terminated, and a misbehavior report will be issued. The rec period wasn't terminated. I got my ticket five days later."*

"Anything else?"

"After rec, I left the cage at the same time Jonesy left his. He wasn't strip searched. Neither was I."

"What does that have to do with anything?"

"If they saw something, they are supposed to strip search us. The CO said he saw me pass something, so why were we only pat frisked? Anyway, if I handed something off, where is it? Why wasn't it recovered? If so, where is that something? What happened to the evidence?"

"Is that it?"

"No, there must be substantial evidence to find me guilty of a rule violation. If you don't have anything, this case should be dismissed."

"I have the CO's misbehavior report. That's all I need."

"That's insufficient. Where is the CO who wrote it? I indicated on the forms I filled out that I wanted to call him as a witness. I want to call Jonesy too."

"They're coming."

"I also want the video surveillance tape for the rec cages that day. It will show all I did was tap fingers with Jonesy. There's no rule against us tapping fingers."

Phillip felt his eyes get misty at this thought. He hated that he wasn't allowed the simplest form of human contact—a greeting between two men. Sitting in his box day after day, he longed for human contact of any kind. He understood how some inmates bugged out because they were deprived of it. They'd slash their wrists or go crazy because medical attention was human contact. The CO extraction unit, the hats and bats team, sent to deal with out-of-control inmates was at least some form of human contact, too. Beatings from COs were considered better than no contact at all by some inmates—the physical pain they suffered at least confirmed their existence.

"The camera was inoperable at the time. These cameras go down on occasion."

Phillip's heart raced, his jaw clenched. "In all the years of coming to these hearings, anytime I've needed video surveillance tapes, the cameras are down."

"I know for a fact it was down because I know the people who work on them."

"Are you testifying, judge?" Phillip knew that if the hearing officer investigated the incident, by law he wasn't supposed to preside over the hearing. But he also realized that argument wasn't going to get him anywhere.

"Just stating a fact."

"If the cameras weren't working on the day of the ticket, I want camera footage of the day before and the day before that."

"We're not going to go back and watch tapes that have nothing to do with this hearing."

Now Phillip could feel his face begin to turn red, his jugular vein started to throb. "Well, they do have something to do with this hearing. Do you know why?"

"I'm sorry, but they do not—"

"Because if you look at the footage from the day before and the day before that, you'll see Jonesy and I were tapping fingers then too."

"Well, maybe you were passing something on those days—"

"Then the camera would show that we did. As if, we're passing something every day but we we're not getting written up on it." Phillip had heard enough. Suddenly, in his mind's eye, he saw himself lunging across the table. He saw his hands wrap around Wolack's pencil-thin neck, twisting his head around and around until it popped off, and blood squirted from the stump like an oil gusher. Phillip imagined the look on the Wolack's face when, for a millisecond before he died, he saw his own decapitated body.

Whoa! He told himself to inhale, hold it, exhale, and to think positive thoughts.

Phillip knew that he had almost lost it then and there. It wasn't the first time. Primitive aggressive fantasies of revenge, torture, and mutilation of the COs and staff consumed a lot of his time in the box. He tried to block out the thoughts, but sometimes he couldn't stop them. He didn't blame himself for having these thoughts. He told himself that anyone locked in a cage all day for decades would be angry at his incarcerator. But the thoughts did frighten him. They were a sure sign to him that he could bug out at any time and could end up a screamer, throwing feces around like a chimp in a zoo.

Again, he forced himself to take control of the moment—to inhale, hold it, exhale, and to think positive thoughts.

Phillip closed his eyes for a second and tried harder to get ahold of himself. He spoke slowly and calmly, "I don't accept that the cameras were just down on the day of the incident. I object, judge, to the denial of the tapes for the other days too."

"Is that it then?" Wolack asked, tapping his pen on the stainless steel table.

Phillip looked down at the floor. He didn't want to let the look on Wolack's face interfere with his concentration. "Judge, I've seen this movie before. It will be my word against the CO's word because there's nothing else. Nobody going to believe an inmate or ten inmates over the word of a CO. I know I'll be found guilty even if there's no evidence whatsoever, let alone evidence that can be *considered substantial. I'll lose because of the blue wall of silence—prison staff backs prison staff no matter what. An independent party needs to conduct these hearings. I've been through these fake hearings—these show trials—so many times. This is just insanity. But maybe that's your goal—to drive me mad, to make me bug out. Is that what this is all about, judge? Is this what's going on here? Are you trying to drive me mad so that I kill myself? Do you want me to hang by a noose made from my bedsheet, ram my head against the wall, or slash my wrists? Is that what you want? It's not going to happen, judge, because I'm not going to let everyone in this state off the hook. If you really believe I killed that officer, the state should have put me to death. But, no, the people in this state want to feel good about themselves, want to think they are above the death penalty. What they don't realize is that they've created a fate worse than death. They've created a system of torture—a system that would have them up in arms at the cruelty if I were a kitten or a puppy. But what they don't know, won't hurt them, right judge? Nobody outside of the system ever sees us. No pictures allowed of us in our cells, right judge? Any pictures of us must be approved and must be in front of a false backdrop, like a forest or a waterfall. No inspections by the United Nations? An inspection would raise security concerns, right judge? But we both know the only security issue is to prevent people from knowing what really goes on in here."*

When Phillip was done ranting, he raised his eyes from the floor and saw Leon Wolack had been transformed into a huge kangaroo eating a butterfly.

This fantastic image was such a surprise that it caused Phillip to toss and turn in bed, mumbling something. He shook his head while his voice grew louder and louder until he woke up and yelled, "David Thompson!"

Phillip shot up in bed. The alarm clock said it was 9 a.m. He had slept for more than nine hours, though it felt like fifteen minutes to him. Yanking out the earphones, he shut his radio off. He propped a pillow up against the headboard and leaned back against it. The dream was about an actual hearing, one like the countless other bogus hearings he'd endured. He tried to make sense of it all from the point where the dream got weird and ended. No kangaroos at Kranston, just a never-ending loop of kangaroo courts and rubber-stamp judgements.

After he ranted to the judge, he recalled Jonesy arrived in cuffs and chains. He took a seat and corroborated Phillip's testimony. Then the new CO came to the table. He said he saw Phillip pass something and that he reported it to his supervisor. Though nothing was done about the alleged passing, the area sergeant testified that they weren't required to do anything about it.

Judge Wolack decided to end the hearing after this testimony, even though Phillip wanted to call other witnesses. He ruled on the record that Phillip was guilty. He wrote that finding in a single sentence on a Bureau of Justice form. No legal justification was forthcoming in the form of a written opinion. There was no review of the facts and there was no discussion of the law. Phillip was just guilty and that was the end of it. He was given the maximum sentence allowed—180 more days in solitary confinement—six months more of box time. It was a sentence to more of the same, which he was going to serve anyway, given the indefinite sentence to solitary he was already serving. It was like getting a life sentence plus 180 days--a fake sentence for a fake hearing, a shining example of the system at its best. Superintendent Kleinschmit affirmed the decision later that day, just as he always did for any CO.

With the help of a Prisoners' Legal Services lawyer, Phillip had filed his appeal with the court in Albany. In response to his appeal, a transcript of the hearing proceedings was submitted by the Bureau of Prisons through the Attorney General. Even though a prison secretary swore under oath that he transcribed the tape to the best of his ability, there were over one hundred instances when he marked the transcript as "inaudible." Chunks of testimony, including a large part of Phillip's testimony and his rant against the system, were supposedly lost somewhere—tangled in miles of brown ribbon—on the tape cassettes.

While the transcript didn't help the state's case, it wasn't a fatal blow, either. The court would routinely remand the case for another hearing if the transcript was faulty enough. The system could do the hearing over and over again until the fake hearing looked right on paper or until hell froze over—*Groundhog Day*, the movie, Prison Edition. Phillip could wait in solitary for it all to play out. What's a few more years?

But the law, on the other hand, was clearly against the state on the issue of Phillip's appeal. The court had previously ruled that substantial evidence of an unauthorized exchange exists only where there is an admission of the exchange by the defendant or a recovery of the exchanged object. The Attorney General could see the writing on the wall. He had neither and conceded defeat. Phillip's perfect record streak remained intact, for all the good it did him.

Even though Phillip's legal victory spared him no time from the box, he had refused to accept the guilty finding. Maintaining a perfect disciplinary record kept alive his slim hope of release from solitary. Yes, so long as he behaved well while they tortured him he had a chance. But winning also gave him the sense of satisfaction of looking his incarcerators in the eye and letting them know, without saying a word, that what they were doing was wrong. So long as he was alive, Phillip believed that his existence served as a constant reminder to them of their unjust treatment.

Oh, sure, they'd say to one another that Phillip got what he deserved. They'd pound their chests—always victorious—as long as they were in the company of other COs. They could put on a brave face for one another, but when they found themselves alone, like Phillip, the system would eat at them and show them no mercy.

Phillip's actions invited the COs to take their jobs and the memory of him home, back to their spouses, their families, and their communities. He knew damn well that COs were reluctant to tell anyone on the outside what they did for a living. He had overheard COs saying exactly that, right outside of his gate or through the ventilation grates. You hear a lot over thirty years when you've got nothing but time on your hands. The COs didn't want to relive their jobs at the end of the day by talking with anyone about them. They wanted to forget their shift—to erase their time inside like it never happened.

On top of it all there was a stigma to the job, the reek of prison that wouldn't wash off. Phillip had heard that people looked down on the COs. They were viewed as knuckle-draggers, Neanderthals who weren't smart enough to be police officers or fire fighters. He had read that COs had highest rates of heart disease, divorce, drug and alcohol addiction, suicide— and the shortest life spans—of any state civil servants.

Over the years, COs would come and go, serve their sentence in the hallways of Kranston and then die before their time, while Phillip lived on. It gave him satisfaction that he was actually killing *them* as they tried but failed to kill *him*. The system spared no one—death and taxes, baby. That single thought put Phillip at peace with the world.

At that point, Phillip decided it was time to get out of bed. He pulled the frayed cord to draw the drapes on his picture window view of the main drag to Albany. He couldn't figure out how David fit into his dream. But with a butterfly-eating kangaroo jumping around in his head, David's presence in his subconscious was the least of his concerns. He let the dream go.

As the drapes ratcheted slowly open, April sunshine flowed over his green carpet giving it the look of a well-manicured front lawn. Phillip put on a too-short terry bathrobe and sat in the rocking chair David bought him at SALs. All the while Phillip was in the box, he tried to imagine what life would be like as a free man. Now he slowly rocked back and forth, content to watch the world pass him by on Central Avenue.

CHAPTER 7

When the world turned green outside his picture window in May, Phillip thought he had lost his mind. First there was the fuzzy hint of red around the branches of the tree in front of the Red Apple Motel. Then, the patches of dirt that bordered the parking lot sprouted spots of color that changed daily, from light to bright to deep green, like the carpet in his room. There were even little flowers that didn't last long—yellow, white and purple—poking up through the shreds of litter leftover from winter.

He hadn't seen that kind of color on the ground, or anywhere else for that matter, since he was a kid. The windows in his solitary cells, when he had them, were always too high to see outside. The concrete floor of the rec cages prevented even the hardiest weed from taking root. Galvanized fencing on all four sides was surrounded by concrete or brick walls that soared high above the tree line. Overhead, you could see only the sky through the galvanized mesh. Rec period was always at the mercy of Mother Nature because the cages had no roofs.

It was a novel sensory experience for Phillip to absorb colors, smells, and textures in person. The Albany Pine Bush Preserve in Karner was in full bloom when he and David pulled into the Welcome Center parking lot one Sunday in late May. The sun rose slowly over scattered gnarled pitch pine trees that dotted gentle sand dune mounds among the low-lying scrub oak. It almost felt as if the ocean should be nearby. But the nearest beach was a three-hour drive east by car and the background noise came from eighteen-wheelers on I-90, not crashing waves. Mixed in and around the scrub oak and throughout the ragged landscape, wild blue lupines were in full bloom.

"Why are we here?" Phillip asked his tour director.

"To take a walk. You can't sit around in your motel room all day. It's not good for you."

"Why so early?" Phillip asked, when David parked the car by the trailhead.

"I wanted to get here before the crowds," David said.

Phillip nodded silently. Almost three months together had taught them both that Phillip did not like crowds and might never get used to them. It was one of the prices he paid for the decades of living in solitary confinement.

"We're going on a treasure hunt," David said, as he opened the Mustang's door and stepped out.

Phillip fumbled to unbuckle his seatbelt. "What kind of treasure? Buried treasure?"

"Nope," David said, as he locked and closed his door.

Phillip opened his door and stretched upright as he stood outside. David's treasure hook had worked. Getting Phillip out of his motel room or the car could be a challenge. "What kind of treasure, then?"

"The best kind—a living kind of treasure," David said, walking past the trailhead kiosk and on down the sandy path.

"Don't we need directions?" Phillip said, pointing to the plexiglass box filled with trail maps.

"Nope. I know where we're going. I've been walking this trail since I was a kid. Are you coming?" David wasn't going to wait for Phillip. He didn't want to leave him too much time to think about the outing. He didn't want to give him an opportunity to invent a reason not to go. David told Annie that Phillip had an acute case of analysis-paralysis. His life experience had made him too wary of everything to do anything. David wanted Phillip to be more spontaneous and he tried to lead by example.

Phillip looked over one shoulder and then over the other. He didn't see anyone in the scrubby woods around them. Still, it bothered him. He was accustomed to the security of walls within reach. He didn't have to watch his back so much when he was in the box or going to and from it. There was always a CO, bars, or a wall behind him an arm's length away. But now he feared that anything might appear out of nowhere behind him; and there was a whole lot of nowhere all around in the preserve.

With his hand, he surreptitiously touched the handle of the carving knife tucked in his sock, hidden beneath his cargo pants. It calmed him. He sped up to catch up to David but his feet sunk to the ankles in the sand like he was running on the beach. He almost lost his balance.

When Phillip finally caught up, David slowed his pace and they strolled side-by-side to the crest of the dune mound and looked down into the grassy meadow below. It was spotted with the twisted trunks of bonsai-like pitch pine and covered in a blanket of lavender blue. As they drew closer, the wave of color became dozens of stems that sported clusters of tiny flowers.

"Aren't these wild blue lupines beautiful, Phillip?"

Phillip stood still and surveyed the surroundings trying to take it all in. "Is that what they call these flowers?"

"Yes."

"I don't think I've ever seen a field of flowers like this before."

"Inland pine barrens like this one are rare, very isolated. I don't think there are any environments like this close to Syracuse where you grew up. There used to be forty square miles of pine bush in this area. Human expansion and development has caused this ecosystem to shrink. It's gotten smaller, much smaller. There are about 3,200 acres left now in Albany."

As David spoke, Phillip thought about the ceiling and the walls in his cell closing in on him. "Are wild blue lupines only found here?"

"They're native to ecosystems like this one, but there are not many inland pine barren areas like this in the country. Maybe in New Jersey and up around Lake Michigan. But you can grow these flowers in a garden. This is crappy soil—it's all sand. Can you believe something so beautiful requires so little encouragement to grow?"

"No."

"Look at them. They aren't just surviving—they're thriving." David started to walk down the path into the meadow of lupines. "Don't they smell sweet?"

"Yes, they do."

"Kind of like honey?"

"Is that what honey smells like?"

"It's close."

Phillip trailed behind him. He had learned that these outings always had an underlying theme to them. "Are you saying I'm like a wild thing, a blue lupine or something, because I survived solitary? Is that what this walk is all about?"

"Geez, Phillip, don't overthink it. Can't we just enjoy the walk now?"

"I'm not stupid, you know."

"I have never suggested you were. You should really stop saying that to me."

"I'm sorry. It's habit. They always treated me as if I was stupid in prison."

"I understand."

"So am I like the wild blue lupine then?"

"You're not going to let this go, are you?" David knew that unless he answered the question, Phillip would think about it all through their walk. He wanted Phillip to learn to just enjoy things for what they were, and not to analyze everything all the time.

Phillip said, "It's a habit, I guess—"

"I understand," David interrupted. He knew he wasn't going to undo thirty years of obsessive behavior in a few months. "No offense, Phillip, but you're not as pretty as a lupine. You're more like a pitch pine over there, scraggly and bent, full of resin and resistant to rot. It's a very resilient tree that sends a single taproot deep into the sand to find water. When you set fire to a pitch pine, its thick bark offers a protective armor, and new growth appears quickly. If you cut a pitch pine down, the stump sprouts new growth. In fact, some of the cones from these trees need the trauma of fire to open and spread their seed. They flourish from disaster. Like you, the pitch pine is hard to kill."

Phillip sported a grin as he walked on. "I like it."

David was glad to connect with Phillip on some level. "It fits you."

"Just call me 'pitch' then."

David gave a snorting laugh. "If I called you that in front of people, it might sound like 'bitch' to them."

Phillip looked at the ground and managed a weak smile. He didn't say anything in reply. David's joke had hit a bit too close to home. Truth be told, he felt like David's bitch at times and that angered Phillip because he was nobody's bitch at Kranston.

It was mentally and physically exhausting to follow David around in an unfamiliar world. Phillip thought the experience was toying with his subconscious and playing tricks on his mind. That's the way it was in the box—your mind toyed with your body; your body toyed with your mind.

Just a week ago, in a dream, Phillip found himself back in Kranston and there David was a CO. On the way to the rec cage, Phillip broke free from his cuffs and stabbed David repeatedly with the carving knife. Fountains of blood sprayed everything deep, dark red and Phillip didn't stop plunging the knife into him until every last drop of blood drained out. It was the same thing a few nights before, but that time, after stabbing him to death, he dismembered the body and ate his flesh before he woke up and screamed David's name. The dreams were growing more intense and disturbing. He was scared and ashamed of them, but didn't know what to do. He sure couldn't tell David about them. He was afraid to lose the only friend he had.

Phillip didn't have any medical insurance. He lost access to medical care provided by the Bureau of Prisons once he was released and he hadn't applied for Medicaid. Even if he got into the emergency room to talk to someone about the sleep disturbances, some psychiatrist would flag him for confinement and observation. That would be just another box at a different venue—except they'd pump him full of drugs, too. Not an option. His plan was to just tough it out and hope the dreams would leave him as quickly as they had come. There was no other choice.

"The thing we're looking for is the size of a postage stamp," David said. He could have said the size of a quarter, but David knew Phillip liked stamps. They were as good as cash in prison.

Phillip's eyes opened wide as he surveyed his surroundings. "Any other clues?"

"They're close to the color of your favorite stamp."

"The purple heart?" The Purple Heart Medal stamp was the one he'd paste on all of his letters to David.

"Yep."

"All I see are the lupines."

"Well, the lupines are nice but they aren't the treasure. Keep looking."

Phillip looked in the brush, at the trees, on the ground. He heard a chirp from foot level and drifted toward the trunk of a pitch pine. David followed close behind. Phillip pointed to something on the ground. It was a baby sparrow.

"He must have fallen out," David said, pointing to the nest above and the mother sparrow chirping away. Phillip saw the nest and the mother and shook his head. He looked down on the baby sparrow chirping and flapping its wings. Suddenly, he lifted his foot over the baby sparrow.

"What are you doing?" David cried, pushing him away. Phillip fell to the ground. "Were you going to kill that baby, Phillip? What in God's name are you thinking?"

"Don't push me, David. Please don't. I'm tired of being pushed around."

"Were you going to kill that baby bird?"

"I want to put it out of its misery."

"It still has a chance. The mother might tend to him."

"The mother needs to learn that she can't save him."

David's jaw dropped when he realized that Phillip saw a reflection of himself in the baby bird. David couldn't imagine how many times Phillip must have wished to be taken out of his misery. It pained him that Phillip couldn't put the prison experience behind him. But at the same time, he knew he was asking too much. He couldn't walk a mile in Phillip's prison flyers. Nobody could fit in those shoes but Phillip.

David extended his hand. "Let me help you up," he said, clasping Phillip's cold hand and pulling him off the sand. "Trust me about the bird, Phillip. Just tell yourself that it's not in prison. Maybe that will help you understand."

Phillip nodded in silent agreement. He had learned to trust David with anything outside of prison. But at the same time, he felt compelled to squash that baby bird. In prison, it would have been the right thing to do. All the cons would see it the same way. Though if it were an inmate and not a bird, no con that killed another would talk about it and risk a murder charge. But every con in the general population knew that a simple pillow could do the job without triggering suspicion. In solitary, it was strictly self-service. They put those air grates above the solitary units for a reason. While everything in prison was cheap, the sheet thread count was always strong enough to hold a dangling body from the air grates.

Phillip couldn't stand to hear the chick squeak and thrash. He stared at the helpless creature; he imagined he could squish it into the ground like he was putting out a cigarette butt. It would only take a second.

"Phillip, snap out of it."

"Huh," Phillip said, now looking at David.

"Let's move on," David said, pointing to the path.

David waited for Phillip to move before following him out of the brush and onto the trail. They were walking through another wild lupine meadow when David spotted the object of his quest.

"Stand still," David said, "and don't move."

"Why? What's wrong? What do you see?"

"Just relax and don't move." David said, carefully reaching out to Phillip's shoulder before he touched it with his index finger.

Phillip grimaced and his eyes bulged. "Is there something on me?" he fretted, twisting his head to see what might be on his shoulder. Was it a bee or a bug? Something was going on and it was behind him where he couldn't see or react. He would never allow that to happen in prison.

He was breathing hard now. His fight or flight instinct had been triggered. But David told him to stay still. Restraining himself took every ounce of will he had. Still, he feared he couldn't hold back much longer. Knots multiplied in his stomach. He felt about to explode. He wanted to grab his knife and swing it in a slashing 360 degree circle of defense.

"Look away," David said. "Don't scare the pretty thing. It's going to be okay."

Phillip exhaled shakily. "What is it, David!? For God's sake, what's on me?"

Slowly, David brought his finger past Phillip's head and stepped away from him. Sitting on his finger, with its wings open, was a butterfly.

"He must have thought you were a flower," David said, smiling. Phillip was wearing his favorite violet-blue turtleneck.

Phillip stood like a statue, mesmerized by the small butterfly slowly opening and closing its wings. The undersides of the wings were pale gray with a continuous band of orange crescents inside iridescent blue spots along the edges. The topside of the wings were powder blue with narrow black margins.

"That's . . . spec-tac-ular," Phillip said in a stage whisper, as he calmed down. "What is it?"

"It's a male Karner Blue butterfly."

"Really? It's named after this town?"

"Yes, it was formally identified here around 1944 by the author Vladimir Nabokov and named after the town. But they are also found in other states with similar ecosystems."

"Didn't he write . . . *Lolita*?"

"Yes he did. Have you read it?"

"No." Phillip moved his head around the butterfly, slowly inspecting every detail "Can we keep it?"

David's eyebrows popped up. "Where would we keep it, Phillip?"

"I don't know. A jar, maybe?"

David couldn't believe that Phillip, of all people, wanted to imprison the Karner Blue. But he understood that he meant no harm. Phillip had the fascinated look of a little boy on his face—a welcome change from the left-over prison stare that was still his default expression. "And what would you do with it?"

"I don't know. Just watch it, I guess. I've never seen a blue butterfly."

"Well, we can't keep him. The Karner Blue is an endangered species. It's against the law to mess with them. One of the reasons they're endangered is because so many butterfly hunters want to add them to their collections. Besides, he'll only live a few days before he dies. We don't want to take that away from him."

"Really? That's all the time he's got?"

"Yeah, he'll mate and the female will lay some eggs and another genera-tion will come to life before the summer is out. Then that generation will produce some eggs that will winter over. The cycle will repeat itself next spring."

"The eggs will survive the winter?"

"Yeah, as long as there's a good snowpack to insulate them."

Phillip nodded. He knew the value of a good snowpack to insulate himself. When the winter wind howled and it was snowing in the rec cage, he was the only con to venture outside at Kranston. The COs would give a shovel to any inmate if they wanted to take a stab at clearing some snow. There was no place to shovel it except to the middle part of the cage. Piling it up there allowed Phillip to create a rectangular walking path around the perimeter of the cage. But more importantly, over time the shoveled snow in the middle accumulated to a height of six or seven feet, high enough to create an igloo. He could make a snow cave, where he could curl up, fall asleep, and protect himself from the bedlam of solitary, at least for part of the hour he was allotted for daily rec. "Why are they endangered?"

"They have a hard time co-existing with humans. The Karner Blue caterpillars only eat wild blue lupine. Habitat like this pine barren, which is favorable to its growth, is disappearing into house lots and shopping plazas. If there's no lupine, there's no more Karner Blues."

A breeze blew across the meadow and the butterfly flew away. David and Phillip chased it over a dune and into another meadow, where dozens of Karner Blues danced above the lupines like they were blown out of a confetti cannon.

Phillip gaped at the scene, wild-eyed; to him it was like a bit of *Fantasia*. He brought his hand to his mouth in astonishment and gasped. His smile was so wide that even his huge hand could barely cover it. "Can I borrow your phone, David? I want to take pictures."

"Sure," David said, taking the cell out of his back jeans pocket. He tapped the camera icon, and handed it to Phillip. "Zoom like this, tap the screen where you want the camera to focus, then tap this icon to take a picture. You got it?"

"I think so," Phillip said, raising the phone towards the swarm of butterflies.

"Try to stay on the path as much as possible. You don't want to disturb the vegetation."

"Okay."

The phone made a shutter click sound every time Phillip took a picture. He took close-ups bending over, lying on his stomach, and on his back. He took distance shots from a variety of angles. David just sat on the path and watched him dance along the strip of sand that wound through the meadow trying to get the best shot. He fit right in, dressed in his violet-blue turtle-neck, a color that was a close match to the female Karner Blue. The entire scene reminded David of when he first brought Christy to see the Karner Blues at the age of seven.

When the camera's memory chip was filled to capacity with pictures, Phillip staggered back to David totally out of breath but with a grin still painted on his face.

"What are you going to do with all those pictures?"

"Hang them in my barbershop."

"That's a nice idea. They'd fit in well. We can take the camera over to Staples and have them download the pictures to make posters. Speaking of your barbershop, did you get all your paperwork in for the grand opening tomorrow?"

"Yes, I think so."

"Tomorrow is a big day."

"Yes."

When David reached Manny Romano by phone three weeks ago, he was between customers in the same Syracuse shop where he had taught Phillip barbering thirty years ago. After he talked to Phillip, he told David he was willing to vouch for Phillip's two-year apprenticeship. He signed the necessary paperwork required by the Bureau of Licenses.

Phillip was fortunate. Changes to the law required that Phillip's apprenticeship training be within one year of applying for a license, but there was no time-frame requirement back when Phillip was working for Manny. He was grandfathered in, so long as he passed a practical exam, which he did with flying colors.

David had rented a space in a small brick commercial building on Central Avenue within walking distance of the Red Apple Motel. The space was like a wide hallway that went back twenty feet to the rear of the building. It had enough space for a waiting area in front, one barber chair in the middle, and a back-office area with a rest room off to the side. There was a frosted picture window in front. Annie hand-painted "Phillip's Barbershop" in blue and a barber's pole underneath the name. David rescued a used barber chair from a cosmetology school that was going to pitch it. Christy picked up some mirrors from around the neighborhood on trash day that they put up on the walls to make the space look bigger. Phillip picked out the black and white checkered linoleum floor from the Habitat for Humanity thrift store. The entire family helped to install it. When Phillip fell in love with some purple neon tubing on Craigslist, David and Christy picked it up and put it up around the perimeter of the ceiling.

They were all excited to open for business. Phillip was just as scared as he was excited. All they thought they needed were customers. Everything seemed ready. But there was no way they could prepare themselves for what would happen when they opened the next day.

CHAPTER 8

On Monday morning, Phillip and David parked the Mustang in the front of the store to make it look as if there was a customer in the barbershop. Sheets of rain blew down Central Avenue from the west. In the parking lot, oily puddles and little lumps of soggy newspaper inserts dotted the pavement. Overhead, ominous clouds promised more of the same.

"Well, here we are!" David beamed. He was hoping that his upbeat attitude would put Phillip at ease.

Phillip knew that his daily routine was the thread that held his mind together. But there was nothing that felt routine when he ventured outside of his room. He could always control what went on in his cell. He couldn't imagine people walking in and out of his cell all day. But that's what he felt it would be like to work in a barbershop.

Not daring to look in the mirror hanging on the wall over the work counter, Phillip went straight to his work station when he and David walked through the front door. He checked his assortment of electric clippers that hung on cup hooks under the counter. He made sure that the lithium batteries on the clippers were fully charged. On top of the counter, he had placed his stainless steel instruments of precision. Combs, scissors, shears, and his straight razor were all laid out on a white terrycloth towel like a surgical tray. Phillip picked up the razor and checked the blade. With his back to David, he took a deep breath and tried to steady himself. But his hands shook like an alcoholic with DTs.

"Why don't you give me a shave while we wait for real customers?" David asked while sitting in the barber chair and leaning back. "We don't open up for twenty minutes anyway."

"I'm not sure that's a good idea."

"Relax, Phillip, you're going to do just fine. You just need to get into the rhythm—into the routine of handling customers one at a time." David was trying to reach Phillip. He knew how much Phillip valued a routine.

But touching somebody—anybody—was not part of Phillip's daily routine and having to touch so many different people, all day long, fell way outside of his comfort zone. Phillip knew this day would come. He had spent days visualizing ways to handle it, but the situation continued to make him lose sleep. Up to that morning, Phillip had never imagined a waiting area full of customers. He stared at six chairs in the waiting area when he walked through the front door. David had placed them there Sunday night after dropping Phillip off at the motel. "What if there's more than one customer in the shop?"

"Then they'll have to wait their turn, Phillip. Don't rush. Take your time and give the customer in your chair your undivided attention."

"But they'll get angry if they have to wait too long."

"They understand that they have to wait, Phillip. That's how it goes in a barbershop."

Phillip nodded. Beads of sweat popped up on his forehead. In solitary, nobody waited for him. And if he made a CO wait, he'd be punished somehow. Now all the customers had become COs in Phillip's mind. The thought made his blood heat and his hands go cold.

"Why don't you lather me up?" David said.

Now David was acting like a CO to Phillip—barking orders. Phillip closed his eyes for a second. He thought about the walk in the Pine Bush and how it put him in such a good mood all day Sunday. He looked forward to hanging the posters of the Karner Blues in his shop. It was easy for him to travel to places in his mind. That's all the traveling he could do during his decades in the box.

He threw a black plastic barber cape over and around David, then tilted the chair back exposing David's neck. At that angle his jugular veins popped into view. Phillip thought he saw one begin to throb. He tried to contain himself—to stem the rising tide of excitement. In anticipation, he skipped the hot towel. Reaching for the electric shaving cream dispenser, he quickly pushed the button with his thumb, and the warm menthol-scented foam flowed into the palm of his hand. His jittery hand smeared pale blue cream all over David's neck to cover the veins. But it was too late.

David Thompson.

The demons were back. Phillip stared down at the man who relaxed in his barber chair and his body shuddered with the emotions that threatened to overwhelm him.

In his dreams early that morning, Phillip had stabbed David to death once again and then woke up screaming his name. The dream was so intensely real he could almost smell the blood. It had taken place just over an hour ago. Now David sat in the barber chair as vulnerable as a sleeping baby.

Phillip watched himself reach down for his straight-edge razor with its stainless steel blade. It was like a closed-circuit TV camera in his head, detached and remote. Phillip asked David to order the longest razor available because his hands were too large to control a regular sized one. They both researched the disposable razor blades on Amazon. Phillip asked David to order the highest-rated brand for sharpness. Only five-stars would do.

For a few seconds, Phillip saw his hands come into focus on the black and white screen in his head. He would grip that blade and slice those veins, then he would stab David like a madman with the carving knife tucked away in his sock. Finally, he saw himself grab both his scissors and shears and stick them in David's heart before he walked through the filthy weather back to the safe zone of the Red Apple. He'd take the carving knife to defend himself later against whatever came his way.

David Thompson . . . must kill David Thompson.

Phillip hated himself for these feelings that he could not control. Deep down inside he knew that David had sacrificed a lot to give him a chance to make it. He wanted to make it too. He wanted to be a barber, to live on his own as a free and independent man. That's what he saw himself doing in his best dreams. He wrapped hope around those dreams like his mom wrapped a yellow ribbon around a tree hoping for his release. But Phillip couldn't help the way he felt; it surged up in his gut like a flood tide—unbidden and unstoppable.

Phillip was furious at the way David plucked him from his room and threw him into everyday life. He wasn't ready. He didn't know if he'd ever be ready. He'd stare outside his picture window and try to imagine himself outside. When he felt strong, he'd sprint to the ice machine and back or make a dash for the laundry room. From his point of view, it looked like progress. But this was too much, too soon.

Phillip's eyebrows drew together and almost ran down his nose. As his face turned crimson, his lips thinned until they disappeared. His body quivered when he grabbed the straight-edge razor. As he turned his back to the entry door, he caught sight of himself in the mirror. Looking back was the face of a man who was about to bug out.

Kill David Thompson now!

David sat there with his hands folded on his lap, eyes closed, and a slight smile on his face. Little did he know that he had purchased the weapon that was about to send him to Eternity.

With a flick of Phillip's left wrist, the razor blade popped open from the handle like a switchblade. He passed it to his right hand like he was crossing over a basketball back on the Syracuse playgrounds. Phillip now held the back of the blade steady with his index finger. He twirled it in the overhead light and the blade glistened. There wasn't even a fingerprint smudge on the mirrored surface. He stood over David breathing heavily. Narrowing his eyes to shield them from the squirting blood that would come, he brought the blade to David's throat.

Suddenly, the shop bell jingled while the entry door opened. In walked a tall man with thinning, straw-blond hair wearing large, mirrored sunglasses. Pulling the razor away from David's face with a jerk of his arm, Phillip turned around to focus on the intruder. David opened his eyes at the bell and sat up in the chair.

The man looked down while he pulled out the clipboard tucked under one arm. His head slowly revolved on his neck—left then right—as he scoped out the shop. He made no greeting.

David popped out of his chair and wiped the shaving cream from his face with a terrycloth towel he snatched off the counter. He wasn't about to make their first real customer wait for service. "We don't officially open for a few minutes, but we can take you early."

Phillip stood there frozen in place, with the razor in his hand. He couldn't believe that he was a split second away from killing David. Waves of guilt and shame flooded his brain, rendering him incapable of speech.

Standing just inside the door, the man was taller than Phillip. Beneath his black wool overcoat, he wore navy blue slacks and an open-collar, powder blue dress shirt. You could see a white t-shirt underneath at his neckline. "It looks like you're already open to me."

"No, no," David said, "Phillip was just trying out a new shaving technique on me."

The visitor removed a ballpoint pen from his coat pocket, pulled the cap off with his teeth, turned the pen around, and stuck the end in the cap before removing it all from his mouth. "The law says if you're shaving a man, you're an open barbershop."

Then it hit David—this guy was a government man, a bureaucrat. He wondered if this incident was another CO shakedown. But he had researched the law. The COs as peace officers had no jurisdiction in a place of business unless, perhaps, there was a crime in progress. There was no crime in shaving a man's face. David ripped off the barber cape. He was primed and ready for this new round of CO-generated BS. He would catch this clown in the act and then turn the tables on him either here or in a court of law. While his brain churned, the lawyer persona politely inquired, "What can we do for you, sir?"

The man didn't say anything. His only response was to put pen to paper on his clipboard and begin writing.

David moved toward Phillip, who stood stock-still, hands at rest on the back of the barber chair, blade held in plain view. For a second, Phillip also wondered if this man was a CO. But he was too overwhelmed with remorse to give it much thought. He had very nearly killed his only friend.

Keeping his back to the man, David covered his mouth and whispered to Phillip, "Is this guy a CO?"

Phillip looked at their subject. The man's sunglasses covered a good portion of his face. But he didn't have to see it to make up his mind. He knew of no CO who was taller than him. He didn't know of any CO who was as thin as this guy. Phillip shook his head.

"Okay," David whispered, "let me handle this. Lose the blade, Phillip."

Phillip folded the blade back into its handle and pressed it against the back of the chair.

David walked over towards the man and stood between him and Phillip. "Are you here in an official capacity?"

The man didn't look up. The only sound in the room was his pen scribbling on his clipboard. "Absolutely," he said, without budging. More scribbling filled the air.

"Could I see your badge or some official identification then?" David asked.

The man stopped writing, put his clipboard and pen in one hand, and reached under the overcoat with the other.

With the coat peeled back, David looked for a glimpse of a holster, a gun. Johnny said COs could carry concealed weapons. But he didn't see one.

The man's eyes fixed on David. In the mirrored sunglasses, David could see his reflection.

Phillip knew better than to look at the man's face. He was focused on his hands and feet and nothing else. Those were the only things that could hurt you. That's the way he dealt with COs. If you showed Phillip only the hands of a CO, he could tell you who it was without ever seeing his face. As a precaution, he stood ready with his blade.

The man pulled out an identification card hanging by a lanyard around his neck. "I'm from the Bureau of Licenses. I'm here to inspect this shop." He waved the ID in David's general direction before tucking it back under his overcoat.

David could see enough of the card to determine a few things. The man looked like the employee pictured minus the sunglasses. The card was laminated and carried the NY State Seal. It looked legit. It didn't stay on display long enough for anyone to read the name typed under the photo.

Still, David was suspicious. The State of New York was a giant morass and it typically moved like molasses in January. He couldn't envision the license material moving from the Application Unit to the Inspection Unit in such short order. But he decided to let it go—let it all play out. If this guy wasn't legit, he couldn't do anything to them except waste their time. If he did something stupid, David planned to document it and use it against him.

"Go ahead," David said.

"Who's the owner of this shop?"

"I am," Phillip said. "My name is Phillip Dawkins."

The man wrote the name down.

"You want me to spell it out for you?"

"No."

"Yeah, I figured you knew how to spell it," Phillip retorted.

With his back to the inspector, David glared at Phillip. With the palm of his hand pointed down to the floor, he slowly lowered it in an effort to get Phillip to tone it down. *Chill, pal.*

Phillip's mind had shifted to the present. It was like he was back in his cell and this inspector was a CO. Any inspection in prison meant a guaranteed ticket. They'd always make something up if they couldn't find anything. Phillip hated tickets based on lies. He fought all of those tickets. Now he realized the same crap he had endured in prison for thirty years was stalking him here on the outside. He wondered if he would ever be rid of it. This was not the life he dreamed about in prison. He didn't feel like a free man. He gripped his razor in a big fist.

"Who are *you*, then?" the man asked David.

"I'm David Thompson, his attorney."

"I see. I'm going to look around the shop now," the man said. He looked at the ceiling and shook his head. "You've got a few water stains in your suspended ceiling tiles." He walked over to the wall on the opposite side of Phillip's station. "You've got some cracks in the wall above the baseboards too. Both these items are violations of 10.21. The overall lighting in here is inadequate. So I'll have to write you up for a 10.14. I saw your entrance carpet when I walked in the door. It's not a light color and it's more than a single loop pile and it exceeds one-quarter inch in height. That's a 10.13 violation. Do you have a receptacle for dirty towels and linens?"

"Yes," David said, pointing towards the back wall.

"Where's the cover to it?"

"On the floor, beside it," David replied.

"Okay, the cover must be on it. The law says you must have a cover. That's a 10.16."

"There's nothing in it to cover," David argued. "We haven't opened the shop yet."

"You just used a towel to wipe the shaving cream off your face when I walked in the door. You should put it in there where it belongs."

"What, and violate the law? I couldn't get the cover on at the same time I put the towel in. You'd probably write me up for that. Besides, I'm not done using it yet. That's why I have it in my hand."

"I'm writing you up anyway."

"Figures. Just make a note in your report that I was still using the towel and there was nothing in the receptacle to cover. Say, will I get a copy of your report?"

"Yes, when I'm done I'll give you and the shop owner a carbon copy. Do you have a covered receptacle for trash?"

"Under the counter, in the cabinet. You pull the cabinet door open and the garbage container rolls out. Phillip, pull it out for the inspector."

Phillip sighed. He marched over to the cabinet and yanked open a ground-level door. Out popped the trash receptacle.

"There's no cover for it," the inspector said. "That's a 10.17."

"Come on," David said, "the receptacle is enclosed and covered by the cabinet."

"I'm still writing you up."

"Of course," said Phillip, standing behind the barber chair with his arms folded across his chest, still clutching his razor.

The inspector moved towards Phillip and stood in front of the chair glaring at him. "I don't like your attitude. You're starting to sound like a real wiseass."

Phillip's face quickly inflated like a red balloon. Speaking in that tone, the inspector became a CO to Phillip. He always wanted to kick some CO ass for the thirty years' worth of crap he'd endured. Now here was his chance. It's not like there was a horde of inspectors ready to back up this clown with hats and bats. He was flying solo. It would be one-on-one. Finally, a fair fight.

David saw Phillip's face and stepped over to stand at his side.

The inspector didn't skip a beat as he continued to rattle off a litany of violations. "Under 10.23 (b), the headrest of the barber chair shall be covered by a properly laundered towel or paper for each customer before the customer is permitted to recline in such chair. I didn't see you use either of those protections with this man here. I'm writing you up. 10.23 (c) requires that a sanitary paper strip shall be placed completely around the neck of each customer before any apron or haircloth or any other protective device is fastened around the neck. You didn't use that either."

"But we're not open for business," David said, "and I'm not a customer."

"Tell it to the judge. I see you're using a neck duster," he said, pointing to Phillip's counter.

"What of it," Phillip huffed, shuddering. David put a hand on his shoulder.

"Dusters haven't been allowed for years. That's a 10.27 violation. I'm also writing you up for a general cleanliness violation under 10.20. The shop looks dirty to me."

Phillip started to move towards the inspector. David grabbed him by the shoulder and pulled him toward the rear of the store. Phillip's face showed that he was about to explode. He reached to open his blade. With his hand on Phillip's chest, David shoved him hard. Keeping his back to the inspector, David whispered harshly to him, "Do you want to go back to prison?"

Phillip didn't say anything. He started to move towards David. He bumped into David's extended hand.

"Phillip? Do you hear me? Do you want to go back to prison?" David whispered.

Phillip closed his eyes and grimaced.

"Don't fall into the trap, man. That's what they want. Don't let them get to you. You've come too far, Phillip. *We've* come too far."

Phillip nodded, dropped his hands to his side, and backed off a few steps.

David turned around to face a grinning inspector.

"Is that it?" David demanded.

"One more thing. I'm writing you up for untrustworthiness and incompetence. That's a discretionary violation."

Phillip lunged forward. "You're calling me a liar. That's what untrustworthiness means to me. Nobody calls me a liar. I may be a lot of things, but I ain't no liar."

David headed Phillip off again and blocked his path to the inspector. "Let it go, Phillip. We'll take this before the judge and then we'll appeal it from him, if necessary." David looked over his shoulder at the inspector. "How much is it for each violation?"

"Let's see," he said, while tallying up the total. Looks like there's ten total violations. They're a maximum of $500 each. I'm going to ask for the maximum given his attitude. So that totals $5,000."

"Five grand?" David shot back. "Are you kidding me? That's ridiculous. Here's an honest man trying to make an honest living and you're doing this to him? You're not enforcing the regulations, you're trying to drive him out of business."

With his nose in his inspection report, the man signed his name in a few bold strokes. He tore off a carbon copy of the report and handed it to David. Still grinning, he said to David, "So you really think this man—Phillip Dawkins—is an innocent man honestly trying to earn a living? Is that what you think? Well, I don't think he's innocent. Not for a second. Eventually, you'll figure that out, probably after it's too late. Serves you right—"

"Hold on there," David interrupted. "What are you talking about? I said he's an honest man and you go off half-cocked talking about how he's not innocent. And what does it have to do with me?"

"I'm done here."

"Yeah, that's right. You said too much. You need to stick to your job of driving good people out of business by writing them up for everything under the sun. If you're not going to explain yourself, you need to keep your personal beliefs to yourself—"

"Watch it there, Thompson!"

"Yeah? Why? You have no jurisdiction over me. You can't write me up for being a state citizen voicing my opinion to a state official."

"I can report you for interfering with a public official doing his job."

"Wait a second, you said yourself that you were done here and I have the completed inspection report to prove it. I can't interfere with a public official doing his job if he's done doing it. So when is the hearing date?"

"It's on the form." With that, the man abruptly turned around and walked out--shoving the entrance door so hard that the shop bells were still ringing when he opened his car door.

David followed the man to the door and through the small window watched him get into his state agency sedan. There was nobody else with him in the vehicle. David wondered why he went on and on about Phillip's lack of innocence. He looked at the report and couldn't read the man's signature. His name wasn't printed anywhere on the form. The hearing address, date, and time were at the bottom. When David saw that the hearing was set for the following day, he almost lost his breakfast. There was hardly any time to prepare.

Phillip dropped into the barber chair and sat rubbing his forehead, staring into the floor. He had never had more than fifty dollars to his name for over thirty years. Phillip's entire family tree never had five grand collectively when they were alive. But the fine was the least of his worries.

He was absolutely disgusted with himself for trying to murder David. He took pride in not being a liar, but here he was living a lie in his interactions with David—pretending to be his friend while just a second away from killing him. He had to tell David about his murderous thoughts, even if meant he'd lose that friendship. He'd rather lose that than end up destroying his friend. If he knew anything, he knew that was the right thing to do. He just hoped that David would be willing and able to get him some help.

Phillip's dream of living happily as a free man was coming apart at the seams. The COs took pride in breaking men. The sole purpose of extended solitary confinement without any chance of release is to break you—break your spirit, crush your hopes and dreams, destroy your ability to be a productive human being. On the first day of solitary, a CO told Phillip he'd die in that cell—that this was his living coffin. Phillip always dreamed that life as a free man would be a challenge but magnificent compared to life in solitary. That was the dream that kept him going for three decades. What Phillip didn't count on was that if they couldn't break him on the inside, they'd try to break him on the outside. Phillip wondered if there ever could be such a thing as freedom for someone like him.

CHAPTER 9

That evening, David was holed up researching barbershop law and regulations in his basement office, while Annie made dinner in the kitchen. Phillip and Christy were out in the backyard batting cage. The cage was made from Kevlar netting that hung like a shower curtain from three lengths of high-tensile wires—one on either side, one in the middle—supported by three fifteen-foot galvanized-steel poles on either end. David and Christy had installed it themselves for their baseball team to use for practice.

Phillip stood behind an L-shaped screen to protect himself while pitching baseballs he retrieved from a big bucket for Christy to hit. For five minutes, he was either hitting them off the end of his bat or he was whiffing as the ball whizzed by him. It was a sure sign to Christy that he couldn't catch up to the velocity of Phillip's pitches.

Christy stepped away from the plate and raised his hand to Phillip to stop throwing. "You're really throwing some heat there. Did you ever play baseball?"

"No, basketball was my sport."

"Where did you learn how to pitch?"

"I guess I learned in prison."

"Was there a prison baseball team or something?"

"No," Phillip said, as he moved to touch the netting. It hung in the same diamond-shaped pattern as the galvanized fencing in his rec pen at

Kranston. It didn't feel like solid steel. It felt silky smooth, soft to the touch, as warm as the air. Phillip recalled the times when he'd take rec in the winter when most everyone else stayed in their cell. He'd clear a path on all sides with a snow shovel. If he wasn't trying to catch a few winks in his igloo, he'd be throwing snowballs against the concrete walls of Kranston. Sometimes he would throw for the entire rec hour, all winter long, until the last bit of snow had melted. The state didn't issue any gloves to him, but he didn't care if his hands froze up. "It's my therapy," he told one CO.

"Mr. Dawkins, are you okay?" Christy asked. He was a few feet away from Phillip now on the other side of the L-screen.

"Yeah, I'm fine Christy. I was just thinking back to my days at Kranston. I learned to pitch by throwing snowballs against the wall all winter long."

"Oh, that explains it."

"Is baseball your sport?"

"Yeah, you could say that. I play rec, though. I don't play for the high school team."

"Why not? You've got a nice swing."

"Well, I made the varsity team. But the coach said he'd never give me the opportunity to play. I know I might not be as good as some of the other players, but I could improve. All I wanted was a chance to earn some playing time. But he wasn't even going to give me that. No matter how much I improved, it didn't matter. I wasn't going to come out of the dugout to play. That's what he said. Can you imagine that?"

Phillip tossed the baseball that was nestled in his glove into the bucket. "Yes, I can. I lived that life for thirty years."

"I'm sorry."

"No need to apologize. It looks like you and me have something else in common." Phillip had grown to like Christy. They had exchanged tales about adjusting to life—Christy as a teenager growing to become a young man; Phillip as a man who hadn't been able to evolve since being a teenager. "So did you quit the team?"

"Yeah, I did. Nobody has ever quit the varsity team like that before. The guys on the team thought I was crazy."

"You're a maverick!" Phillip said proudly. That's how Phillip viewed himself. Not a follower or a leader; he was a maverick.

"I guess."

"What are you doing with so much free time on your hands now that you've quit varsity?"

"I volunteer to ride in an ambulance as an EMT. I'm also doing an internship down at Union College, in Mohawk City."

"What's the internship all about?"

"I'm helping a professor doing neuroscience research."

"What is that? Like study of the brain? Are you studying brain surgery?"

"No, no, nothing like that. It's the study of how the brain works."

"How did you get interested in that? When I was your age, I was interested in muscle cars and girls."

Christy laughed. "I like those things too. When I was a kid, I had wild dreams. I even wrote a daily journal about them. My biology teacher pointed me toward neuroscience and helped me land an internship at the college."

The memory of Phillip's wild dreams that morning began to replay through his head. He couldn't believe he had almost killed Christy's father. *What was I thinking? How could I kill this boy's dad? I never thought about how killing David might impact his son. What's wrong with me?* He held the netting with both hands and looked off into the deepening shade of the backyard. He couldn't look Christy in the eyes. In a deep voice, he said, "I've had some crazy dreams in my life, too." Phillip turned and dropped the baseball glove he borrowed from David into the bucket of balls.

Christy realized then that batting practice had been cut short. "It's no big deal. I've had a dream about satyrs playing football at the high school, about my ears being so filled with earwax that earthworms got stuck in them, about killing my dad. That one is recurring."

Phillip gripped the net when Christy mentioned killing his father in his dreams. He almost buckled at the knees. "Why do you think you're killing your father in your dreams?"

"Oh, from what I've read, he might represent an authority figure to me and, as I grow older and more independent, I'm rebelling against his restrictions. This impulse triggers these kinds of dreams."

"Have you told your father about them?"

"Sure. Sometimes at breakfast, he asks if I killed him last night. We have a good laugh about them."

Phillip thought he might be having similar dreams about David for the same reason as his son. But then he realized that he'd been having his dreams about David at Kranston, long before he arrived at his front doorstep. Plus his dreams were no laughing matter; he had almost acted on them. "You're lucky to have such a good dad."

"Didn't you have one?"

"Not really. He died when I was young. The state was really my father. I spent a lot of my younger years in youth detention centers. I skipped school way too much. In those places, they tried to treat me as a man when I was just a boy. It's like I was going in a different direction from you when I was your age. Then again, when I was in the box they treated me like a boy when I should have been treated like a man."

Annie called from the back porch, "Christy, Phillip, it's dinner time."

"Okay, Mom. We're coming."

Everyone sat down at the dining room table. They held hands and David said a prayer. Dinner was marked by long stretches of silence surrounded by the aroma of fresh biscuits, Niblets corn, and fried chicken.

David was deep in thought, trying to figure out what happened that day and trying to formulate a plan for tomorrow's hearing. Christy was deep into his overflowing plate. Phillip was picking at his plate contemplating the meaning of dreams. Annie was watching the men pick at the meal she spent an hour preparing.

"Don't worry, Phillip," Annie said, "if anyone can figure this barbershop thing out it's David."

When she said this, her smile warmed Phillip just as it always did. He nodded, but guilt then rushed through his brain. His stomach knotted. Here he sat enjoying the hospitality of a wonderful woman whose husband he had very nearly killed. He hadn't thought about the impact killing David would have on her either.

Annie added, "Thank you, Phillip, for all of your help around the house these past few months."

"You're welcome," Phillip said, putting down his knife and fork. He wasn't hungry anymore. "It's the least I could do with David trying to help me set up the barbershop."

Annie beamed, "It's nice having you as a part of our family, Phillip."

Phillip lowered his head and spoke softly, "Thank you for having me."

"You know," Annie continued, "I didn't know what to expect when you first joined us. But then I realized that sometimes you need the perspective of someone outside the family to appreciate what's on the inside."

"How's that?" Phillip wondered.

"Well, for one thing, I didn't know how much David was involved in helping people in solitary. I never gave the issue much thought. But now that I know all about it, I'm proud of all he's done."

"You should be," Phillip declared. "Without people like him, nobody would stop to think about us. He helped raise public awareness about the Mandela rule—no more than fifteen days in solitary. They've made changes. No youths or pregnant women in solitary. But guys like me are the forgotten ones."

Annie leaned over to put her hand on his arm as she assured Phillip, "You're not forgotten here."

Phillip's eyes began to get misty. He had a family now but he had almost destroyed it that morning. Phillip choked up, and when he tried to speak his voice quavered, "Again, thank you for having me. I have to excuse myself now." Phillip got up and headed into the kitchen with his half-full plate in one hand. As soon as he was out of sight through the doorway, he used his napkin to dab at his eyes with the other hand.

Looking up at his retreating back from the table, Annie called out, "I'll wrap that up and you can take it back to your motel room. No sense letting good food go to waste."

David eyed Annie as she twice motioned her head in Phillip's direction. Finally, David got the message. He excused himself from the dinner table and asked Phillip to join him on the back porch. The sun had not yet set, and the filtered light through newly emerged leaves gave the backyard a golden glow.

David eased into a rocking chair with a glass of fruity red wine. Nothing like a little Sweet Walter Red to cap off a good meal. Phillip sat beside him on the front edge of an old, peeling Adirondack chair with a can of Genesee beer. After a long winter, the crickets had finally come to life. A late-breaking spring peeper sang in the distance. The family's two cats, Ritz and Oreo, stood with their faces almost implanted in the porch door screen. Their feline tails wagged a slow beat as they scanned the darkness for the rabbit they'd seen that morning. Christy had disappeared upstairs to do his homework. Annie was far enough away in the kitchen doing dishes that she couldn't hear the two men talk.

"It's been a long day," David said.

"Yes, for sure," Phillip said. Only half listening, he was frantically searching for the words to tell David that he had almost murdered him that morning.

David put his wine down on the section of ash stump they used for an end table and began to rock slowly. "Phillip, you know your business license and your barber license weren't hanging on the wall today. I can't imagine why we forgot to put those up."

Phillip ducked his head as he cringed. He felt horrible. No way out now, he had to come clean. "Maybe it's because I didn't have them."

David stopped rocking and turned his head to stare at Phillip. "What are you talking about? I gave you the checks. All you had to do was to fill out the forms and send it all to the Bureau of Licenses. You didn't do that?"

"Yes, I did. Two days ago."

David's slammed the back of his head on the chair. "I gave you the checks and the forms almost three weeks ago."

"I'm sorry. It slipped my mind."

David looked at the ceiling fan slowly spinning a breeze overhead. "When are you gonna learn, Phillip, that this isn't like doing time in the box out here? Every day means something on the outside; every completed task means something."

Phillip took a sip of his Genesee, pausing to lick the foam off his upper lip. It tasted the same to him now as it did back in 1984, the year before they raised the drinking age from 18 to 21. "I'm trying, David. I really am. It's just that I'm not used to having so many things to do. I don't know how to do them all. I think I've gotten better at it." Phillip's head drooped inches away from the beer. He rotated the can slowly with both hands.

David looked over at him and sighed. "Yes, you have gotten better. That's for sure. But this is a big miss. You can't operate a business without the proper licenses. That comes before everything else, Phillip. It's got to be a priority. It's right there at the top of the list. Do you understand, Phillip?"

"Yes, I do now."

"Geez, opening up shop without the licenses is just asking for trouble. No wonder the inspector showed up this morning."

"How did he know we were opening up shop today, though?" Phillip wondered.

David started to rock again. "I don't know. It takes two days for the mail to get to Albany from here. So I guess they couldn't have seen the paperwork before he showed up this morning."

Phillip looked up from his beer and locked on to David's eyes. "I think they're watching us. I think they are watching our every move. It's just like the CO said when they pulled us over: 'When you guys make a move, we'll be there to take you down.'"

David was rocking faster now, picking up speed as the tension mounted. "You're right, but this guy wasn't a CO."

"How can we be sure?"

"You said you didn't recognize him."

"But there are COs all over the state."

"It doesn't add up. We have a hearing date tomorrow, before an administrative court judge. COs can't do license inspections as peace officers. If COs did do the inspection, this thing will be thrown out of court. No, this all looks legit on the surface. But you're right to ask about how they knew to hit us today. That's a good question."

Phillip sipped his beer, convinced in his core that it was probably a CO raid. He had seen them get away with far worse things. They'd attacked him and then accused him of assaulting them first. Not only did he have the broken bones and missing teeth to prove it—they used that as a reason to keep him in solitary.

David's rocking slowed again as he stroked his chin thoughtfully. "I don't get it though."

"What's that?"

"Well, he wrote us up for everything under the sun, but the one thing he didn't do was to write us up for failing to have a business license and a barber license."

"So he missed something. He's human." Phillip knew COs sometimes looked the other way when they saw certain violations. There was an unwritten code of what offenses to enforce and what to let slide. Some actions just generated too much paperwork to make it worthwhile to write up a ticket.

"Maybe, but perhaps he meant to skip those violations. He might have done it on purpose."

"Why?"

"I don't know, but that's something I'm going to have to check out before the hearing tomorrow."

David gently rocked with the back of his head resting against the chair, as the moon slowly rose over the batting cage in the backyard.

Sitting quietly, Phillip wiped the condensation from his can with his pants. Finally, he squirmed on his seat and turned slightly toward the rocker. "There's something I need to share with you, David," Phillip whispered.

"Sure. What's on your mind?"

"Please understand that I'm real uncomfortable talking about the topic. I'm afraid I might say the wrong thing and offend you. I'm not so good with words here, on the outside. I know what I'm thinking on the inside but sometimes now the words don't match my feelings and I think it comes off wrong."

"I think that's probably happened to everyone, including me. When I was younger, I had a difficult time expressing my feelings for Annie in words. I told her that and she understood. It was easier to express my love through my behavior."

"Hold that thought, David." Phillip didn't want to go down David's path. He didn't know where it was leading. It was like David was taking him on one of his field trips to some place potentially uncomfortable. It was probably innocent enough. But it didn't make it any easier for him to talk about how he was tempted to kill David while David talked about how much he loved his wife. "You need to let me take the lead on this topic."

David was taken aback by Phillip's forthright tone. On the one hand, he was pleased to see Phillip's confidence. On the other hand, his mind raced as to what he might have said or done to bother him so much. "Okay, sure, what's on your mind?"

"It's a difficult topic for me to discuss. I don't want you to react until I'm done."

"Is it something I said or did, Phillip?"

"That's the thing. I don't know. Just promise you won't have a reaction." Phillip heard the music coming from Christy's bedroom and the clanking of dinnerware from the kitchen as Annie loaded the dishwasher. The last thing he wanted was for them to hear that he had an urge to kill David. Phillip wondered if he should wait for a better time and place. But he also thought that with Annie and Christy around, perhaps David would be less likely to fly off the handle. He needed to tell David before he went to bed. Maybe then the demons would leave or at least take a long vacation so he could sleep. But how do you tell your best friend—your only true friend—that you want to murder him?

"Okay, Phillip—"

"Just don't react tonight. We can talk about it some more later. I think that would help us both if we kept talking about it. I know it would help me."

"All right, Phillip, I promise already. What's on your mind?"

Phillip took a deep breath. "Look, David, I know I might be screwed up in the head. I think I was doing okay inside the box. I mean, I adjusted to the box. I really didn't have any choice but to adjust to it. If I didn't adjust, the walls, the ceilings, the COs—they all would have crushed me. You see, once you bug out, once they break you, you don't come back. I've never seen anyone come back. I knew deep down inside that I wasn't much better than the bug-outs and the only thing separating me from them was one bad day, one bad moment. Do you understand?"

"Yeah. I mean, I've tried as best I can to comprehend your living situation. I know that I can never fully stand in your shoes. Oh, sure, I did some time in protective custody. I have a feel for solitary. But I did thirty days, not thirty years."

"Well, I had to make some adjustments to survive on the inside and I've discovered—you've helped me discover—that a lot of those adjustments don't apply to life on the outside."

"Right. I think you and I have talked about that over the past few months."

"Yes, but I've got to talk about this on another level. I have to talk about things going on in my head—deep inside it—things I can't control."

"You mean like your subconscious?"

"Yeah, and it takes place most of the times when I sleep or after I wake up. You see, I think these adjustments to the outside are causing me to have crazy dreams. At first, I thought they were just dreams and, you know, I'd just blow them off. But they have gotten more intense, and more real every day."

"What are the dreams about?"

"You."

"Me?" David's eyes almost popped out. He froze in his chair and studied Phillip's posture. His companion was leaning over, forearms resting on his knees, his head drooping almost between his legs. He couldn't—or wouldn't —make eye contact with David. "What am I doing in your dreams?"

"Nothing. You're dead."

"Really? So how did I die?"

"I murdered you."

Silence.

David's eyes bulged and his head bounced around like a bobblehead in slow motion as he tried to process it all. Yeah, he didn't like the idea of being offed by Phillip—even if it was in a dream. But it was only a dream. And Phillip wasn't a murderer in real life. Christy dreamed the same things, and David knew Christy wasn't going to off him. "Any particular reason why you killed me?"

"No."

David shrugged. "I don't know what to say. I mean, it's just a dream. I wouldn't worry about it."

"But I'm afraid I might carry out those thoughts in real life. I'm afraid I might *really* kill you."

Now David looked at Phillip like he was staring down the barrel of a gun. The thought that the man he was trying so hard to help might kill him was hard to accept. David was tired. He wanted to dismiss Phillip's dream and call it a night. But the horror on Phillip's face was a wake-up call. The dream threatened to become reality in Phillip's head and that's all that mattered.

David now saw Phillip in an entirely new light. Phillip wasn't just someone in dire need of help; he was also a threat. Phillip was not only a threat to him, but also a threat to his family. *Why did I bring him into my life? Why did I bring him into our lives? I should know better. This man is a ticking time-bomb and I invited him into our home. What was I thinking? I should have seen this coming a mile away. No good deed ever goes unpunished.*

David had to probe, but he was afraid to hear the answer. "Why do you think you might act on these dreams?"

Phillip was going to tell David that he was seconds away from killing him that morning. He was going to spill the gory details. That was the plan he promised himself he'd follow after the inspector left and they closed the shop. Make a full confession to cleanse the soul. But the terrified look on David's face, the afterglow of a wonderful meal, Christy's dream lecture, and the simple passage of time had made him reconsider. *Maybe I've said enough already. Maybe I just had a bad morning. There were a lot of new things going on today and maybe I'll handle it better once I get used to the job. I don't have the urge to kill him. It's the farthest thing from my mind. The thought of killing him now is repulsive. I might have said enough to relieve my guilt—to get my mind on a better path. My God, look at all he's done for me. If I tell him any more details, I might lose him. Without David, I'd be dead or back in prison. Maybe that's where I should be anyway. My brain is so scrambled after what they did to me. I need to patch the thing up; I can't fix it alone.* He swallowed hard and said, "It's just that the dreams seem so real."

David rocked a bit and looked skyward. There was a full moon rising and David thought that was fitting for the horror show playing out on his porch. *Afraid* was the word that kept coming to mind. Phillip was *afraid* he might act on his dreams in real life. He was *afraid* he might really kill David. *Maybe so long as a person is afraid to live their dreams, they won't act on them. When is a killer afraid to kill? When does a killer pre-announce that to his next victim? Maybe this is a lot like Christy's dreams.* "Did you have these same dreams in prison too?"

Phillip wasn't going to lie. He thought himself incapable of it. If there was one thing that Phillip owed to his father—or more specifically, his belt —was his unwillingness to lie, though bending the truth could happen. That had been a necessity to survive the box. "Yes, I've had similar dreams."

"About killing me?"

"Yes."

"Did you talk to anyone about them at prison? A psychologist, a psychiatrist?"

"Impossible," Phillip said shaking his head. "The system is so messed up."

"What do you mean?"

"When the demons had me by the throat in the box, I wanted to talk to someone, anyone. But I couldn't. If asked to see a psychologist, he'd give his therapy right outside my cell, my gate. Same with the chaplain. They wouldn't take you to a private room. That is by design. Inmates all around me could overhear anything they talked about with me. And once some of these guys sense a weakness in you, they'll exploit it 24/7, and they'd spread the word to everyone. Then they'd all talk trash all the time. Try and get you to bug out. Reaching out only causes you more pain. And if they found out I was taking pills, they'd yell all day that I was a medication-taker, couldn't handle the box, was going to bug out. Nope, no privacy for you. It's easier to break you then. The COs want to break you so they can control you. Control is always the goal. But once you're broken, it's all over for you. You're a vegetable. But it's a new day for the mental health department—

they will have a long-term patient. And the pharma companies will have a long-term income stream."

David didn't know what to say to Phillip's rant. The insanity he described was too much for any man to overcome; it was also too much to digest in one sitting. Moonlight bathed the backyard and illuminated David's shed. It was a small shed, only 8' x 10', yet it was larger than Phillip's cell. David forced a smile. "You've come a long way since I hid you in the shed back there the first day we met up."

Phillip nodded. "I really appreciate all you've done for me. I feel better now that I've talked to you."

"So, I take it you're not going to kill me tonight?" David asked with the stoic face of a con.

"No, sir. That's the furthest thing from my mind."

"How about my family? Have you ever thought about killing my family?"

"No, sir. Just you."

"Do me a favor, Phillip."

"Anything."

"Promise you'll let me know if you feel like killing me again, okay?"

"Yes, sir. I promise."

David looked at his watch. "I think we should both call it a night. Let's get some rest and pick this topic up another time. I'll get my keys and take you back to the motel."

"Okay," Phillip said, as they both heard footsteps fast approaching.

Annie opened the porch screen door. "David, someone called for you while you two men were out here talking."

"Did you pick up or did he leave a message?"

"I was too busy cleaning up to answer; up to my elbows in dishwater. He did leave a message. It was Johnny McFadden."

"All right, I'll call him up after I take Phillip back to the motel."

"Okay," Annie said. "You guys leaving now?"

"Yep, as soon as I find my keys."

"I saw them in the den. I'll get them for you," Annie said, closing the screen door behind her.

David stood up and stretched.

Phillip sat there, circling his index finger on the top of the empty Genesee can.

"You okay?" David asked.

"I'm not sure."

"What's on your mind now?"

"That name—Johnny McFadden. I recognize it. Would he happen to work at Kranston?"

"Why, yes. Do you know him?"

"That's the name of the new CO that wrote me my last ticket there."

CHAPTER 10

Gusts of wind and sheets of rain pounded the Mustang as it surfed down Central Avenue on the way to the hearing in Albany. Every time David plowed through a puddle, the car shook. Water sprayed like a fountain from the wheel wells onto the crumbling sidewalks with a sound like a huge wave crashing on a rocky coastline.

Phillip said, "It sounds like static blasting from my TV." On some nights when he had trouble sleeping and there was nothing good on the radio, he tried to fall asleep to the static on the TV. The waves of white noise filled up the deafening silence of his motel room. He hadn't said much since last night when he learned that David was friends with Johnny McFadden. McFadden was the CO riding in the back seat during the pull-over; the same one who'd written him his last bogus ticket at Kranston.

"Phillip, I'm sorry I didn't tell you about Johnny McFadden. I didn't think you needed to know. If I knew he had written you a ticket, I would have told you about him. But as far as I knew back then, he was roped into riding in the backseat with the other COs for the pull-over."

"That's what you said last night," Phillip said, looking straight ahead. "Did you ever think that he might be in charge of the ring of COs that pulled us over?" Phillip always thought that the guy furthest behind was the guy in charge. That's the way it worked at Kranston. The COs would never walk in front of a con. They always stood to the side or to the rear, with the most senior CO or prison official furthest back.

"He's a newjack. They're not in charge of anything."

Phillip knew David was right when it came to newjacks. But he wasn't convinced that McFadden was a newjack. The feeling persisted, even though the first and only time he'd seen Johnny was when he wrote that last ticket at Kranston. For all Phillip knew, McFadden was some bigwig from the central office posing as a CO; a guy sent in to hit him with a ticket just for the hell of it. "You sure he's a newjack? You sure he's not some hotshot from the central office sent down to screw me over?"

"Central office? You mean the central office at Kranston?"

"No, the central office for the Bureau of Prisons. The prisons in New York don't run themselves. They're not like other state agencies that are decentralized and run at the institutional level. Everything flows from the central office in Albany. When they say jump, the prison superintendents compete to see who can jump highest."

"Well, McFadden has never worked at the central office. He's a newjack, pure and simple."

"Are you sure of that?"

"I've known him for years. I knew him when he was selling meat out of the back of his pickup. No way."

Phillip didn't say anything. A wave of paranoia had hit when David dropped him off at the Red Apple the night before. He skipped his bedtime routine—no shower, no brushing his teeth, no vitamin, no radio. He just lay down in his street clothes on top of the bedspread and imagined all sorts of wild scenarios involving Johnny McFadden. The good news was that he didn't dream about killing David that night. But Phillip dwelled on the possibility that somehow David might have been involved with McFadden in a scheme to drive him insane. Phillip was used to everyone being against him. That had been his life for thirty years.

David knew Phillip was troubled about McFadden. Ever since he mentioned McFadden's name, Phillip had put back on his 24/7 prison face. He stared straight ahead and moved like he was marching at Kranston. David knew from experience that he needed to chip away at the block of ice now surrounding Phillip. "You've said yourself that the central office is staffed with personnel promoted from within the system."

"Yes, that's right."

"Well, Johnny's been in the system for a year. I don't know if he's even passed his probationary period."

"If you say so."

David parallel parked into a space across the street from the Bureau of Licenses building at the Empire State Plaza downtown. Silently thanking the parking gods for the miracle of a convenient spot, he handed Phillip an umbrella. "You go in and wait in the lobby. Maybe hit the men's room before we find the courtroom. It won't look good if you have to leave the hearing to go to the bathroom."

"Okay." He hated when David treated him like a boy. But then realized he was wise to think ahead like that. Phillip had to relearn bathroom planning when he was released from Kranston. He still was prone to lapses. The one good thing about solitary was you just had to turn around to relieve yourself in the cell toilet. That was life 23/7. Outside in the real world, everything was more complicated. "What about you?"

"Me?" David answered. "I went before I left the house, if that's what you're asking. I've got to come up with some change for the parking meter. So I'll meet you in the lobby in a few minutes."

Phillip popped open his umbrella and bounced across the street like his shoes were spring loaded. It was the stride of a man who had lived an up-and-down life, one filled with more jumping jacks than steps walked. He bounced through the revolving door at the Bureau of Licenses.

David picked up his cell to call Johnny McFadden while searching the glove compartment for the Ziploc baggie full of change he stored there.

"What's up?" Johnny answered.

"You tell me what's up," quipped David. "You told me only the senior-most COs work in the solitary wing, right?"

"Yeah, so—"

"So, you couldn't work in solitary even if you wanted to because you don't have seniority."

"That's right—"

"Well Dawkins said you gave him a ticket—his last misbehavior ticket at Kranston."

"Really?"

"Yeah. So how did that happen?"

"I'm not sure—"

"Come on Johnny—are you playing me for a sap? What do you all have against Dawkins? What did he ever do to you?"

"Dude, I don't have it in for him—"

"How did this happen?"

"Oh, God, that was him!"

"What you mean?"

"It must have been him. There's no other explanation."

"Spill it, Johnny."

"I've worked in solitary a total of two days—"

"But you said you can't work there—"

"Permanently. I can't work there permanently. Not that I'd want to work there at all. It's a nut house."

"You didn't say 'permanently' when I talked with you at the diner."

"We were talking in generalities back then. It wasn't an issue in our conversation, not that I can recall. So I didn't get into specifics—"

"Come on, Johnny."

"Shut up and let me finish. I can be a substitute in solitary when they're short a guy due to sickness or something. The brass tells me where to go every shift depending on their needs. So one day months ago, I got assigned to solitary. The two senior COs on duty with me told me to write up a ticket for some con and I did. They wanted to see if I'd follow orders—part of my initiation into the brotherhood, or so they said. So I did."

"Did Dawkins really do anything to deserve the ticket?"

"I'll tell you if you promise that this is strictly between you and me. You know, lawyer-client privilege and all."

"You're not my client, but I promise not to say anything."

"You'd better not, because you could get me fired if you did."

"I promise, Johnny."

"Then, no, he didn't do anything to deserve that ticket."

"Why did you write him up then?"

"Because they told me to do it. The senior COs said it would be funny and it wouldn't do any harm because he was already in solitary and he was going to be there forever-and-a-day anyway. They said fighting the ticket would keep him busy and content. They said it would be like therapy to him. Truth be told, I think they did it so he'd be focused on fighting the ticket as opposed to bothering them any. It's not the same with most cons in solitary. They've given up fighting tickets. But not him. They said he's been fighting for decades."

"How come you didn't recognize his name from the hearing?"

"Prisoners are numbers to us, not names. Besides, the senior COs filled out all the paperwork. I just signed and showed up to the hearing to testify. Nothing more, nothing less. I don't think his name was mentioned once when I was in the hearing room. If it was, I don't remember it."

"But you referred to him by his name at the diner."

"Yeah, but until now I didn't know they were one and the same person. I didn't see Dawkins when we pulled you two over. Perhaps I should have put two and two together, but I guess I put that solitary wing incident out of my mind. I find myself boxing up all the unpleasant experiences I have on the job and trying to forget them."

David's head was spinning. He didn't know whether to believe Johnny or not. He knew Johnny was a great salesman—he could sell ice to Eskimos. He had seen Johnny spin a web of deceit around the travel baseball profiteers who took advantage of kids and their gullible parents. Johnny was willing to stretch the truth, and even lie if he had to, to get his way and to save baseball for the sandlot kids. But David didn't know if he was on the receiving end of a Johnny campaign this time around. "Johnny, when we were trying to save the baseball program for the kids, you once said: 'You are either part of the problem or part of the solution. Pick a side because there's no middle ground.' I don't know whose side you are on this time around."

"You know, it's just like a lawyer to bring up what someone said years ago and stick it in his face."

"Ah, come on—"

"Sit on your law degree for a second and listen to me."

"I'm all ears, Johnny."

"Hey. I'll admit it. I'm standing on middle ground here. I'm straddling the fence. On the one hand, I don't like what I see here as a CO and I'm on the side of change—I'm part of the solution. On the other hand, I can't afford to get fired—so I guess I'm part of the problem."

"Finally, an admission of sorts."

"Knock it off, counselor, and listen. The reason I called is to help you out. You see, as a newjack I have to do the cruddy work. So the other day, they tell me I have to clean out a secretary's office and throw all of her papers into the trash. After decades with the state, Edith Nowak, secretary to the superintendent, didn't show up one day. They learned that she filed her paperwork with the New York State Retirement System and that she retired, effective immediately. No notice, no retirement party, no nothing. Poof, she's gone and she's not coming back. They told me to clean out her desk and the file cabinets. What a mess. So I found a bunch of papers stuck way in the back of the bottom drawer of a file cabinet in a huge accordion folder with Phillip Dawkins' name on it. There're copies of correspondence going back to the 1960s between someone with the initials EC and a Boris Dietrich. There's also correspondence between Edith and this guy Boris. Plus there's a bunch of other papers and some photographs. I didn't have time to look through it all."

"What do these papers have to do with Phillip Dawkins?"

"I don't know. That's for you to figure out."

"You mean you didn't trash them?"

"Nope. On the way to the dumpster outside, I made a pit stop at my car and loaded the accordion file into the trunk. I'll drop them off at your house today."

David didn't know what to think. He didn't know if the papers were just a red herring Johnny had packaged for some unknown reason or if they were connected somehow to Dawkins. All he knew was that he had to make a hearing that started in ten minutes and he didn't see any harm in looking at Johnny's stash. "Sure, Johnny, drop them off and I'll have a look at them. Thank you for the intelligence work. I've gotta run now. Call you later." David snapped the cell shut, plunked some change into the meter as he popped open his umbrella, and sprinted through traffic. Then he squished through the revolving door, where David found Phillip investigating an aquarium full of fish on display in the lobby.

"Come on, Phillip, the hearing is on the tenth floor. We need to catch an elevator."

David hit the button to call an up elevator. "You just let me do the talking, Phillip."

"Okay."

"Try not to get upset with the judge or threaten the people from the state. All right?"

"Okay." Phillip had left the carving knife at home that day. He didn't want to set off the metal detectors at the Bureau of Licenses. But there were no metal detectors and security was an unarmed rent-a-cop reading a magazine at the reception station. *No metal detector? In a state facility? How could that be?* He felt the system was toying with him, lulling him into complacency, readying itself to crack down on him from behind. *I should have brought the knife.*

The elevator door opened. Phillip, David and a few state office workers hopped on. David pushed the button for the tenth floor then moved his way to the rear with Phillip.

When the doors shut, Phillip realized he was in a box smaller than his cell and it was packed full of people that he didn't know. By moving himself to the very back of the elevator he made sure that nobody stood behind him. He closed his eyes and thought about the butterfly fields. Then he stage-whispered to David, "Do you think those fish have enough room in the aquarium? Did you see that blue one with the big, fan-like fins?" It was a Blue Male Crowntail Betta. "It looked like a Karner Blue."

Some woman sporting blue and red dyed hair, with tattoos on the pronounced cleavage escaping her tank top, stared over her shoulder at Phillip. Phillip saw her and wondered if she had come from a Grateful Dead concert. He thought it might be better not to look back at her, so he closed his eyes in self-defense.

David said, "We'll talk about the predicament of the fish after we address yours."

When the elevator chime rang for the fourth time, David announced this was their floor. Phillip opened his eyes to a fairly empty cab. They both exited and followed the signs. At the end of the deserted hallway was the designated courtroom. David straightened Phillip's blue tie before they entered. He made Phillip dress for the occasion in a loose cement gray suit from SALs, paired with a white dress shirt that only had a slightly irregular collar. The last time Phillip wore a suit was in the 1980s at his father's funeral. He hoped that wasn't a bad luck omen.

The courtroom looked more like a conference room. There were four rows of antique pine pews on either side. They looked more like they belonged in a church than a courtroom. The pews didn't match the mahogany-colored judge's bench. This was the only wooden furniture in the room, which featured institutional gray drywall and a matching acoustic tile suspended ceiling. Humming fluorescent cool-white tubes provided the lighting over worn ocean blue carpet tiles that curled at the edges.

Phillip and David took a seat in the front row behind a plastic 4' x 8' folding table. There was nobody else in the room. On top of the judge's bench were two fifty-five-inch televisions displaying only static. Each one was equipped with a miniature camera on the top. There were two microphones stationed on the judge's bench, too. The sound on the TVs was muted.

When David saw the Cisco-labeled hardware and the absence of a high-back chair for the judge, he figured the judge was going to be patched in remotely. He'd never seen anything like it—the judge would be on television presiding over some courtroom miles away. He had no clue this was coming and had no idea how it would work. *How do I present my evidence to a judge on television? Do I hold it up to the camera?*

Phillip stood transfixed, in awe of the static on the two huge television screens. He thought if they were back in his motel room, they could put him to sleep for sure. At the same time he was dazzled by all the technology. In a flash he grew angry at the Bureau of Prisons—still stuck in the age of ancient, error-prone cassette tapes and outdated cameras. Kranston had 65 cameras that never worked when an inmate needed them. He knew it was a rigged game back at Kranston. He just didn't realize how heavily rigged it was until now.

During his six disciplinary appeal hearings, Judge Leon Wolack was fond of saying, "Well, Dawkins, if New York could afford such advanced technology, don't you think we'd use it?" Now Phillip saw with his own eyes that the state could afford the advanced technology, but the Bureau of Prisons chose not to purchase it because their real goal was to crush inmates by making testimony disappear in reels of magnetic tape that even the Salvation Army couldn't resell.

Phillip got a glimpse of the life-cycle the system had planned for him. After a destroyed inmate had served his bid, the state was only too happy to dump his remains onto the streets. The messed up ex-con then became everyone's problem, at least until life pointed him back to prison again. Ka-ching! Mother Kranston always welcomed repeat customers with open arms.

A slim, middle-aged woman dressed in a floppy white blouse, a charcoal gray pantsuit and sensible pumps approached David. She extended a hand, palm out saying, "If you have any documents you'd like the judge to consider, give them to me now. I will scan them and email them to him."

"I'm sorry," David said, "but are you the attorney for the state?"

"No," she said, pushing back her brunette mane. "The state will not have a representative here today. I'm an assistant to Judge Fairbanks." She waggled her fingers in encouragement. Time seemed to be of the essence in this proceeding.

"Oh, okay," David said. As he shuffled through his papers to assemble his exhibits, he wondered how the state could prosecute their case without an attorney. He handed the exhibits to the woman then asked her, "Where is Judge Fairbanks located?"

"New York City," she replied, turning on her heels and hurrying out of the courtroom.

It was almost time for the hearing to begin. David looked around the courtroom. They were still the only people there. Suddenly, a red light on one of the cameras started to blink. The camera hummed as it scanned the courtroom, stopping when it locked on David and Phillip. There was still static on the televisions. With the red light still blinking, David had the uneasy feeling they were being watched from the other end of the camera. Green lights on the microphones switched on remotely. David leaned over to Phillip. With his hand cupped over his mouth, he whispered, "Don't say anything out loud from now on. The microphones are on." Phillip nodded.

David scribbled a few notes to himself while Phillip stared down the camera. Judge Fairbanks' assistant returned, handing the exhibits back to David before she promptly left the room again. As she made her exit, a man passed her in the doorway coming in.

The new arrival walked up to the table, reaching for a remote-control device. He was tall, older than both Phillip and David, with unkempt, wavy white hair, glasses, and a beard that looked like someone had put a package of steel wool through a blender. It carried a few crumbs and a smear of yellow near his mouth, likely the remains of his breakfast sandwich. The maroon V-neck sweater he wore revealed a once-white T-shirt underneath at the collar and around his midriff where it stuck out over his belly. His sweater was way too short. When he moved, an employee badge hanging from a tattered yellow lanyard bounced on his gut. In a burst of irony, it announced "Excelsior"—the New York State motto.

He pressed a few buttons, which made the static on one monitor off to the side disappear. Now the screen showed Phillip and David on TV. Then the man picked up another remote, pressed a few buttons that turned on the other TV in the middle of the judge's bench. It revealed a brief head-and-shoulders view of the judge staring into the camera. The man then made an about-face. Without uttering a single word or looking at David and Phillip once, he left the room.

Now Phillip was sure that the Grateful Dead was playing somewhere in the building. He whispered to David, "That guy looks like the lead guitarist from the Grateful Dead—Jerry Garcia."

David whispered back, "He's dead, you know. Died in the mid-1990s."

"Really?"

The judge now had his head down, as he shuffled through the papers before him. All David and Phillip could see was what the camera framed— his short, neatly cropped, fuzzy red hair. On the television screen, his hair looked unreal, like the thick, fuzzy mop of a GI Joe action figure. He peered up into the camera, put on a pair of black horn-rimmed glasses, and intoned, "Good morning."

"Good morning, your honor," David said.

"Good morning," Phillip said.

"I can see you and hear you," the judge said. "I take it you can both see and hear me?"

"Yes, your honor," David said.

"Mr. Dawkins, I see you have counsel with you this morning. Is that correct?"

"Yes, sir."

"I have the notice of appearance on record. Mr. Thompson, you are respondent's counsel. Is that correct?"

"Yes, sir. But if it please the court, I may also testify as a witness as I was present on the date of inspection."

"It is so noted. I have just activated the digital recording line. We are on the record."

Phillip took note. *No rickety, old cassette player here.*

"My name is Judge Robert Fairbanks. I am the administrative law judge presiding over this matter at the New York City office of the Bureau of Licenses. This is a hearing regarding the Bureau of Licenses and Phillip Dawkins. Mr. Dawkins and his attorney, Mr. Thompson, are appearing via video conference from the Bureau of Licenses office in Albany, New York. Before we begin, will you both raise your right hands?"

David and Phillip raised their hands.

"Do you both solemnly swear or affirm that your testimony shall be the truth, the whole truth, and nothing but the truth subject to the penalty of perjury?"

"Yes," they responded in unison.

"I am going through the state's documents first, one by one, and will ask you if you have any objections to those documents being entered into evidence, or if there is any reason you believe I should not consider the documents in making my decision. After I review the documents from the Bureau of Licenses, you will have an opportunity to introduce any documents you brought with you, call any witnesses, and make any statement you would like to make. At the end of the hearing, I will write a decision and an order; you will get a copy before you leave. Do you have any questions about the process?"

"No, your honor," David said. He couldn't believe the judge was going to issue a decision from the bench. No need to deliberate on his part. David feared then that the entire process was a charade. Sure, the judge would hear them—right before he found Phillip in violation on all counts.

Phillip had heard a similar spiel at the disciplinary hearings at Kranston. *If Leon Wolack had a cousin in the system, his name would be Judge Robert Fairbanks.*

The judge said, "I have a notice of hearing in front of me dated yesterday. It is signed by a licensed investigator, badge number 576015, signature illegible, at your shop located at 1877 Central Avenue, Karner, New York." The judge then itemized the violations, one by one, and read them into the record. "Do you have any objections to receiving this document into evidence?"

"Yes," David said. "The investigator did not sign the ticket—the notice of hearing."

The judge said, "I see that he tried to sign it. Don't you see those lines above the signature line?"

David squinted hard at the lines on his copy. But they didn't look like a signature—just three slashes with a pen. "I'm sorry. I still have to object to this document because I don't think that's a signature. I think the respondent has a right to know the name of the inspector who is accusing him of the violations."

"Okay, Mr. Thompson. Your objection is noted. I am going to overrule it because it looks like a name to me. It looks like a valid badge number too. I'm going to take judicial notice that the document is produced in the normal course of business at the Bureau of Licenses and admit it into evidence as state's exhibit one. Anything else?"

"I don't understand why the state is allowed to prosecute its case without representation. I think Mr. Dawkins has the right to cross-examine the state and, specifically, the investigator."

"The state has made that decision. The evidence will be weighed with that thought in mind. But if you are making an objection based on their failure to appear, it is noted and overruled. Anything else?"

"Yes, your honor. I have a jurisdictional objection."

"Okay, I'm listening."

David had figured out why the inspector didn't cite Phillip for lack of a business license and a barber license; he planned to work it to Phillip's benefit. "Your honor, under the regulations and prior administrative case law, the Bureau of Licenses does not have authority to issue violations and assess fines against unlicensed businesses and operators. I submitted a brief memorandum of law as an exhibit."

Judge Fairbanks began thumbing through the memorandum. Then he turned his attention to a manila folder, presumably containing the state's paperwork. "Let the record show that the state's file does not contain any evidence that the respondent is licensed either as the owner of a shop or as an operator. Mr. Dawkins, have you ever operated a barbershop before in New York or ever held a license as a barber in New York?"

"No, sir."

"May I continue, your honor, on the same point?" David asked.

"Yes, go ahead."

"The sole remedy under the regulations and case law is for the Bureau of Licenses to refer this matter to the attorney general."

The judge sighed. "I'm going to accept this memorandum into evidence as respondent's Exhibit A. I am going to rule from the bench on this one. I agree with respondent's argument, especially in the absence of anything from the state. Given the circumstances, I rule that this case be dismissed, with prejudice, for lack of jurisdiction. Mr. Thompson, because the case has been dismissed, I will write my decision and put it in the mail to you. There being nothing further, this case is now closed."

"Your honor, I have one more item—"

But before David could finish his sentence, the television showing the judge went to static. The judge had signed off and disappeared into thin air

—poof! Court adjourned. Phillip and David stared at one another in total disbelief.

David had wanted to ask about the procedure he needed to follow to get the investigator's name. He still thought it was fishy that the state investigated the shop on the first day it was open. They didn't know there was anything to investigate then because neither the business nor the barber license had been received and processed.

"What just happened?" Phillip asked.

"Not here," David whispered to him while pointing to the microphones. Their green lights were still on.

Together they hurried out into the hallway, heading to the elevator. "You caught a break, Phillip. Because you screwed up in getting your licenses in order, you screwed the state in its case against you. How's that for justice?"

"So there are no fines, right?"

David pressed the elevator button. "That's right. Thank goodness you screwed up. When they didn't write you up for failing to have licenses, it made no sense to me. But I figured out they didn't do that because if they pled that, it would be an admission on their part that they didn't have jurisdiction."

"Can the state appeal?"

"Yes, but there is only a single administrative judge assigned to appeals in the state on Bureau of Licenses issues. And he has already decided the exact same issue by dismissing the case."

"Wow, that's great news. But what about the attorney general? Won't they refer the case to him?"

The elevator dinged, the door opened, and they boarded an almost-full car. "Let them go ahead and try. The attorney general probably has a case backlog one hundred miles long. I doubt an unlicensed barbershop and barber will be at the top of the attorney general's list of cases to pursue, especially when we get all of our license paperwork in order years before he even looks at the case file."

As the doors shut, Phillip didn't have to close his eyes to travel to the butterfly field. The hearing outcome had restored his hope. He asked David, "Now what about those fish? Is the aquarium too small? What do you think?"

David rolled his eyes.

CHAPTER 11

David took Phillip out to lunch to celebrate their victory. They ate at the Golden Corral—all the chicken nuggets and salad you can handle with free refills on soda—before returning to David's office.

Phillip folded his long legs under the table David had set up next to his desk. The knotty pine paneled space in the basement was turning from cozy to crowded with the addition of Phillip.

David handed him the barbershop mail. Phillip quietly and methodically read every piece of mail with intense concentration, his large hands dwarfing the "occupant" envelopes and brightly colored flyers. Meanwhile David rifled through the huge accordion file that Johnny had left for him at the side-door entrance.

Phillip asked, "What are all those papers you have there?"

"Never mind." He knew Phillip was just a question away from asking about the source of papers. The last thing David wanted to do was to turn a good day into a bad day by mentioning Johnny McFadden's name to him.

"You just pay attention to your mail for now. Look to see if there's anything there about your licenses."

"Okay."

"Don't waste your time reading and rereading every piece of junk mail like you usually do."

"You've told me that before—"

"But you still read and reread it."

"Sometimes I don't know what's junk and what's not."

"Here's a little clue. If some outfit sent you junk a few weeks ago, and then sends you something a few weeks later, they're probably sending you junk again."

"I guess I like mail—any type of mail. It's a holdover from prison."

"And my response to that would be?"

"You're not in prison anymore."

"Correct," David said. "I'm going to make a few phone calls, so keep it down for a minute."

Phillip nodded and returned to reading his mail, gripping it with both hands, like he was reading the Gideon Bible in his motel room.

David picked up his landline handset and dialed his long-time attorney friend, Jim Fletcher.

"Hello? My caller ID says that David Thompson is calling. Could it really be him?"

"How's it going, Jim?"

"I'm doing as well as a drunk might expect," he said, laughing.

"You're a funny guy. Hey, I need a favor from you."

"Sure, anything. I owe you one. What's up?"

"I need you to FOIL the Bureau of Licenses. You know what I mean, right?"

"Sure, you want me to serve them a with Freedom of Information Law request. What are you looking for?"

"A name—the name of the inspector who hit Phillip's barbershop the other day."

"Really? That's news to me."

"Yeah, it happened the day before yesterday."

"Okay."

"I need the inspector's name and any other information in their file."

"Why can't you FOIL them yourself?"

"Because I'm sure they're hiding something. If I FOIL them, they'll see my name and know I'm looking for something in that file. They'll deep-six it before I get my hands on it. I need you to be my straw man, Jimbo."

"Gotcha. How do you want me to proceed?"

"FOIL all of the Bureau of Licenses investigative files going back one year in the Albany area. That request won't alert them that you're after only one file. Have them put all the files in order chronologically and look for the file for Phillip's Barbershop. The hearing was this morning. We won, by the way."

"Nice."

"Copy everything in Phillip's file and call me when you're done."

"Got it."

"Thanks, Jim. Appreciate it."

"My pleasure."

"I'll talk to you later then."

"You bet," Jim said, hanging up.

As soon as he heard the dial tone, David was back to punching numbers into his phone. It started ringing on the other end. "Come on, Julius, pick up already. I know you're sitting at your desk with a coffee in one hand."

On the sixth ring, he picked up. "Special Agent Moore here."

"Yes you are special, Julius."

"Always the joker, Thompson."

"Took you long enough to pick up there, Julius."

"I saw it was you, and I debated with myself over whether I should answer or not."

"So, are you saying I won the debate?"

"Given the choice between the staggering amount of paperwork on my desk and talking to you, yeah you won. Congratulations. So what's on your mind? You're not blowing up oil trains again, are you?" Moore had pursued David as a terrorist suspect before realizing he was innocent. Together, they worked to find the real oil train bombers. The two men had grown to be friends after David's efforts saved the life of Julius's granddaughter—among other children—when an oil train exploded near her Albany elementary school.

"No, sorry, nothing as exciting as that."

"You sound like you have something for me, then."

"Yes, it might lead to something, or it could be a blind alley. But I'm afraid it might involve some paperwork on your end."

Julius sighed. "All right, Thompson, I can at least listen to you. Just don't put me to sleep."

"You mean you don't have an afternoon coffee in your right hand?"

"I'm trying to cut back. Doctor's orders."

"Okay, well maybe this little mystery will wake you up. I'm trying to help out an ex-con by the name of Phillip Dawkins."

"Yeah, I know about him."

"Professionally?"

"No. I read about his release in the newspaper. It raised some eyebrows around here—a guy in solitary for thirty years for a crime he supposedly didn't commit. What about him?"

"Well, it seems there are some people who don't want to see him succeed on the outside."

"What's been going on?"

"CO harassment via an unwarranted traffic stop, a rogue state inspector at his barbershop."

"Really? That's weird."

"I'm just scratching the surface of weird, Julius." David had no intention of ever telling Julius that Phillip thought about killing him. He didn't want Julius to get sidetracked and start investigating Phillip.

"What do you want me to do?"

"I've got a letter—one of many—from someone with the initials "EC" and someone named Boris Dietrich. It's dated January 24, 1966. In it, EC tells Boris that he went through a loyalty background check with the FBI in the late 1940s and tells him how difficult it was for him and his family at the time. I need you to run through the FBI archives and find that report. I need to find out the identity of EC as a piece to the puzzle."

"What puzzle?"

"Long story, but these letters were in a file with Phillip Dawkins' name on it. I don't know if there's a connection or not between these people and Phillip, but I want to look into it."

"You mean you want me to look into it. Do you know we might have a bunch of ECs who went through loyalty checks in the late 1940s?"

"How do you figure that?"

"Harry Truman signed an order in 1947—Executive Order 9835—otherwise known as the "Loyalty Order" to do background checks on people. I think they did close to 30,000 field investigations. I'm sure there were a lot of people who have the initials EC who were investigated. Can you narrow it down any?"

David shuffled through the letters. Some of them were contained in envelopes. No return address. All hand-addressed to Boris Dietrich at a PO Box in Slateville, New York. He looked at the postmarks. "Yeah, I can narrow it down. Look for someone in the upstate New York area between

Montreal and Albany. I've got letters postmarked from both Montreal and Albany. While you're at it, see if you can track down anyone by the name of Boris Dietrich in Slateville, New York. I think that's located close to Kranston."

"All right, that narrows it down. I'll see what I can find."

"Thanks, Julius. I owe you one."

"Yes, you do," Julius said, before hanging up.

"Who was that?" Phillip asked.

"He's a friend who works at the FBI. Phillip, let me ask you something. Who is the superintendent at Kranston?"

"Mr. Martin Kleinschmit."

"Have you ever heard of someone by the name of Boris Dietrich?"

Phillip rubbed his chin, eyes fixated on a colorful brochure from Boscov's Department Store. "No, can't say I have ever heard of anyone with that name."

"How was Kleinschmit as a superintendent?"

"He was a good superintendent."

"How so?"

"He gave me special privileges that inmates in solitary don't get."

"Like what?"

"A pair of long johns, sneakers, shower sandals, stick deodorant, extra bars of soap. That kind of stuff is not allowed by the Bureau of Prison directives."

"How could he do that if it was not allowed by the directives?"

"He said he had broad authority to do things that were in the best interest of the facility. Sometimes that authority could work against you, too."

"Did it work against you sometimes?"

"Yeah, it did. At one time, they had me in restraints moving in the facility. Handcuffs and waist chains are normal for guys in solitary. But they had me in leg irons, too, without a restraint order. That went against directives, but they said it was for the safety of the facility because they thought I was an escape risk."

"So directives aren't really directives at all then?"

"Right, just like promises, directives are made to be broken. Usually they are broken under the cover of safety and security of the facility, but the real aim is to show the inmate who's in charge."

"I suppose it wasn't in the best interest of the facility for Kleinschmit to let you out of solitary confinement—to give you a chance to live with the general population."

"Mr. Kleinschmit couldn't."

"I don't understand. You told me once that your segregated status was reviewed every thirty days by a committee made up of prison personnel and that they would submit their recommendation to the superintendent, but that he had final say in the decision."

"Right, but he really didn't have a say."

"I don't get it. Why were you different than anyone else in solitary?"

"I was a central office case. The brass in Albany were responsible for monitoring my case and telling the superintendent what to do with me. Mr. Kleinschmit said that he wanted to let me out of solitary, but he couldn't because the central office told him to keep me caged up. Yet every other cop killer and guys who had escaped were assigned to the general population."

"What was the purpose of the reviews then if all they were going to do was rubberstamp what the central office wanted? The Due Process Clause of the U.S. Constitution requires that you have a meaningful review of your status. How could it be a meaningful review if the result was a foregone conclusion?"

"Like I've said, the system is designed to break you down. Superintendents aren't super—they are slaves to the central office. Directives are optional. 'Meaningful' really means 'meaningless' so reviews are shuck and jive. Up is down and down is up. It's like living in an alternate reality that messes with you, tortures you, and then finishes you off by frying your brain for good. Do you understand it now?"

"Yes, I think so."

"Don't you see what they're doing now? They've brought their reality into this world—your world—via me. COs do pull-overs, not police officers; phantom state inspectors show up to shake me down and then disappear. In the weeks before my release, so many COs hung around my cell gate and said my life would be great after they set me free. It was all a set-up, a con job. They wanted to raise my expectations so they could crush them."

David would normally consider this as one of Phillip's paranoid rants, but this one had a ring of truth to it. David wondered if Phillip was right or if he'd been sucked into Phillip's delusional world. "But why would they do that, Phillip? Why would they invest all this time in making the life of an innocent man miserable?"

Phillip dropped his mail on to the table, leaned toward David, and got that wild and crazy look in his eyes. David rolled his chair back from his desk. He felt Phillip was about to lunge at him.

Phillip screamed, "It's the system! Don't you get it?"

"Calm down, Phillip—"

"You calm down. You calm down and accept that it's the system!"

"Okay, Phillip. I'm trying to understand—"

"Try harder."

"Okay. Okay already."

Phillip recoiled, sat back in his chair, and closed his eyes. *Inhale through your nose, hold it and count to four, exhale through your mouth. Think positive thoughts.* After four cycles of breathing, the rage drained from his face. "I'm sorry."

"It's okay."

"I have to fight off the demons at times. I know this is all new to you. Just keep in mind: I follow you in your world. You need to learn to follow me in mine."

"All right," David said, watching Phillip go limp at the shoulders. "But can I ask questions like you do about my world?"

"Yes, sure, go ahead."

"Do you think Kleinschmit is part of the system?"

"Yes and no. Yeah, he draws a paycheck from the system—so he's part of it. But he's a good superintendent. He's one of the few good guys in the system. He allowed me to be a porter, to come out of my cell and clean the corridors, to help out any way I could. Mr. Kleinschmit kept telling me I was doing a great job.

"But then the central office called and told him to put me back in my cage. Mr. Kleinschmit apologized to me, but said he had to lock me up again. When Kranston personnel approved a family visit with a distant cousin who's an ex-con, Mr. Kleinschmit approved it but the central office shut it down days later."

"Help me understand. Who at the central office has it in for you and why?"

"The State Commissioner of the Bureau of Prisons is Edmund O'Neil. I think it might be him. He's from Syracuse—you know, my hometown. He might remember Pete Carlson. But there are deputy commissioners, assistant deputy commissioners—a yard-long list of people who could claim to be acting on behalf of the commissioner. There are scads of employees at the central office."

"How could someone get away with impersonating the commissioner?"

"They don't impersonate him in person. They could say it over the phone or have someone else make the call and say that something was ordered by the commissioner—or his office—and nobody would know any better on the other end. Maybe they'd do it when the commissioner was out of the office or on vacation. The prison doesn't shut down—it runs all the time. Decisions have to be made. That's when the underlings shoot out their gremlins in the form of written orders on commissioner letterhead and send it through interagency mail; you know, the state's snail mail system. Anyone with a sheet of stationery letterhead with the commissioner's name on it can issue an order and set the system into motion to wreak havoc. You as a con could work hard to get a privilege, like maybe a commissary buy of coffee. You get the privilege with one order and then a day later—before you get the coffee—that order is countermanded by another one prohibiting the coffee for absolutely no reason except one: The system is designed to destroy you."

"But the commissioner would see these orders when he returned."

"The chances of that happening are slim to none, and Slim has got one foot out the door. There are nearly 50,000 prisoners in the system in more than fifty facilities statewide. They can't keep track of every piece of paper floating around that manages these cons. The left hand doesn't know what the right hand is doing. The order just gets filed away. Out of sight, out of mind. And, if by a miracle someone in the chain of command finds some order out of whack, the blue wall of silence takes over—nobody rats on anyone else. The bogus order sticks forever and a day until a new one comes along. If one ever does. I read everything I could get my hands on about the system—studied all the angles—so I could try to figure out who was keeping me caged up in solitary."

"So why do you think it's Commissioner O'Neil then, when it could be anyone?"

"It's just a hunch and it has a lot to do with what Mr. Kleinschmit said. He didn't come right out and say it but I can read between the lines."

Just then the landline rang. Out of Phillip's eyesight, the handset display on David's desk showed Johnny was calling. David picked it up. "Hello," he said, walking the phone upstairs into the kitchen so Phillip couldn't overhear. David didn't want to let Phillip know that Johnny was calling. Phillip didn't trust Johnny—or any CO—and David didn't want to set him off.

"I've got something for you," Johnny blurted.

"What's that?" David asked closing the basement door behind him.

"I heard they're coming after Dawkins and you again."

"Who told you that?"

"Let's just say I was in the right place at the right time."

"Who's they?"

"The State Police this time."

"You mean COs dressed as the State Police?"

"No, the actual New York State Police."

"You're kidding me. Since when does the State Police carry out the dirty work of a group of COs?"

"This goes higher than the COs at Kranston. Much higher. Probably to the central office level."

"I'm not one for conspiracies across state agencies—"

"Who said it was a conspiracy? It could just be that someone owes someone a favor. But ignore me if you want. Don't say I didn't warn you."

"What else do you know?"

"Only that they are going to raid you when you reopen."

"What do you mean by raid?"

"That's the word they used. That's all I know."

David's stomach churned. The war they were waging didn't look like it would ever end. "Why are they going after us, Johnny?"

"I don't pretend to know. I've got to get back to my post at Kranston. I'm in town and my break is about to end."

"One more thing before you go. Have you ever heard of some guy by the name of Boris Dietrich? You know, the guy named in the correspondence you gave me."

"Never heard of him."

"All right, thanks for the heads up."

"Be careful," Johnny warned before hanging up.

David had his reservations about Johnny, but his warning seemed aboveboard. It made sense. *Word must have spread that we won the hearing. Having failed once, why wouldn't they come back and try to shut us down again?*

But why not just try another inspection? Why raise the stakes with a raid? David didn't begin to have the answers. He opened the basement door and climbed down the stairs while deep in thought. *Why would Johnny warn us about a raid if it wasn't going to happen?* If Johnny was lying or misinformed, David figured they'd know soon enough because he said they would be coming when the shop reopened. David reclined his office chair and stared at the ceiling while rubbing his chin. *We may be outnumbered, but we know when and where our enemy will attack.*

"Phillip, have you ever read Sun Tzu's *The Art of War?*"

"No."

"Sun Tzu said, 'He who knows when he can fight and when he cannot, will be victorious.' I don't know about you, but I'm tired of playing defense. I think it's high time we go on the offensive."

CHAPTER 12

When the Lenco BearCat armored vehicle crept into the barbershop parking lot on June 1st at 10:15 a.m., David knew that Johnny was right. The raid was on. The vehicle looked like a Wells Fargo armored car with a gray-black matte painted finish and no markings. The only identifiers he could see were subtle. It had the Lenco insignia on the front grille and a New York State Police license plate hanging underneath it that read "MRT 3."

David had seen a sister armored personnel carrier at the New York State Fair in Syracuse at the State Police exhibit two years earlier. He knew it was used by the Special Operations Response Team. "MRT" on the plates stood for "Mobile Response Team."

He and Phillip had set this trap a few days earlier. They hung a sign in the barbershop window saying that it would reopen at 9 a.m. that day. As they worked off and on to comply with all the barbershop regulations, David knew someone was watching the shop. There might even be many someones. Through the barbershop front door, as they prepared to reopen, the pair saw plenty of suspicious cars with a driver and a passenger repeatedly slow to a crawl in front of the strip mall. The occupants would leer in the direction of the shop as they passed it at a snail's pace on Central Avenue, running the risk of a rear-end collision from passing traffic.

But this morning the two men weren't inside Phillip's Barbershop. David didn't know what Johnny meant by a "raid" and didn't want to be in the shop to find out. They had parked the Mustang in front of the shop at the crack of dawn. Then they walked in through the front door and straight out the exit door in the rear. It was easy to disappear into the woods, only to circle around and cross an empty Central Avenue. Then they took up a position in a private booth at the Yellow Ribbon Diner. The menus they casually propped against the glass picture window ensured no one could see their faces from the outside. Mission accomplished. He and Phillip ordered breakfast and waited while they drank their way through bottomless free coffee refills.

"Looks like we have our first customers," David said.

"What *is* that thing?" Phillip sputtered.

"That's the State Police's version of a SWAT team."

"Oh my God," Phillip gasped, as he began to stand up.

"Sit down, Phillip. Stick to the plan."

"But I'm afraid of what they'll do to the shop."

"I know, I know," David said, "but you need to sit down. It's too late for us to do anything else. We have to let this play out. Don't worry."

Phillip slowly sat down with a grimace, eyes fixed in a glare on the scene that played out beyond the window.

A few troopers in a cruiser was what David had expected to see—not an entire army. As the rear door on the BearCat swung open, the SWAT team emerged one at a time. Each had a semi-automatic rifle drawn to eye level, scanning for danger. They began to stack up on the side of the BearCat away from the barbershop, using the vehicle's armor as a shield. The troopers were decked out in total camouflage—helmets to boots. Their outfits had no markings to denote they were from the State Police. If David hadn't already seen them at the state fair, he would have thought they were members of the US Army Special Forces.

A few members from the SWAT team ducked and made a dash for the rear of the barbershop. One of the figures behind the vehicle now held a megaphone up to his lips. If he was saying anything, David and Phillip couldn't hear him.

Diner patrons started to notice the activity. Like children drawn to a TV screen, they filtered toward the picture windows that faced Central Avenue. The main road sat empty now, cleared of all traffic. Roadblocks on either side under the traffic lights at the intersections diverted vehicles from the scene. A female state trooper, her arrow-straight spine swathed in a typical navy uniform topped by the signature Stetson hat, marched into the diner out of nowhere. "Please move away from the windows and sit down," she ordered the crowd.

Patrons gawked at her briefly before they drifted back to their tables, where forgotten coffee and muffins cooled. The murmur of voices muffled the diner music from the overhead speakers. "What's going on?" the diner owner barked from her perch behind the cash register. "Looks like World War Three out there. Bad for business."

"There's a hostage situation," the trooper replied sharply.

A chorus of gasps swelled across the room. The wave of murmurs rose to a dull roar as people scrambled for cell phones and tablets.

David's eyes popped. The two gawked at one another across the table with mouths agape.

"Shouldn't we say something?" Phillip whispered.

David shook his head vehemently. "For all we know," David whispered back, "the hostage situation is happening next door to the barbershop."

"I need to go over there and see what they're doing," Phillip said. Again, he started to unfold his lanky body off the booth seat.

"Keep it down, Phillip!" David said in a hushed tone. "Forget it. They've established an outside perimeter and we can't breach it. This is the only safe place to be. The security cameras Christy hid in the shop the other day will record everything that happens."

Phillip squirmed in his seat like a kid in church. He could barely contain himself. Doing nothing in response to unjustified force had been all he could ever do inside the box. He thought things would be different once he got on the outside. But it seemed like nothing had changed. Nothing. Like his box, he saw the barbershop as his space. These troopers were invading it without any reason. *Same as it ever was.*

To make things worse, Phillip had hardly slept the previous night. His bedtime routine didn't do anything to help. He showered for what seemed like hours to relax then took his nighttime vitamin. Didn't help. The static on the TV didn't work; neither did the music on the Easy Listening radio station. When he killed David in his dreams again at 3:15 a.m., he was done sleeping for the night. He had planned to tell David all about it that day like he promised. But now didn't seem like the time, especially since killing David was no longer on his mind.

Now Phillip locked in on a different target: the petite trooper assigned to the diner. It wasn't her small size or her gender that made her a target. He would have taken on the biggest trooper on the force. She was simply the closest person to him who was part of the raid on his space across the street—a sacrificial lamb. He reached down to stroke his lucky charm; the carving knife secured in his sock, riding up his calf.

Suddenly, a SWAT team member stood up and flung a hammer-like device to break the front door window at the barbershop. The guy next to him rose and tossed in what looked a lot like a softball, except that it was solid black. Both SWAT team members then retreated behind the vehicle.

A diner customer called out to the trooper to ask about the ball. "It's a tactical throwable camera," she explained. "It will move around via remote control, transmit images, and help the team assess the hostage situation inside."

Once they broke the front door window, everyone knew the hostage situation was taking place at Phillip's Barbershop. David had to come clean soon or be the subject of intense questioning. The cops would want to know why he and Phillip didn't tell the trooper in the diner that the shop was empty as soon as they saw it was the target of the hostage call.

"Did you see that?" Phillip pleaded. "They broke our window and threw in that . . . that camera thing. Can't we do anything?"

"Keep it down and listen up. We have to slowly make our way over to the entrance—where the trooper is standing. We need to tell her that it's our shop and there's nobody inside."

"Why slowly? They're going to trash our shop."

"You don't want to make it look like we're rushing her. Nothing's more dangerous than a spooked cop. We've got insurance to cover the damages. I made sure of that."

"But we worked so hard to make that shop happen," Phillip whined, his eyes beginning to fill. "This isn't supposed to happen on the outside."

David understood the pain on Phillip's face. The show of force had surprised him too, but it seemed to have shocked the heck out of Phillip. David whispered, "Remember, this is my world. You have to follow my lead here."

Phillip swallowed and nodded hard as if he was trying to convince himself that David was right.

"I'm going to get up and slowly walk over to the trooper. Trail behind me and follow my lead. Don't say anything unless I ask you a question. Okay?"

"All right."

David stood and carefully stepped toward the trooper. The waitresses, busboys, and patrons were all transfixed by the scene that unfolded across the street. An old man sitting with his buddies in a booth shouted, "Look! They're going in." David and Phillip eased upright, turned their heads to look out the window but kept moving toward the door. The SWAT team had formed a line with semi-automatic rifles still drawn to eye level, some barrels jerking left and right, some aiming straight ahead. The two men at the head of the line gripped a battering ram.

The lady trooper made eye contact with David. He and Phillip were the only people moving in the diner. The distant thud of the battering ram against the shop door echoed through the restaurant like a drum beat. The lady trooper's eyebrows popped up in a flash and then she squinted hard at the two of them. Her right hand moved toward her holstered Glock 37. David glanced over his shoulder at Phillip. His face was red, eyebrows lowered, forehead furrowed. He twitched at each thud of the battering ram.

When they got within a few feet of the trooper, David stopped and Phillip halted at his side. "I need to talk with—"

Bam! A loud explosion from the shop rattled the diner's windows like a sonic boom. Phillip lunged toward the trooper, but before he could reach her David tackled him from behind and face-planted him into the checkerboard-patterned linoleum floor.

The startled trooper drew her gun in a flash and aimed it at Phillip. "Freeze!" she hollered.

David didn't have to move from his perch on Phillip's back to whisper into his ear, "Please, follow my lead here. Shake like you're having a seizure." Peering up at the trooper, David announced, "It's not what you think. He's having a seizure—an epileptic seizure. That loud bang must have triggered it. What was that sound anyway?"

Keeping both hands on the Glock, the trooper lowered her gun just a hair. "It was a flashbang grenade."

"What on earth is that for?" David asked.

"With the explosion and a flash of light, its job is to momentarily stun anyone in the barbershop so that the SWAT team can enter."

Phillip started to tremble. He had seen seizures a few times outside his cell in the solitary wing. David reached around him to grasp his shirtfront. "It's okay, Phillip, you'll be okay." He rolled Phillip over onto his back. "They just threw a stun grenade into the barbershop. It wasn't aimed at you. You are not in any danger."

Phillip did his best imitation of a seizure: thrashing, then letting his head loll. But he knew the truth. He had lunged at the trooper to strike her, cut her up—maybe even kill her. He was livid about the raid and the flashbang pushed him right over the edge. *Inhale through your nose, hold it and count to four, exhale through your mouth. Think positive thoughts.*

"He'll be okay in a minute," David assured the trooper. His gaze moved to include the customers who scrutinized them now instead of the ruckus outside.

Phillip started to tremble less and when he finally lay still the trooper holstered her Glock. Phillip gazed calmly up at her stance and David kneeling over him. He gave them a thumbs-up signal.

David said, "You see, he's coming around. He'll be fine now."

"I need to see some ID," the trooper replied.

"Sure. Just let me get it out of my wallet," David said, standing up. He reached into his back pocket and pulled out his wallet, then retrieved his license, and handed it to the trooper. "I started to say before the explosion that I needed to talk with you."

The trooper scanned both sides of the license. Her skinny frame was lost in the baggy uniform despite her exaggerated posture. She wore a name tag that said "Tucker." There was a patch of acne on her neck right under the requisite bun that kept her feminine glory under control. "Thank you for your cooperation," she said, trying to project her voice. It was a lesson she had likely learned at the academy a short time ago. She handed the license back after scribbling down David's name. "I need to check his ID too," she said, pointing to Phillip, who still sat on the floor.

David grasped Phillip's hand and pulled him up. They both sneaked a peek at the scene across the street. A few members of the SWAT team exited the shop with their gun barrels pointed at the pavement. Phillip removed his New York non-driver photo ID card from his wallet and handed it over.

David muttered to Phillip, "They look like they're all done over there." More men in camo exited the barbershop, weapons lowered. A few stood before the store window talking, gesturing to one another with their hands. Troopers wandered around out in the open, along the perimeter of the scene. Some pedestrians clustered on the sidewalk, eyes glued to the unfolding drama. As the woman trooper scribbled down Phillip's name, her walkie-talkie crackled, "All clear. There's nobody in the shop. False alarm."

Trooper Tucker thrust the ID back at Phillip and turned to ask David, "What is it you wanted to say to me?"

"I wanted to tell you that we're the owners of the barbershop you just raided and that there's nobody in there."

"Really? How come you're over here when there's an open sign hanging in your picture window?"

"It's a one-chair shop. There were no customers, so we decided to hold a breakfast meeting over here. We could spot any customer arriving from here and quickly leave to serve them at the shop."

"How long have you been here?"

"I guess a couple hours. The owner and our waitress can vouch for us."

From behind the register, the diner owner hollered, "That's true. They've been warming those benches a long time."

The trooper palmed her walkie-talkie, "Command, Tucker here. Do you copy?"

"10-4, Tucker. What's up?"

"I've got one David Thompson and a Phillip Dawkins with me, across the street, in the diner. They say they own the barbershop. Owner confirms they've been here for hours having breakfast. They approached me and informed me that the shop was empty."

"Copy that. Do they deny making the 911 call from the barbershop landline?"

David said, "Absolutely. We've been over here the entire time. There's no way we could have made any call on the barbershop landline."

Trooper Tucker responded, "Affirmative, Captain. Sounds like a spoofed call. Over."

The radio crackled. "Agreed. Interview them and put it in your report. Over and out."

Phillip asked, "What's a spoofed call?"

Trooper Tucker explained, "It's when someone uses a service to make it look like a call is coming from a certain telephone number—in this case, your landline number. We got a call this morning from someone saying he was Phillip Dawkins and that he was holding David Thompson hostage and was going to kill him. Dispatch said the call sounded legit. So, we responded in force."

"My God," David said, "we could have been killed if we were in the shop."

"Unfortunately, that's happened before when people have been swatted," Trooper Tucker said.

David responded, "Swatted? I don't understand."

"'Swatting' means to falsely report an emergency so as to cause a SWAT team to respond in force."

"It sounds like a way to order a hit on someone," David said.

Tucker gave him a sharp look as she asked, "Do either of you know of anyone who might do something like this to you?"

"Nope," David replied.

"No," Phillip echoed, following David's lead.

Neither of them was going to tell Tucker that they suspected some COs, or the Bureau of Prisons, or maybe even the State Police itself. That would be too much like kicking a hornet's nest then hoping for the best.

After some more questions and paperwork, Trooper Tucker told David and Phillip they were free to go. Dismissed, they walked across the street as the last of the police departed. When they entered the shop, the room reeked of rancid smoke. The place had been sullied and ransacked. David's mouth hung open as he slowly turned in a circle to survey the damage. Phillip just collapsed in the barber's chair.

"How can they do this to us?" Phillip lamented. "How are we ever going to re-open?"

"I'm sorry, Phillip. I don't know what to say." It was far worse than what David expected to happen. It was a huge setback and David knew it.

"I should have stayed in prison. I don't have a chance out here. The world outside is just as rigged as solitary ever was at Kranston."

David had no response to that statement. He called Little Falls Lumber down the street to arrange delivery of some plywood to secure the front entrance. That would buy them some time to get a new entrance door installed. He knew the landlord would be royally PO'd because it was his door. The last thing any landlord needs is tenants who are constantly in trouble with the law.

David made a quick trip home to grab some tools that they used to cut the plywood and nail it up. He stopped to give Annie the short, sanitized version of the debacle at the barbershop, so she wouldn't worry if she saw something on the news.

After they barricaded the door, David took Phillip out the back exit to pick up Christy. His son reacted to the destruction with quiet anger. In a jiffy, the young man downloaded footage gathered from the raid. He had installed multiple hidden cameras in the shop—three in electrical outlets, two in air ionizers placed on countertops, four flush-mounted cameras in the ceiling, even one in the electric coffeemaker. All the cameras recorded audio, too.

The three of them sat in the ruined shop later that evening to review the footage on Christy's laptop. The security cameras showed the SWAT team raiding the shop. It also showed the tactical throwable camera rolling up and down the shop floor like a bowling ball before the raid. Its sudden stops and starts and side-to-side movements revealed that it was controlled remotely from somewhere else by an operator with a joystick. Then Christy patched in the audio recording.

The tactical throwable camera not only recorded video, but it also transmitted audio. Every few seconds, the ball would stop and emit a noise. It sounded like the rolling ball said something. The audio was hard to understand, but it sounded like a repetition of the same phrase over and over again until the SWAT team raided the shop.

David leaned closer to the laptop speakers, "Can you turn the volume up?" he asked Christy. "I want to make sure it's saying what I think it's saying."

"Let me try to tweak the audio with some software," Christy replied.

But Phillip didn't need the audio enhanced. He recognized the voice's cadence and instinctively knew the words. It was the voice that had played in his head ever since he could remember. He now believed it was the same voice that led him to David Thompson's house the day after his release.

After Christy erased the static from the audio, the male voice was unmistakably clear to all three of them: "Kill David Thompson, Kill David Thompson!"

CHAPTER 13

It was one thing for Phillip to hear the voice while dreaming or in his head while awake, but it was quite another to hear it out loud. "Do you hear that? Can you hear that?" Phillip desperately asked.

"Yes," David replied.

"Tell me what the voice says. Tell me!" Phillip pleaded.

"'Kill David Thompson.' The voice says to kill me."

Now Phillip had confirmation that someone else could hear the voice too. "That's the message that's been playing in my head for as long as I can remember," Phillip said. "I thought I was going crazy, but you say you can hear the voice too."

"Yes, I heard it," David gulped.

"Dad, what's this all about?" Christy asked. He was shaken by the voice. Someone wanted to kill his father.

"It was in my dreams, Christy," Phillip explained. "I've heard that voice in my dreams and in my head during the day sometimes. I've had dreams about killing your father too."

Christy turned to David. "I told him about my dreams of killing you." He looked at Phillip. "You've heard that exact voice or that exact message?"

"The message, for sure. I'm not totally sure it's the same voice. It sure sounds like it, though."

"But maybe hearing the exact same message just makes it seem like the exact voice," Christy surmised.

"Maybe. I heard the voice in my sleep, so I'm not sure. When I'm awake and hear the message, it might be my voice that I'm hearing. Maybe I sometimes hear my voice when I'm awake and at other times I hear this other voice in my head. I'm not sure. Until now, I thought it was my voice generating this message all the time."

"Christy," David said, "I hear a muffled sound before I hear the message. I think I can make out another word. Can you enhance the audio a little more?"

"Sure," Christy said, clicking his keyboard.

"Play it back when you're done."

"Okay, here it goes."

The message they all now heard was, "Don't kill David Thompson."

"I don't get it," Christy said. "Which is it?"

David pointed out, "You really can't hear the 'don't' and the emphasis is on the word 'kill.'"

Christy suggested, "Maybe the message was really 'don't kill' but they had a technology glitch."

"Don't even go there, Christy," Phillip objected. "When you've been in the system as long as I have, you learn that technology glitches are convenient excuses. Transcriptions from cassette recordings made during my hearings omit key testimony because they say they can't make it out. Or when I want some video to prove a bogus disciplinary ticket, the prison security camera I want the footage from is always broken. They can say they meant 'don't' yet it clearly came out 'kill.' We know what we heard. And this scheme fits with the rogue COs and the targeted inspection."

"Why would they want to kill my dad, then?"

"Because your dad wants to eliminate solitary confinement. He kept shoving the Mandela Rule in the face of the state. He wants to change the system, so he's now an enemy of the system. The system wants to kill him before he kills it."

David's cell phone went off. "Hold on, it's Jim Fletcher. Maybe he has some information for us. I'll put it on speaker. Hello, Jim."

"Hey, David. I saw the SWAT team raid on the TV news this evening. What was that all about?"

"Oh yeah? What did the TV news say?"

"They said it was a false report. They said your telephone number was spoofed with an untraceable burner cell phone paid for with cash."

"Figures."

"Anyway, I was able to FOIL the state inspection files and found yours in the bunch. Are you sitting down?"

"Yeah, what did you find out?"

"Well, the inspector's signature was illegible, but I was able to trace the badge number to an inspector by the name of Ken Broome. At first I thought someone used his badge number and impersonated an inspector, because he works out of the Central New York Region. He doesn't do inspections in Albany County—you know, where Karner is located—the Capital District Region. But I saw he did other inspections in Albany that day in the other files that came up in the FOIL. However, it was just for that one day. In all the other files I looked at, I didn't find a single inspector who inspected across regional lines. Come to find out, he was only assigned to the Capital District Region for that one day."

"Is there a reason they assigned Ken Broome to hit the shop that day?"

"I asked the same question and the Bureau of Licenses said they didn't have any answers. But then I remembered that the Central New York Region office covers Syracuse and I recalled that's where Phillip was from, and that's where Police Officer Pete Carlson was murdered back in the 1980s—"

"Don't tell me there's some connection between Pete Carlson and Ken Broome?"

"Not directly, no. Ken Broome was born after Pete Carlson died. But get this. Wanda Carlson—Pete Carlson's wife—her maiden name is Broome. It turns out that Ken Broome is the son of her brother. Ken Broome is her nephew."

"Oh my God."

"Tell me about it."

"I don't get why the family is going after Phillip—an innocent man."

"Maybe they don't think he's so innocent."

"If that's the case, why didn't they object to Phillip's release?"

"I don't know. That's a good question."

"You got anything else?"

"Yeah, one more thing."

"What's that?"

"Well, what prompted the investigation was a written complaint…"

"A complaint about what? We hadn't had one customer before the inspection."

"It's not unusual for a competitor to complain—you know, to kill off the competition."

"What competitor complained?"

"It was an anonymous note so we don't know. But I did notice something unusual about the complaint."

"What's that?"

"It was typewritten."

"Yeah, that's a little out of the ordinary."

"One more thing."

"Okay."

"The typewriter they used had a malfunction. The uppercase letters strike lower than the lowercase ones. It's out of adjustment."

"Interesting."

"Yep."

"Well, if you come across anything else, Jim, give me a call. I appreciate your efforts. And send me a copy of that complaint, please."

"You bet."

David said, "Enjoy the rest of your evening," before hanging up.

As the call progressed, the color drained from Phillip's face. When David spoke, a new, shocking truth revealed itself to Phillip. The truth was always shifting, re-creating itself for Phillip since he got out. To him, the truth was as fickle as a weather forecast—something he never needed to concern himself with while sealed in the box.

Once he heard the voice in his head out loud and once David and Christy said they heard the voice too, anything seemed possible to Phillip. A memory bubbled to the top and surfaced in his mind. This wasn't a new experience for Phillip. Memories lost long ago had suddenly reappeared to him since his release—the Syracuse daily newspaper as a kid, his parents' Plymouth station wagon, Manny Romano the barber, the beatings from his father. But this new memory trumped all others. It was triggered when Jim said, "Maybe they don't think he's so innocent."

The memory was from 1985, a few months after he had been released from his latest stint at Hillbrook Juvenile Detention Center. Phillip recalled hanging out with his buddies at their alma mater, Hennington High School, in the Northside section of Syracuse. They were all dropping acid, looking to escape the dreariness of the city. It was Phillip's first trip. He felt a buzz as the LSD flowed through his system, making his clammy hands twitch and tense jaw relax. He felt a surge of energy and an increased awareness of everything around him. Then it all faded to a blur until he realized he was back at Lookout Point, where Onondaga Creek meets Onondaga Lake near the inner harbor in Syracuse. His friends had ditched him while he was tripping and he was alone in a scary place.

At 3 a.m., Lookout Point was small, dark, and unfamiliar. It was a desolate patch of scrubby grass with three graffiti-laden park benches. In front of him, a bunch of deadwood garbage was piled up on the small beach. The lake reeked from sewage and water pollution, courtesy of Allied Chemical and other companies. On either side of the park, there was dense brush and trees. Railroad tracks ran in back of him along the shoreline. He didn't know his way out of Lookout Point. He had never been there before. There was a walkway under the railroad bridge that seemed to go in a direction toward Syracuse. He believed it was his only way out, but the total blackness under the bridge freaked him out. There were no lights anywhere except the faint twinkling across the lake. He lay down on one of the park benches to calm himself, hoping to sleep it off into the morning sunrise. But his anxiety and discomfort only increased as he closed his eyes. He was all by himself and on a bad trip.

Then suddenly a bright beam of light burned his eyes. Someone leaned over him holding a flashlight, trying to rouse him off the bench. At about that same moment, a freight train thundered over the bridge above. The effect was like the flashbang that went off in the shop. Phillip lost it. His dangling hand grabbed a plastic six-pack ring lying on the ground as he yanked the man over the bench onto the pavement.

The dropped flashlight rolled to one side and spilled a glow that shone on the young man's face, making it look ghostly in the black hole of the park. Phillip sat on the intruder as he pushed the six-pack ring down hard on his neck. It felt as if someone had hijacked his body, his hands, and given them superhuman strength.

The plastic ring stretched; he pushed it as hard as he could—squeezing every last ounce of life out of the man. He could hear him gagging, then gurgling, eyes bulging, trying to fight back. He clawed at his attacker's hands, but Phillip quickly got the man's arms pinned to the pavement with his knees. When he went totally limp, the flashlight beam showed Phillip that he had killed a uniformed police officer. He ran into the darkness under the bridge clutching the six-pack ring in one hand, past the patrolman's empty police car with its door ajar and lights still flashing.

Sitting there with David and Christy, he wondered just for a second if he had imagined it all. But the more he thought about it, the more details of the slaying ran through his head. He remembered running through the streets of Syracuse in his new Air Jordans, trying to find his way home. He remembered disposing of the plastic six-pack ring in a full waste can waiting for early morning garbage pick-up near Schiller Park. No, he didn't think it was his imagination running wild. Right then and there, Phillip Dawkins believed he wasn't innocent after all. He truly believed he had murdered Police Officer Pete Carlson.

Now Phillip felt as if he was strapped to a boulder and dropped into the ocean's deepest trench—sinking rapidly, drowning. A single pillar of innocence had supported everything Phillip believed about himself, what he was and had been, for as long as he could remember. In an instant, that prop now crumbled to dust. Staring back at him in the barbershop mirror was the face of a killer. The core of his essence, his soul, evaporated in a flash. Here he was—a killer—and yet he was a free man. The thought made him tremble. The guilt was overwhelming, crushing him. He couldn't breathe. He wasn't any better than the COs or the system. *I should be in prison, behind bars, someplace where I can't kill again.* But he couldn't face the prospect of returning to the box. He felt himself sinking, deeper and deeper, into his own wretchedness. The breathing exercises he had taught himself failed when it came time to think positive thoughts. He needed to blurt it out before he bugged out or passed out, "I killed Officer Pete Carlson."

Christy looked at his dad, his eyes wide with dismay.

"You did what??" David shrilled, in total disbelief.

"I'm afraid you heard me right. I . . . killed Officer Pete Carlson."

"Come on, Phillip, what's going on here?"

"I'm so sorry, but I'm serious."

"And this just occurred to you now?"

"I'm just remembering now what I used to remember. It just surfaced in my brain. I don't know how else to explain it."

"I don't know what to think, Phillip. One day you're innocent; the next you're a killer. Are you sure it's not just one of your bad dreams? Has your imagination gotten the best of you?"

"No, it's too real to be that. I'm sure of it."

"But Phillip, your DNA wasn't under Carlson's fingernails. They conceded that you were innocent. They let you go because you were innocent."

Phillip considered that evidence but chose to believe his own memory instead. "Look, I told you before, I may be a lot of things, but I'm no liar. I killed that police officer."

"But you lied to me before about not killing him?"

"I didn't lie then because I didn't know any better. I can't explain it any better than that."

"If you killed Carlson, then how did that other person's DNA get under Carlson's fingernails?"

"I don't know. I suppose it could have been planted into the evidence long after the murder."

"But, why?"

Phillip was so consumed by his own guilt that he hadn't considered asking why the system might have released him. "David, do you remember what Ken Broome said to you at the end of the inspection?"

"I'm not sure. Something about your innocence."

"Right, he asked you if you really thought I was innocent, because he didn't. Not for a second. He said eventually you'd figure it out, but it will probably be too late and it would serve you right."

"Yes, I remember him saying that now."

"Don't you see what's happened? They planned to put us in the middle of a SWAT raid. They set me up to be a nut job who took you hostage. When they raided the place, they were going to kill me in a hail of gunfire. They'd say they were justified afterward, because of the phone call. Something tells me I wouldn't have been the first person mistakenly gunned down by a SWAT team because of a prank call. Both Carlson's family and the system would be rid of me then. There's no death penalty in New York; so I can accept that Pete Carlson's family might be angry with me. They want to see me dead—even solitary might be too good for me in their eyes. They knew the system hadn't succeeded in breaking me, so they didn't object to my release. They didn't demand a new trial. The system couldn't break me on the inside, so they raised my hopes and set me up to fail on the outside—to break me and then kill me."

"Why didn't they just simply kill you on the first day they released you?"

"That would look too suspicious, too coincidental. Besides, I think the system wanted me to take you out for being such an effective advocate against solitary. Then the plan was to take me out, one way or the other. If I killed you, they'd have legal justification to gun me down. If I didn't kill you, they'd take you out and claim it was an accident. You know, death due to friendly fire. Any which way you cut it, they'd get rid of two problems in one fell swoop."

David wondered if Phillip had a point or if he was drowning in his own paranoia. "Who is the system in our case?"

"Specifically, I'm not sure. But the system is the system. It is what it is."

David rolled his eyes. "It is what it is, then it isn't what it isn't—"

"Exactly."

"What? What is that supposed to mean? When you say 'it is what it is,' that's circular doublespeak to me. It applies to everything. Anyway, if you're right, it looks like the Carlson family is involved somehow."

"Yes. Agreed."

"Maybe it's just the Carlson extended family at work?"

"It's possible, I guess."

"If you're right about all this, that means we're still in danger."

"Yes, I'm afraid that's probably true."

"Phillip, I know it's been difficult to be on the outside when you've been in prison for almost all of your adult life. You've said that you adjusted to the box and that you realize that a lot of thought processes you developed in the box don't work in the world outside of prison."

"Yes, that's true."

"Is it possible, Phillip, that deep down inside you want to go back to prison because you know how to function there? Do you think you might have imagined that you killed that police officer so that you could go back to prison, back to the world that you know where you have a certain comfort level?"

Phillip knew David had a point. He knew that he had often felt like prison was the more comfortable option. He missed the other inmates because at least he had something in common with those men. But he didn't want to go back to solitary—he wanted to be with the general population. That's where he belonged. Generally, cop killers landed in general population. But he knew if they put him back in prison, they'd put him in the box again. That's what the system had planned for him all along if it couldn't kill him on the outside.

He realized now that the system built up his hopes for life as a free man, only to make it just as bad, or worse, than life in the box. That way, if the system took him back in and locked him back in the box, it would break him for sure—make him bug out—because he would have lost all hope for a better life. "No, because if I go back to prison, they'd put me in the box again. I can't go back to the box now. I know that much. So I couldn't just be imagining I killed that policeman to make myself go back to something I hate more than anything."

David heard what Phillip said, but he wasn't convinced one way or the other. He didn't know what to think. "Okay, I had to ask that question. I mean, you've proclaimed your innocence to me on several occasions."

"I really believed I was innocent until now. If I remember correctly—and it's coming back to me now—I think I professed my innocence from day one in prison because, you know, that's what I thought I was supposed to do. I just wanted to fit it in. You don't want to stand out in prison. I didn't testify at trial because my lawyer pled insanity to get me off. But I wasn't crazy. I was just a doped up kid, trying drugs and acting stupid. That one night I was dropping LSD, I lost it and I killed Officer Carlson. But I must have believed my own lies about my innocence back then or come to believe them somehow while in prison. You know, maybe I convinced myself that I was innocent to survive. The thing about pain is that it's always fresh when you remember it. So if I could forget the pain I caused that family, I had a better chance of surviving. Maybe that way, they couldn't break me. I didn't have much to dream about while I was in prison. My only dream, up until I learned of my release, was to make it from one day to the next and hope for a better life in the general population."

Christy hadn't flinched at Phillip's admission. "I can't believe you killed someone, Mr. Dawkins."

Phillip could see that Christy was disappointed in him. "You both have to understand one thing. I'm not the same man who killed Officer Carlson. That was thirty years ago. I didn't know he was married; I didn't know he had three kids at the time. Just thinking about that now makes me sick. How could I do such a thing to that poor woman? How could I leave those kids without a father? I feel horrible about what I did. I'd like to find some way of paying that family back, but I feel as though I'll never be able to earn a nickel at this rate.

"Maybe everyone would have been better off if they fried me in the electric chair. Maybe the death penalty would have been a favor to me and everyone. What's the purpose of my life now anyway? Endless harassment and torture for taking a life? What's the point of that? Do people really want to support that with their tax dollars? If they want me to live, why can't I be allowed to try and do some good with my life to offset all the pain I've caused?

"I know they say that cons don't change—once a con always a con, once a murderer always a murderer. And while that may be true for some of us, it's not true for all of us. Some of us can change; some of us do change. I did change—I remember changing now. It's all coming back to me. In prison, I became a law-abiding American, in a way. I didn't get any disciplinary tickets for years. I didn't break their prison laws, their prison regulations. Not if I could help it. And, you know, not breaking their rules isn't easy when you're locked in a box and the system is stacked against you. But abiding by the rules didn't make any difference. They kept me in a box anyway because they wanted me to bug out. Then after I went mental, they could point at me and say, 'See, this guy's dangerous and needs to be caged and medicated for life.' But I didn't fall into their trap."

Christy eyed his father like he was waiting for him to explain it all.

But David was at a loss for answers. He listened to Phillip, but he was fixated on the small gap between Phillip and his only child, who sat right next to him. *What kind of father brings a murderer into the house, introduces him to his son, and allows the two of them to become friends? What do I say to Annie now that Phillip confessed to killing the police officer?*

CHAPTER 14

David didn't sleep at all that night. He wanted Phillip out of his life. He didn't know for sure if the ex-con had changed or not during his thirty-year stint, but who wants to wear a bulls-eye on his back to find out for sure? As far as he was concerned, if Phillip had killed once he could kill again. Heck, the guy had already dreamed about killing him. And it wasn't just a dream anymore if Phillip had killed before. But more than being a threat to him, David saw Phillip as a threat to Christy and Annie. David knew that Phillip did and could act on his dreams—he could kill him, he could kill Christy or Annie. And who had made it all possible? He wanted to kick himself for inviting a murderer into his family.

At the same time, David realized that he had no choice. He had to keep Phillip close now. If he distanced himself, David thought it could push Phillip over the edge. That could cause him to lash out against any one of the three Thompsons. David took to heart the words of Michael Corleone in *The Godfather*: "Keep your friends close, but your enemies closer." The more David feared Phillip, the clearer it became that he had to keep him close, much closer than he'd like.

Shortly after dawn the next day, David was slumped at his desk in a blue funk when Annie shuffled down the basement stairs half awake.

"Are you okay?" she asked. Her eyes were at half-mast but her wife radar was on full alert.

"Yes, I'm fine," he lied. "Just thinking about what happened yesterday."

"David, I'm afraid. I saw the shop on the TV news last night. You both could have been killed."

"Yes, I suppose so... but we weren't."

"That's a pretty cavalier attitude to have."

"Maybe. I guess when I hit middle age and I saw our friends and family start to die off, I realized my number could come up at any time—terminal disease, car accident, heart attack."

"But, David, this is different. It's not some random event. Someone made that prank call on purpose. Someone wanted to see both you and Phillip get caught in a firefight. What's going on?"

David knew Annie made a good point. "I'm not sure," he evaded.

But David wasn't being forthright and he knew it. He had brought Phillip into the family fold believing that the man was innocent. Yet now it seemed he was far from it. Phillip's murder confession was persuasive. Although he wasn't certain, David believed it was more likely than not that Phillip had been the one who killed Officer Carlson.

David felt he had a duty to tell Annie about Phillip's confession. But he couldn't bring himself to do it. He knew she'd plead family first and seek to protect hers from Phillip. She even might suggest turning him in to the police, but David knew if the police didn't take care of Phillip there would be hell for the Thompsons to pay. David believed in his heart that severing ties with Phillip would not help and could make things worse for his family and even for himself.

Left alone, Phillip sounded like he could dream crazy things and act on them. He could easily dream that one or all of the Thompsons were targets, for whatever reason. *A monster created by the system is as unpredictable as it is dangerous.* Like it or not, he saw his family's fate inexorably tied to providing Phillip with a future in a world gone mad. But he knew Annie wouldn't see it that way. She wouldn't understand or accept that the system was gunning for him and Phillip. In her mind, the system was flawed but basically good. David thought that this naive belief was too embedded in her psyche to overcome.

Pleading ignorance to Annie was the best option available in David's mind, though he realized it was like lying about Phillip's innocence. He hated himself for doing it. He swore off lying to Annie after he lied to protect her from the sordidness of baseball parents who were trying to prevent him from saving the baseball field for the sandlot kids in town. He swore off lying a second time after he concealed from Annie that he was a suspect in Harold Salar's murder. Now he found himself doing it again with Phillip and he couldn't help himself. He also had enlisted Christy in his scheme by having him promise to keep quiet. He didn't feel right about that either. David promised himself if things got really out of hand, he'd tell Annie everything. *But hadn't things gotten out of hand already?*

"You need to be careful, David," she implored. "Maybe you want to talk to our police up at town hall? You know, talk to Pete." Pete McNeal was the chief of police in Indigo Valley and he was David's friend.

David decided right then and there that he'd made the right call with Annie because that's the last thing he wanted to do. For all he knew, the Indigo Valley Police Department was linked to the system too.

"I'll think about it," he said.

"What about Phillip? Is he okay? Maybe we should invite him over for dinner to make sure he's all right."

"He's fine," David snapped and then added, more calmly, "He said he needs some down time." David wanted to keep Phillip away from Annie, away from Christy too, until he figured out what was going on. The phone started to ring. *Saved by the bell.* The caller ID gave the phone number for Julius. "Annie, I have to take this call."

"Okay. I'm going up to take a shower."

As Annie turned back up the stairs, David picked up the phone. "Hi, Julius."

"I think I figured out the identity of EC," Julius blurted. "His initials are really DEC—Donald Ewen Cameron. He's one of those guys who dropped his first name and went with his middle name. Go figure, because I'd take Donald over Ewen any day. What the heck type of name is Ewen anyway?"

"I don't know. Scottish, maybe?"

"Yeah, you're probably right."

"How did you figure out DEC and EC are one and the same?"

"You gave me Montreal and Albany as clues. When I ran those two cities through our database coupled with some years from the 1940s, his name popped up in a 1948 loyalty investigation."

"Who is this guy?"

"He was born and raised in Scotland, got his undergraduate degree and then M.D. with distinction from the University of Glasgow in 1924 and 1936. After getting his medical degree, he moved to Massachusetts to become director of the research division at Worcester State Hospital. In 1938 he moved to Albany, where he became a diplomate in psychiatry and a certified psychiatrist. From 1939 to 1943 he was a professor of neurology and psychiatry at Albany Medical College."

"Okay, so what's the connection between him and Kranston Prison and/or Boris Dietrich?"

"I'm not sure exactly, but I have a theory. In 1943, Cameron was invited to Montreal and became the first director of the Allan Memorial Institute, as well as the first chairman of the Department of Psychiatry at McGill University. He held that position for twenty-one years until 1964. Now, while working in Montreal, he maintained a presence in the Albany area and commuted—"

"A daily commute? That's over three hours each way nowadays!"

"No, no. From what I can tell by the report it might have been once a week or more. The agents asked about him at the Anchorage Motel at Rouses Point on Lake Champlain near the Canadian border. It seems he stayed there several times traveling between Albany or Lake Placid—where he had a house—and his Montreal apartment."

"Why not just move to Canada?"

"He secured his United State's citizenship in 1942 then moved to work in Montreal, Canada in 1943. Per the report, the Immigration and Naturalization Service advised him that if he failed to maintain a domicile in the USA by the end of 1948, he'd lose it. The report indicated that this citizenship was of utmost importance to him so he did everything necessary to maintain it."

"So what's the connection to Kranston?"

"You had to go through Kranston, the town, and past Kranston, the prison, to get from Montreal to Lake Placid or Albany during that time. It was before the construction of Interstate 87. So I imagine he stopped by that town a lot over the span of twenty-one years and made some friends or acquaintances. The report makes note of the fact that Cameron always drove a late model American-made car. A newer car makes sense for him, given all the mileage he was racking up back then. I imagine he was quite the sight rolling into Kranston—a backwater prison town—with a new car and a funky tweed suit he always reportedly wore. He must have gotten to know Boris Dietrich in his travels through Kranston and it sounds as if this guy Dietrich was probably employed by Kranston Prison somehow."

"But the letters were sent to Dietrich at a Post Office address in Slateville, not to him at Kranston Prison, so we don't really know for sure that he worked at Kranston Prison."

"You're right, I suppose, but why else were the letters found in a drawer at Kranston?"

"I don't know. What did the FBI report conclude about Cameron?"

"Many neighbors, acquaintances, and colleagues were interviewed and Cameron was universally hailed as unquestionably loyal to the United States and of sound moral character."

"Whatever happened to him?"

"He died in 1967 from a heart attack while hiking with his son near Lake Placid."

"So three years after leaving Allan Memorial Institute in 1964, he's dead. Why did he leave Allan Memorial Institute?"

"It's not totally clear. I think he saw the end was coming to his research funding there and he wanted to move on. But he did leave abruptly and it was four years before his contract was due to expire."

"Where did he go after Allan?"

"He went back to Albany again and became the Research Professor of Psychiatry at the Albany Medical School and Director of The Psychiatry and Aging Research Laboratories at the Veteran's Administration Hospital in Albany. You know, it's interesting that there seems to be this Albany-Montreal connection with one of Cameron's colleagues and successors at McGill, as well. Heinz Lehmann became Deputy Commissioner in the Research Division of the New York State Bureau of Mental Health from 1981 to 1999, when he passed away. That position required regular commuting between Albany and Montreal too. Lehmann is often credited with being one of the first psychiatrists to discover the benefits of using antipsychotic pills. It seems he used them a lot."

"That's interesting," mused David. "According to Dawkins, the Bureau of Mental Health manages the bug-outs in solitary. Lehmann would have been part of the system when Dawkins was incarcerated starting in 1985."

"The system?"

"Yeah, the prison system. The letters sent to Boris Dietrich are postmark dated from 1964 to 1967, after Cameron left Allan. Did you run across Dietrich's name in your research?"

"No, but I mainly just looked at the 1948 FBI report because that's what you were interested in. I stumbled on the Lehmann connection on the internet."

"What was Cameron researching anyway?"

"The FBI report didn't touch on that point. The report predated his research and only focused on his loyalty. There was an update in his file in the 1960s that tracked him to his last position and to his death, but nothing about his research except for one thing. In his last job he was focused on rejuvenating memory by experimenting with a memory pill on old veterans."

"You know, one of the earlier letters from Cameron said he was sorry that Dietrich had to stop, but he had become overzealous. I don't know the context of the letter. Maybe Dietrich worked with the Allan Memorial Institute. Could you try and track down any record of Dietrich at Allan?"

"What's this all about, Thompson? I mean I've already used FBI resources to help you out. I can't continue to do this on bureau time without having to open a case file and talk to my boss."

"Let's just say my life is at risk here." David didn't feel he could tell Julius that Phillip had admitted to killing Officer Carlson because of the attorney-client privilege. Not that Julius would believe him anyway. David didn't believe for a second that a seasoned FBI agent like Julius would easily accept the idea that New York State might have intentionally set a murderer free. "I can't say any more at this point. You know something? I'll look into Dietrich myself. Don't worry about him. If you'll just check your archives to see if the FBI had opened a file on the Dawkins murder of Carlson back in 1985. If there was one, check to see if you have any DNA evidence in the file. You shouldn't have to open a new file just to check the archives."

"Yeah, I suppose. But any file that old will be in the archives. If it exists, it might take some time before I can get my hands on it."

"That's fine. Do what you can. I really appreciate it."

"Okay. I'll call you back when I find out anything."

"Thanks, Julius."

When David hung up, the word "system" was dancing in his head from his conversation with Julius. He thought about Phillip's theory that the system was out to get them both—one way or the other. It's when the word "pill" joined the dance that David picked up the phone and dialed up Phillip at the motel.

"Hello," a sleepy Phillip answered.

"Phillip, I need to ask you something."

"Okay."

"You mentioned to me that you take a vitamin before you go to bed."

"Yes, that's right."

"But I've never bought you vitamins. Where did you get them?"

"They were in my suit jacket when I was released. I thought the prison pharmacist packed a supply up for me for the transition."

"Stop taking them."

"Why? I think I should take them. I took them in prison. They're good for me."

"You're the one who lectured me about the system."

"Yeah, so—"

"Don't you get it? The state gave you those pills. If you think the system is trying to kill you, maybe it has something to do with those pills."

"I never really thought about it that way. Like I said, I thought the vitamins were good for me. I couldn't get a balanced meal in solitary. Many times it was just the loaf—three servings a day of a dense, tasteless bread—plus a side portion of raw cabbage. So they gave me a vitamin to take."

"I'll get you some real vitamins, Phillip. Promise me you won't take any more of the ones they gave you, okay?"

"All right. You want me to throw them out?"

"No, I want to have them looked at. I'll come over and get them in a half hour. What else did the state give you when you were released?"

"My red transistor radio and headphones."

"Don't use it."

"Why not? I like to listen to the radio so I can fall asleep."

"I'll get you a new radio. You can use that one, all right?"

"It's just a radio."

"Is it? How do you know?"

"Now you sound like the paranoid one."

"Maybe so, but I want to have a look at the radio, too."

"If you say so."

"I do, Phillip. I'll pick that up along with the vitamins in about thirty minutes."

"Okay."

As soon as David hung up, his phone started ringing. Johnny McFadden's wireless phone number popped up on the caller ID. David picked up.

"Hey, Johnny," David said.

"Are you okay? I saw what happened to the shop on the news this morning. Holy crap!"

"Yeah, we're fine. A little shaken up. I need to thank you for the heads up. You probably saved our lives."

"I never thought they'd come after you like that."

"You said they were going to raid us, and they did."

"I thought a few guys would come over and make your life difficult for a few hours max. I never thought they'd come with an army. I never thought they'd use that kind of force."

"What the heck is going on, Johnny?"

"I don't know. For every shift I work, I think my lifespan decreases by eight hours."

"Phillip says it's the system. I think he's got a point."

"Maybe, but don't ever forget that he's nuts."

"Says who?"

"Says everyone I've talked to about him here."

"Maybe you guys made him nuts."

"Don't throw me under the bus. I don't work in solitary, okay?"

"You know who I mean."

"David, you need to be careful of Dawkins. He's crazy, like most of the guys in solitary. That's all I have to say. I warned you about the raid and I was right. I'm warning you about Dawkins now."

David knew Johnny was right about the raid. But he also knew that he was only half right. He didn't know that the raid was a SWAT invasion that could have taken their lives. "Do you know what a tactical throwable camera is, Johnny?"

"Yeah, I saw one at the academy."

"Well, they tossed this thing into the shop and we recorded its audio. It sounds like it's saying, 'Kill David Thompson.'"

"Really? Are you sure?"

"Yeah, pretty sure."

"That's nuts."

"That's just the tip of the iceberg. Hypothetically, what would you say if I told you that he thinks he may have killed that police officer after all?"

"Right, and I murdered the Pope. So he killed that cop and they just let him walk? He's nuts, I tell you. The entire place here is nuts. I think I'm going nuts."

"Don't let them take you too, Johnny. It isn't worth it. It isn't too late for you to get out and find another career."

"I've got too much invested in this to just walk away."

"You be careful, Johnny."

"Yeah, I hear you."

"Have you heard anything more about Edith Nowak?"

"Nope."

"What do you know about her?"

"She's single, lives alone around here somewhere."

"Did her husband predecease her or something?"

"Never married. I saw a picture of her in her desk and I can see why. Fell outta the ugly tree and hit every branch on her way down."

"No family, then?"

"She evidently has a daughter."

"Really? How do you know?"

"I saw some pictures of them both in her desk drawer. My guess is that the girl's her daughter. She looks so much like Edith."

"How old would you say the supposed daughter is in the photo?"

"I'm not sure. I'd guess mid-twenties. You know, she doesn't look too much younger than her mom—she's the spitting image of her too."

"Who's the father then?"

"Who knows? Maybe she's adopted?"

"Or maybe this Boris Dietrich guy is the father."

"Yeah, whoever the heck he is."

"She knows Boris Dietrich. That's for sure. There's copies of letters from her to him dated in the 1990s."

"What do they say anyway?"

"She says over and over how she loves him and wants to marry him like he promised her."

"I still don't get the connection between this guy Dietrich and Phillip Dawkins. Maybe there isn't one. Maybe these letters were just misfiled in a file with Dawkins's name on it."

"I suppose you might be right, but something is going on here. You have to admit it, Johnny. Dawkins and I are being targeted."

Johnny sighed. "Yeah, you're right."

"How old do you suppose Edith is?"

"She looks young in the pictures. I've never seen her before. She worked in the administrative building. Not a place I'd go in making my rounds."

"Younger than fifty-five?"

"For sure."

"That's odd then, unless the photo you saw was old."

"How so?"

"I thought the earliest she could retire as a New York State employee would be fifty-five."

"Maybe so, but you can take an early retirement if you know you're going to die."

David's eyes popped and his heart pounded. It was beginning to add up. Edith's abrupt and early retirement was likely because she was going to die. The clock was ticking now. David knew he had to see her before she passed on and, for all he knew, she could die any time—she could be dead already. She was the only one who definitely knew Boris Dietrich and how he might be tied to Phillip. David knew that if she died before he talked with her, she'd take that secret to her grave. If that happened, David saw the writing on the wall: Edith would seal his fate and Phillip's too. And they'd be the next ones in line to die.

CHAPTER 15

After David visited him to retrieve the vitamins and the radio that morning, Phillip went back to bed to stare at the ceiling. He couldn't imagine what his friend wanted with the only two things he had carried out of Kranston besides the clothes on his back.

He hadn't slept last night, but it wasn't because of the State Police raid on his shop. After about a half hour, the shock and terror of the raid became yesterday's news to Phillip. There might be a twenty-four-hour news cycle on the outside, but in Phillip's head and in solitary the cycle was more like twenty-four minutes. In Kranston, there was no point in dwelling on yesterday's calamities because the next day always brought a new set of challenges to face. Sure, Phillip knew he could have been killed during the raid. But woulda died, shoulda died, and coulda died had been on his daily menu for thirty years. The raid was now nothing more than a piece of the jigsaw puzzle that was the unfinished picture of Phillip's life.

Staring at the pattern of cracks in the motel ceiling, Phillip daydreamed about his past in solitary. Long-forgotten events swam to the surface, but he felt like he was experiencing them for the first time, or like they were someone else's memories. Yet he believed they really were his because they all felt right, and they meshed well with his core memories—the ones he knew were true to him.

Phillip worked to dredge up more recollections about his life in solitary. It wasn't nostalgia that drove him. He was trying to imagine what his life would be like once the system realized its error and stuck him back in the box. He knew that he was the one who killed Officer Pete Carlson. That hadn't changed since the raid. If anything, he was more confident than ever that he was the killer.

Digging back into his mother lode of thirty years of tribulations, he recalled a sweltering hot summer day in 1990. For no apparent reason, two COs showed up at Phillip's cell. "Put on your shoes, Dawkins, and let's get you cuffed up. You're going to see Superintendent Kleinschmit."

Phillip recalled his surprise at the sudden meeting. It didn't usually work that way. If the superintendent wanted to talk to you, he'd stop at your gate during his weekly rounds. You'd chat with him and every con or CO within earshot would overhear it. A private get-together was highly unusual.

One CO put cuffs on Phillip through the meal tray opening. When they opened the cell door, they wrapped him in a waist chain then shackled his legs. Phillip shuffled down the corridor; the clanking of his multiple chains echoed off the walls and floor with each yard of progress away from his cell. As always, his escorts stayed close—one CO at his side, one behind—until they reached the sergeant's office. Superintendent Kleinschmit was at his ease, sitting on the edge of the desk. The COs set Phillip on a chair, closed the door behind them, and took up guard outside.

"You wanted to see me, Phillip?"

"Yes, Marty—"

"I've told you before to address me as Superintendent Kleinschmit."

"Sorry. Bad habit. I try to call everyone by their first name."

"Why did you want to talk to me, Phillip?"

"I want to know when I can get out of the box."

"I don't know. It's in the hands of someone in Albany. You're a central office case and they call the shots."

"This is crazy. I don't belong there."

"You missed the count."

"I was a few seconds late returning from the yard to my cell. I was new here. There were a bunch of cons in front of me that moved too slowly. I've told you all this before—"

"And I've told you that the count is king here. You miss it and it's considered an escape. That's why the CO wrote you that ticket. If you didn't like it, you should have appealed it."

"I didn't know any better way back then. You know appeals to the hearing *officer are a waste of time. They always back the CO. Anyway, I did miss the count. But I wasn't escaping. I was late."*

"After that, you started acting up in the box. Got more tickets for speaking out of line."

"Yeah, you're right. I should've behaved better while you were torturing me—"

"Don't be a wise ass. You were deemed a safety and security risk. You made your bed, you get to lie on it, though I feel bad for you."

"But you have some say. I mean you as the superintendent know what's best for your prison, as far as safety and security goes."

"Yes, that's true."

"So have you asked them to let me out, to give me a chance with the general population?"

"You don't think I have?"

"I don't know. Have you?"

"Yes, of course."

"What did they say?"

"They don't want to let you out of the box."

"Why not?"

"I don't have any idea. They won't say."

"I don't understand. How much longer do you think I'll have to stay here? I've been in the box five years already."

"Five years is not a lot of time."

"Maybe not, if you're looking to do forty, get paid, spend eight hours per day here, and get benefits and a pension. It's been five years. Do you think it'll be another five before I get out?"

"No, no. It won't be that long."

"What's Commissioner O'Neil's problem with me anyway? Cop killers are a dime a dozen in the general population."

"I don't know."

"What can I do to get out of the box? If I follow the rules, it makes no difference."

"I give you things you want if you follow the rules—a pair of long johns, commissary buys of coffee, some sugar. You wanted special music pumped into your wall headphone jack and I made it happen. I do what I can."

"And you do a lot, for sure. I don't know how you can break the directives on my account alone."

"I'm the superintendent and people respect me. It's that simple. They know the consequences of failing me here in my house."

"I appreciate your efforts. I really do. But you didn't answer my question. I asked what I can do to get out of the box. Why not put me on some performance plan? If I meet certain goals, then you'll let me out of the box."

"The system doesn't work that way."

"How does it work then? What can I do?"

"Nothing. Just wait. Time changes things."

"I haven't noticed any change from where I sit. The faces change every couple of years. But I'm still sitting in the box with no end in sight. Same as it ever was. Have you ever spent time in the box?"

"No, and I've never murdered anyone either," Kleinschmit snapped.

"I think that every CO, prison official, judge, district attorney, needs to spend time in the box. Just a month. If five years is not a lot of time as you say, then a month is nothing. If they're working the system, let them experience it in all of its glory. Let them go sleepless—cons screaming, crying, pounding on the cell doors. Let them live on the slop they slip us in those Styrofoam trays. Let them smell the body odor, the blood, the feces, the urine, the cleaning chemicals. Let them see the bug-outs 24/7. Why not give them a taste of the medication too? Let them live without natural light, get their days and nights mixed up. No visits from the family. Let them forget, like I have, who they are and where they've come from. Let them see inmates cutting themselves just to prove that they're still alive. Let them see the cons hanging by a bed sheet from the ventilation grates overhead. Watch the corpses gently twist in the air currents like wind chimes. Once they do their month in this hell, then maybe they're qualified to work in the system."

Then Phillip's memory got fuzzy and faded. Still, the part he had just relived felt fresh even though it happened twenty-five years ago. Phillip thought it must have been an important memory because he could recall it after so many years. He figured its importance must have to do with the commissioner.

When he wondered why the commissioner had it in for him, Phillip had asked a loaded question. By failing to dispute the premise that the commissioner had it in for him, Martin Kleinschmit had put a face to his incarceration in solitary. No more blame Albany or blame the central office nonsense. Commissioner O'Neil was the culprit, the guy keeping him in the box, confirming Phillip's suspicions.

At the same time, Phillip knew he was cornered now. The system was going to get him one way or the other. There was no escape, ever.

He thought he would have a chance on the outside, but he was wrong. Life on the outside, as it stood now, was not an option. The system was going to toy with him before gunning him down—like a cat plays with a field mouse while killing it, slowly, slowly. Phillip lay in awe of the system's wicked ways. The system knew it couldn't break him on the inside, so it transferred him to the outside to finish him off. *Brilliant.*

Instead of wasting him, he thought that the system might decide to lock him up in the box for the murder of Officer Carlson—again. Phillip knew that this time the box would triumph if this option played out. The hope Phillip had nurtured for a better life on the outside or even on the inside with the prison's general population had given him the strength to survive the torture he had endured at Kranston. But hope had been swallowed whole when he realized the reality of the system's reach on the outside. The system had trumped the hope in Phillip's life just as it does for everyone it touches at some point. Without hope, Phillip knew the box would be his coffin in the making.

He thought about fleeing New York to start a new life someplace else. But he realized he'd fail without a support network. People like the Thompsons were like a life jacket to Phillip, keeping him afloat in rough seas. He didn't know or trust anyone else. He didn't have the skills to go it alone in a place and time that was still alien to him. His life experience outside of the box was limited. The one time he'd crossed the New York border was a disaster. That was when he was captured in Scranton, Pennsylvania after the murder. Other than this single occasion, he'd never stepped out of New York State his entire life. The apartment in Syracuse, juvenile detention centers, and the state prison system were all he knew. The thought of crossing the state line once more paralyzed him.

Trapped. The walls were closing in on him again; the ceiling was descending; he couldn't breathe. His relaxation exercises didn't cut it any more. As hope circled down the drain, he saw his entire life flushed in a flash. Phillip suspected he had to create a viable option on his own, in this situation where none seemed possible. He knew he had to come to grips with his fears before a way out could occur to him. He realized he had to put a face to the system for that to happen. Humanizing the system was his last best hope. And the face of the system could only be Commissioner Edmund O'Neil.

CHAPTER 16

David tried to locate Boris Dietrich himself, but a quick Google search for his name and a search of the white pages website yielded nothing. At that point, he decided to call his attorney friend, Jim Fletcher, to track down Dietrich. He realized he had too much on his plate to deal with locating both Dietrich and Nowak. Locating the woman before she died needed to be his top priority.

So David told Jim to first contact the Allan Memorial Institute to see if they could provide any information on Dietrich. Then he took the vitamins and the radio that he picked up from Phillip and delivered them to Julius. He begged the agent to have some FBI techies run tests on them. Julius was hesitant, but once David explained that it was a matter of life or death, he grudgingly gave in and said he'd see what he could do.

As soon as David located Edith, he would do whatever it took to talk with her. He was that desperate for answers. He had to solve Phillip's issues so he could save himself and his family. If he didn't, he felt it was just a matter of time before Phillip lost control and lashed out at one of them. But locating Edith turned out to be a problem. There were no Edith Nowaks listed in the phone directory in New York State.

Next, David proceeded to call every hospital and hospice in the area to see if Edith was on her deathbed somewhere. But he couldn't locate anyone registered by that name. Then, he combed through the file that Johnny had given him to find her home address. One of her letters to Boris mentioned meeting her "a few blocks away" at the Hoosick Tavern. On a hunch, he searched for any Nowak in the village of Hoosick Falls, New York and hit pay dirt. The computer came up with an "E. Nowak" on Church Street.

A phone call out of the blue from some unknown lawyer to Edith wasn't going to get it done, in David's estimation. He knew that a face-to-face meeting was his best chance of getting her to talk. So he hopped in his Mustang for the hour-long trip to Hoosick Falls. The tiny burg was located close to the New York-Vermont border and an hour south of Kranston. This person was within commuting distance of Kranston, which made it all the more likely that E. Nowak was Edith.

It was a nice drive from Indigo Valley, once you passed the urban clutch of Albany and the down-at-the-heels sprawl of Troy. Route 7 wended its way past farm fields and budding suburbs interspersed with piney woods on the way to Hoosick Falls. At 11 a.m. the village's largest employer—a plastics factory—was in mid-shift, so David's Mustang was the only car motoring on Church Street. David thought there'd be a church on Church Street, but he didn't spy one. However, he did drive by three of them on Main Street. The churches were the best-looking buildings in the village.

While Church Street didn't have any churches, it did have two automotive repair garages, a tractor service and sales business, and two convenience stores. Church Street had more active businesses than Main Street did. David thought the two streets ought to switch their names.

The architecture in the village could be politely described as mixed. In the center of this village of thirty-four hundred residents, the storefronts were a mix of businesses, vacancies, and boarded-up buildings. Houses in the nearby neighborhoods ranged from the well-maintained Victorian to a ramshackle farmhouse. Building parcels were of every shape and size. Three things tied the style of all the village homes together: each house sported at least one TV satellite dish, window-mounted air conditioners, and roll-out containers from the same trash company on the curb.

David parked in front of 195 Church Street, the possible home of Edith Nowak. It was a one-story bungalow with a gable over the front porch. The white paint had faded and chipped off, exposing blackish cedar clapboard. The small front lawn didn't look like it had seen a mower yet this season. Dandelions were in full bloom, the crabgrass was starting to overtake what little grass was left, and fluffy white poplar tree seeds floated in the breeze like snow flurries. Fair weather clouds rolled over the village, lending a genial air as the sun popped out in between them. There was a woman rocking on the sagging porch.

David parked his car along the curb and eased out. He gently closed his car door and walked around the front to the curb, stepping up to the side-walk in front of the house. He saw a small tin sign in the shape of a street sign hanging over the bowed porch steps that said it was a Sears House. David knew that these were the first kit houses. In the early 1900s, Sears, Roebuck and Company delivered housing plans and all the materials for people to build their own homes. The materials arrived by rail, so David was not surprised to see the railroad tracks running up against the rear of Edith's backyard.

"Hello, I see you live in a Sears home. Can I ask what model it is?"

"Vallonia," she replied.

"Nice. I've never seen one of these in person before and yours looks like it's an original. You didn't enclose the front porch like most people do to get more living area."

"You sure know your homes," she said, pushing back her jet-black mane on either side. Suddenly, she stopped rocking. Her face hardened as she asked: "You're not from the bank, are you?"

"No, ma'am."

She resumed rocking, but at a slower pace. "I haven't seen you or your Mustang in the village before. What brings you here?"

"I'm looking for Edith Nowak. Would you happen to be her?"

"Depends who's asking."

"My name is David Thompson. I'm an attorney with an office near Mohawk City."

"Did my daughter send you here? Does she still want me to sign those papers?"

"No, ma'am. I don't know your daughter."

"What's your business then?"

"I represent an ex-con from Kranston."

"Over what?"

"I'm just trying to help him put his life back together."

"So you know that I worked there, right?"

"So I've been told."

"Yes, I'm Edith Nowak and I worked there twenty-three years. Twenty-three very long years. You know, I had this smartphone app that counted the days until my retirement and pension. I looked at it a few times every day. I just told myself to hold on, my golden years were right around the corner. And what did all this waiting get me? Nothing, Mr. Thompson. Absolutely nothing."

As she spoke, David slowly walked up her short walkway towards the porch. The walkway was made from old house bricks. The surface was uneven from frost heaves, like ripples on a lake. He tripped when a brick popped up as he stepped on it. It threw his balance off and he fell onto the wooden stairs leading up to the porch.

The woman stopped rocking abruptly. "Are you okay?" she asked, straightening up from her chair.

David looked skyward from his perch on the middle step and saw the skinny frame of a woman. Her pale, oblong face was enveloped by startling jet-black hair on both sides that met under her chin. She stared down at him with an expression of dismay. "Yes, I'm fine, just tripped on a brick," David said, still sprawled out on the staircase.

"I'm sorry about that, Mr. Thompson. I've been meaning to fix those bricks. I'm afraid I've let the place go. There's no reason to fix it up now. Not that it matters to me at this point, but you aren't going to sue me are you Mr. Thompson?"

David picked himself up and brushed himself off as she spoke in a worried tone. "No, Ms. Nowak, but I'd be most appreciative if you could spare some time to answer a few questions."

"I'm afraid I don't have much time left on this earth, Mr. Thompson—no thanks to this village. You know why they call this Hoosick Falls?"

"No, ma'am, I don't," David said, standing in the suddenly bright sun. He grimaced from the pain of the fall and shaded his eyes with a hand to peer up at Edith Nowak.

"Because the most common question around here is, 'Who's sick?'"

David tried to smile through his grimace. He had hurt his hand, too. "What do you mean?"

"Come out of the sun and sit down by me on the porch here, and I'll tell you." Edith pointed to a chair next to her. It was as much a dare as an invitation.

David climbed up to the porch and spotted the rickety, small wooden chair with a frayed cane seat. He carefully sat down, fearing that the seat would rip and he'd fall through. He finally saw Edith up close, dressed in black Capri pants that emphasized her scrawny legs and a size-too-large gray sweatshirt that hung on her skeletal frame. She had deep bags under her eyes, a mole on her cheek, and cracks that ran like a maze in her jaundiced, weathered skin.

Waving a hand toward town, Edith began, "For decades the companies at the plastic plant have leaked this chemical. The stuff is called PFOAs—perfluorooctanoic acid. I've heard it enough times now that I can say it just right. It's not something you would drink on purpose and it sunk straight into our water supply. The aquifer, you know? From there it spread into our wells."

She continued, "At the plant they made Scotchgard, Gore-Tex, and Teflon products and made millions of dollars from it. Now we are paying the price for it. They even called this place the Teflon capital of the world at one time."

Taking a shuddering breath, Edith continued her rant, "Some guy figured the water pollution out a few years ago. The village brass kept it under wraps. They didn't want to cause a run on the village, afraid of a crash in property prices. But people just kept on getting sick. They've finally admitted there's a problem with the water. I've drank that water ever since I was a kid and I'm forty. My daughter drank it. A few weeks ago, I was diagnosed with a rare form of terminal cancer. Who's sick? I'm sick, Mr. Thompson! I'm deathly ill."

David saw his hand had a small cut from the fall that was starting to drip blood. He took a crumpled up tissue out from the pocket of his slacks and pressed it on the wound while he searched for words. "I'm so sorry, Ms. Nowak. I wish . . . I wish I could say or do something . . ."

"Listening to me helps, Mr. Thompson. I really don't have anyone left other than my daughter. And she won't talk to me. Haven't seen her in a few years." She shook her head. "I betcha that water killed my parents, too. This was their house before it became mine. Now it's just a pile of lumber worth a couple grand—just like when Sears delivered it here nearly a hundred years ago. But no bank's going to write a mortgage on it because of my well water. So I can't sell it. It's become my coffin now and a very expensive one at that."

"I'm sorry about your daughter."

"Don't be. She's got good reason to be upset with me." Edith squeezed her eyes shut to block the tears that threatened. Her shoulders slumped in despair. "You see, she wants to know her father, but I won't tell her anything about him."

David didn't know what to say. He wanted to ask if Boris Dietrich was the father. She said she loved him in the letters. He wanted to ask all about the unknown man. But he couldn't risk the interruption. Edith Nowak was singing like the proverbial bird. The last thing that David wanted to do was to say something to seal her lips shut, though that seemed impossible. She was carrying on a mile a minute and the words slipped through her chapped lips like Teflon had coated them over the years. "I see . . . I'm sure you have your reasons."

"Yes, I have my reasons."

He sat silently, trying to project an air of calm and patience. *Wait for it. The reasons are coming.*

"I'm trying to protect my child for her own good and she thinks she doesn't need to be protected. At twenty-four, she thinks she knows everything." Blood started to show through the tissue David clutched in his palm. "Say, it looks like you cut yourself there. Come on in and I'll bandage it up."

David rose gingerly from the rickety chair. He followed Edith through the rusty screen door into the living room. Off to her side, she pointed at a Victorian couch under a pair of double-hung windows overlooking the front porch. "Have a seat." Edith walked stiffly from the living room through an arched opening to the dining room and then disappeared. David spotted a framed photo on the end table next to him. It showed a younger Edith holding the hand of a girl not more than four years of age. There were tulips in bloom in the background. It looked like they were dressed in their Easter best, standing in front of one of the churches David had seen on Main Street. David noticed that there was no white margin on the side of the photo where Edith stood. Bending closer, he saw the photo was creased, as if a part of the picture was folded back, hidden from view.

David heard Edith in another room of the house. There were clicks and squeaking hinges as if she was opening and closing cabinet doors. David quickly picked up the picture and turned it over. It was a cheap plastic frame with the back held on by four bendable metal clips. David thought he could quickly remove the back and look to see the part of the photo that was missing from view.

"I'm sorry, Mr. Thompson." Edith called from the other room. "I know the bandages are in one of these cabinets. I just don't remember which one."

David hurriedly bent back three of the clips. "I appreciate you looking for one, Ms. Nowak." He now heard Edith rummaging through one of the cabinets. He slid the cardboard back cover out from the fourth clip by pulling on the flap that held the frame upright. It revealed a man looking away from the camera, off to the side. He pulled the picture close to his face. Unlike Edith and her daughter, the man wasn't posing for the picture—he was turned away from both of them. David recognized the man but couldn't place him. He got his cell phone out and snapped a picture of the picture.

"I found one," Edith said, from the other room.

A cabinet door slammed and David could hear slow footsteps approaching. He quickly put the back cover on and folded the clips into place. When Edith entered the living room, he was holding the intact picture frame, studying the image. "I was just looking at this photo. Is this you and your daughter?"

Edith walked over, biting her lower lip in distress. She held her hand out and he noticed it shook a little. David handed the frame to her. "Yes," she replied without looking at it. She tucked the photo under her arm and peeled back the paper covering the adhesive strips of the bandage with both hands. "Let me see your cut." David held up his hand and she put the bandage on. "There you go."

"Thank you."

"It's the least I could do," Edith said, taking a few steps to the other end of the couch. She eased down and set the photo on the end table by her side, face down. "Now who did you say you were trying to help out? Lots of prisoners have come and gone in the years since I started working there."

"I never did give you his name. It's Phillip Dawkins. Did you know him?"

"Is he okay? He's not dead, is he?"

David's ears perked up. It sounded as if she knew his life was in danger. "No, Ms. Nowak. Did you think he was dead?"

"No . . . it's just that . . . you mentioned him in the past tense—like something had happened to him."

"I take it you know him, then?"

"Not personally. He was in solitary. As secretary to Superintendent Kleinschmit, I wouldn't have had any contact with him. I know of him through paperwork that I typed up or that passed over my desk, probably on its way to be filed."

"You said typed. You don't still use typewriters at the Bureau of Prisons, do you?" David thought if they still used cassette tapes, maybe they still used typewriters. It was worth asking since the complaint with the Bureau of Licenses over the barbershop was typed.

"No, no. We have computers now, though they're pretty old. The only person who might type is Commissioner O'Neil. He's got an ancient Royal at his desk at the central office in Albany. The same one he's had for years. But that'll be gone soon. I hear he's retiring." She sighed before continuing. "My former boss, Superintendent Kleinschmit, is going to become the new state commissioner for the prison system."

"Do you know O'Neil?"

"Martin Kleinschmit is a good boss, a good superintendent."

"I asked you about Edmund O'Neil."

Edith fidgeted in her seat. "Sorry. Mr. O'Neil hired me when he was the superintendent at Kranston. But I haven't talked with him for years."

"When did he hire you?"

"Back around 1990, I guess. You sure do ask a lot of questions, Mr. Thompson."

"Just one more should do it." David waited until the end for this question. He knew it might be the one topic that shut Edith up for good. But he felt it was time to roll the dice. There was no Boris Dietrich anywhere except in Edith's file cabinet and David had gotten that information illicitly from Johnny. "Who is Boris Dietrich, if you know him?"

Edith sat there frozen—lips pressed tightly together, eyes narrowed to slits—staring into space, as the ancient grandfather clock ticked away in the corner of the living room. "No, I've never heard of him," she said with a short negative shake of her head.

David knew she was lying, but he wasn't about to call her on it. Not now. Doing that would run the risk of losing her as a source for good, for however long she lived. And she was all he had to go on at the moment. "How about Ewen Cameron? Have you ever heard of him?"

Edith abruptly stood and heaved a sigh. "No, I've never heard of him either. I think you should leave now, Mr. Thompson. I have a doctor's appointment scheduled in an hour and I have to get ready."

David got up. "Sure, thank you so much for your time. I really appreciate it."

Edith nodded as she followed him slowly to the screen door.

David fumbled for parting words as he pushed the door open. What do you say to a dying woman? "I hope your doctor's visit goes well, Ms. Nowak."

"Hope is all I have on my side, but thank you," she said, closing the door firmly behind David.

After limping his way to the curb, David sat in the Mustang and pulled out his cell phone to Google the Bureau of Prisons. He found its website and clicked to open it up. After a few more clicks, he was staring at a photo of Edmund O'Neil, the Bureau of Prisons Commissioner. His biography said he was married and mentioned his four children. David compared his snapshot of the man in Edith's photo to the official studio photo of the commissioner on the website. Though their ages differed, the two men could have been twins. David glanced at Edith's house through the passenger window of his car. A curtain panel in one of the living room windows was drawn back and he could see part of Edith's head as she peered out. He could not linger to digest what he had learned. David started up the Mustang and drove away.

Edmund O'Neil has five children, not four.

CHAPTER 17

Two nights later, Phillip and David were parked in the Mustang in the Palisade section of Mohawk City. They sat diagonally across the street from a two-family home on North Ferry Street in the historic district that was first settled by the Dutch in the 1600s. In the 17th Century, a palisade surrounded the settlement to protect the residents from marauding Frenchmen and Indians. The street where they sat led to a dead end at the Mohawk River. It was a location that had once been a prime address, but no longer.

In the Palisade, the more weather-beaten homes were located closer to the water because that's where the floods hit first and most often. Every spring during ice-out the streets would fill with frigid, filthy water as huge floes that jammed under the bridges at a turn in the Mohawk caused the river to back up and spill over its banks. During summer and fall, a sudden deluge could fill the underpasses and low-lying streets to the brim, trapping unwary motorists. It was historic, and more than anything else, it was old.

Janet Nowak's two-story building was just a few houses up from the river. The rundown houses on either side of her home displayed yellow condemnation notices in the windows. Gang graffiti decorated the chipboard that blocked entry at the front doors. In the glow of the gaslight-style street lamps, you could still see the flood lines on the weathered clapboard and crumbling brick from the hurricanes that had pummeled the region in the past few years.

"Duck!" David barked as he slid low behind the steering wheel. The car sat under a large oak, shaded from the street lamp. Phillip dove to the floor on all fours on the passenger side and tried to squeeze his head under the glove compartment. A dog license and ID tag jingled as the figure's hard-soled shoes clumped on the broken sidewalk like a throbbing heart. The shadow of a man and his canine friend passed by the car.

David shimmied himself back upright in the bucket seat and peered into his rearview mirror. He watched the retreating figure and listened to the footsteps fading up to higher ground, toward the heart of the city. "It's all clear. You can get up now."

"I can't," Phillip gasped. "I'm stuck."

"Jeez, give me your hand," David sighed.

Phillip's huge paw engulfed David's extended hand and he tugged on it until Phillip popped out from under the dash.

"You don't have to crawl under there when I say duck," David gently explained. "Just lean forward and drop your head below the window line."

"Okay. Bad habit I guess."

David nodded. "I understand."

"Can you tell me now why we're staking out this house?"

"Janet Nowak is Edith Nowak's daughter. Edith is the Kranston secretary who's retiring, who had papers in a file with your name on it. Her daughter, Janet, lives here in that house across the street, alone. Figured that out this morning when she left for work. She has a state job here in Mohawk City at the Workers' Compensation Board."

"How do you know she lives there by herself?"

"I asked around, talked to a cashier at the convenience store on the corner."

"Never heard of Edith Nowak."

"You'd have no reason to know her. She worked in the prison's administrative offices."

"What's her daughter have to do with me?"

"I'm not sure. Maybe nothing. But we still gotta check this out. We don't have much else to go on at this point."

"Check what out?" Phillip asked.

"We're going dumpster diving tonight."

"What does that mean?"

"We're going to pick through Janet Nowak's trash."

"Isn't that against the law?"

"No, not really. Everyone here uses a commercial garbage service that owns the trash containers and loans them out to customers. Tomorrow is garbage day. Once Janet takes out the trash to the curb, it's considered abandoned property. So we can take her garbage and do whatever we want to with it."

"Really?"

"Yep. Further up the hill, where the B&Bs are, the college students make quite a killing picking through the stuff they put out for the trash."

"Why would we want her trash? What are we looking for?"

"Her DNA."

"Really? I don't understand. How do you get that in the trash?"

"We find something with blood on it, some hair, a Q-tip with earwax, dental floss, a discarded toothbrush, some other bodily fluid."

"That's crazy. Why are we looking for her DNA?"

"I think she's Commissioner O'Neil's daughter."

Phillip thought for a second. "You've got to be kidding me."

"No, I'm dead serious. O'Neil has been married to the same woman for decades. Has four children by her. Janet would make five. Her mom tells me that Janet doesn't know who her father is and this has caused a rift between the two of them. It sounds like Edmund O'Neil and Edith Nowak have a secret to hide. I think he's the father."

"I still don't get what that has to do with me. It seems like such a waste of time. I just want them to leave me alone, so I can cut hair for a living."

"It's not a waste. Trust me. Remember, I know best for things that take place outside of the prison walls." David was not laying all of his cards out on the table for Phillip. He had figured out another possible angle to the relationship between Edith Nowak and Edmund O'Neil earlier that day. It was so salacious and provocative that he hesitated to tell Phillip about it at all. One thing he knew for sure: now was not the time or place to get into that discussion.

Phillip crossed his arms, shook his head, and his voice took on a petulant edge. "Did you get O'Neil's DNA already or do we have to stake out his house and pick through his trash too?"

"Fortunately, no need to go there. Picking though his trash would be problematic. He's got a wife and children who all still live with him. I couldn't isolate his DNA in his trash. It could belong to anyone in the house. Even his pets. I had to come up with a different plan for the commissioner.

"So I followed him yesterday out of his office. Same building as the Bureau of Licenses that we were at for the hearing. The building directory listed him as being on one of the top floors. I took a trip up to his floor just to scope it out. It looked like the agency had just moved into that space. Workers were hanging a big sign that said 'Bureau of Prisons' in the corridor right off the elevator. There were a bunch of suits coming and going, mostly men. They had security buzzers on the office doors that could only be activated by a state swipe card.

"Here's the thing--I saw employees hold the door for others so they wouldn't have to pull out their cards. So you can beat that system if you have to. But there really wasn't much I could do up there.

"I guess I could have loitered in the halls, wait for him to come out, and follow him to the bathroom to see what developed. But I'd stick out if I just hung around and had no place to go. I wouldn't look like I belonged. I'd stick out and draw someone's attention. Besides, getting his DNA from the bathroom didn't sound too appealing or too promising either. I wasn't going to swab his toilet or urinal. I could be getting anyone's DNA or nothing at all.

"So I left and waited in the lobby for lunch time. When I spotted him as he got off the elevator, I trailed along to the cafeteria hoping to get a utensil or a piece of food with some saliva. Sadly, no such luck.

"But after lunch, I saw him pop a piece of gum in his mouth. He talked awhile with some other suits at his table before getting up to leave. I followed him out. I wanted that wad of gum. Yet I thought it was hopeless to expect he'd toss it out before he hit the elevator. Then I got lucky.

"Near the elevators, he stopped at the barbershop in the lobby for a trim —he's got quite a head of white hair. It was a one seat shop. I followed him in and sat down like I was a customer in waiting. He tossed the gum out in a tissue before he sat down in the chair. When it was my turn, after O'Neil left and the barber was distracted, I went to the garbage pail, pretended to throw something out, picked the gum in a tissue up, and stashed it in my pocket."

Phillip's jaw dropped at David's lengthy explanation. "Couldn't you have gotten a lock of his hair and get his DNA from that?"

"No can do. You'd need a hair follicle—the root—to get any usable DNA, and O'Neil didn't go to the barber to get his eyebrows plucked."

"What did you do with the gum?"

"I had to send it in to a commercial testing service. It's not as if Ancestry.com or 23andMe runs DNA testing on gum."

"What's Ancestry.com or 23andMe?"

"People buy a kit and send in their DNA through spitting in a tube. They use it to develop their family tree or to discover their ethnic or racial origin."

"We're not doing that, though, right?"

"That's correct. We are doing something like a secret paternity test for now."

A rumble sounded in the distance. David held his index finger to his lips with one hand, while he rolled down the window with the other. The rumble turned into a scraping sound coming around the corner of Janet's building, down her driveway. The other half of the two-family home had a separate driveway off on the far side. From around the corner of the building a silhouetted figure appeared dragging out a garbage can to the curb. David could see the figure was wearing a dress and heels. It had to be Janet. She set the garbage can off to the side of the driveway and looked up the street toward the city before turning toward the river and facing David and Phillip. They both froze, hoping that the darkness would shield them. But she continued to look in their direction.

David started to sweat bullets. He kicked himself for bringing the Mustang. Not many cars park on a dead-end street to begin with. Even fewer people choose to park on one lined with condemned houses. The Mustang stood out like a nightlight in a dim hallway. It was a white 1974 classic. David imagined Janet was thinking that she had never seen his car parked on the street before. *I should have brought Annie's Prius. If only she didn't have a bloodhound nose. She'd pick up the lingering smell of garbage in it instantly.*

But a second later Janet turned around, walked back up the driveway, and disappeared. The echo of her heels clicking against the asphalt faded before David heard a house door slam shut. Then there was only the sound of crickets.

David wiped the sweat from his forehead and brow. *She's got just one can.*

All the more reason to believe she lives alone. "Okay, Phillip. We're on. It's show time!"

"What do you want me to do?"

"Here, take the keys. Open the trunk. Make some room. Throw some stuff in the back seat if you have to."

"Okay."

"I'll get the can and bring it back here and we'll empty it into the trunk."

"We're taking all that trash with us?"

"It's not like we have the option to pick through it here."

"I guess not."

"Let's go. Don't slam your door shut. Just ease it closed enough to turn off the overhead light and keep quiet."

"Okay."

Phillip slid out and circled around back to pop the trunk while David skulked down the sidewalk to get the can. The glow of blue light from a computer shone through the drawn curtains in Janet Nowak's front picture window. Slinking softly like a ninja in his cocaine-white New Balance cross trainers, David moved under the window sill and slipped past the front porch. Christy had been after him to get a pair of kicks that weren't so white. "Those are old man kicks," Christy opined. Now David wished he had taken his advice.

David bent at the knees, clasped his arms around the plastic can, and lifted it. Holding his breath against the odor, he strolled casually back to the car like he was carrying Annie's grocery bags. Phillip already had the trunk open and had made plenty of room.

"Left to right," David said, holding the can

"What do you mean?" Phillip asked, while removing the can's lid.

"Let me do it," David said. He lifted and tipped the open can to let a series of white trash bags plop one by one into the trunk. "Freshest trash—the bags on top—starting left, and flowing to the oldest stuff, from the bottom, on the far right."

"What for?"

"Not now, Phillip. Let's just get this done and get out of here. Quietly close the trunk." David took the empty can in one hand, the lid in the other hand, and skittered back to the end of Janet Nowak's driveway. He set the can back down on the curb at the same spot where he took it. He put the lid back on exactly the way he'd found it. Then he scampered back to the car, quietly clicked his door shut, and told Phillip to do the same. David slowly drove off—turning on his headlights only when the Mustang reached the end of the block.

Thirty minutes later, six white trash bags were lined up in the Thompsons' two-car garage like giant marshmallows. David was undoing the red ties for the first one in line. Phillip was at the other end of the production line.

"Put on those latex gloves, Phillip, and we'll dig through the most recent trash first."

"Okay. But can you explain—"

Just then Annie poked her head into the garage through the door that led to the kitchen and eyed David.

"Oh, it's you, David. I thought I heard something. I didn't know you were back. What are you up to?" she asked before spotting Phillip standing off to the side.

"Ah . . . Phillip is helping me with the trash."

"Hi, Phillip, I didn't see you standing over there," Annie said, as she stepped down into the garage. She scurried toward Phillip. "I'm so sorry about the barbershop," she lamented as she extended her arms to embrace him. Phillip stood stiffly at attention as Annie hugged him. "We'll get your shop going, Phillip, don't worry. David will figure it out."

David could not take his eyes off of Phillip's hands. They quivered as he slowly brought them up from his side to place them on Annie's shoulders to hug her back. David felt some vomit pop up and coat the back of his throat. He didn't know if it was the odor from Janet Nowak's trash or the sight of a murderer hugging his wife that almost made him throw up.

Phillip looked at David and nervously smiled. As Annie held him, he lifted his hands from her shoulders and shrugged while opening his hands, palms upward. David's eyes narrowed as he shot the other man a sharp stare. He wanted to believe Phillip's insistence that he was no longer the same man who killed Pete Carlson. At the same time, he feared for Annie's safety. He didn't want her to be a test case to see if Phillip truly had a change of heart and was no longer a killer. On top of it all, David wanted to smack Phillip for taking even the slightest pleasure in hugging his wife, the love of his life.

Then David remembered that he had only himself to blame for the situation. Days had passed since the raid and he still couldn't bring himself to tell Annie about Phillip's confession. He had no intention of doing so and it wasn't attorney-client privilege holding him back. He knew that Phillip would not mind if he disclosed it and might even tell her himself. *I need to stop bringing my work home with me—need to separate my work life from my family life if it's at all possible. Is it for me, though?*

He was keeping secrets from Annie again despite promising himself he wouldn't do it anymore and despite hating himself for doing it. *Some things never change; I'm one of those things.*

Annie pulled away a bit, her arms still around Phillip's ribs. She backed her hips up into Phillips hands as she peered up at him. "We'll get through this together." Just then Christy popped his head out of the door leading to the kitchen. Annie didn't skip a beat, "Don't worry, Phillip."

"I'll try not to, Mrs. Thompson."

"Please call me Annie."

"Okay."

David had seen and heard enough. His eyes locked on Christy's. He touched his belt buckle with his right hand. It was an indicator signal David always used to fall back on when he coached Christy's baseball team. The sign indicates to the players on base or at bat that the next signal was the instruction: take a pitch, hit and run, or steal the base. With Annie's back to them, David touched his belt buckle, then pointed at her, clenched his fist, hammered it, looped his index finger around in the air, and pointed toward the kitchen.

Christy looked at his dad's hand gestures in total amazement. The signals were a mix of an umpire calling a runner out or ejecting some fan, coach, or player from the ballpark. But Christy got his dad's message loud and clear. He wanted his wife out of the garage. Now.

"Excuse me, Mr. Dawkins," Christy interrupted. "Mom, can you come in and proof my English essay before I go to bed?" Christy knew that making his mom feel wanted and useful was the easiest way to get her back in the house.

"Sure, honey," she said, following Christy inside. She looked over her shoulder at Phillip. "We'll have you over to dinner soon and we can talk more."

David rolled his eyes. A family dinner with Phillip was the last thing he wanted. When Phillip was with the family now, it put David on high alert for the safety of Annie and Christy. Phillip's presence also served as a constant in-your-face reminder to David about all his mistakes and short-comings.

"That would be nice, Mrs. Thompson . . . I mean, Annie. Thank you."

"You're welcome. Are you going to clean this mess up, David?"

"Yes, ma'am."

After Annie left, the two men again stood over the line of garbage bags.

"Let's get to work, Phillip."

"Okay. Can you tell me now why we put the garbage bags in the order they fell out of the can?"

"Sure. The more recent the garbage is, the fresher the DNA in it will be. We want the freshest DNA possible to get a valid reading."

"I guess that makes sense."

"Could you get the wheelbarrow leaning against the wall over there? We'll dump one bag at a time into it and sort through it in there."

"Okay."

While Phillip fetched the wheelbarrow, David undid the red tie and opened the bag. When Phillip returned with the wheelbarrow, David dumped the bag into it. Instantly, a putrid odor flooded the garage. David turned his head away in disgust. Phillip started to gag and then coughed up some phlegm.

"I'll open the garage door," David said. "There's a tissue box on my work-bench for you."

David pushed a button and the opener motor overhead began to hum as it lifted one of the two garage doors. Phillip spat his loogie into the tissue and folded it up.

Gingerly, David started to pick through the accumulated trash with his latex-gloved hands. "Check this out, Phillip!"

"I'm coming."

He looked around for a garbage can but couldn't find one.

"Jackpot!" David exclaimed.

Phillip set his used tissue on the workbench and hustled over to see what he had found. David opened his latex-gloved hand to reveal a small, opaque object in the shape of a crescent moon.

"What is it?"

"A nail clipping."

"That has DNA in it?"

"Yes, but let's see if we can find some more. I'd imagine a person trims their finger nails or toe nails all at once . . . ."

"I guess."

David put the nail clipping in a miniature paper envelope from the DNA kit, while Phillip poked around. He moved a crushed toothpaste carton and some tissues smeared with flesh-toned make-up and bright red lipstick.

"There's another one," David exclaimed.

"Where?"

"There, by your pinky finger. I'll get it." David picked up the next nail shard and tucked it in the envelope.

Ten minutes later, they had collected seven nail specimens.

"That should be enough. I'll ship it off to the commercial testing service tomorrow and we'll see if we have a match with Edmund O'Neil's gum."

"How long should that take?"

"Not more than a few days. I paid extra to get an expedited report."

"All right. I still don't see what this has to do with me."

"If I can establish that O'Neil and Edith Nowak are Janet's parents, perhaps I can use that as leverage somehow to get O'Neil to leave you alone. It's obviously something that O'Neil wants to keep secret."

"But Janet Nowak is a woman now. Maybe keeping the secret doesn't mean as much anymore to him."

"He's one part of the equation. The other part is the mother, Edith Nowak. She doesn't want her daughter to know about this. Then there's another part of the equation I haven't told you yet." David had withheld this information from Phillip while he tried to figure out if there was any reason why he shouldn't disclose it. He couldn't think of any, so he figured it was as good a time as any to tell Phillip now. "Edith Nowak is forty years old. She told me that and I confirmed it. She has her birthday posted on her Facebook account."

"So what?"

"Janet Nowak is twenty-four years old. That's what her mother said when I visited with her. I ran a background check on Janet this morning using a website and I double-checked her age."

"Okay."

"That means that Edith Nowak gave birth to Janet when she was sixteen years old. Seventeen is the age of consent in New York. So if Edmund O'Neil is Janet Nowak's father, he committed statutory rape."

Phillip's face grimaced in disbelief as all the color drained out of it. "Isn't that . . . a felony?"

"Yes, a Class E felony, which is currently punishable by up to four years in prison."

"But this happened over twenty years ago."

"Right, and the statute of limitations is five years. So he can't be prosecuted now. But he could have been in big trouble back in the 1990s, when this took place. He was about forty years old back then—married with a family. There would have been no defense to statutory rape for him."

"But why wasn't he charged?"

"The DA can't prosecute what he doesn't know about. Edith Nowak must have dropped out of school to have the child or maybe she was home schooled. There's plenty of ways to slide under the radar of the DA."

"Why didn't Edith or her parents press for charges to be brought then?"

"Good question. I suspect there was a deal made. Looking at O'Neil's biography on the state website, he was the superintendent at Kranston at the time. This was before he was made Commissioner of the Bureau of Prisons. I find it interesting that Edith started working at Kranston about the same time and that O'Neil was her boss."

Phillip sat down on a stool near the workbench and peeled off his latex gloves one at a time, while he tried to process it all. He stroked his chin, then began shaking his head as he stared off into space. "What you say makes sense. But I don't see what it has to do with me. I think this may be a waste of time."

"It might not have anything to do with you, but perhaps we can somehow use the secret as leverage. It's a tool to find out what's really going on with you. Even if he can't be prosecuted, Edmund O'Neil does not want his wife and children to know. Twenty years later, this still could cause a divorce or estrangement from the children. The disclosure would harm his professional reputation and his legacy, too. There's really no choice, Phillip, except to pursue this lead until it ends because we've got absolutely nothing else to go on at this point. Zip, zero, zilch, nada."

CHAPTER 18

The next afternoon, David and Phillip were sitting downstairs in David's office trying to figure out a way to open the shop again. Christy was at school and Annie was at the first day of a two-day conference in Albany.

David's cell rang. The caller ID flashed Julius's name and number.

"It's Julius!" David yelped. "Maybe he has some information for us. I'll put him on speaker and you can listen. Just don't say anything, so he doesn't know you're here, okay?"

Phillip nodded. "All right."

"Hey, Julius, what's going on?"

"Dr. D. Ewen Cameron. That's what's going on."

"Really? What about him?"

"You know, I really got into researching this guy. I've never heard of him before and I've lived in Albany all of my life."

"I've never heard of him either."

"Well, there's a lot of information about him on the internet. You can just Google his name. But there's not much in the local media archives about him. Maybe it's a chapter that people around here would like to forget."

"How's that?"

"His research."

"What about it?"

"Torture is a word that comes to mind. But I think you first have to consider the historical backdrop for you to fully appreciate what I'm going to tell you about him."

"Okay," David nodded, even though Julius couldn't see him, and set the cell phone on his desk.

"It appears Cameron was doing work for the forerunner of the CIA—the Office of Strategic Service or OSS—during World War II. His involvement can be traced back to around the time of the Pearl Harbor attack in December 1941. Some people say he worked on a truth drug committee and tried the serum out in the veteran's hospital in Albany."

"Do you think that's true?"

"I don't know for sure, but there's plenty of evidence to suggest that this tidbit fits in with his MO."

"Okay, what else did you find out?"

"Allen Dulles, the future director of the CIA and an OSS American spy at the time, first met Ewen Cameron prior to the Nuremberg trials. Cameron was asked by the United States, quite possibly by Dulles, to perform a psychiatric examination of Nazi Rudolf Hess to determine if he was fit to stand trial in 1945. Cameron was briefed by Dulles before he gave Hess a psychiatric examination and determined he was sane. It was the first time the two men met. Apparently, they hit it off. Cameron achieved worldwide fame overnight by examining Hess. Then he used this notoriety as a springboard to become our go-to guy to explain and solve the German threat going forward."

"What threat? The war was over, right?"

"Yeah, but just hear me out. I have to lay it out one step at a time. You'll understand in a few minutes."

"Okay."

"At the end of the war, Cameron emerged as a self-proclaimed expert on the German culture and on the underlying causes of the war and the Holocaust. He wrote a paper entitled 'The Social Reorganization of Germany.' In it he identified all the problems of the German culture—the need for status, worship of order, regimentation, authoritarian leadership, and the fear of other countries. He said there was a need for a major 'transformation of the existing cultural organization in the postwar period' in Germany. The driving narrative at the end of the war was to do everything and anything to prevent World War II from happening again. Every good marketing campaign needs a tagline; our country's brain trust and the defense industry used this narrative for a few years.

"The big fear posed by Cameron was that German youth who had been adolescents during the Third Reich would be the greatest threat to world peace in years to come. In a later paper, Ewen Cameron had a solution to address that threat. He suggested that each surviving German over the age of twelve should receive a short course of electroshock treatment to wipe out any remaining vestige of Nazism. In other words, he wanted to erase their memories."

David's eyebrows popped, "Really? Nothing ever came of that, right? We didn't go around trying to erase the memories of Germans, did we?"

"No, not Germans. But we did it to Canadians instead."

"You mean at the Allan Memorial Institute, where Cameron was the director?"

"Right, but you're getting ahead of me."

"Okay. Sorry, can't help myself. This is wild."

Julius continued, "Later on, in the 1940s and early 1950s, the driving narrative to support our defense budget and the defense industry shifted away from doing everything and anything to stop another World War II. Instead it focused on doing everything and anything to stop the spread of Communism. People were still trying to come to grips with how the atrocities of World War II—like the Holocaust and the murder of millions of Jews and others—could have happened. What possessed the German people to willingly engage in such inhuman behavior?

"In 1949, Cardinal Joszef Mindszenty, an outspoken anti-Communist, confessed during a trial that he engaged in espionage against the Hungarian Communist government. People speculated that he had been tortured and brainwashed by the Communists. The word 'brainwashing' entered the American vocabulary in a 1950 newspaper article talking about how the Chinese government forced citizens to join the Communist Party. Remember, we were in the midst of a Korean conflict and American GIs taken prisoner by the North Koreans were paraded before cameras, seemingly willingly, to denounce capitalism and imperialism. The McCarthy anti-Communist hearings were about to start in 1954. The brain trust of Ivy League boys running the country thought we were losing not only the arms race, but also the race to understand and to utilize brainwashing. That's when Ewen Cameron grabbed the baton and ran a record-breaking lap to try and win the brainwashing race."

David sat stunned, shaking his head at the phone, "You can't be serious. Brainwashing race?"

"Dead serious. Those were the times in which we lived back then and that was the atmosphere in which Ewen Cameron flourished."

"Well, that explains why the FBI did a loyalty investigation into Cameron back in 1948. They wanted to make damn sure he was on our side."

"Yes, that makes sense, given what happened next. Cameron went on an absolute tear, writing and speaking to build an unassailable platform in his profession. He was a social media whiz before there was any social media as we know it today. He conquered whatever media was available to him. Between 1947 and 1950, he wrote and published three books. One book in three years was quite an accomplishment back then and remains so even today. But one book per year on top of what else he was doing? I'll bet the man never slept.

"I tried reading one of his books—*Life is for Living*—and it damn near killed me. It was full of anecdotes and I found it interesting on the surface. But I could not figure out the point of all of these endless observations about the challenges of life at that time. It never led anywhere. You step back from it, and the book is pure psychobabble—all two hundred and fifty-some-odd pages of it. I thought the stupid book was trying to brainwash me."

"Maybe it should have been titled, *Life is for the Brainwasher?*" snickered David.

"That's not too far from the truth, as far as he was concerned. His writing didn't stop at the bookshelf. He was churning out professional papers too, at a furious pace. At every opportunity, he was traveling all over the country and speaking to some group of professionals in the field. He was all over the newspapers and on the radio.

"But that's not all. During the 1950s he headed the American, Canadian, and World Psychiatric Associations, the American Psychopathological Association, and the Society of Biological Psychiatry. He attracted a large number of postgraduate students and visiting scholars from around the world. Year after year they showered awards on him: the Adolf Meyer Memorial Award, the Samuel Rubin Award, and the Montreal Mental

Hygiene Institute Award for outstanding contributions to the mental health of the Canadian people. Honorary fellowships and memberships were sprinkled all over his resume. He even had his own PR man. Yeah, you heard me right; this nut job had a PR man. Ewen Cameron was a mental health rock star."

"On top of all this," David interjected, "Cameron was the director of the Allan Memorial Institute, right?"

"Correct. From 1943 to 1964, Cameron was the director and a Professor of Psychiatry at McGill University. He ran his research and treatments at the Allan. An associate wrote some years later that Cameron would arrive at the Allan around 8 a.m. with dictation belts recorded several hours earlier, which kept one secretary busy typing all day. He had committee meetings in the morning, whirlwind rounds on the wards with an entourage of residents, then more meetings, lunch at the Royal Victoria Hospital, as a rule. In the afternoon, he saw private patients, making a final round of the wards before going home after 7 p.m. At home the pace wasn't any slower. He was married in 1933, was raising a family—had three sons, and a daughter—while making the commute between Montreal and Albany or Lake Placid frequently."

"That all seems impossible for one person. Perhaps he cloned himself."

"Ha, you think you're being funny. Reportedly, Cameron read science fiction every night before he went to bed. It was his lifeblood. He was a man who loved gadgets. I read that he tried to build an automatic baby feeder, like B.F. Skinner's baby-tending box, for his own kids. I'd wager that if he could have cloned himself, he would have."

David found this fascinating, but disturbing. "Tell me about his research."

"It has its roots in science fiction and a gadget. Aldous Huxley wrote a dystopian science fiction novel entitled *Brave New World* in 1932. In the not-so-distant future, the book suggested, we would get subliminal messages played while we were sleeping. Babies born in the hospital would get messaging delivered by under-the-pillow speakers. Interestingly, after this was published some guy had the idea of making a phonograph with a timer and an under-pillow speaker to teach people to learn such things as a foreign language. Cameron asked one of his aides to contact the inventor to check it out. When the aide told him of the inventor's claim that anything could be taught during sleep, Cameron took the idea and ran with it.

"You see, Cameron was trying to change the mindset of his subjects in his experiments through messaging. He wanted to pound his messaging into the brain—he called this 'psychic driving'—to make it stick for good. Further, he wanted to do this in the most time-efficient way possible; like he wanted to create a mental health production line.

"The messaging was bizarre, according to patients who are still living. 'You are a horrible mother and wife' was given to one patient before positive messaging was instilled. Cameron got frustrated because his messaging wasn't being accepted while the patients were awake. I'm not sure why that came as a surprise to him. It was like someone nagging you constantly, every few seconds, repeatedly, day after day, week after week. It would drive anyone crazy.

"So why not have them sleep and get the messaging that way? He invented his own messaging machine gadget, a tape recorder, that replayed the same message over and over again while the patient was sleeping.

"But if messaging via sleeping showed promise, why not have the patients just sleep all the time to get the messaging? Why not have them sleep all day long? So he drugged them up, creating sleep cocktails composed of Thorazine, Nembutal, Seconal, Veronal and Phenergan, and other drugs. Threw in some LSD, too, to make them more apt to accept the messaging. But why stop at sleeping all day long? How about all week long? Even all month long? How about longer? And he did exactly that.

"Then, why take any chances on outside stimulation that might interfere with the messaging. Let's make sensory deprivation chambers and make them sleep in there. And that's exactly what he did.

"Are patients' past memories, behaviors, and relationships getting in the way of messaging? Forget psychoanalysis. No need to waste time talking your way to a healthy mental state when you can wipe the patient's mind clean through electroshock. He called this 'de-patterning.' But you had better get all the memories out to get the messaging to stick, including any memory of the torture you just put these poor people through. So you wake the people up from their endless sleep and you shock the crap out of them. The recommended voltage was usually 110 volts for that kind of therapy back then; Cameron used 150 volts. The normal dosage was a single shock lasting a fraction of a second. Cameron's shocks lasted longer, up to one second—thirty times more powerful than normal. They were zapped two to three times a day, as opposed to the more usual once a day, or once every two days. These poor people had their circuits wiped clean. It was like an Etch-A-Sketch for the mind. Their bodies forgot everything, including how to go to the bathroom, how to walk, how to eat.

"More was always better to Cameron. More messaging, more sleep, more drugs, more isolation, more shock. You could never have too much of a good thing.

"These poor unsuspecting people—mostly women—would be admitted to the Allan supposedly because they had schizophrenia, depression, or some other mental malady. Husbands, families, everyone thought these women were going to get the best medical care available in the world for whatever ailed them because, well, Cameron was the world's leading psychiatrist at the time. But what they didn't know was that the treatment was really based in science fiction, not in medical science.

"Cameron would do everything and anything to drive his messaging home in a time when we would do anything and everything to keep Communism from spreading. Cameron was a man of the times in a way. But I think the entire platform he created for himself in psychiatry served, in part, as a front for his science fiction experiments. Do you know what the real kicker is to this lunacy?"

"No, what?"

"These people paid to be tortured. They thought they were paying for the best medical care available, when they were really paying for some quack to get his jollies from doing experiments he culled from comic books."

David wished he had been taking notes. "How the heck did he get away with this?"

"Because Ewen Cameron was God. One of his former patients said she thought he was God back then and could do no wrong. In the 1950s, Cameron would go on to treat Allen Dulles' wife, Clover, who suffered from depression, as did her mother. But I bet Clover never received anything more than Cameron-lite treatment. If Dulles, the head of the CIA under Eisenhower at the beginning of the Cold War, trusted Cameron to treat his wife, he'd trust him to treat anyone because Cameron was God to him too. That's the image Cameron created for himself and that's the image that everyone accepted back then. And you don't mess with God. Cameron attracted a ton of research money because investing in God is a sure and noble thing.

"He was unstoppable. 'There but for the grace of God goes God,' was reportedly the chatter of nurses, junior colleagues, and underlings when Cameron was afoot doing tornado rounds at Allan Memorial. So nobody ever openly questioned God about his so-called research. Yeah, some peers questioned it privately, but taking on God wasn't going to put money in their pockets or further their careers. So they just watched it all play out like they were waiting for an accident to happen.

"That accident didn't happen until more than ten years later. Nobody really questioned Cameron's status as God until the source for part of his funding was revealed, long after he died hiking the Adirondacks in 1967. In 1977, it was made public through US Senate hearings that Cameron was funded by the CIA for his work from 1957 until 1963 through a special project—code name MK-Ultra. Oh, it's debatable whether he ever knew that the money funneled through a grant from Cornell's Society for the Investigation of Human Ecology to his program was from the CIA. But it didn't really matter. He had other funding through other sources, like the Canadian Government and the Rockefeller Foundation. He was going to do his brainwashing research anyway because that was the path he was on before the CIA started funding him. But once it was made public in 1977 that the CIA funded his research, all hell broke loose. You see, if someone takes money from the CIA, he can't be God because God doesn't do business with the devil. Everything was seen in a different light then. Cameron went from God to Lucifer in a flash and suddenly former patients surfaced with stories of torture at the hands of Ewen Cameron."

"Did Cameron have any success with his research at all?"

"No. Wars are good at destroying things. His war against memory was no different. Minds were wiped clean. Cameron hoped to create a new and improved person from these cleansed minds. But he only got halfway there. Even Dr. God couldn't put Humpty Dumpty back together again."

"Did you run across Boris Dietrich's name during your research?"

"Negative."

"Did you find an FBI file on Officer Carlson's killing back in 1985?"

"Double negative. Still looking. Archives is backed up."

"What about the radio and the vitamins? Were you able to run tests on them?"

"Yeah, but the preliminary results came back negative."

"Tell them to look again, and to look harder, especially after what you just told me."

Julius could do a passable Morgan Freeman impersonation, when he was in the mood. Today he drawled, "Maybe you should come to work for the FBI, David. That way you can become my official boss."

"I'm sorry, Julius. It's just that I think we're on to something."

"David, did you forget Ewen Cameron is dead?"

"Are you sure?"

"Come on, David. If he wasn't dead, he'd be about 114 years old today. He's not involved in whatever is going on with Dawkins and you."

"I'm not so sure. I mean, why would that correspondence from him still be in that file cabinet at Kranston?"

"Who knows? Be careful, David. Paranoia is a disease that's contagious."

"Just promise that you'll ask your techies to take another look, please."

"All right, I'll ask them to check these things out again."

"Thank you."

"Is that it, boss?"

"Stop it. You know how much I appreciate what you're doing."

"You're welcome, David. I'll be in touch." With that, Julius hung up.

Phillip hadn't moved during the entire conversation. He stared upwards, through the basement window, into the window well surrounding it. A chipmunk scurried around the well, rummaging through leaves from last season.

"You heard what Julius said, Phillip. Does any of what he said resonate with you?"

"What he was talking about took place in Canada a long time ago. I'm not sure how it can have anything to do with me. What do you think?" Phillip asked, pointing at the window.

"About the chipmunk?"

"Yes. Do you think he can get out of the well by himself?"

"I've never seen one get stuck before. It's only eight inches deep. That chipmunk will make it. I'm hoping we'll be as lucky."

CHAPTER 19

The following Wednesday, Phillip and David were hunkered down in David's office again, attempting a round of brainstorming, when the side entry doorbell rang.

"I'll get it," Christy said. He'd just gotten home from school and was up in the kitchen crunching away on celery sticks slathered with peanut butter, his favorite afternoon snack. Annie was at the final day of the two-day conference.

"Dad," Christy called down from the kitchen, "there's a Federal Express package for you."

David hurried to the bottom of the basement steps. "Okay, toss it down."

Christy flipped it into the air with one hand and David caught it against his chest. "Thanks, Christy."

"Sure, Dad," Christy replied, before turning back to the kitchen.

David placed the white polyethylene overnight package in the center of his desk. "It's here!" he said to Phillip, with a little "ta-da" gesture.

"What's that?"

"The secret paternity test results," David said, gripping the envelope at the top seam. "Now we can confirm that Janet Nowak is the child of Edmund O'Neil."

David pulled the seam apart and yanked out the paperwork. The cover letter said that the DNA profiles were successfully extracted from the gum and fingernails. The letter went on to say that DNA profiles for both subjects had been uploaded to the company website. They could be shared with other DNA sites for possible matches.

After the usual legal caveat that the report's conclusion was not admissible in a court of law because the company did not oversee the DNA's chain of custody, the report said there wasn't a match. Edmund O'Neil, identified as case number 569725, was excluded as the father of Janet Nowak, identified as case number 569741. No wiggle room; not even a glimmer of hope. The letter said "The probability of paternity is 0%."

Disappointment that bordered on despair crowded out disbelief on David's face. His nose crinkled, his eyes squinted shut. He spun the letter in the air onto his desk and covered his face with trembling hands. He swallowed hard and took a deep, shuddering breath. His only lead had hit a dead end.

Phillip stared at the office wall, expressionless, and waited for the verdict. After a minute he turned to David and asked, "So what does the report say?"

"No match," David snapped. "You can read it yourself if you'd like."

Phillip showed no visible reaction. He resumed staring at the wall. "That's okay. No need."

David leaned back in his chair, stabbed both hands into his hair, and let out a huge sigh. "We're back again at square one. We've got nothing to go on."

Phillip nodded. "I'm sorry. I didn't think this would lead anywhere."

All of David's frustration concentrated in his expression as he glared at Phillip's blank face. "I'm waiting . . . "

"For what?" Phillip yawned and stretched his yard-long arms out at either side.

"For you to say, 'I told you so.'"

Phillip turned his head to David. "I wasn't going to say—"

"You came pretty close. You told me you didn't think it would lead anywhere."

Phillip calmly gazed back at David, eyes half-closed. "I didn't mean anything by it. I was just stating, you know, a fact."

"You're sitting there like this is no big deal. Maybe you've got some ideas on what we should do now."

Phillip thought for a few seconds. "I don't know. Give it time? Time has a way of changing things when we can't." Phillip didn't realize that he had just parroted Superintendent Kleinschmit's line to David until after the words left his mouth.

Even then he didn't think twice about it because he knew it was the only answer he could dredge up. He wasn't about to share his plan to pay Commissioner O'Neil a visit; maybe let the carving knife he left back at the motel room do the talking. He knew that plan wouldn't go over well with David.

"Time?! That's your idea?" That's the last thing David wanted to hear. He felt the situation suddenly spinning out of control. It was like being in a vehicle that hydroplanes on a wet road. That feeling never sat well with David.

As a lawyer, he always had a plan; often he had at least one more in reserve. Passing time by twiddling his thumbs was never one of those choices. He was always pushing against time, not waiting for it to pass. He wanted to save time by finding a prompt solution, so his clients could move on without some legal crap overhanging their lives. He wanted Phillip to be off on his own, gainfully employed and happy already, yesterday even, to spare his family the threat of Phillip—the killer—lashing out at them.

"Yes, that's the only idea that comes to mind." Phillip sat there gazing at the photos of David and his family that decorated the office walls. "Maybe you picked the wrong gum out of the trash?"

"Impossible. I picked the tissue out from on top. I could see the gum sticking out from between the folds."

David witnessed Phillip eying his family photos on the wall. The continued focus made him feel uneasy. Two weeks ago, Phillip had confessed to David that he wanted to kill him. Maybe it was time for an update.

"Phillip, can I ask you something?"

"Sure."

"Have you had any more dreams or thoughts about killing me since we last talked?"

Phillip considered the question at length. It took a few moments to search his memory. "No, I don't think I have." His expression remained blank, almost placid; his voice was calm.

David didn't like how long it took Phillip to answer. He didn't like the uncertainty in what he said, either. There was no margin for error when his family was concerned. David yanked out his desktop keyboard and started clicking away. A long-shot idea came to mind; he was putting it in play.

With a couple of motions of his infrared mouse, he went to Mission DNA's website. Mission is a free, open-source genealogy database like GEDMatch. Anyone can upload a DNA profile to the site and look for matches. So if you've got your DNA profile from consumer DNA sites like Ancestry, 23andMe, Family Tree DNA, MyHeritage, or any other source, you can upload it there. The site runs a scan to see if their files contain any other matches to your genes from outside of your chosen consumer DNA site's database.

Unknown to Phillip, David had snagged his DNA in a tissue filled with mucus that he had dropped on the workbench in the garage. He'd sent it off to one of the consumer sites without a second thought. Phillip's right to DNA privacy didn't matter. David's family came first. He put Phillip's mucus in a test tube, paid for expedited service, and registered his profile to Mission DNA the night before. But there were no hits.

Now David uploaded Janet Nowak's and Edmund O'Neil's profiles to see if there might be any hits for them in Mission's database. He was flailing in the gene pool for any clue that might give him another lead.

"Waiting for Father Time to adjust things in our favor is not an option, Phillip. I can't hold out thirty years," David quipped while navigating his computer mouse. "Neither can you, this time around. Have you checked the mirror lately? You're not getting any younger. You can't sit around in your room like you're in solitary and expect to make it on the outside." With one final click, the two new profiles were uploaded.

Phillip fidgeted in his chair. He resented David's criticism. Not because it was misguided. Phillip knew the analysis was spot on. He had thought repeatedly about going to visit Commissioner O'Neil since he first came up with the idea. But that was five days ago. He still didn't have anything close to a plan. The idea was nothing more than a daydream that wandered in and out of his mind as he watched the world go past his motel room picture window. He meant to do something about it but couldn't; David's comment was a reminder of what he hated in himself.

"What's wrong with you today, Phillip?"

"What do you mean?"

"You're yawning and acting like a zombie."

"I'm sorry. I've been having problems sleeping."

"Is something bothering you?" *Like maybe you're dreaming of going after Annie or Christy?*

"I just don't see how I'm ever going to make it on my own." Phillip was beginning to sound morose.

"I don't either. Not now, anyway. But I won't give up. I don't understand how you were able to manage solitary for thirty years but you get easily flustered with how things happen in the outside world."

Phillip shrugged. "Two different skill sets, I guess. I'm having challenges adjusting to the outside."

"That's to be expected. But you can come up with ideas too. My God, you developed a mindset that allowed you to survive in the box. Surely you can develop a mindset for surviving outside of the box. More than anything, Phillip, you need to learn to *think* outside of the box."

David's desktop pinged, signaling the receipt of an e-mail. David saw the sender was Mission DNA. The subject line read, "You have a match!" He opened the email. "Hold on Phillip. Looks like I've got something here."

"What?"

"Janet Nowak's DNA matched someone else on Mission's database."

"Really?"

"Yes." David leaned toward his screen. His lips started to move as he read. But nothing came out. His face went white, his jaw dropped. He put his hands on his cheeks to keep the front of his head from melting into his lap.

"Whose?"

"I don't believe it. I cannot freakin' believe it!"

"Whose DNA is it?"

"Yours."

"What are you talking about?"

"Your DNA matches Janet Nowak. The report says as a related male, there's a 99.9% probability that you are her father."

"What?" Phillip screamed.

CHAPTER 20

Phillip couldn't believe his ears. His face flashed from alabaster white to crimson red in a burst of adrenaline. His gray eyes nearly popped out of their sockets, the bags under his eyes faded. He reared up from his table directly across from David's desk and stood there trembling. "How did my DNA get in that database in the first place?!"

Phillip had survived thirty years in the box because he wouldn't let the system abduct his soul. Now his best friend, his only friend, had abducted it and had sent it off to share with the world.

"Calm down. I put it in there," David said.

Christy came running down the stairs with a worried look on his face, while he alternated glances between his father and Phillip. "What's going on?"

"Your dad put my DNA on a database without asking me first."

"Your DNA? How did you get his DNA, Dad?"

"When we were in the garage combing through Janet Nowak's trash, he blew his nose and put the tissue on the workbench. Later that night, after I took him back to his motel room, I took a mucus sample from it and sent it in for analysis."

"Who gave you the right to steal my DNA?" Phillip protested, looming over the table and desk where they worked. With each breath, anger inflated his body, until David imagined he would float to the ceiling like a furious helium balloon.

"I didn't steal it. You still have it. I just posted your profile into their system under an anonymous case number. I can delete it at any time."

"Why did you do that, Dad?" asked Christy in confusion. He looked uncomfortable at the escalating situation, as if the room were shrinking around the three men.

"I did it on a whim. We were down to our last lead. I didn't think it would lead to anything. I really thought Edmund O'Neil was Janet Nowak's father. I can't believe you're the father."

"Wait, Mr. Dawkins is Janet Nowak's father?" Christy looked both uncomfortable and dismayed.

"Apparently so," David said.

"You had no right to take my DNA profile and post it without my permission." Phillip had endured a lifetime of insults to his mind and body in Kranston; he'd lived in a limbo where he had no control of any kind. It was supposed to be different on the outside.

"That's debatable," David replied, "under the circumstances. Given the results, I think you owe me an explanation."

"For what?"

"You're Janet Nowak's father. How did that happen?"

"I'm not her father!"

"The DNA analysis shows that there's a 99.9% probability that you are her father—"

"It's wrong, then."

"How can that be, Phillip?"

"I've never had sex with her mother."

David took out his cell and showed Phillip the picture he'd taken of Edith Nowak from the photo in her living room. "Recognize her?"

"No, I've never had sex with her."

"Really? So, did your boys just swim out of solitary confinement, across the yard, into the administrative building, to crawl up Edith Nowak's leg?"

"I've never had sex with that woman, I tell you! I don't even know her. I haven't had sex with a girl since before I went to prison."

"How do you explain it then?" David decided the best defense was a good offense. It was the only course he could take in the face of Phillip's anger.

"I can't," said the ex-con, shoulders rising then falling in a confused shrug.

"You know, Phillip, all along you've said that pursuing these DNA leads was a waste of time—that they wouldn't lead anywhere. Maybe you didn't want me to pursue them because you knew that this would all lead to you eventually."

"That's not true." Now Phillip began to sound shrill, as defiance set in to replace his dissipating anger. His eyes searched the corners of the room, looking for an answer to this conundrum.

"It all makes sense to me," David posited. "Edith Nowak didn't want to tell her daughter that she was the bastard child of a convicted murderer. That's why she refused to share his identity with her. That's what led Janet to become estranged from her mother."

"No, that's not true. She's not my daughter." A touch of desperation tinged Phillip's reply; his eyes moved faster around the perimeter of the space, not landing on David or Christy. He was searching for an escape route.

"The commissioner and superintendent knew this happened under their watch. If anyone found out there'd be hell to pay—allowing a convicted murderer in solitary to have sex with an employee. Did you rape her?"

"Are you kidding me? How could I rape anyone if I've been in solitary for thirty years?" Phillip's large hands landed on his hips as he shook his head in exasperation.

"Maybe during rec hour?" Now there was a double entendre for the ages, David realized.

"You mean I lured her into my rec pen and raped her? That's not possible. She never set foot in solitary. I was under guard all the time while in the rec pen, in my cell, in the shower—at least two COs were with me at all times outside of the box." Phillip was deflating now, his body hanging over the table, resting on his flexed arms as the white knuckles hit the surface.

"Did she *rape* you then?" David asked aggressively.

"You can't be serious. How could that even happen?"

"I don't know. But I suppose it doesn't make any difference or not if she raped you. Back then, sex with an inmate would have led to disciplinary action against Edith, including suspension or dismissal, even if it was consensual. And if this happened with the superintendent's knowledge or approval, he'd be fired. Were you at Kranston in the 1990s?" David was getting a little irritated, both with the situation and with Phillip's obstinacy.

"Yes, but I never had sex with this girl. Did you say she was sixteen at the time?"

"Yes."

"How did a sixteen-year-old even work at Kranston?"

"You can work when you're sixteen. She could have lied about her age too, for all I know, to get the job. Who was the superintendent back then?"

"O'Neil or Kleinschmit. I can't exactly remember."

"Why are you protecting Edith Nowak?"

"I'm not." Phillip paused for a minute, then repeated, "I'm not."

"Did you somehow use this incident to gain leverage for your release?"

"What are you talking about?" Now the ex-con was incredulous. Sex and blackmail, from a cell in a solitary confinement unit? Sure.

"Maybe you told Superintendent Kleinschmit that if he didn't release you, you'd tell everyone about your affair with Edith Nowak. So he managed to have the DNA switched with the DNA in Officer Carlson's murder file to get you out."

"Stop it. You're being ridiculous—switching out DNA." By now Phillip had dropped back into his chair, where he sat just shaking his head slowly.

"Am I? The New York State Police is currently under investigation for manipulating DNA analysis to match samples to known suspects in crimes. DNA-swapping with known criminals is certainly possible in that environment."

"The police officer's family would have protested my release if—"

"Really? I think the family got sick and tired of seeing you survive the box, year after year, decade after decade. They wanted you dead from day one. But New York does not have capital punishment—the death penalty. For thirty years you survived and they suffered. They wanted vengeance. What better way to get it than to let you out and let the family do what New York State could not do? That's why Ken Broome, nephew to Officer Carlson's wife, inspected your shop and wrote you up for multiple violations. For all I know, the family was somehow involved with the CO traffic stop and the raid on the shop too. Of course, Kleinschmit knew they were going to go after you. That was fine by him. He'd let the family take care of his problem. One half of the affair with Edith Nowak would die with you and the other half would die when the cancer finished off Edith Nowak."

"Why would I admit to you that I killed Officer Carlson then? I had nothing to gain from doing that."

"Sure you did. You were afraid I'd figure it out at some point. You thought you'd beat me to the punch. If you told me before I figured it out, you thought I couldn't divulge your admission because of the attorney-client privilege. You wanted to string me along so I'd continue to help you."

"But I wanted to kill you, David. I told you that. Why would I want to kill the only person I can rely on? Who would help me then?"

"You tell me. You should know. We're talking about what's going on in your head, not mine."

"There was no sex, I tell you. You don't think I'd forget having sex with a woman after living in the box all these years, do you?"

"Well, Phillip, your memory hasn't been the best. Things from your past just seem to pop out of nowhere into your head—like your admission that you killed Officer Carlson."

"I can't argue with that, David. Maybe . . . maybe I had sex with her but I can't remember it? Maybe that's what happened?"

"I suppose that's possible," David admitted.

"Dad, if Phillip says he didn't have sex with her, I believe that's what he believes."

"Christy, please stay out of this."

"Dad, I am involved with this, like it or not. I didn't ask to become involved. It just happened. If neither of us can talk about Mr. Dawkins with Mom, then let me at least share my thoughts."

At times like these, David wished he had established his office outside of the home. Every day was Take Your Child to Work Day in the Thompson house. David knew it was his fault. He had set up an open-door policy when Christy was a little boy, getting off the bus from grade school. But ever since Christy became a teenager, Take Your Child to Work Day had become Challenge Your Father at Work Day.

"All right, what are you saying Christy?"

"I'm saying that he believes his memory, even though his memory might be incorrect. I learned about this in my neuroscience internship. I think he's telling the truth about what he believes."

"And what makes you believe him, Christy?"

"He and I are a lot alike. He left the real world when he was my age. We are at the same place now in our heads, but at different points in our chronological lives," Christy explained. "Doesn't matter. I know when one of the kids in my class is lying. Mr. Dawkins isn't. He's already said he's not a liar. I believe him. You shouldn't be so hard on him."

"Oh come on now, Christy. I've got to question him and his memory to get at the truth. If I didn't question him, we wouldn't be considering the possibility that he might have had sex with Edith Nowak but just not remember it. My God, I don't believe I just said that out loud. But in the context of what's been happening with Phillip and what we've learned from the file on him at Kranston, I guess it's possible. But why don't you remember it, Phillip?"

"I don't know."

David just shook his head. "Well, it seems you're in good company, Phillip."

"What do you mean by that?" Phillip asked. This discussion was seriously taxing his appetite for human interaction.

"It seems there are a few people who want to forget that you're the father of Janet Nowak. There might even be some people who don't know you're her father. Janet might like to know who her father is, but if we told her I think she might want to forget it too."

"I believe Mr. Dawkins, Dad. I believe he's telling the truth about what he remembers."

"But you didn't believe that he killed a man when he told us that he did."

"True, I did say that," Christy affirmed. "But don't take it out of context. I said that in reaction to his admitting it. Like he later said, he doesn't think that he's the same man today as the guy who killed that police officer thirty years ago. I believe him."

"I'm glad you're so confident, Christy. I'm thirty-five years older than you and I don't know what to believe, but you've got it all figured out."

"I believe he's being truthful, Dad. I realize his memory is messed up. But I believe he's being honest with us about what his memory is at any given time."

"Can we all agree that Phillip's memories can and do change on a dime? Phillip, what do you say to that?"

"Yeah, I'm afraid my memories do change," he shrugged.

"I agree," added Christy.

"With all due respect, Phillip, if this is the case, then what's the current value in anything you say? You know what? Don't answer that question.

Forget I asked it. We have enough to deal with without fighting amongst ourselves."

David leaned back in his chair, took a deep breath, then figuratively bit his tongue. He wanted to remind Christy, "Phillip had dreams about killing your dad." He wanted to say, "Now you're willing to stake my life on your belief in Phillip?" He yearned to ask Phillip just how close he'd actually come to murdering him. For a clincher, he wanted Christy to name all of the people that he's known for thirty years and leave it at that. But David didn't want to get into an argument with Christy, not in front of Phillip at least. Doing so would run the risk of helping the two of them forge an even deeper bond.

It troubled David that his son would identify and side with Phillip, a man who was potentially both a murderer and rapist. It was a blunt reminder that he had only himself to blame for bringing Phillip into their lives. He couldn't remove the ex-con without putting Annie, Christy and himself in danger. Withdrawing support from Phillip would be like lighting a fuse and David was deathly afraid Phillip's head would explode in a fit of rage.

But even though he wanted to remove Phillip from their lives, he knew that he couldn't do it right now. With the background information on Dr. Ewen Cameron coming into play, there was something larger than Phillip going on here, something larger than all of their lives combined. David's mind was racing, putting new pieces of information together, reconfiguring old information. Suddenly, a new theory blossomed in his head—one that scared him to death—a theory he certainly couldn't talk about in front of Phillip and Christy.

CHAPTER 21

After driving Phillip back to his motel room later that afternoon, David was at an intersection on Central when his cell started ringing. The caller ID said it was Julius. The FBI agent was just the guy David wanted to talk to right now. He kept trying to poke holes in his new theory but he couldn't. He desperately needed to talk to someone about it. Julius seemed to be the only one available. David pulled into the Price Chopper Supermarket parking lot to take the call, secure beyond the prying ears of his family and Phillip.

"What's up, Julius?"

"Good news. We do have a file on the Dawkins murder case from 1985. It turns out Dawkins fled to Pennsylvania, over state lines, before he was arrested in Scranton. That triggered FBI jurisdiction over his apprehension. Also, the City of Syracuse police asked for our help on the day of the murder. I'm told we sent an Evidence Response Team."

"Great. Does that mean you have DNA evidence in the file?" David's hands began to sweat.

"I don't have the file yet. It's in transit. But they did tell me there's DNA in it. What's it to you?"

"I have Dawkins' DNA profile. I want to see if it matches with what's in the file. I want to find out if Dawkins really did kill Officer Carlson."

"That makes sense." Julius had a dry wit and a way with words.

"But if it doesn't match, it doesn't necessarily mean that Dawkins didn't kill Officer Carlson," David spit out.

"Huh? I'm confused. How's that?"

"It might mean that the man who we know as Phillip Dawkins is not actually him. It's someone else. I think the man we know as Phillip Dawkins might really be Boris Dietrich."

"Have you lost your ever-loving mind?"

"No, I don't think so," David blurted out as he hurried to get his story straight before Julius hung up on him. "Let's look at the facts. We have letters from Edith to Boris saying over and over how she loves him and wants him to marry her like he promised. What does that sound like to you, knowing that Edith has a kid with an unknown father?"

"Yeah, I admit it sounds like Edith wanted to marry Boris to make things legit."

"Right, and here's something that'll be news to you. I ran a secret paternity test on Janet Nowak based upon her discarded DNA. Guess who won the pin the tail on the daddy game?"

"I give up." Julius drawled, with a touch of sarcasm.

"Phillip Dawkins."

"What? Wait, how old is the daughter, Janet Nowak?"

"Twenty-four."

"How could Dawkins father a child when he's been in solitary for thirty years?"

"Exactly. He couldn't. There's no way, which is why I think he's Boris Dietrich. That might explain why the DNA I got from Phillip doesn't match the DNA at the crime scene but matches the DNA profile of Janet's father."

"You mean they switched Dietrich with Dawkins? Seriously, Thompson, get a grip. How is that even possible?"

"Dawkins got visitors like every five years or so, right? How many people in the outside world remember what he looks like? Most likely the person who gets access to talk to him is someone who has never seen him before and will never see him again. Maybe an envoy from the United Nations, a prison rights lawyer, a reporter. There's plenty of opportunity to make the switch."

"Didn't you visit him?"

"Yeah."

"Does he look the same to you?"

"Yeah, but I saw him five years ago. They could have made the switch before I even met him."

"Somebody must have known about it."

"Yeah, definitely some COs should be in the know. But not many. There's a core group assigned there—the senior COs. But they could be CIA plants for all I know. That wouldn't surprise me," David continued. "Bottom line is that Dawkins was just another nameless, faceless man in a box. Other cons rarely, if ever, saw him. If you were a lifer, you could decline rec and never come out of the box. It's easy to make people forget you if they're already trying to forget you."

"What about the age difference between Dietrich and Dawkins?" Julius broke in. "Dawkins was born in like 1966. Dietrich sounds like he could have been a young man back then. There must be a twenty-year age difference between them."

"But there's no evidence Dietrich ever served time in prison up until the switch," David continued. "We thought he might have worked there, but we can't find a trace of him except in the letters. As far as we know, he could have been a free man before they made the switch. But when you're in prison, you age faster. When you're in solitary, you age even faster. And thirty years in solitary? That's the current record in New York State. Dawkins could have easily caught up to Dietrich in age appearance after being in solitary for decades. Who knows? They might have done some plastic surgery too."

"Yes, that's a stretch, but it seems possible," Julius replied. "Do you think Dietrich is putting on an act impersonating Dawkins? Do you think Dietrich even *knows* he's not Dawkins?"

"I don't think he knows. His memories as Dawkins are shaky and can change in a flash."

"So you think Dietrich has been brainwashed to believe he's Dawkins?"

"Yes, I think that might be what is going on. But, the thing is, I don't know when it took place. It could've happened years ago so that Dietrich now has his own memories as Dawkins from his time in solitary on top of the actual ones that were transferred to him from Dawkins."

"For real?" Julius sounded gob-smacked.

"Yes. You gave me that idea when you told me about Dr. Ewen Cameron's background. I've read a lot about him since then."

"But Ewen Cameron died in 1967."

David dived back into his theory, "What's to say he didn't establish a research lab at Kranston that continues today? Like you said, he stopped there frequently in traveling from Albany to Montreal. He used predominantly female subjects at Allan Memorial Institute. But let's face it, back then the CIA was interested in brainwashing men, not women. They wanted to not only brainwash enemy men, but they also wanted to prevent *our* men from being brainwashed. How could Cameron be sure his findings applied to men, especially American men? He needed to have male subjects to prove the efficacy of his research to the CIA. Now I read that experimenting on Americans like Cameron did was illegal back then and that's why Cameron did his dirty work on Canadians. So, if he was going to do any research in the USA, he'd have to do it secretly. What's more secret than a maximum-security prison with a solitary confinement wing filled with men who have been forgotten? There's no such thing as a surprise inspection of solitary confinement facilities at New York State prisons, if there's any inspection at all. Show me photos or videos of men in solitary in New York. They don't exist. In this state it's okay for us to violate the Mandela Rule. Fifteen days or fifteen years? Who cares? Nobody cares about these men. Our media doesn't care about them. Reporters go after Third World countries for their human rights violations, but they don't look in their own backyard. But even if they did care, the Bureau of Prisons wouldn't let them in to look around. Nope, they'd say it was a security issue—like they've done for decades. What a perfect set-up to get away with absolutely anything— for the CIA to do its thing."

"But there's no evidence that these experiments ever took place at Kranston," sputtered Julius.

David was ready for that. "CIA Director Richard Helms ordered most of the MK-Ultra records destroyed in 1973 before existence of the program was uncovered in 1977. So we'll never really know everything. It's safe to say that the CIA destroyed the most damaging information in that purge. Anything going on at Kranston would fit that bill because it would have been illegal."

"What makes you think these experiments are taking place today?"

"Before MK-Ultra and other programs were exposed, the CIA denied the existence of these experiments. Why would they admit to their existence today, if they were still going on? So, if you believe nothing has changed with the CIA over the years, you can't deny the possibility that this secret program still exists today."

"But Cameron's experiments demonstrated he could only wipe memories out. He couldn't replace them with anything for an extended period."

"That was then; this is now—fifty years later. If the experiments continued, they must have made some progress. They had all the time in the world to record Dawkins' memories and transfer some of them or all of them to Dietrich. All they had to do is sit down with him and record his memories, like they were having a friendly chat with him. What else did Dawkins have to do in the box but talk? Out of all the inmates held in solitary, Dawkins would have been the perfect subject because he was the longest-held man in solitary. It's no wonder they never let him out to join the general population. Why they never let him out of the box was a big mystery to me, but now it all fits."

"If you're right about Dietrich assuming Dawkins' identity, what ever happened to Dawkins?"

"I imagine he's dead. He was an only child and had no immediate family. Who was left in the world to claim his body and foot his funeral costs? When nobody claims a body, they pop the inmate into a plywood box, write his name on it with a Sharpie, and bury it in an unmarked grave in a field out back of the prison. But I guess there's the remote chance he's still alive and in storage at Kranston today."

"Why would they release Dietrich to the outside?"

"They wanted to test their research in the real world. They wanted to see if he would kill on command. I was the target, maybe my family too. With my murder, they could claim success to the CIA. Maybe continued funding depended on showing results. If they could show they had a killing machine and eliminate a threat to their research by killing me all at the same time, so much the better. Once Dietrich completed his mission, they'd either kill him or take him back to solitary. He was their Manchurian candidate."

"Why do you think they harassed Dietrich so much on the outside?"

"No different than what Cameron tried to do with his victims by isolating them on the inside. They wanted to keep the pressure on Dietrich —isolate him on the outside—so he'd follow through and kill me."

"Do you imagine Officer Carlson's family is in on this?"

"I don't know. I doubt it. I think the family may be part of the experiment. The spooks want to see if the relatives notice any difference between Dietrich and Dawkins. If they could fool the family, they could fool anyone."

"How about Edith Nowak? Does she know that Dietrich is Dawkins?"

"I don't have a clue. But if she knows that Dietrich got tortured to become Dawkins, I'm sure she's not losing sleep over it. She's probably still ticked at him for not following through on his marriage promise."

"Do you think the Kranston superintendent or the state commissioner are behind all this?"

"I don't think so. I think this is way bigger than the two of them. I think the CIA is directly involved. They probably have their own people in place at Kranston. How else could they keep it secret for so long? I don't know how much knowledge the superintendent and commissioner even have of the program."

"David, if the CIA is involved, then this is way bigger than the both of us," Julius suggested cautiously. "I don't think the FBI is a part of this, but one thing I know for sure: the higher-ups here won't like me poking and probing the CIA. I'm just a grunt trying to do a good job for my country and keep my nose clean so I can retire ASAP. The FBI guys running this show in DC are way too political and will rip me a new one if they want to keep a lid on this."

"I understand. I don't want to mess your life up," David replied in his most soothing voice. "You know I appreciate what you're doing. I'll play this any way you like to shield you."

"I'll just finish what I started. They'll ask even more questions now, if I back off. It's too late for that. But I need to be more careful going forward."

"Got it. Be honest with me, Julius. Do you think I'm crazy here?"

"No, it adds up, though it does sound crazy. But remember what I said before about you getting all paranoid?"

"What's that?"

"I told you to be careful because paranoia is contagious. Well, you caught it first and now I might have caught it from you."

Immersed in his reverie about the tangled web surrounding Phillip, David wondered how long his Mustang had been sitting in front of the supermarket. The sun was getting low in the sky and he was hemmed in by empty shopping carts. It was a wonder someone hadn't called the cops on him.

David wanted to know the truth about what was going on with Phillip

Dawkins and he needed to know it now. His instincts told him that knowledge was power—the more he knew, the more he could leverage it all to somehow fix everything.

David realized that only the truth could save him, his family, and even Phillip—if he was still alive. At this point he would stop at nothing to get the real story.

That night David cranked up his computer and read all he could find on Cameron, his research, and the CIA operations in the 1950s. It dawned on him then that while knowledge might be power, too much knowledge could end up killing him too. He was walking a very fine line in a dangerous game. At any time, the CIA henchmen might arrange an "accident" for him if they decided he knew too much. They could effectively stop the spread of his knowledge with his death. Before he could fix anything, the CIA could fix him—for good.

CHAPTER 22

The next morning at 9 a.m., David sat across from Jim Fletcher at his Mohawk City office. He watched as the other lawyer rummaged through a few layers of papers on his desk. The sun pierced the cloudy film of his second-floor picture window that overlooked the gilded dome of City Hall. A sash window was open; it gathered a breeze that stirred a few dead flies lying belly up below the screen among the paint chips on the sill. Cicadas in the surrounding trees screeched intermittently. The vibration hummed in the downtown air over the sound of traffic like a dentist drilling out a cavity. Their early whining forecasted a hot and humid day ahead.

"You used to have a window air-conditioner in your office, Jimbo."

"It broke yesterday," was the terse response.

"You're going to need one today," David prophesied.

"As soon as I get a paying client, I'll go right out to Wally World and grab one."

"On that topic, I insist that you bill me for this work."

"Thank you. I appreciate it. Oh, here it is." Jim handed David a stapled pile of papers that he had fished out of one of the piles.

"Is that the document you told me about on the phone?"

"Yep." Jim was looking a little pleased with himself.

"What is it?"

"It's a small section from a memoir written by Dr. Robert A. Cleghorn, published in 1990."

"And why should I care about this guy? Nice name, by the way. Any relation to Foghorn J. Leghorn, the cartoon rooster?"

Jim chuckled. "I don't know about that. But he was the director of the Allan Memorial Institute in Montreal."

"Wait, I thought Dr. Ewen Cameron was the director."

"You know about Cameron?" Jim gasped. He seemed crestfallen that David was up to speed.

"Yeah, I had my contact at the FBI do research on the man because of the letters from him in the file at Kranston." David proceeded to tell Jim all about the letters in the Kranston file from "EC" to Boris. He briefed him on the background work Julius had done on Cameron.

"Well, Cleghorn immediately followed Cameron in the role of director at the Allan in 1964," Jim added. "He established the Laboratory for Experimental Therapeutics there in 1946. He was only remotely involved with Cameron's research work—he was doing his own thing there—but was intimately familiar with it. After the CIA's relationship with the Allan and Cameron was exposed in 1977, I think Cleghorn wanted to go on record as to the goings-on that took place there under Cameron. He was afraid of the shadow Cameron would cast on his legacy. So he published this section of his memoir in 1990, five years before his death."

"What's your take on it?" David asked, riffling through the pages.

"I think Cleghorn, the shrink, needed a shrink of his own to deal with his relationship with Cameron," Jim replied with a shrug. "He calls him Chief throughout, compliments him, and in the next paragraph he criticizes him, almost overshadowing the compliment."

"So Cameron was God to Cleghorn but not really."

"Exactly. Cameron was a great man but . . ."

"Okay, that's interesting. How does this relate to what I'm dealing with here?"

"Well, in one of Cleghorn's critical moments he mentions that Cameron had a 'blind spot for psychopathic personalities.' So much so that he hired at least one of them as a lab assistant."

"Maybe that apple didn't fall too far from the tree."

"Good point."

"So when Cameron wasn't around, did this psychotic run the asylum?"

"Apparently so. Cleghorn asks rhetorically in his memoir, 'Who was his second in command?' His answer: 'There wasn't one.' According to Cleghorn, this lab assistant liked to give electroshock treatments to anyone who walked through the door and he could never give enough of it. Cleghorn called it 'therapy gone wild.'"

"So, who was this guy?"

"Cleghorn doesn't identify him. Maybe he was afraid of being sued for libel if he printed his name. He calls him an 'oddly-assorted young man' who was 'indigestible.'"

"Indigestible?" David snorted. "Interesting word choice there."

"For sure. Anyway, I asked the Allan Memorial Institute if they could help me identify this guy. They were of little help. Then I read about some former patients who were suing everyone associated with their treatment. I contacted them. These ladies are pretty old today, but two of them said the name of this guy was Boris Dietrich. They have hospital records that even mention his name. They're sending me copies of those documents."

"Great work, Jim! Thank you." David sensed a bright spot on the horizon.

"No problem."

"What happened to Dietrich?"

"Cleghorn says later that this guy was 'indubitably a menace' and he had to force him out after Cameron left."

"Well, that explains things."

"How so?"

"In one of Ewen Cameron's letters to Boris, he calls him 'overzealous.' That fits Cleghorn's description of him."

"Interesting."

"My bet is that Cameron got him a job at Kranston through his contacts as a favor to Dietrich, when they forced him out. In that way, Cameron could continue his work there on men exclusively, after being ousted as the director at the Allan Memorial Institute."

"That makes sense."

"But after Cameron died in 1967, Dietrich lost his support and influence for doing the research. At some point, perhaps Dietrich became a menace to the CIA at Kranston. Maybe they didn't know what to do with him, while at the same time they had decided that he knew too much."

The pieces all fit together in David's mind. The CIA had determined that

Dietrich had outlived his usefulness; so the agency had decided to try out the brainwashing tactics on one of its own. Dietrich became disposable. *Why just eliminate Dietrich when the agency could use him to further their mad research in the process? There's nothing more efficient than using someone and then losing him in the process. They would simply recycle the man into someone else.*

David knew all too well that his assassination by Dietrich was the measure by which the grand scheme either succeeded or failed in the eyes of the CIA. He also knew that if the experiment failed, that wouldn't stop the CIA. *These creeps always have some contingency plan in the event of failure.* David knew he was an accident waiting to happen at the hands of the CIA-- if Dietrich didn't kill him first. It was a no-win situation for him. He had to do something about it before it was too late.

CHAPTER 23

While David was meeting with Jim Fletcher that morning, Phillip lay wide awake in his bed at the Red Apple. His anxiety was now matched by his determination to make a new life for himself. He was not going to sit at his motel picture window and watch life pass him by on Central Avenue today. He refused to be the fish trapped in the aquarium or the chipmunk stuck in the window well.

As far as Phillip knew, he *was* Phillip Dawkins. Phillip had no reason to believe he was really Boris Dietrich. It never crossed his mind. He didn't have any memory of being the psychotic man who delivered electroshock torture to countless victims as Boris Dietrich. The screams of agony echoing down the corridors of Allan Memorial Institute during electroshock sessions did not exist in his mind. The memories of the victims' faces—flushed, grimacing, eyes bloodshot—crying, begging for release from the pain of voltage frying their brains and flesh, were absent as if they had never occurred.

Even though he heard Julius Moore say that Ewen Cameron successfully wiped memories clean through frequent, massive dosages of electroshock treatment, Phillip didn't reckon that he might be a victim. He didn't consider that any memory of the electroshock treatments he received could have been erased, too, in the process of wiping out his memories of life as Boris Dietrich.

After showering and shaving, the man who knew himself only as Phillip

Dawkins donned his favorite violet-blue turtleneck and cargo pants. He tried to convince his inner convict to leave the carving knife at home, but he couldn't do that. He needed it for protection; he needed it for peace of mind; he needed it to get his ex-con self out the door. When he was all set to go, he opened the shabby curtains to look out at the world that awaited him. As he pulled the frayed cord, the sun hit his torso and the lavender glow lit up the room. The view was crystal clear and it was a beautiful day in the neighborhood.

Phillip had cleaned the smudges off his picture window the night before with some glass cleaner he borrowed from the motel clerk. The TV weather forecaster said that it would heat up and grow humid that day, but so long as the view was good, Phillip felt he was ready to head out. Fluffy clouds sped overhead racing the traffic on Central Avenue. Annie and David had paid him for doing chores around the house. Today he planned to put that money to good use. It would be the first time Phillip ventured outside without an escort since the day he arrived on David's front doorstep.

While riding with David or looking out his motel window, Phillip had seen the buses travel up and down Central Avenue. There was a bus stop a short walk away. When he shopped for food with David at the Price Chopper Supermarket across the street, he saw you could buy a bus pass swipe card at the customer service counter. It was as good as cash money to the bus driver. All he had to do was purchase the card like anyone else without calling attention to himself. That was his first planned destination for today.

After doing his breathing exercises to calm himself, Phillip picked up his wallet, keys, pen, and a pocket-sized spiral notebook off the dresser. He distributed his booty among the many pockets of his cargo pants, stepped out into the beautiful morning and then locked the door behind him. With the soft, fabric lunch bag Annie had bought him in one hand, he strode across the rutted parking lot like he owned the place. Stepping over the cracks in the concrete sidewalk to the striped crosswalk, Phillip hit the big red button on the light pole like he was an old pro. He watched the red hand on the screen across Central Avenue as if he didn't care if it ever turned into the walking man figure. Not that he wasn't afraid, but he learned fast in prison never to act scared. If you looked weak or lost, it was like declaring open season on yourself. He figured that this same rule applied to living on the outside of Kranston too.

When Phillip entered the Price Chopper, he picked up a circular from the rack in front of the potted petunia hanging baskets. He did this not because he planned to do his weekly shopping, but because he saw a customer in front of him do it. To Phillip, after decades of sensory deprivation, Price Chopper was like the Great Bazaar of Tangiers—a swirling symphony of sights, sounds, and smells. It was too much to tackle right away, without his wing-man David protecting his flank. He hung a left at the crowded checkouts, weaving through the patrons loaded with groceries and notions. Then he got in line at customer service, leaned on one of a dozen stanchion posts tied together by drooping velvet rope, and waited his turn. He was stroking the velvet absently with one hand when he heard the voice of the woman behind the counter.

"Can I help you, sir?"

For a split second, Phillip didn't realize she was talking to him. No one had called him sir in as long as he could remember. He stepped right up and brightly replied, "Yes, ma'am. I'd like to buy a bus pass."

"Would you like a monthly pass or a pay-as-you-go pass?"

Uh-oh, decision time—another problem he never had in the box. "Which is more expensive?"

"The monthly pass costs more upfront. It's for commuters, "she explained patiently. "If you don't plan to ride every day, the pay-as-you-go pass is a better deal."

Phillip jumped in with both feet. "Thank you. I'll take the pay-as-you-go pass. How much is it?"

"It's one dollar per ride. But after the second ride on any given day, you can ride the bus all you want for free."

"Okay, I'll take twenty dollars' worth of fares then." Phillip forked over a twenty dollar bill out of the wallet that Christy made for him out of duct tape. He accepted the pass from the woman with a nod, placing it in the spot where the twenty had been. Then, he picked up a bus schedule and map from the counter display rack. He was excited to learn that he could ride the bus all day long on the cheap. That fit nicely with his plans.

Phillip's head swelled with accomplishment; he felt good that he'd done something all by himself. Maybe too good. *Go back to the motel room now. You've done enough for one day.*

But the new Phillip suppressed the voice in his head and pressed on. Skirting the confusing aisles jumbled with unfamiliar products, he made his way around the outer edge of the store past Frozen Foods, Dairy and Meat. He made it safely to the deli counter and picked up a roast beef sandwich—his favorite, thanks to Annie. She made them for him whenever he visited the house. Then he spotted a bottle of Coke in a cooler there and a bag of Doritos—his prison comfort food—on a display rack. So he grabbed those too. He was looking for all the support he could get to continue the ordeal of his solo outing. He nearly sprinted down the candy aisle on the way to the cash register. Phillip was amazed by how he could smell the sugar right through the cellophane bags; it made his head spin. After paying in cash, he loaded his three old friends into his lunch bag. His final test was to use the public restroom before heading for the bus stop.

When the Route 905 bus pulled into the New Karner station, Phillip boarded. The bus ran between Mohawk City and Albany. That morning, Phillip was headed eastward down Central Avenue for Albany. It was the same road that he and David had driven on the way to the hearing; it was the same route that would bring him to the office of Commissioner Edmund O'Neil. But that wasn't his destination today. No, today was a dry run to the Bureau of Prisons office combined with a shopping expedition.

Part of Phillip wanted to tell David what he was doing that day. He wanted to show David that he could function on the outside all on his own. But he wasn't about to share this expedition with David. He wanted to keep David out of it. What David didn't know couldn't hurt him. Phillip wanted to protect him, Annie, and Christy.

Inside the CDTA bus, Phillip once again ran right up against the world outside the box. The bus was filled with commuters, students, kids, and the disabled, with a sprinkling of all ethnic backgrounds. It was like his rec pen and the United Nations on wheels. The delegates were both standing and sitting. They either stared straight ahead like zombies focused on some inner agenda or they sat absorbed in what they were reading. Sometimes it was a book, but more often their focus was on their cell phones. Half the people on the bus were attached by the hand, and maybe via earbud, to a glowing screen.

Phillip didn't understand their fascination with the cell phone. He'd spent the better part of his life trying to get out of a box and yet these people wanted to live in one.

Phillip found a window seat on the sidewalk side. He pulled his pen and notebook from his left pants pocket and resealed the Velcro flap. He began to scribble the names of promising destinations and their addresses as the bus passed them. He was looking for a cell phone store, a clothing store, and a public library. It took him two complete round trips on the route between Mohawk City and Albany to collect the information he needed before deciding on his itinerary. He passed the main office of the Board of Prisons four times and recorded the travel time between the Red Apple Motel and the main office in his notebook.

Mohawk City had a branch library right on the bus route. That was Phillip's first stop. He figured he could research his next two stops there on the public-use computer. The desk clerk at the Red Apple told him they had free computer terminals at any public library.

It was the first time in his life he'd been in a library other than a school library. That was his hiding spot when he skipped class in high school. He could go deep in the stacks and pretend he was searching for the perfect book on world history. While held in solitary, he never even saw the prison library. He only heard stories about it, when the porter dropped off books at his cell. But in the end he read all the books they had at least three times during his three-decade stint.

This city library branch was a new, one-story brick building. Nice but small, about half the size of the Dollar Store next to it. When he opened the door to enter, a frosty blast of air conditioning hit him in the face. It still smelled of the formaldehyde off-gassing from the heavy duty indoor-outdoor carpet tiles on the floor. He recognized the Corcraft metal book-shelves and the butcher block lounge furniture that emerged from prison workshops all over the state. That sight made him relax, like spotting something from home.

When Phillip passed the glass entrance vestibule, he spotted kids running around inside as if it were gym period at school. Moms were in the children's section studying the bookshelves for something to keep the kids quiet for the afternoon.

Off to his right there were six computer terminals, each boxed in by its own blue-fabric privacy screen, like the ones you might see on Election Day at a voting booth. Phillip surveyed the backs of the men and women who were mouse-clicking away inside their own cubicles, as the screens flashed colorful pages over their shoulders. Phillip had heard of click farms but he'd never seen one. He spotted an empty spot at the end of the row.

He approached the reference desk, thankful that there wasn't a line like at prison. It was staffed by an older, white, blue-haired lady, wrapped to the neck in a buttoned-up cardigan that featured daisies with sequined centers. She was taking books out of the return bin.

Phillip shuffled up to her and pointed toward the terminals. "Excuse me, is that . . . cell open over there?"

"Cell?"

"The computer—"

"Oh, the computer. Yes, it looks like it's free. If you'd like to use it, you need to sign it out." She lifted her eyeglasses that dangled from a chain around her neck and pushed them back on her nose. One red-painted nail pointed to an empty line on the form. "Just sign there and you can use it for a half-hour."

Phillip lifted a little yellow pencil stub off the counter and signed his name and the time. "Could you show me how to use it? I've never used one before."

"Sure. What exactly do you want to do on it?" Phillip was surprised that she was so willing to help. He half expected a stern rebuke from her and a finger shake in his face for his ignorance. That's what was served up in the box anytime he had a question. *Dawkins, you should know how the system works after all these years.* "I want to search for things."

"Okay, I can show you how to do that."

"Thank you."

When Phillip sat down at his station, the librarian whispered instructions over his shoulder. Her flowery perfume made a fragrant cloud that overwhelmed the carrel space. She showed him how to use the search field in the Google browser and explained how it differed from the URL address field. Next, she showed him how to use Google Maps to locate places. There was a printer hooked up to his computer, she added, if he needed to print anything out. Then she set Phillip loose. In a few minutes there was a short line of people waiting to use the computers. Phillip realized that he had just thirty minutes to catch up on thirty years.

He Googled his name, for starters, and couldn't believe all the information about him that popped up instantaneously. There were a lot of old newspaper articles on him, many about the events that he didn't remember. There were some articles about his release from Kranston along with a few pictures of him that he'd never seen before. The amount of information on Phillip Dawkins and its easy accessibility startled him. Some of it was flat-out wrong. He felt exposed, naked before the world, and forever cast in the events of that one fateful night back in 1985.

He knew for sure then that he had to make it on his own on the outside. Nobody was going to hire him or give him a chance after they Googled his name. He wondered if he could erase any of it. He tried hitting the delete button, but nothing disappeared.

Phillip looked at the clock on the computer. He had to get to his other research pronto. No time to dwell on what he couldn't change. He Googled Edmund O'Neil's name and then Martin Kleinschmit. He learned everything he could about them and wrote it down in his spiral notebook. There was nothing on Boris Dietrich.

Switching gears, he went to Google Maps and found a satellite image of the Bureau of Prisons office in Albany. Using the street view option, he zoomed in and saw workers coming and going from the building or lounging about outside on a smoke break. He studied their clothing as carefully as an anthropology field worker researching foreign tribes. This helped him make a list of what he needed: dress shoes and socks, suit, buttoned-down shirt, tie, belt, and briefcase. He made note of the color of the lanyard—midnight blue—that held the state ID. He went to Google Images to get a close-up view of a state ID and printed out a few color copies.

Finally, he searched for a cell phone store that sold a cheap phone with only call and texting features. They called them "burners" on the internet. He learned Walmart sold them and he found a store on his bus route. He signed off the computer with a minute to spare, thanked the librarian, and left the building. Outside he took a deep breath of fresh air, blinked at the sunshine, and got on the next bus.

A seat next to the window was available and Phillip took it. He opened his little cloth satchel, then started eating his lunch, as he pondered where to buy the clothing and shoes. The suit he wore for his Bureau of Licensing hearing was too baggy. He was short on cash; clearly he couldn't afford a new business ensemble from a retail store. SALs—the Salvation Army Thrift Store—would have to come to the rescue again. This time he promised himself to stay away from the '80s look.

At each intersection the bus stopped, let a few people off, took on new passengers, and changed the make-up of the riding population. Down near Quail Street a fellow in his early twenties sat down beside him. As the bus started moving, the man kept glancing either at him or outside the window, Phillip couldn't tell which. Then the guy tapped him on the shoulder and Phillip looked over. The man had dark olive skin, a scrawny build, twitchy hands with nails bitten to the quick, and thick black hair. More than anything else the guy looked half asleep, but he was sweating profusely. He wiped his brow with one shaky hand and flashed Phillip a small Ziploc bag packed full of little white pills with the other. In a froggy voice he asked, "You want some Oxys?"

"Huh?" Phillip couldn't figure out what he was talking about.

His seatmate continued, "OxyContin, dude. You know, hillbilly heroin?"

"Heroin? Are you serious?" Phillip drew back, up against the window wall. He wanted to get as far away as he could from this kind of trouble.

"For sure. It's good stuff. Crush it, do a rail, and fly." The man smiled at all the possibilities, revealing two rows of rotting teeth in red, swollen gums.

"No thanks," Phillip shook his head vehemently. "You wouldn't be sitting next to me if you knew what I did the last time I tripped—"

"Nah, this stuff is boss." The man nearly hummed, rocking his body slightly in the seat, happy with his product and his life.

"No, not interested. I don't want to go back to prison." Phillip was emphatic in his denial.

"You did time?" Those half-mast eyes widened in surprise. And the man drew back slightly.

"Yeah, hard time. You don't want to know." Looking out the window, Phillip hoped the druggy would take the hint and just go away, far away.

"Where were you at? Attica?" Lots of enthusiasm emanated from his new best friend. Phillip looked at him with disgust.

"Kranston."

"Wow, I know some guys who were there. They said it was bad." He leaned in, sharing sour breath and stale body odor up close, another issue Phillip never had to deal with in the box. The only COs who got even marginally close were the guys who delivered his meals and those who walked him out to the cage for rec. Some of them might have been a little ripe, but they rarely got nearer than a baton's length away.

Phillip gave a brief nod. "Yes, it was. Did you ever do a bid?"

"No."

"Don't. Get clean. Stay out. If you go in, you could end up in the box and that'll be all she wrote, pal. Don't end up like me."

His seatmate fell back into sales mode. "You need to chill, man. I'll give you some of these. Half price for you—"

"Forget it," Phillip snapped. "My life might be in the crapper, but at least I can control my own death out here."

"What is that supposed to mean?" the guy whined, not ready to give up on a sale.

"Long story, and the next stop is mine. As far as you're concerned, ask yourself if you want to die tripping. I don't. I know that much." He stared into the vacant eyes of someone whose conscience had taken a different bus out of town a long time ago.

"Sure you won't try some?"

Time to get out of here. Phillip reached up and pulled the stop request cord above the window. A chime went off at the front of the bus and he felt the vehicle slow to a stop. "What are you? Some kind of narc or something?"

"No!" The druggy put a lot of wounded pride into that single syllable.

Phillip stood up. He still wondered if this guy was sent by the system to entrap him. *He's not white, so he's no CO.* He shuffled past the man to the aisle and held on to the overhead bar with one hand as he made his way to the door. When the bus stopped, he got off facing SALs.

It looked like a branch office of the local landfill. After business hours, drive-by donors had junked a sofa, some mangled exercise equipment, and an assortment of crap at the curb with the expectation that SALs would magically sell it all. Phillip strode through the mess with the confidence of a post-apocalyptic warrior. Mad Max on a shopping expedition.

SALs was housed in a one-story sheet-metal-framed building about the size of a small supermarket. Waves of heat shimmered over the roof. The lemon-yellow finish on the exterior walls had faded to chalk dust. The bright red Salvation Army sign hanging over the entrance shone was a beacon of hope. The water-stained "sale today" sign in the large window was right where Phillip had last seen it weeks before when they bought the gray suit—except that it was drooping now. The tape adhesive at one upper corner had given way.

The twin glass entrance doors were stuck at the seam; Phillip had to jerk them open. When he entered, a rush of hot air greeted him. It was like he had cracked the door to a preheated oven. The store had no AC and no window shades, so it concentrated heat like a solar dream. The strong aroma of moth balls was circulating right at nose level. Two airplane propeller-sized fans roared on full-blast in the open doorways at the rear.

Phillip stationed himself in the men's suit section and yanked the hangers toward him along the rusty bar, one at a time. With each screech of a poorly aligned hanger, he eagle-eyed the merchandise. After a few minutes, he located a navy blue suit coat with matching slacks that looked his size. He went into hunter-gatherer mode as he made his way through the store. First he picked a blue tie to match, then a white dress shirt, followed by a slightly stretched belt, new socks still bound by a cellophane label, a dented Samsonite briefcase, and a pair of brown penny loafers new in the box.

Lugging his finds to the back of the store, he tried it all on in a plywood dressing room. Under a flickering blue-white fluorescent light, Phillip looked at himself in the cracked mirror. The sleeves on the jacket were a bit short but passable. The waist on the matching slacks fit okay, if he used the belt, but the inseam was too long. He felt he could fix that. Annie had taught him to sew and even bought him a sewing kit. Everything else fit well enough.

It all came to $19.32, leaving Christy's duct-tape wallet just a little lighter. At the raised checkout near the store entry, the clerk put everything in a large plastic garbage bag for him and handed over a receipt.

It was a relief for Phillip to get back on the air-conditioned bus and rest his feet as it headed back down Central to the plaza that held Walmart. He felt a sense of elation. *Getting good at this!*

Inside the Walmart entrance—smelling popcorn and hearing the canned announcements blaring overhead—he piled all of his SALs purchases and belongings into a blue shopping cart with a bent wheel and headed into the store. An older, heavyset woman, dressed in a Walmart vest that matched his cart, said "hello" to him as she leaned on a cane just inside the door.

Phillip's instant reaction was to think of his knife. He knew of several cons who were jumped at Kranston for their stuff and he'd never possessed so much stuff in his life. A second later, he realized that he'd overreacted— she couldn't and didn't plan to jump him. He'd never seen a Walmart greeter before, never even been in a Walmart, at least as far as he could remember.

"Hello," Phillip bellowed back in his prison voice.

"Can I help you?" she smiled.

"Do I look like I need help?" Phillip retorted. In an instant, he wished he hadn't said what he did, the way he did. *She's not a con.* Behavior on the outside had a lot of new rules.

The woman didn't flinch. Rude comments from store patrons were infrequent but all in a day's work. "I'm sorry, sir. I didn't mean anything by it. I just wanted to know if you needed help in finding anything."

"That's okay. I'm sorry I snapped at you." Phillip tried to look appropriately contrite as he surveyed the supercenter that stretched on forever in every direction. "I guess I do need a hint. Where are the cellphones?"

"Straight back, in the rear of the store, electronics section. But you'll have to leave your bag here."

"What?" He drew up in a defensive posture, hands reaching for the bags of precious stuff.

"You'll have to check your bags at customer service," she repeated patiently. "It's the rule."

Phillip looked confused. Those were the magic words—he couldn't argue. But how was he going to complete his mission and protect his stuff at the same time?

"Don't worry," the woman added cheerfully. "You'll get it all back when you leave the store."

Phillip didn't want to give up custody of his belongings. But he saw a woman doing the same thing at customer service so he decided to play along. He convinced himself it was okay to check his bags. He figured it was like being frisked before going into the pen for rec time, though Walmart was the biggest pen he'd ever seen.

So Phillip checked his belongings with the dreadlocked lady in the blue smock behind a long L-shaped counter. With an empty cart, he made his way to the rear of the store, looking over his shoulder every thirty steps to make sure nobody was following him. The coast was clear, even though this pen was teeming with people, all of them bent on buying more stuff than Phillip had ever seen in one place.

At the electronics counter the sheer number of cell phones overwhelmed him. There were Smartphones and IPhones and flip phones in every color. He didn't know how to find what he wanted. He needed to ask someone for help but was afraid to. He'd never asked for help at Kranston. Even if you needed help in the worst way, you had to carry on and pretend you didn't. Asking for help always ended badly.

"Can I help you?" a pimply faced teenaged boy asked, as he stood next to Phillip staring at the array of choices. His Walmart smock was too big and he hadn't yet grown into his hands and feet, but he seemed at ease working both sides of the counter.

Phillip looked him in the eye and the boy smiled back. "We sure have a lot of phones, don't we?"

"Yes, you do. Too many." The need for so many choices made Phillip very uneasy.

"Do you know what you're looking for?"

"Something simple to use. Nothing fancy. I want to be able to add minutes by paying cash. I need voice and typing."

"You mean texting?" the kid replied.

"Yes, that's what I meant." Phillip had to work hard at not being defensive. He decided this boy was like the lady at the front entrance, just helping —not a threat.

After a few minutes, Phillip chose the cell that the clerk recommended and paid for it there at the register in the electronics department. The clerk put in the battery, activated it, and taught him how to use the keypad. On his way back to the front of the store, he found a white lanyard in the school supply department along with some magic markers, a glue stick, and a package of white construction paper. Mission accomplished. He checked out and retrieved his belongings from customer service. He wondered if he was the only one who looked through his bag to make sure everything was still there before taking the bus back to the Red Apple.

Later that evening, Phillip was seated hunched over his desk in his motel room. He was hard at work under the only lit lamp in the room. He had already used the magic marker to color the lanyard midnight blue—the same color as the ones the state employees used. He cut out a copy of a State ID he found on the internet at the library with the Sheffield staghorn-handled carving knife from David's dining room. He used the copy as a template to create his own.

For the first time since moving in, he had the windows open in his room. The drapes billowed in the gentle breeze of a cool summer night. Above the street noise drifting in, David's words reverberated in his mind: "Every day means something on the outside; every completed task means something."

If only David could see me now.

CHAPTER 24

The next morning, David and Annie were eating their cereals of choice together in the dining room, watching the squirrels plot to empty the birdfeeder. It was their daily ritual before going off to work—one upstairs, one downstairs. Christy had left for school to take his last final exam before being set free for the summer. David rose from his chair at the screech of the boiling kettle in the kitchen. He was pouring hot water into a cup of Irish Breakfast tea for Annie when the landline started to ring. David glanced at the base station on the far counter. A nameless telephone number flashed red on the caller ID screen.

"Who's calling?" Annie asked.

"No name. I don't recognize the number. Probably a robocall looking to sell us a timeshare. Fat chance."

Annie snickered as she lifted a spoonful of Corn Chex cereal to her mouth. With Christy looking at colleges, there was no room for indulgences in the Thompson budget.

"I'll get it," David said. "It will just take me a sec to verify it and block the number."

"Okay," Annie shrugged at the opportunity to avoid a confrontation. She was a people pleaser, even with telemarketers, so David got to be the bad guy.

David picked up the handset. "Hello?" he said in his best formal, discouraging voice.

"Good morning, David. You'll never guess who this is."

David recognized the voice. *It's Boris.* He mentally bit his tongue. "Ah . . . Phillip, is that you?"

Annie lifted her gaze out of her cereal bowl. Questions broadcast from her countenance with the lift of one brow.

"Yes," Phillip smugly replied.

"But this is not your motel number. I hear traffic in the background. Are you at a pay phone?" *Where in the world did Phillip find a pay phone?* David was trying to get one step ahead of the situation.

"No, I bought myself a cheap cell phone." Now he truly sounded pleased with himself.

"Really? Where did you get it?" David reminded himself not to be confrontational. *Aim for casual interest.*

"Walmart. I went out into the outside world yesterday."

"Okay. Where are you, by the way?"

"Are you surprised?" Phillip sounded like a kid with a frog in his pocket.

"You never cease to surprise me, Phillip."

"Aren't you proud of me for leaving my room and figuring it all out?"

"Yes, I suppose I am." David suddenly felt as if he was having a conversation with a grade schooler. "I guess right now I'm more worried about you than anything." At that moment, David realized the depths of his dilemma. While he was worried about Phillip, he was terrified of Boris. His head spun as he contemplated the double whammy of Dr. Jekyll and Mr. Hyde. Which was worse, the convicted murderer or the sociopath scientist?

"You can't have it both ways, David. You can't want to get me out of my room and then worry about me when I do."

"You're right. Sorry, I'm a parent and that line of thinking is par for the course. Look, we can talk about this when I see you. I don't want to burn up your cell minutes. Now where are you?"

"At a bus stop. I just missed an express bus going downtown. I'm waiting for the next one."

"Where are you going?"

"I'm going to pay a visit to Commissioner O'Neil."

"What?" Suddenly David's hair was standing on end. "Are you crazy?" So much for the casual approach.

Annie pushed away her cereal bowl, dabbed at her lips with a napkin, and turned her full attention to David's conversation.

"No, I don't think so," Phillip snorted. "Not any crazier than any other guy locked in a box for thirty years."

"Is this an arranged visit?" David was grasping at straws as he desperately hunted for a way to sideline this runaway train. "Do you have an appointment to see him?"

"Hell no. You think he'd see me if I called to make an appointment? I'm the last person on earth he wants to see."

"What do you plan to do when you get there?" David felt like a police dispatcher, frantically trying to keep the perp on the line while he contrived a plan.

"I want to talk to O'Neil and then we'll take it from there."

Oh, boy. David felt his stomach plummet. "What do you mean, 'take it from there'?"

"You know, play it by ear . . . ."

"No, I don't know. Why don't you tell me?" David tried to keep a light, interested tone while he pumped Phillip for details.

"When I talk to people, sometimes my memory is jarred and things come back to me," Phillip continued earnestly. "I think O'Neil is behind all of these incidents, all of my problems. If I confront him and fix things, maybe I can have a life on the outside. It's my only chance."

"There has to be another way." David felt sweat beading on his upper lip and in his palm where he gripped the portable phone.

"I don't see one now." Phillip wasn't mad, just matter of fact.

"You said to me once that with time things have a way of working themselves out." David found himself wishing for another decade or so to sort out this mess.

"Not this time around. You know, the more time passes, the better your chances get of dying right alongside of me."

"Phillip, don't say things like that." *Careful now. Don't provoke him, just stall.*

"I call them as I see them. Always have, always will."

"Please tell me you're not going to hurt him."

David's request was met with static from the cheap phone and the sound of traffic whooshing down Central Avenue. "Phillip, are you going to hurt him?" *Don't hang up; please don't hang up on me.* Now David knew what it felt like to be a mother coaxing her daredevil kid off the third-floor roofline.

"I don't know what's going to happen. Anyway, it's my decision; it's my life. I just wanted to call and say thank you in case things don't work out. You are a good friend to put up with me and to try and straighten me out. Your family is wonderful and you're very lucky to have them. Please thank them for me."

"You don't have to do this."

"Yes, I do. It's my only option. You know as well as I do that they'll either put me in the box again or they'll kill me here on the outside. Two different means that lead to the same end. I will not survive the box this next time around. Hope used to give me a reason to survive the box because I believed I was innocent. Now that I know differently, I'll have no hope. The system will win this time around. I will not die in the box if I can help it."

"There has to be another way out of this mess."

"I don't think there is and I can't take you, Annie, and Christy on a trip through hell to find it. You deserve better than trying to fix all the mistakes I've made in my life. I know I'm not the same person that I was when I killed Officer Carlson. I know I'm a much better man now than when I was nineteen. But that doesn't make any difference to anyone else. I'll always be a cop-killer in the eyes of other people, no matter how hard I work to change myself for the better. That one day, that one bad choice out of all the questionable choices I ever made, will define me for the rest of my life. I don't want that one day to destroy you in the process. You're a good man, David Thompson."

"Phillip, you need to listen to me now."

Click.

"Are you still there? Phillip?"

David looked at Annie in disbelief. "He hung up." The phone lay in his limp hand at his side, now giving off a dial tone.

Annie stood up and quickly stepped over to David in the kitchen. She took his free hand and tilted her head to one side as she inspected his face. Her forehead crinkled; her lips pursed like one of David's Cheerios for a few seconds. "What's going on, David?"

Her voice was gentle, but implacable. He could almost hear the Wife Gears turning in her head. *Busted.* David didn't want to say a thing to Annie about the SNAFU with Phillip. He wanted to just let things play out. He felt that Commissioner O'Neil and Boris Dietrich deserved one another. Perhaps their meeting would settle some of the issues facing and threatening him and his family. Maybe Commissioner O'Neil would arrest or kill

Boris and that would be the end of all of his problems. If Boris managed to kill O'Neil—well, that would work too, as long as Boris shared the same fate or was arrested promptly for the murder. In either scenario, Boris would be out of David's life and the system might then choose to leave him and his family alone.

"Who is Phillip going to hurt?" Annie asked.

David sighed. He had said too much during the phone conversation. "The Commissioner of the Bureau of Prisons."

"What?" Annie looked appalled.

David looked down. "You heard me right."

"I don't understand. Why would Phillip hurt him?"

"He believes the commissioner is behind all of his troubles."

"Why does he think that?"

"It's a long story."

"Well, you better make this long story short because we've got to hurry to help Phillip out."

David's eyes popped and he swallowed with a gulp. He didn't expect that Annie would be so quick to jump in and help out. "I don't think I should get involved, Annie. You heard me—I tried to talk him out of paying this guy a visit. But he didn't want to listen. It's Phillip's choice at this point."

"We've got to do something, David. He's a good friend. Why he's almost a member of our family."

David rolled his eyes and prepared to step deeper into the hot mess his day had become.

"What's wrong, David?" She let go of his hand and put both hands on her hips. "This is not like you. The David I know would be in the car right now on his way to help Phillip."

"Maybe the David you know doesn't want to get himself killed. You can't help someone who doesn't want to help himself."

"You're expecting an awful lot from Phillip. He doesn't know how to act in our world. He's been in solitary for so long."

David thought it was time to come clean. Maybe a little dose of truth would change her mind. "Annie, there are some things you don't know about Phillip."

"Really? Like what?" Annie asked skeptically.

"Phillip believes he killed that police officer—"

"What?" Annie shifted from skeptical directly into disbelief.

"You heard me right."

"You said he was innocent. He must be innocent or they wouldn't have let him go."

"Phillip believes they let him go so he could help them come after me."

"What? Why would they come after you? Who's they?" Annie snapped.

"I don't know—"

"Come after you for what?" Now she was like a dog with a bone.

"Maybe because of my views on solitary. Maybe something else."

"When did Phillip tell you this?"

"After the hearing. That night at our house."

Annie leaned back against the kitchen counter as if the news had taken the wind out of her. Shaking her head, she continued, "This doesn't make any sense. I can't believe he killed that officer."

"He firmly believes that he did."

"And how was he going to come after you?"

"He said he was sent to kill me."

"Now I've heard everything. Did he ever threaten you in any way?" Annie's voice vibrated with annoyance.

"Not directly, no."

"What do you mean by that, David?"

"He did say he had dreams about killing me."

"When were you going to tell me this?"

"I think I just did."

"Well, dreams don't necessarily mean anything."

"Yes, I know."

"David, don't you see he's mixed up?"

"Of course I see it."

"I don't care what Phillip believes at this point. You need to help him."

"Annie, are you okay? That doesn't sound like you. I thought you'd be angry with me for not telling you about this sooner."

"Don't think that I'm not. No time for that now. We'll get back to it. Right now you've got to do something to protect Phillip and that state guy —the commissioner."

David couldn't believe that Annie wanted him to get involved. She didn't comprehend the potential dangers. "What do you want me to do, Annie?"

"Do you think you have time to beat Phillip to the commissioner's office?"

"Maybe. Phillip is waiting for a bus to take him to downtown Albany. That's where the commissioner's office is located. I might be able to intercept him before he gets there."

"Do it then. Get a wiggle on."

"But you need to know something else, Annie." Now David wanted to make sure Annie knew everything before he raced down to O'Neil's office on a rescue mission.

"What now?"

"Phillip may not be Phillip."

She looked at him with an exasperated huff. "Seriously? What is that supposed to mean?"

"Phillip might really be someone by the name of Boris Dietrich."

"What? God, you're making my head hurt. What on earth are you talking about?"

"I'll explain it to you, but I'm not sure where to begin. It's complicated."

"Stop, David. We don't have time. Answer me this: Do you think it's possible that Phillip didn't kill the officer?"

"Why yes, I suppose—"

"And do you think—I can't believe I'm saying this—do you think Phillip might really be Phillip and not this Boris guy?"

"Yes, that's possible."

"Do you agree that no matter what, Phillip is not the same man he was thirty years ago?"

"Yes, assuming he is Phillip."

"Well, that's good enough for me."

"But Annie, there's a whole lot more to this than meets the eye." He wanted to tell her about MK-Ultra and that the CIA black ops guys might be involved in trying to kill him.

"Now answer me this, David: If something happens to Phillip and you're wrong about all this stuff, will you be able to live with yourself?"

"I'd feel awful for sure."

"Me too. And what about Christy? How do you think he'd feel? He's close to Phillip, you know."

"I hadn't thought of that."

"You'd better get going, David. Do you want me to come with you?"

David's mouth hung open. His stomach was doing somersaults. He couldn't believe he'd gotten himself into this mess in the first place. Now he couldn't believe Annie was pushing him to do a search and rescue operation. But he knew deep down she was right. He couldn't live with himself if he was wrong about Phillip. If he was wrong, Christy and Annie might never forgive him either.

"David? Snap out of it and work with me here. The clock is ticking."

David swung into action. "No, we can't risk both of our lives. One of us has to stay safe for the sake of Christy. You stay here."

"Okay. Please be careful, David. Don't forget your cell."

"I've got it in my pocket. I just need my wallet and my keys." He thought about grabbing his Civil War Sharps carbine—the only gun he owned. But he suspected that running around the streets of Albany, or inside the state office building, with a rifle in his hand might just get him killed. David bolted to the hall closet and shook his coat as he lifted it from the hanger. He felt his wallet bump in the pocket and heard his keys jingle. "I'm all set," David said as he stormed toward the door.

In the meantime, Annie had written down the phone number Phillip had called from onto a sticky note. "Here's his phone number," she said, handing it to David before grabbing his arm and pulling him close. "I love you, David Thompson." She gave him a bear hug and a quick, hard kiss on the lips.

David left the house full of determination; he hoped the farewell kiss wouldn't be his last.

CHAPTER 25

David sped up Central Avenue toward the bus stop closest to Phillip's motel, but there was no Phillip waiting near the CDTA shelter. He jerked the Mustang to the outer lane; the tires screeched as he pulled a U-turn. As he passed Jimbo's Shooter Supply, David prayed that Phillip hadn't shopped for a gun there.

Suddenly, traffic came to a halt. Up ahead, David could see the light arrays of several emergency vehicles flashing in both lanes of the Albany-bound traffic. There was some kind of accident ahead. But David didn't see a red express bus between himself and the accident. That would have been the color of Phillip's bus. If Phillip's bus was between him and the accident, David figured it would have blocked the light arrays of the smaller emergency vehicles ahead of it. But he could see their lights perfectly. He pounded the steering wheel when he realized Phillip's bus must be traveling ahead of the accident. He pulled out his cell and dialed Phillip's telephone. It rang but there was no answer. After eight rings a voice said that there was no way to leave a message. Phillip hadn't activated the phone's messaging feature.

Phillip had hopped on an express bus to downtown shortly after hanging up on David. Now he was riding the elevator, straightening his tie, on his way to see O'Neil in the state office building. The directory in the lobby said he was on the twenty-third floor. Another suit was along for the ride.

"It's a nice day outside," the other suit said.

"Sure is," Phillip replied.

"Too bad we have to be inside today."

"You said it."

The chime sounded and the elevator came to a stop. The other suit got off. "Have a good one."

"You too," Phillip said, rolling up on the balls of his feet. When the doors closed, he chuckled as he reached for the lanyard around his neck and tucked his fake New York State ID partially behind his lapel. His artwork was not perfect, but he hoped it was good enough. The point of the sheathed carving knife tucked in his sock pricked his ankle so he shimmied it up his calf a bit.

The chime went off; the door opened. Phillip strode off as if he owned the place. A sign on the wall opposite the elevator pointed the way to the Bureau of Prisons executive offices and Phillip veered left in that direction. The hallway was filled with working stiffs—men and women—milling and walking about. There was a security station dead ahead. No metal detector in sight. A pimply face male guard was sitting behind a desk. He was on the phone talking to someone. As people passed by him, he bobbed his head in approval. Phillip got behind two men heading for the executive offices. When they laughed, he smiled and shook his head just as they did. When all three of them got to the security desk the officer there gave them the head bob.

Phillip trailed behind the two men, gradually creating more distance between him and them. He didn't want to invade their space and raise their suspicions. One swiped his ID card over the scanner at the entrance to the executive offices and the red light turned to green. They opened the door wide and shuffled into the office. The hydraulic closer overhead whooshed as the door closed slowly—slow enough for Phillip insert his foot in the opening and for him to enter the office. *No card, no problem.*

As Phillip made his way around the huge perimeter of the open floor office space design, he ignored the sea of cubicles in the middle section. He knew that the commissioner would not be stationed there. Those spaces with mounds of manila folders piled high were reserved for the underlings who served their masters sitting in the windowed offices.

Phillip was only one of 60,000 inmates to the top brass, but the top brass were everything to Phillip. He believed that the commissioner and his servants were the master puppeteers behind his day-to-day existence under the control of the Kranston staff. In his mind, they decided if he should stay in solitary or go to the general population. Knowing how the brass worked was a matter of life and death to him.

He made it his life's work to learn about how these bureaucrats thought. At his cell gate or through the ventilation shafts, he had overheard COs and prison officials at Kranston talking forever about the central office in Albany. Phillip talked to the suits from that office when they made rounds every once in a blue moon at Kranston. Anything and everything in the prison library having to do with incarceration in New York was devoured, reread, and memorized.

Phillip had scoped out the Bureau of Prisons office building on Google Maps at the public library. He saw how one side of the Bureau of Prisons office overlooked the New York State Capitol, home to the Senate and the Assembly, the epicenter of power in New York State. If the prison brass were going to be anywhere, they would be in window offices looking down on the New York State Capitol. Phillip knew that appearances were everything with the Bureau of Prisons.

Phillip read each nameplate as he strolled by the outer window offices and headed for the larger corner office, with its two large windows on either side overlooking the capitol building. The nameplates mounted on the wall next to each office door carried the name and title of the occupant. He knew he was getting warmer as he walked by chiefs, assistant directors, directors, assistant deputy commissioners, deputy commissioners, and then a senior deputy commissioner. Pecking order based on seniority was sacred in the Bureau of Prisons, as Phillip knew all too well through his experiences with the COs.

The nameplate on the corner office door read "Mr. Edmund O'Neil, Commissioner." The door was just slightly ajar but still wide enough for a gaunt figure like Phillip to slip through. The Wizard of Corrections was sitting at his desk, his back to Phillip, facing one of the windows, one leg crossed over the other at the knee. He was reading a spreadsheet in his lap. The face of the prison system gently rocked himself by pushing and releasing his one grounded wing-tipped shoe. He nibbled at the temple end of his eyeglasses. When Phillip closed the door behind him, the door latch clicked into the strike plate. O'Neil's black, bushy eyebrows snapped to attention as he spun his executive office chair around to see if someone had closed his door from the outside without his permission—again. His hair was thick, neatly combed and parted, and all white just as David had described it. Hanging on the wall behind O'Neil was a large photograph of the seventh hole overlooking the ocean at the Pebble Beach Golf Course in California. Phillip put together the golf photo and the tan O'Neil sported— O'Neil was shooting rounds every chance he got.

O'Neil spotted Phillip standing in his crisp, navy blue suit with his photo ID dangling from a lanyard around his neck.

"Can I help you?" O'Neil snapped.

"Yes, I think you can," Phillip quipped. "My name is Phillip Dawkins."

"Dawkins . . . Dawkins," O'Neil said, stroking his chin. "Hmm, that name sounds familiar. What department do you work for in the Bureau?"

"I don't work for the Bureau of Prisons, sir."

"Really? Where have I heard that name before?" O'Neil asked, leaning back in his chair, almost twiddling his thumbs.

Phillip was surprised that the mention of his name didn't get any reaction from O'Neil. "I'm an ex-convict, sir. I was released a few months ago because new evidence was discovered that proved my innocence."

O'Neil popped out of his chair as if Phillip's carving knife had poked him in his butt. He backed up a few steps from his desk. "How did you get in here?"

"I walked in, sir, like anyone else."

"You used a fake ID to get in here?"

"Not really. Nobody bothered to look at it."

"I told those morons from the General Services Bureau I wanted beefed up security in place before we moved into this space. They promised but they didn't deliver. Typical state pencil pushers. What do you want from me?"

"A few minutes of your time." Phillip made note that O'Neil was surprised and concerned but he wasn't begging for his life. Not yet, anyway. *It's like he thinks I'm really innocent.*

There was a series of family 8 x 10 photos high on a bookcase—four children in front and sitting, O'Neil and his wife in the back standing—all taken in front of the same sky blue screen sprinkled with white, puffy clouds. Looking at the photos from left to right, the family grew up before Phillip's eyes.

"Nice looking family," Phillip said, pointing at the bookcase.

O'Neil bit his lower lip. "Thank you."

"You had a family picture taken every year?"

"Yes . . . for the church yearbook. Look, you can't just barge in here without an appointment. You have to follow procedures. I have a good mind to call the police."

"I'm not going to let you do that, Mr. O'Neil," Phillip snapped. *A little electroshock might shut him up.* "And you know as well as I do that you'd never make an appointment to see me. Look, I don't want any trouble. I just want to ask you a few questions. Now why isn't Janet Nowak in your church family yearbook photos there?" Phillip instinctively believed that O'Neil still thought he was Janet Nowak's father. Maybe he really was, for all Phillip knew because he sure didn't believe that *he* was the father despite what David's DNA test said.

"What about Janet Nowak—I mean, who is she?"

O'Neil just tipped his hand right there—he knows her. "You know who I'm talking about. Edith Nowak is the mother of Janet. We both know who the father is."

Silence.

Phillip waited for the denial but it never came.

"What do you want from me?" O'Neil demanded.

"I want to ask you a few more questions and then I'll leave. And I won't say anything about Edith and Janet Nowak to anyone."

"Okay, but don't come any closer."

"Is it true that I was a central office case and that you directed the people at Kranston to keep me in solitary?"

"Are you kidding me? I've got 60,000 prisoners to manage. What makes you think you were so special that I would single you out to keep you in solitary?"

"You were from Syracuse and that's where the killing took place."

"I don't care. I haven't been back there in years. There are thousands of cons from Syracuse. I'm not targeting them and never did."

"You mean to tell me there's no such thing as a central office case?"

"Sure there is, but I don't recall your name ever being on the list. Can I go to my computer and print something out for you?"

"Okay, but no funny stuff. I can see your hands on the keyboard. I can see your screen."

"What I'm going to print out are the central office cases for last year."

O'Neil fiddled with his mouse; after a few clicks he hit the print button. Off to Phillip's side the printer started humming and ran off six sheets of paper with names listed in columns in alphabetical order.

"Pick up that report and read it yourself."

Phillip removed the papers. The first page had the title of the document, "Central Office Cases," and a date for the calendar year. Phillip shuffled through the papers but didn't see his name listed. "My name isn't on here."

"That's what I thought. You're not a central office case, see."

"How do I know this isn't some list of names you keep handy in your computer just in case you're asked this question?"

"Are you serious? Do you think people barge into my office every day to ask me this question?"

"I don't know."

"Trust me, they don't. Certainly not if we had our security in place."

"Superintendent Kleinschmit says I was a central office case."

"Well, he's mistaken. But it's not like he knows who's a central office case anyway. It's not like we share the list with him or any superintendents. We just keep the list internally so that we give special attention to paperwork coming over our desks involving particular inmates."

"Why was I held in solitary for so long?"

"Long? It's the system. It's the way it works."

"You mean it's the way it doesn't work. It never worked for me. I was a good inmate, followed the rules as best I could, and you still kept me in the box."

"I'm not the system. I'm just part of it. If you think I can just wave my magic wand and get you out of solitary, you're sadly mistaken. I've got the union to deal with and all of these shop rules we've let creep into the system. The union has more power over personnel decisions than the prison superintendents or even me. If we try and get a CO fired and the union moves against us, they make us go before an arbitrator who has the ultimate say on punishment—usually an unpaid suspension even if they used excessive force."

Phillip's mind turned to Johnny McFadden and all of the rogue COs. There were plenty of rotten COs protected by the blue wall of silence. He never considered that his confinement to solitary might have been union orchestrated. But Phillip wasn't buying it. "So you're telling me that the COs were the ones who kept me in solitary?"

O'Neil said, "Well, the COs are a big part of the system."

"Why did three COs perform a traffic stop on me and my friend after I got out of Kranston? Somebody told them to do it."

"What are you talking about?"

"Are you telling me you don't know? They pulled me over for a traffic stop."

"No, I don't know about any traffic stop. Please realize that I've got twenty-nine thousand employees. If it really happened, the Bureau would frown upon such behavior. Did you file a complaint with the Bureau?"

"Who was I supposed to complain to?"

"The Office of Special Investigations."

"How was I supposed to know that?"

"I just told you."

"You mean I had to breach your security and walk in here unannounced to find that out?"

"You could have called the Bureau of Prisons' switchboard."

"I've tried to call you to get some information since my release. You've got no real people to answer questions. Just a bunch of recorded menu options that don't apply. What's your special investigations case backlog?"

"I don't know. About one thousand cases, I think."

Phillip let out a long, fading whistle. "Let me guess. Are most of your investigators former COs?"

"Yeah, I suppose, but they're qualified—"

"Never mind. We both know my complaint would stop with the blue wall of silence—just like in prison when it was my word against a CO's word. It would drown in the backlog until they announced it was dead about ten years from now. Isn't that how the system works?"

"We're trying to change some things in special investigations. Time has a way of changing things."

"That's what Superintendent Kleinschmit used to say."

"He's right."

"Isn't he taking over your job when you retire?"

"Yes, that's the arrangement."

Phillip lowered his voice—almost to a whisper—and said, "He's a good superintendent."

For a few seconds, O'Neil sat there with a stupid grin, nodding. "But I can't ever really retire."

"Why's that?"

"Because I've been sued as commissioner and some of those cases will drag on for years. I'll be sued after I leave too, until every statute of limitations has run out. They'll subpoena me, I'll have to give depositions, have to testify at trials. The cons will never leave me alone. It's like I'm the cause of all of their problems."

Phillip's lips pressed together and a tight, sly smile emerged. "It's a great system, isn't it? Don't worry, Mr. O'Neil. Time has a way of changing things, right? At least the state pays you when you show up in court, right?"

"Yeah, they'll pay me. But I'd gladly give it up if they'd just leave me alone. You can see by the photos in my office that I've got a family. I made a lot of sacrifices to support my family over the past decades. No doubt, I've made some mistakes. I'd like to spend some quality time with my wife and children before I leave this planet. Quality time means that I want to forget about my time with the Bureau of Prisons. It's not that I didn't appreciate my time here. I'd just like to put it behind me as one phase in my life. I won't be able to do that."

"You and me both, Mr. O'Neil, except I didn't appreciate my time at Kranston."

"I see."

"How would it be if you spent your retirement in a box, Mr. O'Neil?"

"What do you mean?"

"That's what life's been like for me in solitary—"

O'Neil's gaze locked on Phillip's gray eyes. He could no longer deny the recognition. "Now I remember your case."

But Phillip believed that O'Neil knew about his case all along. "Thirty years. How would you like me to lock you in your bathroom for that long? Feed you under the door. Board up your windows. Blast a recording of people screaming all day long. Set up a cage in the backyard for your rec hour. Beat on you every few days. How does that retirement sound?" O'Neil looked away. "Look at me, Mr. O'Neil. Look at me!" O'Neil slowly turned to face Phillip. "I'm not a case. I'm not a number. I'm a person, flesh and blood, just like you." Phillip's eyes started to well up. "Now I see that old Royal typewriter over there on the stand. I want you to type this on it: 'Solitary confinement beyond fifteen days is torture.'"

"I have to reach into my desk drawer to get some paper."

"Go ahead, but I've got my eyes on your hands. If you take something out that's not paper, I'll kill you as sure as I'm standing here." Phillip was all ready to pull out his knife and carve O'Neil up before pushing him through the window to the pavement below.

O'Neil's hands trembled as he reached in the drawer. He pulled some sheets of typewriter paper out, separated one from the rest, and spun the knob while he fed it into position. "What is it you wanted me to type again?"

"Focus, Mr. O'Neil. Type: 'Solitary confinement beyond fifteen days is torture.' Make sure the first letter of each word is capitalized." Phillip wanted to see if the typewriter's uppercase letters struck lower than the lowercase ones, like the typewritten complaint filed with the Bureau of Licenses.

"Okay, I'm done," O'Neil said, with his voice cracking.

"Let me see. Hand me the typed page." O'Neil ripped it out and handed it to him. Phillip's eyes became slits, his face reddened, he clenched the paper and shook it at O'Neil. Yet all the letters struck level with one another. Phillip wasn't angry because the typewriter hadn't malfunctioned like the one used to type the complaint. Certainly, that frustrated him. He simply wanted to believe that O'Neil was the only one behind every second of every day he spent in solitary. But the typewriter told a different story. No, Phillip was angry that O'Neil had typed "years" instead of "days." "Do it again and do it right this time. I said days, not years."

"I'm sorry. I'm very nervous."

"You know what the Mandela Rule is, right?"

"Yes."

"Well then get another sheet and type it out. As a matter of fact, type it out ten times like before—first letter of each word capitalized."

"Okay," O'Neil said, loading another piece of paper. He began typing.

"What is with you? How could you mistake days for years?"

"Like I said, I'm nervous."

"I think your mistake just shows me that you really don't think much of the Mandela Rule. Do you think it shouldn't apply to us? Do you think we're too good for some stupid United Nations finding? Is that what you think?"

"No," O'Neil said as he typed away. "It's just that it's a new rule and these things take time."

"Time? Don't talk to me about time. Every day of delay means more torture for some lost souls in New York, across the country. How many do you torture per day now? How many are in solitary?"

"I don't know—"

"You don't know because you don't want to know. It might cause you to think about what you're doing. It might cause you to lose sleep to know that you're the Commissioner of Torture in New York. You don't want to take that title into retirement, do you? Is that the legacy you want?"

"I'm only one person in the system."

"You're the single most powerful person *in* the system, Mr. O'Neil. If anyone has a magic wand, it's you. Stop with your smokescreen. Show some leadership, for God's sake. Are you old school, Mr. O'Neil? Maybe that explains why you keep an old typewriter around. Is that what your problem is? How long have you been in the system?"

"Forty years."

"Forty? That's a long time. How old were you when you started?"

"Twenty."

"What was your first job?"

"I was a CO."

"Well, you must have dished out some solitary, even if they weren't using it like it was going out of style back then. Isn't that right, Mr. O'Neil?"

"It was necessary at times, yes."

"I'll bet you miss the good ol' days. I can see you and your CO buddies today backslapping each other at retirement parties, longing for the good old days when nobody questioned solitary. I can see you yucking it up: 'Remember when we put Dawkins in solitary back in '85? It was like the roach motel for him; he could check in but never check out. Those were the days.'"

"Times have changed since back then."

"Have they really changed, Mr. O'Neil? Yeah, you guys have to work a little harder and smarter to keep us in solitary. But the results are the same. Look at me. If they hadn't sprung me because of my innocence, I'd still be in the box today. So you worked yourself up to superintendent at Kranston after being a CO, isn't that right?"

"Yes, eventually."

"And from there, you went on to become commissioner. Rising through the ranks—a true American success story?"

O'Neil spun the typewriter knob and handed the paper to Phillip. "I'm finished."

Phillip pushed the paper back. "Read it to me."

O'Neil look puzzled. "You want me to read this back to you ten times?"

"Yes, that's a good idea."

"Okay, if you say so. But—"

"No buts. Just do it."

"All right. Solitary confinement beyond fifteen days is torture."

O'Neil read it over and over again out loud to Phillip. At first the words soothed Phillip. Here was the New York State Commissioner of the Bureau of Prisons reciting the Mandela Rule. Phillip closed his eyes the fourth time O'Neil recited the line. But soon his eyes were wide open. "Stop reading. You shouldn't have to read it. You should know it by heart. I know what the problem is now. I can hear it in your voice the more and more you recite that line. You know what the problem is, Mr. O'Neil?"

"No, but I'm sure you're about to tell me."

"You're not saying it like you mean it."

"In all fairness, you're forcing me to say this."

"You're right. But I shouldn't have to force you to read it. You should want to read it and it should come naturally to you. You should genuinely believe what you're saying. But you don't, do you Mr. O'Neil? Let's be honest. You don't think the Mandela Rule is worth the paper you typed it on. You think it's ludicrous."

"Like I said, times have changed—"

"But have *you* changed with them?"

"I'd like to think so."

"Oh come on now, you really don't think a few years in solitary is any big deal, do you?"

"It wasn't when I was a CO later in my career."

"Thank you. At least you're being honest with me, finally. Do you see what the problem is now?"

"No, not—"

"You're the problem. Not just you, but anyone who's been in the system for too long. You all privately think this Mandela Rule is a joke. There's no way things are going to change with people in the system who love dishing out solitary. There has to be a massive retraining effort. The culture has to change in the Bureau of Prisons. And that change has to start at the top."

"Maybe that's why I'm stepping aside and retiring."

"Oh, I'm not buying that you're doing anything noble here, Mr. O'Neil. I'm not buying that at all. You're retiring because you figure you've got a fat pension that you've worked for all of your life. Like you said before, you want to leave the Bureau of Prisons behind. You want to leave this phase of your life behind and move on to enjoy your golden years."

"Well, maybe things will change. Kleinschmit is going to be taking over my job. Even you said he's a good superintendent."

"Maybe so, but that doesn't make him a good commissioner, especially since everyone around him still loves the box."

O'Neil grabbed a tissue from the container on his desk and wiped the perspiration from his forehead.

"It's not hot in here," Phillip observed as he moved around the desk to sit down in one of the two upholstered chairs facing the desk. "You've got this wonderful central air conditioning flowing from the registers. What's wrong, Mr. O'Neil? Are you nervous? Are you afraid of me?" A voice in Phillip's head said, *Ask him about Boris.* He pushed it aside.

"Should I be?"

"No, you shouldn't be—not if you believe thirty years in solitary is no big deal. There shouldn't be any problem with me after I've been in the box that long. Right, Mr. O'Neil?"

"If you say so."

"No, I didn't say that. Not even close. I'm just mimicking what you said. I've got issues, Mr. O'Neil. Plenty of them, thanks to you and your kind." Phillip lifted his pant leg, pulled the carving knife out of the sheath, and twirled it in one hand. It shimmered in the cool, fluorescent office lights that hummed with applause, at least in Phillip's mind. The perspiration started to pour off O'Neil's head. His lips quivered.

"I have every reason to slice you up right now and to watch you spurt blood like a fountain. There'll be a bloodbath on this brand new beige carpet of yours. I can smell the newness of the fibers. But the metallic odor of blood would overwhelm it as you squirmed on the floor trying to cling to life. I'll personally pick you up by the legs and squeeze, shake, and pound your body like an almost-empty bottle of ketchup to get every last drop out. There'd be so much blood that it'd probably stain the subfloor underneath. They'd scrub and scrub, but it wouldn't make any difference. They could never get the stain and the smell out. This office would be a constant reminder of what solitary could do to a man. Killing you might even cause some long-needed changes. I'm sure you've heard of Tom Clements, former head of Colorado prisons. He was shot dead by an ex-con who did time in solitary. When his doorbell rang a few years back, Clements answered it and the ex-con said, 'Pizza delivery man' and then—Bam! Bam! Bam!—shot him dead. Read about him the other day on the internet. His killing sure brought about some changes in Colorado. But I'm not going to kill you, Mr. O'Neil. Not today, anyway. But I may move in next door to you, maybe live over the fence in the home in back of you. I know where you live. You and I can be neighbors. I'm sure you won't mind living near me. There's no law against it. You can introduce me to your wife and children. We can have barbecues in the summer, coordinate garage sales. I can watch your house while you're away, pick up your kids from school when you get tied up. You and I can even chair the neighborhood watch committee. After all, a few years in solitary shouldn't give you anything to worry about, right, Mr. O'Neil? It's no big deal. If I can take living it for thirty years, you can at least take living *next* to it for that long. My condition wouldn't bother anyone else in the neighborhood because they wouldn't know any better. But you know what goes on in solitary at Kranston. You know what you've made me. Have you ever done time in solitary, Mr. O'Neil?"

"I've worked in solitary as a CO—"

"Not the same thing, Mr. O'Neil. Not even close. All you prison people are the same. You say solitary is no big deal. Let's see you do it then. Let's see the prison union chiefs do it, too. I'm not talking a day of PR time. I'm talking at least thirty days. Otherwise, it's all talk."

"Are you done yet, Dawkins?"

"If I could tattoo the Mandela Rule on you, I would," Phillip said, tucking the knife way under his pant leg. "The name is Mr. Dawkins to you, sir. I know your name game. All the cons had to call you and the other prison brass mister on the inside. That's what we were told. But you, the COs, and all the other prison personnel could call us by our last names. In this way you thought you could distinguish yourself from us cons, because you thought you were better than us when the truth is everyone—even you—is just *one bad day* away from becoming one of us."

"Don't compare me with a con."

"Solitary is torture, remember? Sentencing someone to solitary in violation of the Mandela Rule is a crime against humanity. You've already had your *one bad day* a thousand times over. You're one of us now. Welcome to the dark side, Mr. O'Neil. The system spares no one—not even you." *Ask him about Boris. There's that voice again.*

"All right, you've had your say. Anything else on your mind before you leave peacefully?"

Phillip recalled David's conversation with Julius about Cameron and the CIA. He wondered if the CIA was a part of the system but decided not to ask O'Neil. If it was true and if O'Neil knew about it, he knew he would deny it. That's what all CIA operatives did without fail because they knew if they didn't they'd put their own lives in jeopardy. Phillip knew that if he voiced his suspicion and the CIA was really involved, he'd only make them even more desperate to kill him and David too. Phillip couldn't do that to David; he couldn't do that to Annie and Christy. There was nothing to gain by asking O'Neil about the CIA's involvement, and there was way too much to lose.

Ask him about Boris.

Phillip thought by visiting O'Neil he might jar his memory to recall something from his past. But nothing had come to him during the visit, except the name of Boris . . . Boris Dietrich. He recalled that David was trying to identify him.

"Who is Boris Dietrich?"

O'Neil's jaw dropped, his eyes bulged. He pushed his chair back from his desk with his legs and it rolled toward the window.

"Well, let's have it, Mr. O'Neil. Don't make me take my knife out again."

O'Neil wiped droplets of perspiration from his upper lip. "Where did you ever hear that name?"

"Where I heard it is irrelevant. Judging by your reaction to it, I think you know that name. Who is he?"

"I don't know anybody by that name."

"Your reaction to hearing his name tells a different story."

Suddenly, the office door unlatched and David slipped through the opening and closed the door behind him.

"What are you doing here?" Phillip asked.

Out of breath, David said, "I've come to take you home,."

"Who are you?" O'Neil demanded.

"You shut up," Phillip retorted.

"Phillip," David said, staring down O'Neil, "I think we should leave now."

Phillip stood there as stiff as the Lady of Justice statue on O'Neil's desk. He was trying to process it all. He couldn't lash out at O'Neil because he didn't want to involve David in anything he might do to the bureaucrat. His talk with O'Neil hadn't jarred his memory much. The absence of his own name from the central office list confused him. Even the typewriter didn't implicate O'Neil. Phillip decided there was nothing to be gained from staying any longer. As much as it pained him to admit it, there was no closure to be had here. A new option hadn't presented itself as he had hoped. It was time to make an exit—to regroup, to reassess.

"Okay," Phillip said. "But before I go, Mr. O'Neil, I suggest that you keep quiet about our talk here today, unless you want the word about Edith and Janet Nowak spread all over New York State and beyond."

David stood there in a daze, not knowing what to make of the situation. As far as he was concerned, Phillip had relations with Edith and was Janet's father. But O'Neil didn't respond to the ex-con's demand. He sat there slouching in his chair, hands drooping beneath the seat, like he was guilty of something. *Does O'Neil somehow believe that he's the father?* That idea was too much for David to grasp at the moment. He just wanted out. He put his hand on the door lever in anticipation of leaving. "Okay, Phillip, it's time to get going."

"All right, but I think he knows who Boris Dietrich is."

When David heard this, his knees buckled. He used the door lever to steady himself and glanced at O'Neil's slack-jawed face before looking at Phillip. *Does O'Neil think—does he know—that Phillip is really Boris Dietrich?* David wasn't going to wait to find out. The last thing in the world that David wanted to have happen then was for Phillip to learn that he was really Boris Dietrich. The guy would explode; all hell would break loose. There'd be a bloodbath. "We can talk about it in the car," David said firmly.

"But—"

"No time for 'buts,' Phillip. We need to go NOW before a goon squad comes and traps us in here. I evaded security to get in. It's only a matter of time before they figure us out. I don't think anyone here wants that to happen. We could all be killed."

All Phillip needed to hear was the word 'trap' to get him moving. The last thing he wanted to do was to die trapped in a box at Kranston or in the box known as O'Neil's office. Phillip knew that while his life was out of control, his saving grace was that if needed, he could exert some control over the time and place of his death. And the last place he wanted to die was in a box of any kind.

Phillip moved quickly towards O'Neil, who covered his face with his hands.

"Don't do it," David implored.

Phillip rolled O'Neil out of the way and yanked his phone line out from the wall jack. "All done," he said.

David opened the door a crack before they both slipped out.

In a flash, Phillip wrapped the phone wire around the outer door lever and wrapped it to the lever of the adjacent office door.

"Follow me," David said, in a hushed voice.

David hoped O'Neil stayed put until they were out. Side by side they strode down the passage between the window offices and the vast sea of cubicles in the center of the office. There were a few employees standing over the cubicle walls talking with one another, too busy yacking to notice the pair. Phillip pushed the entrance door hard and it flung open. They sped by the few people walking in the hallway.

"We're taking the stairs," David whispered, pointing straight ahead to the fire exit stairwell. They walked past the elevator banks. The security guard was sitting at his station with his back to them. Phillip then figured out how David had gotten to the office without an ID. The security office was focused on the elevators. There wasn't anyone guarding the stairs.

The kerplunk of opening doors and the rumble of voices echoed in the stairwell as they both shot down the steps, with David leading the charge. After twenty plus stories they were dizzy when they flung open the ground floor door. In the lobby they race-walked to exit through the revolving door entrance. Once outside they broke into a jog side by side. When Phillip spotted the Mustang across the street, he blew by David like a gazelle. Phillip was in basketball mode like a point guard running a fast break. Phillip headed for the passenger door on the other side. David threw his keys into the locked door, opened it, and lunged to the other side to unlock the passenger door so Phillip could hop in. David peeled out before Phillip fully closed his door, and off they went toward Mohawk City and home base.

"God Almighty, I wish you hadn't done that."

"Done what?"

"Paid O'Neil a visit."

"I didn't have a choice. They weren't going to let me live a new life on the outside unless I did something."

"But you exposed us as knowing much more than they could have ever believed possible."

"Knowledge is power; you got to use it to make things right."

"But by showing that you know too much, you re-energize them to kill us."

"It was a risk I had to take."

"If the CIA is involved, that's how they work. The world is littered with the remains of people who knew too much."

Because Phillip firmly believed that O'Neil was leading the effort to kill him, he thought a visit to him would spur some other option to fall into place. He hadn't considered what would happen if it didn't. "I wish you hadn't come to O'Neil's office; I wish you hadn't tried to save me."

David didn't respond. As much as he hated to admit it, he realized now that he'd made things worse for himself and his family by trying to rescue Phillip. He'd shown O'Neil that *he* knew too much, too. *No good deed goes unpunished.* Then it hit him that the CIA might be paying a visit to his house right now. His family might be in danger. Gritting his teeth, he lifted his hands and pounded the steering wheel like a jackhammer. Then he put the pedal to the floor.

CHAPTER 26

On the way home, David barely stopped the car long enough to let his passenger out so he could walk the rest of the way to the motel.

While Phillip was closing the door, David leaned over and called through the open window, "Please stay put in your room until you hear from me. I'll call you tomorrow."

Phillip didn't say anything, just nodded. David put on his signal, pulled out into traffic, and applied his foot to the gas so the Mustang sped off. The car flew back to his suburban refuge in record time.

When David burst through the door at home, he saw Annie and Christy at the dining room table eating lunch. He grabbed a napkin off the table to mop his brow as he breathed a gusty sigh of relief.

Annie stood up to walk over to David's side. She placed a hand on his arm, then leaned in to study his face. "Are you okay?"

"Yes, I'm fine," David replied, searching out the window for any sign of strange vehicles parked on the street.

"You look like you've seen a ghost," Christy said, pushing his half-eaten sandwich aside. He focused on his father, far too keen on the scent of new developments to be bothered with finishing lunch.

"That's not too far from the truth. How did your exam go?" David walked into the kitchen with a casual air. He stood at the window to check the backyard. Nothing out of the ordinary there. Yet.

"Fine, but what about Mr. Dawkins?" Christy persisted.

"Yes," Annie said, "Were you able to stop Phillip before he got to the state office?" She was back at the table, but her attention was all on David too; lunch could wait.

"Not exactly. But I was able to stop him *at* the state office before anything bad happened." David tried to stanch the flow of information, for all the good it would do him.

"That's good," Annie said. "Where is he now?"

"Back at the motel room."

"Why didn't you bring him back here?" Annie asked.

"Ah . . . because he needed to rest." It was a flat-out lie. He hated to do it, but David had another more pressing reason. He wanted to create space between himself and Phillip, between his family and Phillip. If Phillip had stirred the pot to excess, David wanted him to suffer the consequences alone. If all they wanted to take out was Phillip or Boris—or whoever this guy was—David hoped that a single kill would satisfy them. He didn't want to put himself or his family in the crossfire for Phillip if he could help it.

But he wasn't going to stop at Phillip. David now wanted to separate himself from his family too for a while, to create another layer of protection —a geographic layer. "You know what? Christy's done with school and the summer is here. Why don't we all take a vacation? We could all use one, that's for sure."

Annie tilted her head, her eyebrows lifted. "What are you thinking, David?"

"I'm thinking we could rent a nice place on Lake George for the summer. You two could go up there. You could work remotely. They have fiber-optic internet service in some areas around the lake. Christy can have his friends up."

"What about you, David? Where are you going to be?"

"I have some work to do down here. But I'll join you on the weekends. Maybe even Phillip can come up after things settle down for him."

"I know you, David Thompson. I know what you're trying to do. You're trying to protect us." She poked a finger at him, almost like an accusation. This was going to be a tough sell.

"Why shouldn't I? It looks like Phillip killed that police officer."

"Christy and I talked about that. We're not sure that he did. Furthermore, even *if* he did, we believe he's a different man than he was back then."

The wife was hanging tough. She had her arms crossed and the faintest hint of a pout around her mouth.

"She's right, Dad." Christy was poised to chime in when David was saved by the phone ringing in his pocket. He pulled it out. The caller ID said it was Julius. "Hold that thought. I need to take this call. What's up, Julius?"

"You were right," Julius blurted.

"About what?"

"The vitamins and the radio."

"What about them?"

"The vitamins contained a strong dose of LSD in one part of the pill. The lab folks missed it the first time because they tested a different part of the pill."

"That means someone was drugging Phillip."

"Yes."

"And the radio?"

"It had this chip in it. Very sophisticated technology that was hidden quite well. My tech guys removed it and found a subliminal message that was barely audible. It played repeatedly when the radio was turned on."

"Unbelievable. It's Cameron and his psychic driving all over again. It smells like a CIA op for sure. What's the message?"

"'Kill David Thompson.'"

"I don't like the sound of that, but it all adds up. That's the message Phillip heard in his head."

"You were right on both counts."

"I kind of wish I wasn't."

"Understood. You need to send over your DNA results for Dawkins so I can compare it to what the FBI has from the murder scene."

"Will do."

"Other than looking at that, there's nothing much else I can do without opening up a case file. I'll have no control of it after that. If the CIA is involved, I don't know what we'd end up doing here, if anything. It might make things worse for you if word floats up to the big boys and girls at the political level of either the FBI or CIA."

"You're right."

"That's all I've got for now. I'll be in touch."

"Thanks, Julius. I'm grateful for all you're doing."

"Take care of that family, David."

"Yes, I will." David hung up and joined Christy and Annie at the table. He dropped into a chair with another sigh. "That was Julius, my friend at the FBI. Someone was drugging Phillip with LSD and telling him to kill me."

"What?" Christy and Annie exclaimed in unison.

David went on to explain Cameron's research—electroshock to wipe memories clean followed by drugs and messaging to replace them with something else. Then he explained what Julius had found.

"That's incredible," Annie said softly, shaking her head in disbelief.

"That's insane, Dad," Christy said, stroking his chin with a look of wonderment. "That's all news to me. I've never run across anything like that in my neuroscience studies."

"I don't think that dark snippet from our history is something they want to include in your textbook."

"I suppose. You know, all this goes to support what Mom and I were saying about Phillip."

"What do you mean?"

"If what you said is true, Phillip is not responsible for wanting to kill you. That's not him. It's someone else trying to force him to do it. Even if he did kill that police officer decades ago, I don't think he's the same person today."

"Me either," Annie added with a nod for emphasis.

"But what if Phillip is really Boris Dietrich?"

"What do you mean, Dad?"

David went on to explain to Christy about how Phillip's DNA showed he was the father of Janet Nowak and how that wasn't plausible. He explained, however, that it was possible if Phillip was Boris; then he showed how that theory meshed well with everything else.

"It's an interesting theory, Dad. But there may be competing, alternative theories that you haven't considered."

"Like what? If you've got one I'd like to hear it."

"I don't know. But there must be some other way for Phillip to end up being her father. Use your imagination, I'll bet you can come up with a theory."

"Christy, no flights of fancy, please. I'm looking for a theory grounded in facts."

"So am I, but the truth is that we don't have all the facts. We're trying to piece together something that happened thirty years ago with a person whose memory looks like it's been altered, even manipulated."

Annie jumped in. "Whether he's Phillip or this guy Boris, he's not a terrible person from what I can tell." Annie always trusted her gut instincts.

"You two don't know Boris Dietrich. He was a sadist with electroshock back at the Allan Institute. Don't you guys think we should be held accountable for our past actions?"

"Yes, David, to some extent I agree with you. But this man we know as Phillip is not a bad person now. He's been neglected and tortured. He has every reason to be an absolute savage beast, but he's not," Annie reasoned. "Don't you agree?"

"I suppose, but I don't want him to repeat his past with us, even if it's just a reflex."

"Neither does he," Christy said. "He's been honest with us about his past. He's been protective of us. From what Mom told me, I don't think he wanted you to go down to the commissioner's office because he wanted to protect you."

"Think about it," Annie added. "If Boris was really Phillip they've made him harmless in comparison to what you described Boris as being in his past. Why would these evil people behind all this want to tame Boris? I guess that's one big reason why I don't believe he's Boris. I don't think he'd hurt a fly."

David pondered what Annie said. He thought about the fish in the aquarium in the state office building, about the chipmunk in the window well, about the Karner Blue butterfly—about how Phillip interacted so well with those small creatures. *Maybe Phillip wouldn't hurt a fly.* Then David thought about the baby bird on the ground—about how Phillip wanted to crush it to take it out of its misery. But even then, Phillip didn't want to kill the baby bird for the hell of it; he wanted to shield it from suffering a slow, painful death.

Annie pressed, "If he isn't Phillip, then where is Phillip?"

"I don't know," David replied. "You two make some good points. I honestly don't know what to believe about Phillip now. One thing I do know, Phillip—as we know him needs to know about the LSD and the radio chip. I think he'd be relieved to know that these evil thoughts were not his own, but were implanted in his head."

"You're right," Annie said.

"I agree," Christy chimed in.

"Oh, and David," her lifted eyebrow accompanied the rising tone of her voice. "I think I can also speak for Christy here; we don't plan to leave your side. Not even for the lure of a summer on Lake George."

"That's right, Dad."

"All right." David didn't like the idea, but he was outnumbered. He decided to let it go for now, perhaps revisit the topic later. David walked off toward his office door, "I need to call Phillip right now." The radio chip and the LSD brought the CIA into focus. It sounded like Cameron's research was not only alive but even thriving within the walls at Kranston. David knew all too well that the CIA played by its own perverted rules when it came to men like Phillip who had become a liability.

David had discovered the legendary Frank Olson treatment in his research of Ewen Cameron. It took decades to uncover, but when CIA employee Frank Olson started having reservations about his agency's torture experiments in the 1950s, he decided he wanted out. Before he could resign, the CIA slipped him some LSD. Olson had a bad trip that caused him to lose his mind. Within ten days Olson was dead, reportedly having committed suicide by crashing through a hotel window, falling to his death in New York City. That was the testimony of his hotel roommate, who also happened to be a CIA employee.

In the 1970s, the CIA was forced to admit to slipping Olson the LSD, but it stuck to the suicide narrative. That held until Olson's body was exhumed in 1994. James E. Starrs, a George Washington University professor of law and forensic science, found no evidence that Olson had crashed through a window. He did find evidence that the former CIA operative had been struck in the head before falling. Olson appeared to have been murdered and dropped from the window because he knew too much—posed too great a risk of ratting out the CIA. All this was consistent with a 1953 CIA assassination manual unearthed in 1997. It stated that "the most efficient accident, in simple assassination, is a fall of 75 feet or more onto a hard surface." Olson fell around 140 feet from the thirteenth floor, about double the recommended amount, for good measure.

David saw the writing on the wall for Phillip and for himself. They both knew too much. Worse yet, if the CIA was involved, the Feds would know through O'Neil that they knew too much. It was Frank Olson all over again with a new twist. Not only did they want to off Phillip by feeding him a steady dose of LSD, they wanted him to waste David in the process. It was a CIA twofer, sort of like the Doublemint gum commercial jingle—"double your pleasure, double your fun." But the only people having fun were the spooks. *How many unknown Frank Olsons have they murdered over the years?*

Down in his office, David emailed the DNA report on Phillip to Julius. Then he got up to pace while dialing up Phillip on his cell.

"Hello?" Thank goodness Phillip answered.

"Phillip? It's David. How are you doing? Are you okay?"

"Yeah . . . I'm fine. Why do you ask?"

"Are you in your motel room?"

"Yes."

"Listen up, Phillip. Julius, my FBI friend, he confirmed that your vitamins were laced with LSD."

"Oh my God!"

"Yeah, and your radio had a chip that played a subliminal message to you while you listened to it."

"What?"

"You heard me. Your radio had a computer chip that repeated just one message—'Kill David Thompson.'"

Silence from the other end of the line.

"Did you hear me?"

Now David heard breathing—heavier and heavier—until it sounded like there was a gust of wind blowing on the other end.

"Phillip, are you there?"

"Those bastards!"

"Phillip, listen up—"

"Son of a bitch. I think O'Neil is really Boris Dietrich—"

"Forget Dietrich, already. I know how this must anger you, but you need to focus and listen to me. You can't eat or ingest anything that you don't know everything about the source, or anything that's been left in your room unattended. They could try to drug you again at any time. Be careful of your television or any electronic device that they might have accessed. Know that they could be trying to message you again. Do you hear me?"

"I can't believe it. I can't believe they did this to me."

"Believe it. At least now we know what's going on. It wasn't you. You didn't want to kill me. They wanted you to kill me. Then they wanted to take you out once you finished me off."

Silence.

"Did you hear what I said?"

"Yes, I understand."

"Good." The landline began to ring. David couldn't believe it when he saw the caller ID was flashing Edith Nowak's name. "There's a call coming in that I need to take."

"Okay."

"Please be careful, Phillip."

"I will. Thanks for the heads up."

"I'll be in touch," David said, before hanging up the cell and grabbing his landline phone.

"Hello?"

"Is that you, Mr. Thompson?"

"Yes."

"This is Edith Nowak."

"Yes, Ms. Nowak."

"I need to talk with you in person. Can you come out tomorrow morning?"

"Yes. Sure."

"How's 10 a.m. sound?"

"Fine. Can I ask what this is about?"

"Edmund O'Neil. I need to tell you the truth about him. I can't talk about it over the phone. I'll see you tomorrow then."

"I'll be there."

"Thank you," she said, before hanging up.

What is she going to tell me? That Edmund O'Neil is the mastermind? That he's really Boris Dietrich the way Phillip believes?

CHAPTER 27

David sat on the same couch as he had before in Edith Nowak's living room. It was a dreary Saturday morning and another layer of dust had fallen on Edith's tchotchkes since David's last visit. Nothing else had changed.

"I'd offer you something to drink, Mr. Thompson, but my hands don't work well. Every time I get chemo, my fingers go totally numb, like I don't have them anymore. I can't manipulate things with my hands without dropping them."

"That's okay. I'm fine. You said you wanted to talk."

"Yes. I don't have much time left. The chemo isn't working. It's killing me faster than it's killing the cancer. I'm going to stop treatment. I'm going into a hospice shortly. They'll drip me morphine until God takes me."

"I'm so sorry to hear that. I wish I could say or do something." David fumbled his hands in his lap, acutely uncomfortable with talking about her impending death.

"You can do something. You can listen to me." Edith was weak but emphatic.

"All right."

"Ever since we first talked, I've felt this need to talk with you again. I don't exactly know why. Maybe it's to relieve my conscience or something. I don't know. Maybe it can help you and Phillip Dawkins, though I'm not sure how." Edith sighed. "Here goes."

"When I was young, real young—in my teens—I was introduced to Edmund O'Neil, who was Kranston's superintendent at the time. We went out to a shady bar here in Hoosick Falls, the kind of place where they didn't check for underage drinkers. One thing led to another and, well, I had an affair with him at the time. I was young and didn't know any better." Edith's eyes became glassy. She tilted her oblong head toward the ceiling, blinking hard as if to keep the tears from streaming down her face. "I got pregnant with Janet. I thought there was something between us but he had a family and, as I found out, he wasn't going to ever leave his wife or his kids. But he felt sorry for me and hired me as his secretary. He paid child support too, on the condition that his wife and family never find out about Janet, and that Janet never find out he was her father."

"So you believe that Edmund O'Neil is Janet's father."

"I know it." Edith spoke with the calm assurance of someone who was there.

I know otherwise. "Is that all you wanted to tell me?"

"I think so."

"I think maybe you left something important out."

"What do you mean?"

"Like you were under the age of consent when it happened, that this amounted to statutory rape, and that Edmund O'Neil could have gone to prison."

"Yes, you're right. How did you know?"

"I did the math. So, why wasn't this reported to the authorities?"

"I was estranged from my parents at the time, living on my own. Isn't that ironic? My daughter is estranged from me now. Anyway, I was supporting myself then. I never finished high school, had limited skills. I needed the work. He promised me a job and he delivered. I was secretary to him before I became secretary to Martin Kleinschmit, after Edmund left for the commissioner job in Albany. He gave me financial security and supported the child. I thought he might leave his wife for me. But after a while, I realized he was all talk. By then it was too late."

"You mean the five-year statute of limitations had expired?"

"Yes."

"But why haven't you told your daughter about him? She's over the age of eighteen. He's not still supporting her, right?"

"He's still paying me for her. I still need the money. He won't pay me if she knows about him. That's been the deal since she turned eighteen. When I die, he's promised to pay her anonymously via an attorney through a trust that's been set up."

David was blown away by her story. Edith thought that Edmund O'Neil was Janet's father when David knew it was Phillip. *The DNA doesn't lie. But is she lying to me or does she really believe O'Neil is the father? I don't know.* "Out of curiosity, did you or someone else run a paternity test?"

"I didn't have to run one. I didn't have sex with anyone else but him that one time."

"One time?"

"Yes."

"Did O'Neil have a paternity test done?"

"I think he might have done it. I think Mr. Kleinschmit arranged for it. Yes, now that I think about it, Mr. Kleinschmit did have one done. It sounds like something he would do. He's such a good man."

"Did you ever see the test results?"

"I don't think so. No, I didn't have to. He admitted that he was the father."

"Why are you telling me all this?"

"I don't know. I think I'm supposed to do it; it's an urge that won't let go of me. I don't know why I feel compelled to share this with you. I know you won't tell anyone because of the lawyer-client privilege and all."

David's head was a muddled mess. He didn't have the heart to tell her that the lawyer-client privilege rules did not apply to her; she wasn't his client. But he didn't have a reason to tell anyone else either, so he didn't say a thing to Edith. *Does she really believe O'Neil is the father?* Johnny had given him love notes that Edith had written to Boris Dietrich. She wanted Boris to marry her like he promised, according to those letters. *Does this mean that O'Neil is really Boris Dietrich?* "Ms. Nowak, the last time I was here, I mentioned Boris Dietrich's name. Do you recall?"

"Yes, but I'd rather not talk about that name." Her thin frame shuddered in the chair.

"I won't say it then, but can you tell me who he is?"

"No, just talking about that name makes me nauseous."

"Do you recall ever having written letters to anyone by that name?"

"No. Why would I write letters to someone I didn't know?"

"I don't know. I'm just asking." David wasn't going to tell her Johnny had discovered those letters in her file cabinet. If that little tidbit was revealed, it might just get him kicked to the curb.

"Please, I don't want to talk about that name anymore. I don't know anyone by that name, but it feels like they've shot me up with chemo when I hear you say it." Edith's face turned gray, her hand shot up to cover her mouth, and she lurched forward. She moved her hand just long enough to blurt out, "You'll have to excuse me a minute." Then Edith leaped up and wobbled down the hallway to the bathroom, where she slammed the door behind her. David heard her heave before the splash of vomit hitting the water in the toilet bowl.

David sat there frozen, while down the hall Edith hurled. He was dumb-founded by this turn of events. Edith sounded like she really believed that Edmund O'Neil was Janet's father. On the other hand, maybe she knew that Phillip was the father. It could be she wanted to hide that from everyone, take that secret with her to the grave. *Maybe she doesn't want it known to her daughter or to anyone that she bore an illegitimate child to a convicted murderer. Maybe she wants to throw O'Neil under the bus to keep me from pursuing the idea that Phillip is the father.*

David thought about confronting Edith with the fact that he had proof Phillip was the father. But he couldn't face the fallout or the lifelong regret he'd have if it turned out he was wrong or if somehow Edith actually believed O'Neil was the father. *Either way, I'd end up killing her before the cancer does. Let her believe what she wants to believe and let her take that comfort to the next world.*

In a few minutes, Edith limped back into the room and slumped down in an upholstered Queen Anne chair across the living room from David. The sixties fabric beneath her shaky knees and wobbling head was a solid pea green, which just emphasized the bloodless pale tone of Edith's complexion.

"I'm afraid I'm going to have to ask you to leave, Mr. Thompson," Edith said, wringing her hands and wiping her clammy face.

"I hope it's nothing I said—"

"No, not directly. I'm having some awful thoughts. I'm not sure where they're coming from. I don't know if they're memories or if my imagination is running wild. I think it's the chemo. It *must be* the chemo."

"Do you . . . do you want to talk about them?"

"I think not. I'm afraid if I say them out loud, that'll make them stay with me long after you're gone. If you could, please shut the door behind you when you leave. I think I'll just sit here awhile."

"Okay, Ms. Nowak," David said, getting up from the chair. "If you'd like to talk again or if there's anything I can do, please feel free to call me."

Edith was looking in David's direction, but her eyes were focused over his shoulder, outside the picture window.

With tears welling in her eyes, Edith said, "If I don't see Janet before I die, could you just tell her that I loved her?"

"Yes, Ms. Nowak, I can do that."

"If I tell everyone I know to tell her this, I'm hoping she'll get the message."

"I'm sure she will."

"Good day, Mr. Thompson."

"Goodbye, now," David said, before turning to the front door. As he stepped toward the exit, the floor board creaked beneath his foot. He turned to close the door behind him and glanced at Edith, head tilted back, staring at the overcast sky outside the picture window.

A few moments later, he was sitting out front in his Mustang. He could see the top half of Edith's head set back and off in the right-hand corner of the picture window. She hadn't moved from her chair. He dialed up Phillip on his cell phone, but there was no answer. Then he tried his motel room phone, but still no answer. David decided to pay a visit to the Red Apple to check on him. He looked up one last time and he saw Edith sitting there frozen in time, staring at the clouds as it started to drizzle.

When David turned the key in the ignition, it hit him that he'd seen this facial expression before. Phillip stared out the picture window like this when David visited him in his motel room. It was the same vacant look Phillip sometimes wore in David's office. As David struggled to put the Mustang's ancient transmission into drive, it triggered a subliminal thought about Cameron's psychic driving. When he got the car into gear, David had an epiphany.

Edith Nowak has been drugged and brainwashed just like Phillip.

David turned his head to look at the picture window one last time before he drove off. He didn't see Edith's forehead any longer in the right corner of the picture window. She'd moved. David got a glimpse of her standing on the other side of the window staring at him. In her hands, she held a rifle at her waist. *Good God, is she going to shoot me?*

CHAPTER 28

As David sped off looking out the passenger window, he saw Edith track him with her head like a laser sight in "locked-on" mode. He knew his rifles. Edith's gun looked like an old 22 caliber, at a glance, about the same age as his Mustang. David thought maybe she used it to shoot varmints in her vast backyard as many rural New York Upstaters do. It's about the only way to deal with a rogue groundhog. Except in this case she wasn't facing the backyard. She was staring at him in his car on the street in front of her house and he was the only varmint in sight. *Maybe her chemo is laced with LSD. Maybe there's no chemo at all. It could be just LSD straight up or some other psychotic drug cocktail.*

He'd never forget *that* face. There Edith stood like a mannequin in a dirty department store window with a crooked smile on her haggard face. It was the very first smile he'd seen from her. The truth had seeped through her attempts to suppress it and it was aimed right at him. *Oh my God, she was going to shoot me dead in her house, but couldn't quite bring herself to do it. Or did the chemo disable her fingers so badly that she couldn't? Did she get the same psychic driving message as Phillip had? "Kill David Thompson." Did I trigger something in her by asking about Boris Dietrich?*

It hit David then that he could not trust anything she had said to him. Not a single word. It wasn't that David thought she was intentionally untruthful. Not at all. He feared that, like Phillip, Edith might honestly believe something based on a memory that could change on a dime or could have been implanted by the CIA. Even though David believed much of what she told him, he had no yardstick to separate fact from fiction. Everything she believed was suspect because all of her memories were suspect.

While he was high-tailing it out of Hoosick Falls, David decided he needed to tell Phillip about his visit with Edith. David wanted to let him know that he wasn't the only victim of this mess. He thought that this might comfort Phillip, calm him down, and just maybe help him to unearth some memories about Edith or his own past.

David rode over the curb with his back tire as he darted into an empty space in the Red Apple Motel parking lot. The Mustang dropped into place with a thump that did not bode well for his shocks. He popped out of the car and knocked on Phillip's door. There was no answer. The drapes were wide open so David peered through the picture window. The bathroom door was ajar. There were no lights on; there was no sign of life in the dingy little room. The bed was made. *Oh, no, he went to O'Neil's office again.* David dialed Phillip's cell phone. No answer. The voicemail still hadn't been activated.

A door squeaked behind him and David wheeled around at the sound. The motel clerk was taking the office trash out to the dumpster. It was the same clerk who collected the rent from David every week.

"Hey, do you know where Phillip might have gone?"

"Phillip?"

"Yeah, the guy in 113."

"Right, the tall guy. He left a few hours ago."

"Was he on foot?"

"Yeah, he walked across the street and got on a bus, I think."

"Was it a red express bus?"

"I guess so."

"Any idea where he was headed?"

"The only red express bus on that side of the line goes to Albany."

"Okay."

David was now furiously rubbing his face with both hands as he desperately searched his brain for a plan. Nothing like a little frustration-induced friction to get the gray matter moving. He was about to fly down to O'Neil's office on a second search and rescue op, when he decided to stare in Phillip's window one last time.

The room was clean, as if the maid had readied it for the next road-weary occupant. There was a white envelope centered on the empty surface of the desk. At first David thought it was a tip envelope for the maid. But then he wondered if it might be something else. He jogged over to the office where, with some difficulty and a twenty, he pried a spare key out of the clerk.

It took a few minutes to fling open Phillip's door and snatch the envelope off the desk. The envelope was sealed, with David's name scrawled on the front. His hands trembled as he ripped open the missive and read the contents.

Saturday Morning

Dear David,

Hopefully, you're not reading this letter. I plan to finish my mission, get back here, and rip it up before you ever open it. But if I don't make it back before you see this, it might mean I'm in trouble or dead.

If that's what happens, you should know that I'm busing over the river to Martin Kleinschmit's house to pay him a surprise visit.

Edmund O'Neil raised more questions in my head than he answered. I think Martin Kleinschmit has the answers.

I don't expect any trouble with him, but I'm leaving you this note just in case.

Oh, and don't be ticked off at me for not having told you or invited you to tag along. You can't be involved. You have a family that depends on you.

Thank you for being such a wonderful friend.

I will always cherish the kindness you and your family showed me.

Phillip

David slammed the letter on the desk, dropped down into the chair, and buried his face in his hands right up to the hairline. He was tempted to tear his hair out. "Damn it, Phillip!" He knew that the ex-con was right about one thing. If he tried to follow Phillip, it might further seal his fate as a man who knew too much. He had a better chance to escape that fate if he stayed away. He could just pretend he never saw this letter if Annie asked questions later on. Besides, if Phillip was really Boris Dietrich in disguise, then there was less of a reason to save him. Still, if David was wrong about

Phillip being Boris, he knew he'd have to live with the consequences. One guilty conscience, coming right up. In rising frustration, David pounded his fist on the desktop. "Jesus, Phillip!"

David's cell phone began to play the theme song from *Superman*. Christy had installed the ringtone as a prank. David cringed and made a mental note to have him change it back to the sound of an old dial phone ringer. David sighed as he read the display. Julius was calling.

David picked up. "Yeah, Julius . . . ."

"You all right? You don't sound like the Mr. Sunshine that I know."

"Long day, Julius. I'm sorry."

"Well, maybe this news will raise your spirits."

"What do ya got?"

"There's a match."

"DNA?"

"Yeah, the DNA at the crime scene matches Phillip's DNA."

"My God, he was telling the truth then—he did kill that officer."

"Apparently so."

"They knew this when they let him out. They freed him to kill me then."

"It seems that way, yes."

Suddenly, David's eyes widened as a realization hit him. He sprung up out of the chair. "Oh. My. God. Oh my God—"

"What's wrong?"

"It also means that Phillip is Phillip. He's not Boris Dietrich. We know that Phillip was Phillip when he killed the officer. He couldn't have been anyone else back then. And his DNA from back then matches the man we know as Phillip today." David didn't care who Boris Dietrich was back then. It only mattered that Phillip was Phillip.

"You're right—"

"I've got to go, Julius. Phillip is going to pay the Kranston superintendent a visit. I've got to go stop him if I can." Now David had all the motivation he needed to launch another search and rescue mission. And he needed to hit the road, pronto.

Julius said, "Really? I don't know if I can help you out—"

"You can't. I don't want you involved. I don't want the FBI brass coming down on you for sticking your neck out. You said it right the other week. If the CIA is involved and you're discovered to be poking around, there's a whole world of hurt waiting for you."

"I feel bad. Call me, though, if you find yourself in a bind."

"Are you at your desk?"

"Yes."

"I need you to find Martin Kleinschmit's home address. He's the super at Kranston."

"Spell it."

"K.L.E.I.N.S.C.H.M.I.T"

"Let me plug it in and see what we get."

"Thanks."

"Bingo. Surprisingly, there's quite a few of them in New York. Any idea where he lives?"

"No. Wait a second. Phillip said he was going over the river to see him. He was headed to Albany. That must mean he's crossing the Hudson."

"Right. And it must be close to a bus line, I'd imagine. So he's local, or at least has a house locally."

"Makes sense—"

"There's only one Kleinschmit who lives locally. Looking at the bus route maps, he lives close to the Route 233 bus line, across the Hudson, in the village of Hampton Manor."

"Can you transfer from the 905 to the 233?"

"Yes, down at the Greyhound Bus Terminal in Albany."

"What's his address?" David grabbed a pen from the desk to write it down on the envelope.

"Fifteen Thoroughbred Drive, Hampton Manor, 12144."

"Got it. Talk to you later."

"Be careful out there."

"Will do. Thank you, Julius." With that, David hung up, shut and locked the door behind him, dashed to the office to fling the key at the motel clerk, and mounted his Mustang for the ride to Hampton Manor.

He tried Phillip one last time on his cell. Still no answer. This time David texted him instead. *Phillip, I just met with Edith Nowak. She claims to have had sex with O'Neil once. Said Kleinschmit ran paternity test that showed him to be father. Doesn't add up. She also seems to be an electroshock and memory experiment victim. Where are you?*

David then punched Kleinschmit's address into his GPS phone app. The internet calculated the quickest route—a forty-five-minute drive, if the traffic cooperated. He figured that Phillip had an hour-plus head start on him. That was way more than enough time for him to find trouble. David regretted the day he first told Phillip to venture out of his motel room into the world. At that instant, *he* wanted to lock Phillip in a box—the same feeling he had about Christy sometimes—to protect him from himself. While peeling out onto Central Avenue, it struck David that he might have two sons now.

CHAPTER 29

After David plucked him from his one-on-one meeting with O'Neil the day before, Phillip felt rebellious. He ignored David's instructions to return to his motel room. He didn't want to be alone with his thoughts; he didn't want to be trapped in his room. The need to move was mindless, like itching under his skin. It likely sprang from a fear that O'Neil would send someone after him.

Instead of heading to the safety of his room, his feet took him out to the bus stop. He got on the Route 905 bus and rode between Mohawk City and Albany for the rest of the day. Every time the bus passed the Red Apple Motel, he'd scrutinize the area to see if there was any activity around his room. Nothing.

Slowly Phillip gained confidence that the fear he instilled in O'Neil had legs, but he still felt he had to act soon. He believed the commissioner would keep quiet about his visit for now. The man didn't want his relationship with Edith Nowak revealed to his family, to his close colleagues, and to everyone in the system.

But Phillip knew from his own experience that fear could not be sustained without the delivery of a refresher—just as the COs did with their steel-toed boots on follow-up visits to his cell. Without that kind of reminder, he knew that O'Neil would talk to someone about his visit soon enough. Then they'd target him again. He needed to act while the commissioner was still punch-drunk with fear.

David's text about his visit with Edith Nowak vibrated in Phillip's pocket as he moved across the street into the woods near Kleinschmit's driveway entrance. He pulled out the phone, read the message, and filed the information away for future reference. He didn't answer David's query about his location. He still wanted David to stay out of it for his own good and the safety of his family.

Kleinschmit's house was just as Phillip saw it in his mind—a two-story, large, modern stucco home with a long, crushed stone private driveway. He didn't recall capturing it this clearly in Google Maps on the library computer. He remembered that the bird's eye shot of the home was blocked by trees overhead. The street view was virtually useless because the house was set back on Thoroughbred Drive, hidden by trees and shrubbery. Still, the home replicated his vision of it.

Phillip saw one car, a tuxedo black Lincoln Navigator, lurking in the driveway. He had overheard some COs talking about its magnificence outside of his cell gate one night. It was hard for Phillip to believe that someone would pay just under a $100,000 for something twice the size of his box. Even more mind-blowing was the idea that a prison super could afford it.

Circling slowly around the house in the woods that protected the residence, Phillip reached Kleinschmit's endless backyard. It was a manicured lawn the size of five football fields. At the far end there was a large fenced pasture, a barn, and a pair of horses frolicking about. Close to the house, the green velvet expanse of lawn broke for a long, rectangular in-ground pool framed by travertine blocks and intricate ceramic tile patterns.

Such a pretty picture. Not a threat in sight. Why did it fill him with a sense of dread? His gut knotted and churned for no reason that he could see or explain.

In the distance, Phillip spotted the figure of a man reclining poolside on a chaise lounge facing him. Phillip knew from the Kranston scuttlebutt that Kleinschmit was a lifelong bachelor without any family. He thought the man tanning himself poolside in the warm summer sun must be Kleinschmit.

Phillip made it to the far end of the in-ground pool undetected by the sun worshipper. He stepped carefully in his secondhand sneakers across the stone and concrete pool deck, moving toward him in plain view. Phillip noticed the man's rhythmic breathing and pursed lips. He looked asleep.

At the narrow far end of the pool with his back to the house, Phillip recognized Martin Kleinschmit. The superintendent lay facing skyward, propped up on one of a dozen poolside chairs that showed no sign anyone's wet butt ever sat on them. Draped in an open, plush terry cloth short robe, the lounger showed no sign of hearing Phillip. As his chest slowly rose and fell, the man's genitalia bulged in the gentle embrace of his red Speedo. Kleinschmit's tall, slim body glistened in the sunlight and radiated an aura of expensive sunscreen. He was hiding behind a pair of Ray-Ban aviator sunglasses that reflected the rare cloud in a blue sky.

Halfway up the length of the pool, Kleinschmit blurted, "Good to see you, Dawkins. I've been expecting you."

Startled, Phillip stopped in his tracks and rose up to full height. He then slowly brought his feet together, as if standing at attention by his gate at Kranston. "Hello . . . Mr. Kleinschmit."

Kleinschmit lifted one hand gracefully, palm up, gesturing to the phalanx of patio chairs that lined the long side of the pool. "Sit down, Dawkins." He emanated phony graciousness, like a Mafia don greeting a supplicant.

Phillip looked over his shoulder as he spun around, like a dog chasing its tail, scanning the scenery for anyone else in the yard. Nobody. Then he glanced at the house windows. The reflections from the backyard prevented him from looking inside. Nothing there either. "I'll stand if you don't mind."

"Suit yourself." Kleinschmit clasped both hands behind his head as he crossed his legs. Phillip saw his top foot sway left, then right like a clock pendulum. He thought of what Kleinschmit used to say to him: *Time has a way of changing things when we can't.* He mumbled it out loud.

"Did you say something, Dawkins? Speak up, man. What brings you here?" His tone had a taunting quality, verbally poking Phillip in the gut.

"Since you expected me, you must know."

Kleinschmit laughed sardonically, his lips twisting in a mockery of a smile. "You want answers. Right?"

"How did you know I was coming?"

"They all do."

Phillip was taken aback. *What does he mean by "all"? Does "all" include Edith Nowak? He didn't mention O'Neil's name—must not have talked to him. He didn't know I was coming. Not today, at least. He's bluffing.*

"I don't like the look on your face, Dawkins. I wouldn't try anything rash if I were you. There might be a high-powered rifle with your head in its crosshairs. There are lots of trees around, lots of windows in my home. COs come over here all the time and stay for the weekend. It's like a retreat for them."

Phillip hadn't considered the possibility of a threat from the trees—like guard towers and COs armed with sniper rifles. The reflective glass blocked the view through the windows, so he couldn't see inside. Like prison, there could be a hundred guards out of sight who would come running if Kleinschmit summoned them. Phillip felt like he was back at Kranston with Superintendent Kleinschmit flaunting his power.

His voice, the sound of his raspy voice, was making Phillip break out in a cold sweat, go weak at the knees. The sense of foreboding became a tidal wave of terror washing over him. He could feel the surrounding woods closing in on him; the sky was collapsing, crushing him. "I know I killed that police officer. I remember it."

"Really? Are you sure?" Kleinschmit lay relaxed on his lounge, like a cat in the sun.

"As sure as I'm standing here. I want some answers."

"We all want answers, Dawkins. We all think we want the truth. But there's the truth and then there's the real truth. And most of us can't handle the real truth. We'd rather believe anything but the real truth because we'd shrivel up like a slug on a hot rock and die if we faced up to the real truth.

"Take your case. Now you say you know you killed that police officer. Maybe so, but maybe it weighed on you as the years passed. Maybe you grew a conscience all alone in the box. Maybe you couldn't live with yourself knowing that you killed him. Perhaps you thought about his wife, his kids, his family. You got weak. Your remorse got the best of you. Maybe we had to give you anti-psychotic meds to stabilize you. Maybe that's the truth. Can you handle that truth or do you just want me to tell you what you think you want to hear?"

"Just tell me *the* truth. And I never took meds!"

"Ah, memories are a very fragile web, Dawkins. You can lose them, you know. We exist as a collection of our memories. That's what defines us, what separates us from one another. It's what makes us unique. Without our memories, we don't know who we are or why we're here. The longer you stayed in the box, the more you lost your memories, your sense of self, and you became a hollow version of the person you were. You became a long-haired, wild-eyed zombie. You might have forgotten about taking those meds, but maybe you wanted them because you needed them. You needed them to get high and forget. Maybe we found you hanging yourself from the ceiling air register grates with your bedsheets. Maybe we cut you down, gave you CPR, brought you back to life."

"That's not true. That never happened."

"Are you sure, Dawkins? Maybe you just don't remember it. Anything is possible when it comes to memories. But I remember it like it happened yesterday."

"I've lost some of my memories. I've regained some. I've had some that turned out to be false. You messed with my mind!"

"Maybe we stopped you from killing yourself."

"You did me a favor, then?"

"Maybe you were on your way to checking out. Maybe you were of no use to anyone—even yourself."

"So you saved me from myself? Is that what you're saying?"

"You're getting upset, Dawkins. Maybe you'd like something to drink—calm your nerves? I've got some good scotch here." Kleinschmit waved a hand toward a bottle of golden liquid that sat next to his chaise on an end table.

"No, not from you. When you saved me from myself then, why didn't you let me out of the box?"

"You'd become a legend in the system, the longest-held prisoner ever to survive in solitary. You were notorious—an invitation to cons in the general pop to make a name for themselves by taking you on. We didn't want to see you get killed, not on our watch. They'd ask a lot of questions then. We would be buried in paperwork. You also had too much power for us to let you roam free in the general pop. You got too much respect for being such a survivor."

"Come on. Whatever notoriety I achieved was because you didn't let me out of the box after you first put me in. You never gave me the chance. I earned a chance. I earned an opportunity to live in the general pop. If it didn't work out, you could always put me back in the box. And if things really didn't work out, I could have had an accident and you could have dug me a grave out in the fields. Put me out of my misery."

"At some point it became too late to let you out, both for your own good and the good of the facility."

"So you locked me up in a box for my own good?"

"Those were my instructions."

"Cons die in prison all the time. What made me so special? Why couldn't I have a chance to live with the general pop?"

"It wasn't my call. You were a central office case."

"That's not what O'Neil said. He printed out the central office list right in front of me and my name wasn't on it. For years you blamed the central office for my stay in the box. You blamed the system, when it was really you pulling all the strings."

"You talked to O'Neil then?"

"You're damn right I did. Yesterday."

"And did he tell you I was to blame?"

"No, I just put two and two together when he showed me the central office list."

"Did he voluntarily agree to meet with you?"

"Let's just say my visit was unannounced."

"You really shouldn't have done that, Phillip. O'Neil will call me first thing on Monday. I know him. He's going to be pissed at you. He's going to want to punish you." Kleinschmit's voice projected regret, but his body showed some tension now.

"Really? How can he get more pissed at me than he already is? I know you two wanted me to kill Thompson, so then you could kill me, or lock me back in the box. I was as good as dead before I stepped into his office. I had nothing to lose because you still can't kill a man more than once."

"You're entitled to your opinion. And how do you know all this?"

"You had me take vitamins at night at Kranston. Every night they'd deliver them to my gate. The CO would not leave until I took them. They were laced with LSD."

"Come on, Phillip. It sounds like paranoia has gotten the best of you."

"The bottle you gave me when I was released—I had it tested. Laced with LSD."

"Nonsense, Phillip. Why would we do that?"

"You already said you gave me anti-psychotic drugs. Why not LSD? You knew I had already tried it—you had to have known about that the first day at intake when they put me away."

"Oh come on now. I was good to you. Sneakers, long johns, shower sandals, stick deodorant, extra bars of soap—I got them for you even though the bureau directives didn't allow for them. Why would I do this for you and then drug you?"

"To calm me, to make me more receptive to your messaging."

"What are you talking about?"

"You piped special music into my wall headphone jack."

"Right, classical music. Another thing I did for you."

"You knew I went to sleep listening to the music. You pumped subliminal messaging into it—'kill David Thompson.' It was the same messaging you pumped into my radio. I had it tested. There was a chip in it with the same command—'kill David Thompson.' I was a manufactured assassin dispatched to do your bidding."

"Ridiculous."

"Really? Then why else would you release me when you knew I killed that police officer? You knew I killed once while high on LSD. You thought I would do it again. The officer's family knew something about it. Why else would the wife's nephew inspect my shop?"

Kleinschmit's eyebrows twitched.

"Yes, I found out about him, too. The family must have known you'd finish me off one way or the other. That's why they didn't object to my release. They want to see me dead."

"Nonsense."

"You made my life miserable on the outside, so that I'd be more susceptible to killing Thompson. What exactly did you do to me in Kranston?"

"That's not important."

"Why not?"

"If you don't have a memory of it, it never happened."

"Just tell me the truth!"

"The truth is *your* memories."

"So the truth is ever-changing then? It's like the weather? If you don't like the truth, wait a while and maybe it will morph into something you like better?"

"The truth is but a fleeting memory. When that memory is gone, the truth never happened. When a new memory emerges, that becomes the truth. What do you remember?"

"I see what you're doing now. You're probing my memories, my truth, to see if I'm still of any use to you. Maybe you think you can save me with some memory maintenance. Maybe you think I'm a total loss because my

memories are coming back to me and my truth is changing. I don't understand why you did this to me. I thought you were a good man, a good superintendent."

"Phillip, do you recall your relationship with your father and mother?"

"A *good* man . . . ."

"Focus, Phillip. Do you recall what your father and mother said
about you?"

"What does that have to do with anything?"

"Just answer."

"No—"

"Your father said he *never* wanted to have you. Your mother said she
hated you."

"NO!" Phillip screamed with his eyes shut. A flash of light seared
through his brain as if a CO had cracked his skull with his baton. He
cringed, grabbed his head, and buckled at the knees. He blindly wriggled a
hand at his side, searching for the feel of a patio chair to fall on. His eyes
opened, tears streaming down his face, as he found a chair and collapsed
into it.

Yet nobody was near him; nothing had struck him. It was all in his head.

He eyed Kleinschmit preparing to get out of his chair. As the man's
knees swung sideways and his torso bent, Phillip reached under his pant leg
and drew his knife. "YOU SIT DOWN RIGHT NOW OR I SWEAR TO
GOD I'LL CUT YOU TO PIECES!"

Kleinschmit slowly sat back down, perched upright on the edge of his
chaise lounge. "Are you okay? I was just coming over to check on you."

"Spare me your BS." Phillip braced his heavy head with both hands on
his cheeks, thumbs under his chin. It was pounding harder and harder, like
it was going to explode. He started to cringe. Kleinschmit's voice kept
ringing in his ears, over and over: *Your father never wanted to have you. Your
mother hated you.* "Why did you say that to me?"

Kleinschmit sat motionless, eyes fixed on Phillip. He took off his shades
with one hand and neatly placed them on the end table, between a bottle of
thirty-year-old single malt whiskey and a half-full glass of it, no ice. His hair
was black, slicked back, darker than his graying eyebrows. It formed a
widow's peak on his forehead. With his skin wrinkled and sagging a bit
below his jaw, his face made him look older than his toned body alone
suggested.

Phillip gripped the handle of the upright knife, blade flashing in the sun, his hand trembling. He could hear Kleinschmit's raspy voice, but Kleinschmit's lips weren't moving. *Your father never wanted to have you. Your mother hated you.* "Shut up already. What are you, some kind of telepath?"

Kleinschmit smiled, showing his yellow teeth. He reached for a pack of unfiltered Camels leaning against a half-filled black ashtray. "Do you mind if I smoke?"

"Yes, I do. I hate cigarettes. Keep your hands where I can see them."

"Your father smoked, didn't he?"

"Stop talking about my father." Now the smell of tobacco smoke swirled in Phillip's head. *Your father never wanted to have you. Your mother hated you.*

A gentle breeze blew, bringing the smell of something sweet to Phillip's sensitive nose. "What's that scent in the air?" Phillip looked around the pool and saw weeping shrubs in bloom. Their fragrance was sweeter than the lupines of the Karner Blue. "What are those flower shrubs over there?"

"Juliana Hers Weeping Lilac. Aren't they beautiful? I'm a big lilac fan. You can see they're all around the house."

Phillip recognized the fragrance but couldn't place it. All he knew was that the smell was making him nervous for some reason. Could this same shrub have bloomed in his childhood, in Syracuse?

"You don't look well, Phillip. Maybe you'd like to go inside and get out of the sun?"

"Why did you do this to me? I thought you were a good man." Now a voice echoed in his head. *Martin Kleinschmit is a good man, a good superintendent.*

"We could continue this talk inside, if you'd like."

"No. I'm not going in *that* house," Phillip said, pointing to the concrete-gray stucco mansion. He wasn't sure why he was so terrified of the house. At that moment, he feared it more than he did Kleinschmit. When he saw his reflection in the large picture window, he stood up. He looked at all the windows. They were all white paned windows. The reflections weren't naturally occurring. Every piece of paned glass had been tinted to reflect so you couldn't see inside. Even the basement windows were tinted. He took a step toward the house and it suddenly all came together. A memory surfaced.

"Now I remember, Kleinschmit. It's all coming back to me now. The smells, the fragrances, your voice, the windows, this house. I've been here before. This is not an implanted memory either. It can't be. Why would you implant a memory about me being in your own house?"

"I think you're imagining things, Phillip. Your mind is playing tricks on you."

"No, I don't think so. I remember being in this house, in the basement, through that sliding glass door over there. Behind that door is a white operating room of sorts. I was lying on my back on a table—it was shiny, and metal—looking out that window. I remember because I was naked and the steel was cold. Maybe stainless steel. There was a light overhead. It was really bright. My hands and ankles were strapped down to the table. There was a huge machine that hummed. A man in scrubs with a surgical mask applied some jelly to my temples. My head was in a vise-like contraption. Someone put something in my mouth, maybe a bite block. I struggled but I couldn't move. I was terrified. The man said I wouldn't remember the treatment at all. I felt two cold electrodes applied to my head. Then the machine hummed louder and louder until . . . until . . . that's all I remember."

"You know, Dawkins, hallucinations are part and parcel of the experience of solitary."

Phillip knew there was more to his memory, but he couldn't unearth the rest. "This isn't a hallucination. And if you haven't noticed, I'm not in solitary anymore. You held me against my will and fried my brain with electroshock. You're nothing but a sick, sadistic son of a bitch."

"Well, that's quite an assessment coming from an admitted cop killer. Your memory is about a hallucination you had in solitary. And even though you left solitary, it never *really* leaves you. Isn't that right, Phillip?"

Just then there was a loud whinny from one of the two horses in the pasture below. Both men looked in that direction. The stallion nickered, shook his head, and nudged the mare's neck with it before she urinated like someone had turned on a hose full blast. When she was done, the stallion stood on his hind legs and lifted his front legs onto the mare's back, while trying to mount her from the rear. When he got into position, it took less than thirty seconds of thrusting before the deed was done. He dismounted and galloped off.

Kleinschmit said, "Well, looks like Caligula has covered another one for the season, all by himself. Glad I didn't have to get involved. That'll probably be his last."

"What do you have here, some kind of stud farm or something?"

"Yes, it's a side business. There are a lot of mares that come through here during mating season looking to hook up with him. He was quite a racehorse in his day. A lot of his offspring compete about an hour north of here up at Saratoga Racetrack. Now, Phillip, I don't have an operating room in the basement with steel beds and whatnot. Go see for yourself. The sliding door is unlocked."

"Okay, let's walk over there and take a look." If Kleinschmit said that there wasn't an operating room on the other side, Phillip didn't expect to find one. But what he hoped to find was another trigger that would force another memory to surface. He pointed his knife at the house. "You first."

Kleinschmit got up and walked toward the door. Phillip was close behind with his knife extended. When they got near the door, Phillip said, "Lie down on the lawn, face down. Kleinschmit looked over his shoulder. His glacier-blue eyes narrowed then zeroed in on Phillip. "Right there," Phillip said, pointing his knife at a patch of grass a few feet from the door. "Do as I say."

Phillip kept his eyes on Kleinschmit as the super got down on all fours before lying flat on his stomach.

Phillip slid the door open wide and poked his head inside. The finished room had large ceramic tiles on the floor. The walls were sheet-rocked, bare, and painted off-white. There was a white desk by the door but otherwise the room was empty. It reeked of cigarettes. The ceiling was made of suspended white tiles with swirls that looked knotted together.

"See, there's nothing there. It's all in your mind. Maybe you heard about my house and had dreams about it. Maybe those dreams became hallucinations."

But Phillip now recalled the cigarette odor in the room. He spotted a black, oblong ceramic ashtray full of butts on the desk. He'd seen it before. He remembered it. Now he could envision Kleinschmit's icy-blue eyes piercing him like shards of glass from between a scrub cap and surgical mask against the backdrop of the knotted ceiling. "I've been here before. I know it. There were other men here too."

"Phillip, we can't just take prisoners out of the facility and take them to my home."

"Don't give me that. It's happened before. The Kranston library has the state investigative report about Green Haven Maximum Security Prison—about how inmates were routinely driven to the home of the superintendent to do work around his house or to attend parties. I read it and know the real deal."

"That was years ago, Phillip. Do you recall being driven here?"

"Green Haven might have been years ago but so was my visit here. No, I don't remember being driven here, but just because I can't remember something doesn't mean it didn't happen. If I've learned anything the past few months, it's been that. For all I know, I was drugged and unconscious while you drove me here."

Your father never wanted to have you. Your mother hated you.

Kleinschmit's voice in Phillip's mind was now almost too loud to bear. It burned his ears and he had a vision of himself being nailed to a cross, blood flowing from the nails pounded through his wrists. Clutching the knife, Phillip's right hand slowly drooped to his side, tip pointed down, while he rubbed his forehead with his left hand.

Kleinschmit's eyes widened at the impending opportunity. "What's the matter, Phillip? Let me get up to help you. There's a chair inside you can sit down in."

"YOU STAY THERE OR I'LL KILL YOU! I'm not going in *that* room. It's coming back to me now. I'm starting to remember things. Not only did you electroshock me here to wipe my mind clean, you blared a recording 'round the clock telling me—in your voice—that my father didn't want me and my mother hated me. You . . . you drove a wedge between me and my parents."

"Phillip, how could I drive a wedge between you and your parents when you didn't have a relationship with them to begin with?"

"With all their faults, they were still my parents. Why would you do such a thing? Why? You were such a *good* man, such a *good* superintendent." As soon as Phillip said that, the pieces fell into place. "After you turned me against my parents, you sought to replace them. You fed me a recorded message that you were a good man, a good superintendent. You had your own walking, talking PR machine in me that told everyone you were a great man. I even believed it and couldn't recognize all the bad things you did to me. It was the old good cop-bad cop routine—except it played out in my head, all of the time. My parents became evil and you became God."

"There you go again, Phillip. Maybe it's time for you to leave."

"I'm not going anywhere. You're the one who took my porter job away, not the central office. The central office didn't keep my distant cousin from visiting, you did. You're the one who got the COs to write bogus tickets to keep me in solitary. You probably even told the hearing officer to decide against me on my appeals. When my segregation status was reviewed every sixty days, you either told the committee to decide against me or you overruled it. You wanted to keep me in solitary so you could experiment on me in secret. Who's behind this? The CIA?"

"I don't know what you're talking about—"

"Well, there's no sense asking you. You won't admit that this is a CIA op. You don't want to compromise the agency. If you did, you know they'd come after you."

"You're delusional. The CIA isn't involved in anything we do at Kranston."

"Who's in charge of this project?"

"I don't know what you mean. O'Neil is in charge of the Bureau of Prisons, if that's what you mean. But you already knew that."

Just then, Phillip spotted something square covered in white vinyl on top of the white desk just inside the door. He reached a long arm inside and ripped the vinyl cover off. There sat a powder blue 1965 Smith Corona Sterling Typewriter loaded with a sheet of paper. "Look at what we have here. A typewriter. Now why would you have something so old in such a modern home as this?"

"It was a gift. Commissioner O'Neil gave it to me. He likes to collect typewriters."

"When did he give that to you?"

"I don't know—a few years back."

With one hand holding his knife, Phillip reached in the room to type some lowercase letters with his free hand. Then he pressed his thumb on the shift key and typed some uppercase letters. He jumped when the typewriter bell sounded to let him know he was running out of room. As he ripped the paper and brought it close to his eyes, the sound of the bell continued to reverberate around the empty room before finally fading. He couldn't help but think he'd heard that bell before. "I don't believe it. Would you look at that?"

"Look at what?"

"The uppercase letters struck lower than the lowercase ones, just like the typewriter that was used to file a complaint with the Bureau of Licenses. Your typewriter is out of alignment."

"I wouldn't know. I don't use it."

"Well, somebody has used it. Maybe one of your COs came over and typed something up for you or maybe you just forgot that you used it. Like you said, memories can be a tricky thing. Or maybe you're just lying through your teeth." And as Phillip said that, another memory surfaced. It made his blood run cold. He felt the chill deep in his gut.

"I remember now lying on that metal table, face down this time, strapped down at the hands, ankles, and neck. I was naked. I think it must have been before you tried to wipe my memory clean with electroshock. There were other men in the room, maybe COs, maybe the CIA. Everyone was behind me; I couldn't see anyone. Someone was massaging my buttocks, putting some lotion on them. I think hands put jelly on my anus, started probing it, and lubricating it with something, maybe a finger. The men in the room were laughing. Then I felt something thrust into my anus, in and out, in and out. I recall my rectum was in horrible pain. OH MY GOD, OH MY GOD, DID YOU . . . DID YOU RAPE ME HERE? IS THAT WHAT YOU DID TO ME?"

"You really need to listen to yourself. Do you really think there was a conspiracy to kidnap you from prison to rape you here? If we really wanted to rape you, we'd pair you up at Kranston with some ass bandit as your shower-mate, and then we'd drop your soap on the floor."

"I WASN'T TALKING ABOUT SOME ASS BANDIT AT KRANSTON. I WAS TALKING ABOUT THE CIA. I WAS TALKING ABOUT COs. I WAS ALSO TALKING ABOUT YOU!"

"So you have memories of me raping you then?"

"No . . . I don't."

"Do you have memories of me here at my house?"

"No . . . but I do remember a man overseeing this torture. He hid behind a surgical mask and scrub cap. He had your eyes. Wait . . . now it's coming back to me. There was a hole in the table lined with padding. My genitals and my penis were lined up with that hole so that they hung down below the table, underneath it. You catheterized me, made me piss out every drop of urine I had in me. Then I felt you put some rod or something deep into my anus. I screamed when it went in. You thrust it back and forth and pumped electrical current through it. I heard laughter. I felt so ashamed and angry you stuck something in my butt. I recall the tingling turned to pain and then back to tingling. I felt so violated. Then I realized that somehow I was getting an erection. YOU USED ELECTRICAL CURRENT TO GET

AN ERECTION OUT OF ME! And then you fooled around with the current and . . . I don't believe it. YOU CAUSED ME TO EJACULATE BENEATH THE TABLE. I lost complete control of my body. I was so thoroughly ashamed, angry, and disgusted but at the same time I was ejaculating. That sounds like rape to me. Why did you do that? Did you and your pals get your kicks out of dehumanizing me? YOU'RE SICK, KLEINSCHMIT, A TOTAL PSYCHO."

"You've lost your mind, Phillip. You need help. Let me help you."

"Right, Kleinschmit. 'I'm from the government and I'm here to help you.' I don't think so. It's coming back to me now—it's *all* coming back. There was another table beside me, several feet away. There was a person lying on it. I couldn't see that person's face, just the feet, because that person was pointed in the opposite direction. The legs were smooth, no hair, and the feet had a pedicure and coral pink nail polish. Yes, that person was a woman. She didn't move or say anything. After I ejaculated, someone ducked under my table and everyone left my side and went to the other table. You put her legs up in stirrups and—OH MY GOD, NOW I KNOW WHAT YOU DID, YOU SICK SON OF A BITCH. YOU TOOK MY SEMEN AND PUT IT IN HER. YOU WANTED TO IMPREGNATE THAT WOMAN WITH MY SEMEN!"

"Phillip, let me help you. You had wild hallucinations like this while you were in solitary. You almost killed yourself several times. I got you help, allowed you to live with yourself, helped you to erase all the bad memories of your childhood and the memories of murdering that police officer."

Phillip was half listening, and half watching the horses run with one another in the pasture below. "You ran a stud farm for horses and a stud farm for me." Now Phillip understood that the woman lying next to him was Edith Nowak, and that he really was the father of Janet Nowak. David was right. The silhouette of the woman he'd seen in Mohawk City was his daughter. He wished he'd seen her face, but at the same time he was glad he didn't. "YOU RAPED EDITH NOWAK WITH MY SPERM. IT'S LIKE I RAPED HER. HOW COULD YOU DO THIS TO ME? WHY DID YOU DO THIS TO ME?"

"Maybe you raped Edith Nowak yourself? Did you ever think of that? Maybe you had access to her when you were a porter cleaning the cellblock. Maybe you two ducked into a supply closet to have sex—"

"I don't have any *memory* of that."

"It was erased. Sometimes when we treated you, we mistakenly erased memories."

"I don't believe you. Is that what you call electroshock torture? Treatment?"

"It's been around for decades and has successfully treated people like yourself. O'Neil knew all about electroshock therapy and its benefits."

"Shut up, already. The internet says that nobody even knows how it works. If you erased my memory of raping Edith Nowak in a supply closet, then how do I have this memory of you impregnating Edith Nowak with my sperm in this very room? You certainly didn't implant that one."

"It's a hallucination. People get them when they've been locked up in solitary for a long time."

"Give me a break. When I saw your home, it was like I've been here before. I remembered the fragrance of the lilacs. I knew I was in this room before you even opened the door. The reflective windows, the swirls on the ceiling tiles in this room, the ashtray, the tiles on the floor, the dirty grout between them—it all came back to me in a flash. I also remember seeing the horses out through this sliding glass door while lying down on the table. I *know* the sound of the loud return bell on that typewriter."

Suddenly, Phillip put it all together. David texted that Edmund O'Neil had sex with Edith Nowak *once* and that Kleinschmit had run a paternity test proving O'Neil was the father. "YOU'RE A PSYCHOPATH, KLEIN-SCHMIT, AN ABSOLUTE PSYCHOPATH! You knew O'Neil had sex with Edith Nowak when she was underage once. But you didn't know if once was good enough to impregnate her. So you raped me, stole my sperm to ensure that Edith Nowak became pregnant. You lied to O'Neil about the paternity test, maybe you even manipulated the results, and used that poor child to prove to O'Neil that he raped Edith Nowak. Janet Nowak was not only proof of intercourse, but the timing of her birth was proof that she was underage when it took place. You presented an airtight case of statutory rape to O'Neil but told him you could fix it all and keep it under wraps—"

"You're delusional, Phillip—"

"Am I? You must have used Edith Nowak's rape to gain leverage over Edmund O'Neil. You used your knowledge of the rape to secure and solidify your position as superintendent at Kranston. You helped buy Edith Nowak's silence by getting her a job in the prison and stringing her along about a future together. You used the rape to buy O'Neil's silence about the torture program you conducted at Kranston. You know, there must be over fifty prison superintendents in New York State in line for the job as New York State Commissioner of the Bureau of Prisons. Why did you get the job? Because you used the rape as leverage to get it from O'Neil, that's why. You knew if someone else took the job, they might find out what you had been up to all these years. You had to get that job to make sure that nobody would find you out and you could keep your CIA project going undetected."

Kleinschmit rolled over, sat upright on the lawn, and peeled off his robe. "Where's the proof, Phillip? Who is going to listen to your wild hallucinations? Do you think people are going to believe some ex-con who lost his mind in solitary? You need to leave now. I'll forget this ever happened if you leave right now and never come back."

Phillip's cell phone vibrated in his pocket. He yanked it out with his free hand while he clutched the knife upright in the other. It was a missed call from David followed by a text from him:

Jim Fletcher just called me. He researched the name change records for several counties in and around the prison. He got a hit for Boris Dietrich in Washington County. The man previously known as Boris Dietrich changed his name to Martin Kleinschmit decades ago. I repeat: Martin Kleinschmit is really Boris Dietrich. You need to be careful. Are you at his house? Please call.

Phillip's eyes narrowed, his head went a bit dizzy as his entire body flooded with rage. "Hey, Kleinschmit, do you remember what you said to me about 'time' when I was in the box looking to get out?"

"Time?"

"Yeah, you said, 'Time has a way of changing things when we can't.' Guess what, Boris? Your time is up!"

"YOUR FATHER NEVER WANTED YOU. YOUR MOTHER HATED YOU."

"NO!" Phillip screamed, clutching his head with both hands. The knife slipped from his grip.

Kleinschmit's eyes turned to slits in his grimacing face. Pivoting on his red Lycra-encased backside, he rolled onto all fours—like a cat in a Speedo—and lunged for Phillip.

CHAPTER 30

David was a half-hour away from Kleinschmit's house when Jim Fletcher had called to tell him about Boris Dietrich. As he drove over the Dunn Memorial Bridge that spanned the Hudson River at Albany, he tried to sort it all out. So many lines of lies and deceptions making a rat's nest of evil that he could hardly keep it all straight.

At one time, Edith Nowak knew Boris Dietrich and fell in love with him —not Edmund O'Neil—even though she believed O'Neil fathered her daughter. The letters Johnny McFadden discovered revealed that Boris Dietrich had promised to marry her. That's what she had wanted desperately back then. But somehow she had no recollection at all of Boris Dietrich now.

David could only imagine that Kleinschmit had wiped her memory clean of Boris Dietrich; gone without a trace. No ties to Boris could survive in the circle of people at Kranston. He needed a new identity after being forced out by Cleghorn, the director who followed Cameron at the Allan Memorial Institute. Maybe he knew he could never get or hold a job as Boris Dietrich. Maybe he feared that one day his ex-patients would try to track him down. In any event, David speculated that Cameron landed Kleinschmit a new job at Kranston before he died.

While Kleinschmit was obligated to conceal his past, David understood that at the same time he still took pride in it. David saw a connection between the initials in Martin Kleinschmit's name and the CIA's MK-Ultra project. He envisioned Kleinschmit laughing up his sleeve when he chose that name in the 1960s. He may have regretted it ten years later when the MK-Ultra code name first became a national sensation in *The New York Times.*

Kleinschmit was the one man in the system who reached out to Phillip to make his confinement tolerable by bending the rules. But now David could discern the sinister motives behind Kleinschmit's apparent kindness. Each favor brought him one step closer to control of Phillip's mind. Phillip had always said that Kleinschmit was a good man, a good superintendent. Edith Nowak had echoed Phillip's sentiment almost word for word. Now David understood that Kleinschmit had implanted this powerful message in their minds to help obscure the truth. If, for even a second, it occurred to them that Kleinschmit had done some evil things, his positive messaging would subdue and smother those thoughts before they could take root.

The Mustang hit a pothole coming off the bridge and David's head touched the ceiling. He looked down at the speedometer. The car was doing 55 MPH in a 40 MPH zone. *Phillip will blow a gasket when he reads that Martin Kleinschmit is Boris Dietrich.* While David worried about how Phillip might react to that news, he was much more afraid for Phillip's personal well-being. He feared Phillip was in real danger. If Kleinschmit had practiced mind control on his prisoner for decades, David thought it wouldn't take much for him to reassert a hold over him. Tightening the grip of his left hand on the wheel, he reached over with his right to grab his cell phone from the passenger seat. Phillip hadn't texted a response. There was no voice-mail message either.

When David finally pulled onto Thoroughbred Drive, he was stunned by the enormity of the few homes that lined the street. Each one looked like it could double for a Ramada Inn. He could not fathom how a prison superintendent would afford to live here. The mansions all lay back in the woods, shrouded by trees and shrubs, hardly visible from the road. There had to be at least a half-mile between each estate.

Even the roadside mailboxes were opulent statements—works of art that stood in obvious competition with one another. No Rubbermaid clunkers or wooden boxes on a pole in this neighborhood. Kleinschmit's mailbox for Fifteen Thoroughbred Drive at the cul-de-sac terminus was welded atop the head of a lifelike cast-iron lawn jockey. David spotted a black Lincoln

Navigator parked down the winding driveway, so he knew there was a good chance someone was home.

David eased onto the manicured lawn at the side of the road and slipped out of the car. He didn't want to pull into the driveway. He knew the crushed stone would pop under his tires and announce his arrival. He peered through the bushes and examined the front of the house.

There was no sign of Phillip or anyone else: no lights, no sound, no movement. He heard the distant neigh of a horse, but nothing else except the shushing of the leaves rustling in a soft summer breeze. He figured he'd scope out the side and rear of the home first, then maybe ring the doorbell. He could pose as a lost tourist, looking for directions. *Maybe Phillip isn't here. Maybe he didn't make it yet or has left already. Maybe he changed his mind and headed back to the motel after he read my text.*

David circled around the house through the woods. The closer he came to the rear, the more frequent and louder the horse whinnying became. Suddenly, there was a rustling in the leaves, dry twigs snapping in quick succession. Then he heard the steps, the sound of something running. He swung his head in the direction of the noise and recognized the white tails of two deer—doe and fawn—scampering away deeper into the forest.

When David had worked his way through the trees that paralleled the house and gained a clear view of the huge backyard, he spotted a lone horse in the field below. The animal was running along the length of the fence, stopping to neigh at the house every few seconds. The horse sounded distressed.

David looked over toward the house, scanning for activity at the windows, then glanced toward the pool area. He saw a bathrobe in a white heap on the lawn between the stone deck and the house. Next, he noticed something drifting in the water; maybe it was a raft or some kind of pool float. At a loss for what action to take, he worked his way closer to the house.

The mansion was closed up tight. All the windows and doors were shut; there was no sign of anyone. When he got a closer look at the pool, he saw the water had a pinkish cast. He didn't know if Kleinschmit had dyed the water or if it was just dirty with algae. But then the pool float came into focus as he drew closer. It wasn't a float at all. It was a man's body, suspended face down, arms and legs extended in a limp embrace of death.

"Phillip!"

David rushed to the side of the pool. His haste was wasted; the body was lifeless. A pool-water return slowly twirled it around while the current gently pushed it down toward the rear of the yard. The pink water was actually diluted blood; the water was a much deeper crimson red close by the man's head. David was about to jump into the pool to pull the man out when he spotted the red Speedo and realized that it wasn't Phillip at all. It was someone else. *Oh my God, that's got to be Kleinschmit.*

In a daze, David backed away from the pool and almost tripped over a chair. His heart was pounding, his hands trembled, his feet felt like they were cast in cement. For a full minute, he was immobilized by shock before his brain kicked in again. *What should I do?* He debated calling 911. He could jump in the pool to try to pull Kleinschmit out.

He quickly looked all around the house and didn't see another person, only the horse that wouldn't shut up. His eyes locked onto a pattern of blood spatter on the concrete pool coping nearest the house. The man in the water was still dead. His head bobbed over by the pool skimmer now. The circulating water sucked blood from his head wound through the skimmer to the pool filter. When it pumped back from the filter through the water returns, streamers of blood shot out and dispersed, turning the pink pool water to red. It had been less than five minutes. David spun and darted for the woods.

Bolting out of the yard was a fight-or-flight response for David. Since there was nobody to fight, flight seemed like the logical option. And fly he did. David hadn't run this fast in decades. He kept looking over his shoulder and tripping in the tangled underbrush, even falling a few times. His knees were weak. He couldn't erase the memory of Kleinschmit doing the Dead-man's Float in his own blood.

As he plowed through the forest, David's head reeled from this new series of events. The man in the bloody pool was dead. If he was Klein-schmit, death couldn't have come soon enough. David knew there was nothing he could do to reverse that outcome. He felt that he owed it to himself and his family to stay out of it. Nothing good could come out of getting involved.

If he pulled the body out of the pool or if he called 911, David would have to answer a lot of questions. The cops might even consider him a suspect or a co-conspirator with Phillip. Having already seen the inside of the Albany County Jail, he was in no hurry to survey what Rensselaer

County had to offer. If he got involved, he could end up having to implicate Phillip to save himself. No way. If the system wanted Phillip, he wasn't going to help them out one bit. They'd have to get him on their own.

David backtracked his way to where the Mustang sat quietly in the sun. Sliding into the front seat, he inhaled a single shaky breath before turning the ignition, shifting into gear, and speeding away. He kept a lookout for Phillip walking along the road shoulder, but he didn't spot a single pedestrian. A thought raced through his mind. *What if Phillip was injured? Maybe he was hurt somewhere on Kleinschmit's property? Was that why the horse was so upset?* David didn't stop to search for Phillip on Kleinschmit's land. His self-preservation instincts had spurred him into flight without a second thought.

When David pulled into the Red Apple Motel lot, the door to Phillip's room was partly open. David barely parked the Mustang before he was out of the car. He flew into the room shouting, "Phillip! Phillip, are you here?" The bathroom door was shut but he heard the sound of someone spraying something inside. He pushed the door open, nearly hitting a startled middle-aged woman. She was the maid, in the middle of cleaning the shower. "Where's Phillip?"

"You mean the tall one, the man who was here?" she asked in a Spanish accent.

"Yes, where is he?"

"He checked out a little while ago."

"Where did he go?"

"I don't know. He just packed up all of his stuff and got on the bus."

David pulled out his cell. There was no phone message or text.

Phillip Dawkins had vanished.

CHAPTER 31

For the rest of the day, David sat in his office glued to the television news station he had set on mute and the radio all-news station broadcasting just loud enough for him to hear. He was watching and listening for information about Martin Kleinschmit's death. The internet was off limits for news. The last thing he wanted to do was to create a digital stream of breadcrumbs by looking for news about a death that hadn't yet been reported publicly. He knew that trail might circle around to bite him in the ass one day.

At dinner in the dining room with Annie and Christy, David sat where he could see the screen on the small, countertop television in the kitchen. With the volume set on low, David was primed and ready; the remote lay next to his dinner knife as if it was part of his place setting. When the television flashed the headline, "Up Next: A Mysterious Death in Hampton Manor," David grabbed the remote and rose from the table to walk into the kitchen.

Frowning, Annie said, "David, what's so important that it can't wait until after dinner?"

"There might be news about Phillip on the TV."

"Really?" Annie said, getting up from the table.

"What about him?" Christy asked, popping out of his chair.

Christy and Annie stood on either side of David, eyes glued to the tiny screen. "Shh," he said, clicking up the volume, "here it comes."

The earnest, young male reporter was stationed in front of the superintendent's mansion, as an ambulance and police vehicles flashed their light arrays in the background behind the yellow crime-scene tape. "New York State Police and local rescue crews were summoned to this Hampton Manor address this afternoon, after a stable hand reported to work and discovered his boss floating face down in the pool. The employer, Martin Kleinschmit, was pronounced dead at the scene. Police say Mr. Kleinschmit appeared to have slipped at the pool's edge before hitting his head on the concrete coping and drowning in the pool. Police say they are continuing to investigate the incident but don't suspect foul play at this time. They are, however, looking for a man who might have more information on the incident. His name is Phillip Dawkins and this is a picture of him. Anyone knowing the whereabouts of Phillip Dawkins is asked to contact the State Police at the telephone number below. This is Bill Small reporting live for News Channel 9 from Hampton Manor."

David's mind raced as he clicked off the television. They showed a picture of Dawkins in the clothes he wore on the day he showed up at David's door. It must have been taken the day he was released. The report didn't mention his prison record. They obviously didn't want to alarm people.

"Oh my God, David. Who is Martin Kleinschmit?" Annie asked.

"He was the superintendent at Kranston prison where Phillip was holed up," David said, before swallowing hard. "And he was also Boris Dietrich in an earlier life."

"Whoa!" Christy blurted. "*He* was Dietrich and not Phillip?"

"Yes. Jim Fletcher called me yesterday and told me that Boris Dietrich changed his name to Martin Kleinschmit decades ago."

"Now that lines up with all that electroshock stuff that was going on there," Annie said.

"Yes, it does—"

"But David, why do the police want to talk to Phillip about Martin Kleinschmit's death?"

It was time for lawyer David Thompson to make an appearance. "I'm not exactly sure," he responded. Yes, he wasn't exactly sure but he had a pretty good idea of what went down. Phillip said he was going to visit Kleinschmit the same day Kleinschmit was found dead? Yeah, right, just a coincidence— one worthy of an induction into the Coincidence Hall of Fame.

"You must know something, David. Why else would you be watching the news on TV? You hate watching the news."

David felt Annie's intuition radar zeroing in on him. "I know enough to get me in trouble and that's about it."

"What do you know?"

"I can't say."

"You can't or you won't?"

"Can't because I love you both and I don't want to drag either of you into this mess. The less you know, the better off you'll be. If you're ever questioned by the police or anyone else, you can honestly say you don't know anything about the incident."

"David, it's time to spill the beans on this so we all know what's at stake."

"What gives, Dad?"

"Sorry guys, but I have to pull rank on both of you."

"I thought our marriage was a partnership, David. You know, equal partners."

It wasn't the first time David regretted living with Annie, before he married her, while he was attending law school. She learned too much for *his* own good. *Damn law school should just give her an honorary degree, already.* "Yeah, well, sometimes one partner is more equal than the other."

"How does that work, Dad? If both partners are equal—"

"Now, Christy, you stay out of this one. Sometimes you're too smart for your own good. For God's sake you're still a kid, so why don't you act like one for once and not care about your parents' squabbles? You know, think about the next cell phone you want and how your life will be so much better for having it."

"David, that's not fair. That's not Christy and you know it. Enough—"

"Enough? I don't think so. I'm just getting warmed up. Annie, you know just enough law to be dangerous. Most times we do operate like *The Three Musketeers*. You know, one for all and all for one. But when circumstances change, we need to change with them. Now is one of those times. You both need to leave this house right now and get far, far away from me. Annie, I'd like you to take Christy and go spend a few days with your father—"

"Dad, I don't get it. Why are you kicking us out of the house?"

"I'm getting to that. You see, most lawyers don't work out of their homes. Sure it has some advantages. I've seen you off to the bus since you were a tyke. I've been there for you every step of the way. I've gotten to see you grow up into a fine young man. But right now if I had an office outside of the home I'd be kicking myself out of here to go there. I'd be sleeping on the couch in that office until they came for me—"

"Who's they, David?"

"I don't know—maybe the State Police, maybe the Bureau of Prisons, maybe the CIA, maybe the entire system. You heard the news report. Phillip is a person of interest. If they don't find him, they'll come looking for me soon enough. They know I'm close to Phillip and they know I don't have an office outside of the home. So they will end up at our front door and I'll need to deal with them."

"But David, we want to be here to support you—"

"You'll do more to support me if you don't get involved. If I don't give them what they want, they'll look to you two to get what they want. They'll try to interrogate you: think of some way to use you as leverage against me. How will that help me? How will you be able to support me when you're all tied up in this mess too? How will that help us? I want you both to be out of sight and, hopefully, out of mind when they show up here. We must divide ourselves now to conquer this situation. This is one time when the sum of ourselves separated is greater than the whole of us together."

"But David—"

"No buts today, Annie."

"Mom, I understand what he's doing now. I think we should leave."

I've won Christy over. It's two on one now. Time to seal the deal with Annie. "I'll keep in close touch with you guys. Text or call to check up on me, if you'd like. I'll let you know if I need you."

"Promise?"

"Promise, but please hurry."

Within fifteen minutes, Christy and Annie had packed the essentials for a few days away. The bags were loaded into Annie's Prius that was headed twenty minutes north to her father's place. The coast was clear.

David sat in his living room with oil and a rod, cleaning his Civil War Sharps carbine, the only gun he owned. It wasn't that he anticipated using it —there's not much anyone can do with a rifle that can only fire three rounds per minute. It's no help at all if the entire law enforcement system is breaking down your front door. But he needed to occupy himself. This was a way to take the edge off while waiting for Armageddon.

And it didn't take long before there was a knock at the door.

CHAPTER 32

David knew it was them when he heard a rap on the front door. Everyone who was anyone in David's life knew to come to the side door because he'd disconnected the front doorbell. It was a simple but elegant call-screening system that even tech-savvy Christy appreciated. The undesirables endlessly pressed the doorbell button to no avail. Eventually they would give up and leave without disturbing anyone in the house.

That is, unless the undesirables were so persistent that they actually put knuckles to wood. The last person who had knocked at the front door was Phillip, on the first day David had met him after his release. But David knew it wasn't Phillip knocking this time. He knew Phillip was staying away to protect the three of them.

David unlocked the deadbolt and cracked the door slightly. "Yes, can I help you?" He used his best, pseudo-polite, get-off-my-front-porch voice.

Two middle-aged, crumpled blue suits perched on the doorstep. They both stood about six feet in their wingtips, with the same medium build. One guy sported unkempt salt and pepper hair; the other had dealt with a receding hairline by reverting to a shaved head. Salt and Pepper had his top shirt button undone. His solid navy blue tie was loose and cockeyed. Baldy's turkey neck rolled over his choke-hold collar and brown polyester tie. Wrinkles accentuated their white dress shirts, and it wasn't just from wearing seatbelts.

Baldy intoned, "We're detectives from the New York State Police Bureau of Criminal Investigations." Both men flipped open and shut their badge cases like they were street dealers in a three-card monte game. Now you see them, now you don't. "We'd like to come in and ask you a few questions, if you don't mind, Mr. Thompson." He used his best, pseudo-polite, don't-make-me-break-down-the-door voice.

David scanned the street behind them for a moment. He saw an unmarked blue Chevy Tahoe parked in front of his house, with a black one parked in back of it. David spotted two people in the black unit, on high alert in the front seat eying the scene at his door. The blue one was empty, which told David its occupants were on his doorstep. "Hey, I'd like to see those badges again." The detectives looked at one another and then slowly removed the cases from their suit pockets. David held out his hand through the door opening crack.

The detectives glanced at one another again. "Don't worry, I'll give them back." David took the badges and studied them. He read their names and gave the badges back before stepping outside and closing the door behind him. David took out a pen and a spiral pocket notebook from his back pocket and began writing the detectives' names down. "I'm writing your names down. Please understand that it's nothing personal. Recently I got pulled over by a pair of corrections officers impersonating police officers. Ever since then, I've made it a point to look at the badges more closely. Now what can I do for you two gentlemen?"

Baldy said, "We'd like to step inside and ask you some questions."

"Do your friends want to come in too?" David said, gesturing with his head at the black SUV.

"No," Salt and Pepper said, "they're fine."

"Are they from the State Police, too?"

"No," Baldy replied.

"Where are they from?"

The two detectives glanced again at one another. "We can't tell you at this point," Baldy asserted.

"Is that right?"

"So can we come in?" Salt and Pepper asked again.

"Do you guys have papers to serve me at this point?"

"What are you talking about?"

"You know, like a search warrant?"

"No," Salt and Pepper said. "We just want to ask you some questions. We thought we could do it inside because it's cold out here."

"Don't worry about me. I'll be fine out here." David wasn't about to let them step over the threshold. He didn't want them to see all the family pictures around his home. He didn't want them scoping out his house to find information to support a search warrant. As far as he knew, the State Police also were involved in this in some way. The tactical throwable camera with its kill-David-Thompson message was proof positive. "What's on your mind?"

"We're looking for Phillip Dawkins," Baldy said. "We want to talk to him."

"Okay."

"Well, do you know where he might be now?" Baldy asked.

"I don't, but even if I did I couldn't tell you."

"Why is that, Mr. Thompson?" Salt and Pepper asked.

"Attorney-client privilege."

"Phillip Dawkins is your client?" Baldy scoffed.

"Yes."

"Since when?" Baldy needled.

"I can't say."

"Why not?" Salt and Pepper asked.

"Attorney-client privilege." David couldn't tell them about the timing of his representation, as it might implicate Phillip in a crime. No matter what, though, David wasn't about to tell them that Phillip unknowingly became his client the minute they showed up at his door. He decided to invent and play the attorney-client privilege card to put an end to the questioning before it got started.

"Is Mr. Dawkins in your house?" Baldy inquired.

"I already answered that I didn't know where he was. I think that covers your question. By the way, there's nobody in the house but me."

"Where were you earlier today?" Salt and Pepper asked.

"What does that question have to do with locating Phillip Dawkins?"

"Are you hiding something, Mr. Thompson?" Salt and Pepper asked. "If you aren't going to answer our questions, it might implicate you—"

"Implicate me in what? What crime are you investigating?"

Baldy was up to bat now. "We're investigating the death of Martin Klein-schmit in Hampton Manor."

"I saw that incident reported on the television. The reporter said that the police didn't suspect foul play."

"We don't at this time, but we still need to investigate it," Baldy said.

"How do you think he may have died?" David wanted to confirm that they were still working from the same script that the TV newsman had read.

Baldy glanced back at the black SUV, took a deep breath, then exhaled. "We think he might have slipped at the edge of the pool and hit his head on the concrete lip before drowning."

"Well, you showed up here looking for Phillip Dawkins. I already told you he's not here and I don't know where he is, and that's all I'm going to say. Unless you have a warrant, I think our conversation is over. And by the way, you can tell your friends in the black SUV that I've made arrangements for everything I know to be made public in the event that any harm comes to me, my family, or to Phillip Dawkins."

Baldy's eyes bulged and his mouth dropped open for a few seconds. "Those two in the SUV will want to know if your arrangements include a list of names."

David had no clue what he was talking about, but he ran with the ball. "Absolutely everything, including my lists. They'll understand." It was a total bluff on David's part. He hadn't set up any such thing yet. But he needed to put that idea out there to buy some protection until he did make those arrangements. "Have a good evening, gentlemen." With that, David stepped into his house and shut the door.

David peered out a sidelight to the front door as the detectives schlepped to the black SUV. His heart thumped; sweat trickled down his forehead. He didn't have a Plan B if they all decided to converge on the house.

When the vehicles finally drove off, David breathed a sigh of relief. His ploy had worked. After he gathered himself, he texted Annie that he had met with the police and that everything was fine for now. She and Christy could return home the next morning.

Leaning against the front door, David wondered what list of names Baldy was talking about. He had sifted through the stash of papers Johnny had retrieved from Edith's file cabinet and there wasn't a list anywhere in the pile. Besides, he didn't think anyone knew about Johnny's haul and delivery to David.

David didn't buy Baldy's theory of how Martin Kleinschmit accidentally died any more than Baldy apparently believed it. The explanation sounded like it was right out of the 1953 CIA assassination manual: "the most efficient accident, in simple assassination, is a fall of 75 feet or more onto a hard surface."

In David's mind, there was no difference between a fall of 75 feet and a slip and fall by the edge of a pool, so long as the target ended up dead. But he didn't believe for a second that Kleinschmit was assassinated by the CIA like Frank Olson. He feared that Phillip had something to do with Kleinschmit's death, and that the CIA—the people in the black SUV— were using that accident theory to bury their new brainwashing operation. The last thing the spooks wanted was for a state murder investigation to uncover their operation at Kranston. They couldn't risk being publicly exposed in a courtroom by David or any lawyer in Phillip's defense of a state murder charge. There was only one way for them to deal with Phillip. They needed to arrange for him to have a fatal accident, too.

Just then an epiphany hit David and he flew down the stairway to his office. When he had given up on his crusade against solitary, he didn't bother to tell the Bureau of Prisons. The bureau kept sending David documents to comply with his previous Freedom of Information Act requests. The system was slow as a glacier but equally unstoppable. So his requests were still being complied years after they were first made, long after he had given up the quest. David had simply piled up their mailed responses in a corner of his paneled office. He never even bothered to open up the large brown envelopes that bore the NY State Seal.

Within seconds, he was tearing open envelopes and scouring the contents for anything that resembled a list. A half hour later, David's sweaty fist curled around a list of first names, followed by the first letter of their family names, ending with a numerical eight digit code. He found the list stapled to the back of a bunch of spreadsheets that contained statistics about prisoners at Kranston.

Aghast at the implications, he flipped through the pages of the list backward to find the beginning. There were hundreds of names, maybe over a thousand names, mostly women. It just ran on and on: Marie G 1246920; Gladys W 15736269; Shirley D 18954723; Mary K 18957846; Louis F 19429821; Marian M 19864327. When he got to the top of the list, he saw the typed heading to the document. It read, "Allan Memorial Institute Participants."

Oh my god. I don't believe it.

David searched for and located the boilerplate cover letter that always accompanied a Freedom of Information Act response. Dated two years earlier, the letterhead read "Kranston Maximum Security Prison." The letter itself was signed by Edith Nowak on behalf of Martin Kleinschmit, Superintendent.

Bada bing, bada boom.

Now it all made sense. David had read newspaper articles stating that there were fewer than 100 participants in the Allan Institute experiments. Nobody knew for sure because CIA Director Richard Helms had ordered most of the MK-Ultra records destroyed in 1973. But David held evidence in his hands that proved there were close to a thousand victims.

Most if not all of the people on the list were probably dead. But if the existence of the list splashed into the headlines, it would be a public relations nightmare for the CIA. Family members of the victims, if they could be identified, would scream bloody murder and deluge the CIA with lawsuits for years to come.

Now David knew the primary reason he was a CIA target. It wasn't simply because he had campaigned against solitary. It was because he accidentally received this list from Edith Nowak. Kleinschmit and the CIA knew that he had it and they were terrified. They all wanted to kill David to bury the list with him.

CHAPTER 33

The next Saturday, the Thompson family gathered for supper in the dining room. Their dinner prayer included Phillip, just as it had every night that week.

As portions of turkey, mashed potatoes, and salad were being passed around the table, Annie took her turn to ask the inevitable first question of the meal. "David, have you heard anything from Phillip?"

"Yeah, anything, Dad?" echoed Christy.

David sighed. "No, I'm afraid not." His shoulders slumped at the thought of endless unanswered questions.

"Where do you think he went?" Christy asked.

"Oh, I think he's hiding somewhere. He can make himself small. He can live in small places." David didn't mention that he had checked their shed for Phillip. But he saw no sign that the man had set foot there since the day David hid him under a tarp when he first arrived on their doorstep. "They had a brief TV news report from Most Holy Redeemer Cemetery today about Martin Kleinschmit. At the end of it they mentioned Phillip again."

"Oh, was it Kleinschmit's funeral today?" Annie asked.

"Yes, it was quite a show. There were COs in dress blues with white gloves serving as pallbearers. Bureau of Prison officials sang his praises before they lowered his casket into the ground, while a guy in a kilt played 'Amazing Grace' on the bagpipes."

"Sheesh, what a crock," Christy muttered.

Annie scowled. "I don't like to say it, but that man had an accident coming to him." David had told them both in detail about Martin Kleinschmit and his experiments on Phillip—the electroshock therapy, the messaging indoctrination, the LSD.

"Maybe it wasn't an accident," David said. He wanted to suggest that Phillip might have been involved in Kleinschmit's death. Annie's and Christy's enthusiastic support for Phillip needed to be contained without revealing too much.

David hadn't told them he'd followed Phillip out to Kleinschmit's house and found the superintendent dead in the pool. In his mind, he was asserting the attorney-client privilege not only against the state police, but also with Annie and Christy. The less they knew the better, just in case the state cops ever made a return visit. Since their house call the week before, David hadn't heard a peep from them. Things were quiet, almost too quiet.

"I'm very worried about Phillip," Annie said.

David replied, "Yes, you've mentioned that before—"

"Why doesn't he reach out to us?" she asked.

"Maybe it's for the better," David said. He saw his opportunity to plant another seed of doubt that he could draw upon later, if needed. "I got the DNA report back from Julius Moore, my FBI contact. He confirmed that Phillip did kill that police officer."

"Really?" Christy said.

"Yeah, really."

"It doesn't matter," Annie said. "I'm still worried about him."

"I figured that—"

"Why do you say that, David?" Annie blurted.

David's instinct was to compliment her while defusing her. "Oh, it's just that you're such a giving and caring person..."

"Unless you're Martin Kleinschmit," Christy cracked.

David chuckled. "Yeah, never get on the wrong side of your mother."

"So I've learned," Christy said, smiling.

Annie shook her head with a grin. "You two . . . but I still think Phillip's a different person than he was thirty years ago. He didn't kill you, David."

"Yes, I can personally attest to that."

"You know what I mean. He had those thoughts in his head about killing you—the ones you told us about that were implanted and inflamed by messaging and drugs. Yet he fought them off. He tried to protect you. I think he's trying to protect you and all of us right now."

"Mom makes sense," Christy added.

"Yes, she does. That's why I married her."

David's cell vibrated; he plucked it from his rear jeans pocket and began reading a text to himself. "Oh my God, it's Phillip!"

"What does he say?" Annie pleaded.

"He wants me to meet him tomorrow morning in the Pine Bush at 6:30 a.m."

"Is he okay?" Christy asked.

David's thumbs were already at work texting him a message. "I'm asking him, right now."

"Can we go too, David?" Annie asked.

David now regretted saying anything about the text. "He sent the text to me. I'm not sure you should go."

"Does it say we *shouldn't* come?" Annie asked.

David took a deep breath. "No, it doesn't."

"I want to go," Christy said. "If he's hurt, I can treat him. I'll bring my EMT bag with me. You can't bring him to a hospital."

David hated to admit it, but the kid made sense. Out of the three of them, as someone with emergency medical training, he was the only one who could care for Phillip. If they had to bring him to the hospital, they'd have to identify him. If they lied about his identity, the authorities would find him out soon enough. It would be game over for Phillip and they'd all be caught up in the mess.

David first needed to find out if Phillip was really hurt before putting his family at risk. If Phillip was in good shape, David would tell Christy to stay home. David picked up his cell, pulled up the contact number for Phillip, and dialed. But Phillip didn't pick up and he couldn't leave a message because the voicemail feature still hadn't been activated.

Over the next few hours, David continued to frantically text Phillip, but he never got a response.

"If he's not responding, he's probably hurt," Annie worried.

"I don't know, Annie. Maybe he just turned off his cell to conserve his battery or to prevent them from tracking him."

"Dad, they can't track his burner phone. They don't have his number. He probably paid cash for it."

"Yeah, but he doesn't know that. Phillip isn't tech savvy and he's paranoid. But you're right, you should come if we don't hear from him by tomorrow morning. Besides, if I have to carry him, I'll need your help."

"Well, if Christy is coming with you, then I'm tagging along too," Annie insisted.

David knew he wouldn't be able to keep Annie home short of locking her in the closet if her teenage son was going.

The Three Musketeers had been reunited again. One for all, all for one.

CHAPTER 34

Dawn was breaking when David, Annie, and Christy rolled into the Pine Bush parking lot in Annie's Prius wagon. On the way over, David had kept an eagle eye on his rearview for anyone who might follow them. But there wasn't any traffic around this early. It was 6:15 a.m., so the parking lot was empty. The visitor center didn't open until 10 a.m. on Sundays.

The three of them entered the trailhead at a fast walk. Christy was carrying his EMT bag, just in case.

"Where is he, David?" Annie asked.

"He said to meet him near a tree."

"There are a lot of trees here, Dad."

"Don't worry, I know the tree. Phillip and I hiked here once, so I know the tree he's talking about. When we get to the top of this dune, it will come into view." The text told David to meet Phillip under the pitch pine where they found the baby bird. It was a spot he would always remember.

The sun popped above the horizon, piercing the morning mist as they reached the top of the dune and stopped to catch their collective breath. Walking in sand, even on a trail, is harder than it looks. As they stood in the stillness a breeze shimmied the blooming lupines in the valley below. The season's second and final brood of Karner Blues was about to hatch. David looked toward the base of the designated tree, about thirty yards down the trail. But there was no sign of Phillip standing there.

"Do you see him, David?"

"No, but I see the tree. Let's keep walking."

As they moved down the dune, the bole of the tree came into clear view. But Phillip was nowhere to be found.

"What's that?" Annie asked, pointing to the base of the tree trunk.

"It looks like there's a knapsack on the ground, leaning up against the tree," Christy said. "It probably belongs to Mr. Dawkins."

"But where is he?" Annie asked.

The three of them stood under the tree's sparse canopy turning in circles, searching in the cover provided by the scrub oak for some sign of him.

"Phillip!" David whisper-shouted. "Phillip, are you here?"

But there was no sign of him. The breeze gathered strength into a wind gust. As it blew, the pitch pine branches above them creaked like the worn hinges on an ancient door.

When the gust subsided, much of the creaking stopped. But above the trio the rasping persisted, like the ghostly sound of a barely moving rocking chair.

When David looked up toward the source of that sound, he saw a wrapped purple bedsheet suspended from a branch directly above him.

David backed away to get a better view. The bedsheet was hanging by a rope and swayed in unison with the creaking sound that was now fading. David figured that something was wrapped in the sheet, weighting the rope down, causing it to stretch and creak. Just then, David made out the soles of a pair of men's shoes hanging above him followed by the shape of lower legs wrapped tightly in that sheet. "Oh my God!" he screamed.

Annie and Christy looked up and gasped. Something in the shape of a person gently twisted in the dawn air above them.

Annie rushed into David's arms. She hid her face in his neck and began to cry. "David, please tell me it's not Phillip. Please tell me it's not him."

David stared in shock at the figure, and felt moisture began to gather in his burning eyes. His throat closed so tight that he couldn't immediately answer his wife. He simply wrapped his arms around the most important thing in his life and embraced her.

As a ride-along volunteer EMT, Christy had been to grisly crime scenes before, but a body hanging in a tree was a first. He ripped open his EMT bag and grabbed his rescue knife—the same knife he used to smash car windows and cut seat belts off crash victims. Within seconds, his lithe young form went into monkey mode scaling the trunk of the tree. When he inched out on the limb and reached for the rope, he called down, "Dad, can you try and catch it?"

"I'll try," David said, wiping the tears from his eyes. He released Annie and gently moved her out of the way, sitting her down on a fallen pitch pine. She was openly sobbing now. "Hold on a second," David said, quickly scraping leaves, branches, and pine needles into a pile with his feet.

"Hurry, Dad! I'm not sure if he's still alive."

"Okay, I'm set. Can you tell if it's Phillip?"

Christy started to saw at the rope with his blade. "No, I can't see his face. It's blocked by the sheet."

David stood on the impromptu brush pile, hands extended up over his head, feet shoulder length apart, looking up at the grotesque shape hanging ten feet above him. *Maybe it's O'Neil? Did Phillip somehow kidnap O'Neil and hang him?*

"Here it comes," Christy shouted, as the rope fibers frayed and then snapped.

The body dropped straight down and David did his best to grab it around the middle as it hit the ground. He laid his burden down on the pile of brush as gently as he could and peeled back the sheet around the head.

"Is it him, David? Please tell me it's not him." Annie had her hands over her face and her shoulders shook from the stress.

David's face fell as a man's eyes came into view. They were open, blood-shot red, with no sign of life, looking right through David. Then the rest of his face came into view. "NOOOOO!" There was a hangman's noose wrapped around Phillip's neck. "It's Phillip!"

"Oh, dear God!" Annie wailed.

David tucked his fingers under the rope and furiously tugged at the noose, trying to loosen it. Christy scurried down the tree and took Phillip's hand to check for a pulse. David's eyes locked on Christy's but Christy shook his head. They both yanked the noose until it came loose, then pulled it off over his head.

David put his palm on Phillip's chest. There was no discernable heartbeat, so he began thrusting it down every few seconds.

Christy gently touched Phillip's eyelids, then his jaw, then his neck. Finally he stood up and turned to his father as tears began to slide through the emerging beard shadow on his young face.

David glanced up at Christy "Come on, Christy. We can't give up so easily."

"It's no use, Dad—"

"Why not?"

Christy wiped his nose with his sleeve. "There's rigor mortis in his eyes, his jaw, and his neck. He's been dead for a few hours."

David stopped, threw his head back with his eyes closed and fists clenched. He dropped to his knees on the forest floor and let the tears of frustration and sorrow leak onto the hands that were now in his lap.

"I'm sorry, Dad," Christy whispered. He sat down next to his father and put an arm around his shaking shoulders. Annie stumbled to David's other side and put her arm around him too. David hadn't seen her cry so hard since the day her favorite aunt died ten years earlier. The three of them embraced for what seemed an eternity until Christy pulled the sheet back over Phillip's head.

David rubbed his eyes and face dry. Then he cleared his throat of gathering anger and spat out, "Those bastards killed him."

Annie and Christy exchanged confused glances. "What are you talking about, David?"

"They tracked Phillip down and captured him. It was them who used Phillip's phone and texted me last night to come get him this morning. They strung him up; they murdered him. They tried to make it look like a suicide, an accident." Suddenly, David stood up and scanned the woods and the fields around him. He knew they were somewhere spying on his every move. But there was nobody in sight. The Pine Bush was quiet except for the wind and the birds.

"Who's they?" Annie asked.

"The CIA. That's what they do, you know. It's called the Frank Olson treatment. When an operative is of no use to them anymore, they terminate them and make it look like an accident. Look at Martin Kleinschmit. Slip and fall? I don't think so." David hated himself for bringing Annie and Christy with him. Now the CIA would know they were all involved with Phillip. *The Three Musketeers* had all just become potential targets for termination.

"What do we do now, David?"

"I don't know. I really don't know." David knew he and his family had left DNA all over the scene. He shouldn't have cut Phillip down and touched his body. If he had known it was Phillip and was sure that he was dead, David would have just left him hanging there and walked away with his family. He could have reported the accident anonymously. Woulda, shoulda, coulda. But it was too late.

Christy stood up and went to where Phillip's knapsack leaned against the trunk of the tree. There was an envelope duct-taped to the side of it. David's name was handwritten on the front. "Dad, you need to see this. There's an envelope with your name on it."

"Really? Bring it over here."

Christy peeled it from the knapsack and handed it to his father.

David opened the envelope. "It's a letter to me. It looks like Phillip's handwriting."

Annie sniffled and took a shuddering breath. "Could you read it to us, David?"

"Okay. Here it goes." David had no way of knowing that in his goodbye note Phillip had written a manifesto for lost souls.

Dear David,

I'm so sorry to leave you and your wonderful family. I didn't decide to take my life on a whim. It was something I've thought about long and hard over the past month. The way I see it, I really don't have any choice.

I apologize that you're finding me this way and for handing you this mess to clean up. I wish I could have somehow done this without involving you. But it seems you can't clean up after yourself if you take your own life, no matter how much you want to.

Whoever is pursuing me now has been relentless. I've been camped out in the Pine Bush since I left Kleinschmit's home. I disguised myself as best I could and walked through the woods to the same Stewart's store on the corner every morning to get the paper. My story hasn't dropped out of coverage. Every day there's some-thing about me in the news. A few days ago, I saw a leaflet with my picture thumb-tacked to the Stewart's community bulletin board. Yesterday, when I got to Stewart's, I saw a black SUV with its emergency lights flashing. I sensed they were getting close. Even if I moved on, it was just a matter of time before they tracked me down and cornered me. I know they wouldn't stop until they had me, and I could not let them take me alive.

There is nothing more of any meaning to my current life on this planet. I can't change what I did to that police officer thirty years ago. It was wrong and I'm sorry. I feel horrible about what I did to him and his family. I'd like to show that I'm not the same man any longer. I'd like a second chance to prove myself. I think everyone should get a second chance. I thought this country was all about second chances. But I guess that idea doesn't apply to me. I'll forever be judged by that one day.

I'm not saying I should be a free man. I did wrong and I understand and accept my life sentence. For me, my second chance was in the opportunity to join the general population. But if by some small chance they took me alive, you know as well as I do that I'd be back in the box, especially now that Kleinschmit is dead. I cannot and will not go back to the box. I know I'd end up killing myself there, if they didn't kill me first.

I learned long ago that while I have very little control over my life, at least I have control over my death. You can't worry about what you can't control. There's no point in it. So I've been less and less concerned about my life as they have pursued me on the outside of Kranston. Some days I was downright apathetic about my life, and I know you commented about my bad attitude on more than a few occasions.

Ever since I killed that police officer, I have lost control of my life. You know they put me in a box and tortured me for decades. I guess they figure two wrongs make a right. I died a little every day, inch by inch, and it was constant torment.

The people who are politically and morally against the death penalty have no idea they live in a state that has something worse than the death penalty. They have a system that tortures its prisoners in solitary until they are either thrown into the streets or they die in prison. The first outcome is downright dangerous to everyone. The second outcome is a waste of resources and a waste of a life.

THEY SHOULD TERMINATE US INSTEAD OF TORTURING US. The unstated goal of this day-to-day torture is for us to kill ourselves. You know, to do the state a favor. They want us to execute ourselves in our sealed boxes—our coffins —because they can't do it alone, although they've been known to do their best to help out. All this happens while the people on the outside live in ignorant bliss. They believe they live in a state that doesn't have the death penalty, so they feel good about themselves. This goes on in far too many states today.

I understand that some prisoners need to be in solitary. Maybe I needed to be in solitary, for a time at least. But as I learned, once I was in the box for me there was no way out.

As I've told you I was not allowed to attend my administrative segregation review hearings. I'm not allowed to have an attorney there either. Under the law, the reviews are supposed to be every sixty days—maybe it's every thirty days now. It doesn't matter. They view the review process as a joke because they have skipped doing them altogether recently for long periods of time.

Now they've taken back the bare due process bone they tossed us with these reviews. They don't follow their own rules. You know, a review every 120, 240, 480 days—it's all the same to them because they know the results will be the same. They just rubber-stamp my solitary sentence, regardless of whether I've been clean of disciplinary tickets for five years or if I've had hundreds of tickets. It makes no difference. There is no program designed to reward good behavior with release to the general population.

While I have lost control of my life and there's nothing I can do about it, I can't live with myself if I don't try to control my death. NO INMATE WANTS TO DIE IN PRISON. It's like serving an afterlife sentence. While my actions in my life here on earth deserved a life sentence, my soul—the entity I've become over three decades —doesn't deserve a sentence of eternal damnation behind prison walls.

If I died in prison, I'd have no next of kin who'd claim my body. Any relatives that I have left are distant, they don't know me and they'd have to pay my funeral expenses if they claimed me. If they didn't try to bail me out in life, you can bet they aren't going to bail out my cold dead body.

I know you'd try to claim it, but I doubt they'd give it to you because you aren't next of kin. That's what the rule says and they'll choose to enforce this rule. The last thing they'd want is an outside autopsy of me. Kranston wants my body because it's also a show of power to every other inmate that there is no hope for them either. Everybody in the system knows me and they would know the system beat me. I can't take the chance that they'd keep my body.

Prison is all about crushing hope. If they have me, they'd bury me in a plywood box with some cheap marker that would disappear in a year. Nobody would be allowed to visit me. Not a chance anyone would put a penny on my headstone. I'd be six feet under and lost in some prison burial field. I cannot die in peace knowing that this was my fate.

I want to die here in the Pine Bush. It's a place I've grown to love. I never experienced anything like the sweet scent of the lupines and the dancing Karner Blues.

You were right, David, I am like a pitch pine. And I chose to die by hanging from one of my own.

They want you to believe that Kleinschmit died in an accident. Well, if self-defense is considered an accident, so be it. He came after me and I defended myself. We were locked in a wrestling match by the pool when we fell in. His head split open when it hit the pool's edge. But I know nobody is going to believe the word of an ex-con over the life of a prison superintendent. When he just floated there without moving, I set the mare free and ran the same way she did.

But don't cry for him. At least he got the death penalty and wasn't tortured. He deserved to die. My talk with him caused memories to surface in my mind. I recalled being electroshocked in the finished basement of his house. I'm sure of it. And David, you were right. The DNA doesn't lie. I am Janet's Nowak's father. I remember that they raped me, stole my sperm, and implanted it in Edith Nowak. She was unconscious and lying on a table next to me in the basement. I've learned since then that the process is called electroejaculation. They use the procedure on impaired men who are unable to normally impregnate women.

You see, Kleinschmit knew O'Neil had sex with Edith Nowak once (per your text) when she was under age. He knew he needed to have something to come of it to gain control over O'Neil. It would be leverage so he and the CIA could continue the brainwashing experiments. I don't think O'Neil was part of the CIA op. It was going to be O'Neil's child no matter what any paternity results said. Kleinschmit got in the middle of it and sold O'Neil on the idea it was his child. He brokered a deal that O'Neil could live with. Kleinschmit and Nowak would shut up about O'Neil's indiscretion if he got Nowak a job and paid her off, and if he didn't interfere with Kleinschmit's experiments at Kranston. These deep, dark secrets cemented their relationship for all time.

I regret that I'll never be able to know and love my daughter. But it's for the best. Please don't ever tell Janet Nowak that I was her father. Let that mystery die with me. If she found out I was her real father, it would haunt her forever. I cannot ruin my daughter's life the way mine has been ruined.

I don't want anyone to learn of my death, David. No funeral services for me. I want the system and the CIA to think I'm alive and well. I want them to hunt me until the end of time. I can die peacefully knowing that they'll chase me forever and that they'll never catch me. Serves them right. The idea that I'm alive and running free might give some cons in solitary the hope they need to survive.

That's where you come in, David. I don't want you to bury me. I want you to have me cremated and spread my ashes in a field of wild blue lupines here in the Pine Bush. I've made arrangements with Steven Benson, Winding Brook Road, Gloversville, to cremate me in a large ceramics kiln he owns. He's an ex-con friend who spent five years in solitary. He owes me big time. You can find him in the phone book. Take me there and he'll take care of the rest.

You'll find sixty handwritten letters I've composed to Edmund O'Neil in my knapsack. I figured if he's so afraid of his life being ruined by exposing his secret daughter, I might as well blackmail him from the grave to try and change the rules for solitary confinement. With Kleinschmit gone, he needs someone else in his life to blackmail him. Tag, I'm it!

I already sent him one yesterday, with instructions not to retire. There's a copy enclosed. Just pick and choose a few letters and put them in mailboxes around the state or other parts of the country every year, as you see fit. It will be our experiment to see if we can change the system from the top down.

Be careful. Think about using a remailing service or dropping the letters in a rural post office box. Keep away from cameras. No licking envelopes or stamps. If you wear latex gloves when you touch them, you should be golden. Oh, and most importantly, I recorded the conversations I had with O'Neil and Kleinschmit on my cell phone. That's also in my knapsack. Those recordings will provide some solid life insurance for you.

In my knapsack, you'll also find the carving knife I stole from you on the first day when I came to your house. I must apologize for doing that. I felt vulnerable that day. I felt like someone was going to jump me because I wasn't used to being in open space environments. Of course, on top of it all, I had those wild thoughts about killing you, thanks to Kleinschmit.

Don't mourn me, David. Tell your family not to cry for me either. Trust me, I'm in a better place now. For the first time that I can remember, I'm free and truly happy.

I'll always be there for you, David. I'll always be there for Annie and Christy too. I'll be there in spirit. Look for me.

Your friend forever,

Phillip

The three of them sat silently staring into the sand, not knowing what to think or say to one another.

Finally, Annie spoke. "Do you think the letter is really from him?"

David recognized the handwriting from the letters he received from Phillip while he was at Kranston. The pages were numbered just like the letters Phillip sent David. It was also written on the same type of narrow ruled paper. And Phillip always used both sides of the paper as he did with this letter. "Yes, it looks and sounds like it's really from him."

"I don't think anyone made him write that letter," Christy said.

"I think you're right," David said. "The CIA wouldn't have let him write a lot of this. It wouldn't be in their best interest. They certainly wouldn't have let Phillip give us those recordings or those letters he penned to O'Neil."

"So it doesn't sound like the CIA was involved," Annie said.

"No, I think he managed to elude them. To me, it looks like Phillip took his life on his own and this is his suicide note."

"I wasn't going to say anything, Dad, but it looked like he died with a smile on his face."

"Yeah, I saw that. He did say he was the happiest he'd ever been in the letter."

Annie shook her head, took out a tissue and blew her nose. "Electroshock? Electroejaculation? Confinement in a box no bigger than my closet day and night? No hope for release, no matter what his behavior? I think it's awful what they did to him. Just plain awful."

"You're right, Annie."

"What do we do now?" Christy asked.

"In his honor," David replied, "I think we should do exactly as he asked."

"Agreed," Annie said.

Christy nodded his head.

"We've got to move fast," David said. "People will be out on these trails soon enough. We've got to use this sheet of his to carry him out of here before anyone sees us. Annie, grab the knapsack and the EMT bag. Christy, grab the other end of the sheet so you and I can carry him out."

"I'm going to miss him," Annie said.

"Me too, Mom."

"Come on, let's get out of here," David urged.

As he and Christy carried Phillip away, David thought about the conversation he had with Phillip as the helpless baby bird lay under that very same tree a few months ago. When Phillip spotted it, he lifted his boot up and over it. He almost crushed it before David stopped him.

"Were you going to kill that baby bird, Phillip?"

"I want to put it out of its misery."

"It still has a chance, Phillip. The mother might tend to him."

"The mother needs to learn that she can't save him."

CHAPTER 35

Two weeks later, early on a Saturday morning, the four of them were driving in the Mustang on their way to the Pine Bush. David was behind the wheel, Annie rode shotgun, and Christy sat in the backseat next to Phillip.

Phillip was contained in a 6" x 8" used Amazon cardboard box complete with its smile logo. Steven Benson, Phillip's ex-con friend, had cremated Phillip's body in his kiln. Then he sealed his bones and ashes in a plastic bag before packing him up. It was the last box that Phillip Dawkins would ever have to endure.

An echoing silence filled the Mustang, as everyone in the car was lost in thought. After holding their own informal short service, David and his family planned to honor Phillip's request and set his spirit free in a field of wild blue lupines. It would be the second memorial David attended that week in as many days

Yesterday, he had attended a wake for Edith Nowak. She died the day after Phillip took his own life. The obituary in the Albany *Times Union* requested contributions to the American Cancer Society in lieu of flowers in her memory, though the same paper reported a week ago that she died from a gun accident in her house. Julius told David she had taken her own life; her closed casket confirmed that story. The events of thirty years ago, the electroshock torture, the messaging, all had claimed her before any metastasizing cells could finish her off. Estranged from her daughter Janet over the secret identity of Janet's father, Edith had died with a broken heart in her chest and a .22 caliber rifle under her chin.

Johnny McFadden stood in his dress blues just inside the door of the funeral home at Edith's wake. He said his CO union rep had volunteered him for ceremonial duty at the service that would follow. David pulled him aside for a catch-up chat.

"So, how's it going, Johnny?"

"Your friend Dawkins has caused quite a stir. Every available law enforcement person in the region has been out looking for him."

"So I've heard." Julius had told David the same thing.

"Well, I know better than to ask if you have any idea where he is. And if you do know, please don't tell me. I don't want that kind of information at this point."

"Why do you say that, Johnny?"

"It doesn't matter to me anymore because I'm looking for a new job. I need to get out of this line of work. The system spares no one, you understand? It eats at the souls of the keepers too. I'm treating my kid like she's an inmate. My temper has gotten worse, according to my wife. I can see where this is going and I'm getting off this ride. I need to get out before it's too late for me."

"There's no chance of things getting better?"

"There's been a lot of chatter about changing the system for the inmates from the top down this past week. More so than usual. Some guys believe it will be better for us COs, but the old timers—the men in charge—are entrenched in their views. They've vowed to fight any change to the system that consumed their lives. I believe it will get worse before it has even the slightest chance of getting better."

"I understand. Good luck in your new employment hunt. Excuse me. I need to get in line here for the coffin before viewing hours end." David wanted to pay his respects to Edith; at the same time he wanted to meet and console Phillip's daughter. When it was his turn, he knelt before the polished wood box and said a prayer. *Edith, I know you lived a life in anguish these past few months. I hope and pray that you're at peace now.*

After he rose from the padded prie-dieu and turned away from the coffin, David looked at the receiving line that led off to the side. He saw Edmund O'Neil hug Janet. David realized he was there as her mother's former boss, not as her father. He had his wife and family in tow beside and behind him.

At a distance, David recognized echoes of Edith in Janet's face. But right before he introduced himself, he saw she had Phillip's fierce gray eyes. When she reached out to shake his hand, he saw and felt her large hands. Yes, she was Phillip's daughter.

"Hello, I'm David Thompson. I'm sorry for your loss. I had the pleasure of knowing your mother."

"Hello," Janet replied. "I'm sorry; I don't think I know you. Can I ask how you knew my mother?"

"I knew her socially. She always spoke so highly of you. I just wanted to tell you that she loved you very, very much." In relaying her mother's message of love for her, David had fulfilled his promise to Edith Nowak.

Janet's eyes welled up and she smiled sadly through the tears. "Thank you. You don't know how much hearing that means to me."

David spotted a brooch on the shoulder of her black dress. He'd seen it in the Pine Bush gift shop when he visited once with Phillip on one of their outings. It was a Karner Blue butterfly made out of stained glass and silver.

David said, "I really like your pin."

"Thank you. You know, I received it in the mail a few days ago. I didn't order it. It didn't come with a note or anything. There was no return address. I have no idea who sent it."

"Ah, maybe you have a secret admirer then," David said.

Janet chuckled. "Now there's a nice thought. I thought it was just sent to me by mistake. But I like your take better."

David longed to tell her that the jewelry was a present from her father, Phillip. He longed to tell her that her father loved her too. But he knew he couldn't. Some things are best kept secret and this was one of them. He left the wake with a sense of satisfaction. One more door had been closed.

When the Mustang entered the Pine Bush parking lot at 6:30 a.m. for Phillip's last trip, David said, "Guess who I saw at Edith Nowak's wake yesterday?"

"Janet Nowak," Christy guessed.

"Besides her," David said, as he positioned the Mustang next to the trail-head. The lot was empty for the time being. He held his peace, waiting for a response to his question.

The three of them opened their doors to get out. As he swiveled in his bucket seat, David said, "Christy, could you grab Phillip please?"

"Got him," Christy said, as he grasped the box where Phillip remained.

"We give up," Annie said, as the four of them entered the trailhead. "Who did you see?"

"I talked with Edmund O'Neil in private for a few minutes."

"What did he have to say?" Christy asked.

"He withdrew his retirement papers from the state comptroller's office. He plans to keep working as commissioner."

"That's a shocker," Christy said.

"Phillip would be proud of him," Annie said. "Where is Phillip's lupine field?"

"Just over this next dune," David said. "A little further down the rail from where we found him."

"What else did O'Neil say?" Annie asked when they reached the dune's summit. They stopped to catch a breath and take in the view. Soft early morning rays sparkled on the dew that clung to the wild grasses and flowers spread out before them.

"He's going to look into changing the rules for solitary confinement. Maybe create a step-down program where prisoners can transition back into the general population. He could even introduce a solitary confine- ment review process that's actually fair. Look over there. You can see Phillip's field through the trees. Let's keep moving. I don't want anyone to see us and question us when we set Phillip free. We're probably violating some law doing this."

The three of them moved down the dune and past Phillip's tree.

"Wow, who knew that this O'Neil fellow could demonstrate such leader- ship so late in his career," Annie commented.

"I gave him a bit of a nudge. I told him that my recordings, lists, and all of my papers would be released through several law firms in the event anything happens to any of us. As far as he's concerned, that includes Phillip. I told him to share this with all of his acquaintances on a need-to- know basis. I said we'd shut up if they left us alone."

"How did you arrange for that?" Annie asked.

"I gave copies to Jim Fletcher and a few other lawyers in town. I wrote a long narrative about what happened in the form of a signed and notarized affidavit. Paid all the lawyers a hefty fee. They have everything in their safes and know what to do if something happens to us. But I don't think we'll have any problems. O'Neil doesn't want this to go public and neither does the CIA. It's the best life insurance for us our money can buy."

"Did O'Neil ask about Mr. Dawkins, Dad?"

"Yep. I said I didn't know where he was. Then I gave him the attorney-client spiel."

"Do you think they'll actually make any changes to the system?" Annie asked.

"I don't know. O'Neil said it will be a tough sell because of the corrections officers union and the old timers in administration."

"Maybe it's time for Mr. Dawkins to drop another letter to him in the mail," Christy said.

"Yes, perhaps Phillip can offer him some words of encouragement. After listening to Phillip's recordings, it seems Mr. O'Neil is afraid that Phillip may move in next door and pay him and his family a visit. Maybe he needs a reminder of what's at stake if reform doesn't take root. But let's not kid ourselves. Even though he's the top dog, he's only one man. And who knows how much the CIA is involved since Kleinschmit died."

The rising sun was peeking through the trees over Phillip's field when they arrived. The crickets were fading; bumble bees were at the breakfast table feasting on the waist-high wild blue lupines. The flowers were past peak but the field still featured plenty of spires in bloom. Bunched together, they looked like sturdy, long violet fingers reaching up from the ground toward an azure sky. A honey-like fragrance wafted to the heavens as the temperature rose.

The three family members walked off the trail into the lupines and stood side by side. Christy set Phillip down on the ground at their feet.

"Do you guys have anything you'd like to say before we set Phillip free?" David asked.

Annie and Christy looked at one another. "You go first, Mom, unless you want to pass."

Annie sighed. "David, there are so many thoughts and emotions rushing through my head. There's a lot I'd like to say but I don't want to ramble on because I don't want anyone to see us here."

"I understand. Maybe you'd like to say something about what Phillip meant to you? Christy can do the same if he'd like. Then I can offer a prayer."

"I'll try," Annie said. She stood between Christy and David, reached for their hands, and held them tightly. "Phillip, I want to thank you for being a part of our lives. You really opened my eyes. I always thought that people in prison were bad to the core. You taught me that this wasn't true, at least not for you, and it probably isn't true for many others behind bars. Some people can and do change. I saw all the good in you despite what you did when you were so young. I feel horrible about what was done to you in prison. It was wrong. Lord knows you deserved better, and I hope you find the peace you deserve in the afterlife."

"Christy?" David said.

"Mom shared some of my feelings. Mr. Dawkins taught me a lot of things, but if I had to choose one it would be about being mentally strong. One day I sat in my closet for an hour just to see what life was like for him. Let's just say it was hard, and I couldn't imagine doing it for thirty years. But he did and still tried to be a good man, even with all the horror that he went through. I'm not sure I could do that. I'll never forget his inner strength. I'm going to miss him a lot." Christy looked to his dad with misty eyes.

"Dear God," David said, "please bring justice to those in the CIA and others who used Phillip for their evil ends. That's all I'm going to say about those who were directly involved in bringing about his death. Now for the rest of us, let me say this. Dear God, please forgive Phillip. He owned up to killing that innocent police officer. He owned up to the eternal damage he caused that officer's family. Every second of every day for thirty years, he paid a very high price for his sin. God, please forgive us all for our sins in how we treated Phillip. Forgive us for lying to ourselves. We believed that we were merciful and compassionate for not putting Phillip to death for his sin. Instead, we wrapped Phillip up in a nice little soundproof box that was invisible to us, and we created a system that would either drive him mad and/or kill him. God, please forgive us for torturing Phillip for his sin by sentencing him to a box. We lied to ourselves and tortured Phillip over most of his adult life. I believe we committed a sin far greater than Phillip's sin. But in the end, only you can be the judge of that. One person does not make a system. Our collective will over the span of generations has created this system. The system belongs to all of us, and so we own all of its sins. An unjust system is shared by everyone who tolerates it. All of us had a hand in torturing Phillip Dawkins. God, I pray that you can forgive all of us. Finally,

I pray that Phillip's life was not lived in vain. I pray that his life and death will change the system for the better. Amen."

"Amen," Annie and Christy echoed.

David picked Phillip up and split open the packing tape on the box with his car keys. He removed the plastic bag and unzipped the seal on the top. "Dear God, we now give you Phillip and ask for your mercy. We have come here today to set Phillip free in a general population of wild blue lupines. We pray that Phillip will now have in his afterlife what he could not have in this life on earth." The scattering of cremains was imminent.

David dipped his hand into the bag, took out a handful of Phillip's ashes, and threw them up in the air. A gentle breeze spread Phillip among the lupines. Annie whimpered through the hands pressed to her mouth. David and Christy fought back tears. The slowly falling ashes nudged some Karner Blues out of their repose and the butterflies briefly took flight. The second and final brood of the season was enjoying life in the Pine Bush. When the bag was almost empty, David held it upside down and shook it until the last vestiges of Phillip floated away.

When the scattering was done and Phillip had found his rest, the three hugged one another in a family embrace. As they separated to begin the walk back to the car, Christy said, "Wow, Dad, don't move."

David froze. "Why not?"

"Look, there's a butterfly on your shoulder," Annie said, pointing to it.

David turned his head to look. A butterfly faced David, slowly flapping its wings. The wings vibrated as they moved, as if it was stretching them. It was the motion of a newly hatched butterfly, fresh from the cocoon, drying out and preparing for its brief life journey.

"It's a Karner Blue," David said.

"Is that what they call it? It is a beautiful powder blue color," Annie said.

"I love the orange crescents underneath," Christy said. "Is it a male or female?"

"It's a male," David said.

"Looks like you have a friend, Dad. He won't stop staring at you."

After a breeze faded to stillness, the butterfly lifted off and flew among the three of them in a jerky flight pattern. It touched David on his forehead, Christy on his nose, and Annie on her cheek before zigging and zagging around them.

David smiled as it all came together. Phillip had mailed the Karner Blue brooch to Janet. He had departed his life on a pitch pine wrapped in a sheet like a caterpillar in a chrysalis waiting to emerge. The last line in his goodbye letter announced: *I'll always be there for you, David. I'll always be there for Annie and Christy too. I'll be there in spirit. Look for me.*

As the butterfly climbed toward the sun and faded from view, David said, "Peace be with you, Phillip."

~ The End ~

I sincerely hope that you enjoyed *Caged to Kill*. If you did, please share your experience with your friends and family.

I urge you to *please* read the afterword to this book that follows. I think you will be very interested in the backstory to this novel.

I also invite you to read the other two standalone books in the Lawyer David Thompson Legal Thriller Series: *Saving Babe Ruth* and *The Killdeer Connection.*

Please sign up to join my Readers Group by entering this link address http://subscribe.tomswyers.com/JoinReadersGroup. You'll get updates and special offers only available to members.

Finally, please take a few seconds to write a few words about your reading experience with *Caged to Kill* on Amazon by entering this link: http://smarturl.it/ReviewCagedtoKill. Positive reviews encourage authors to write more. Your support is so very much appreciated. Thank you!

AFTERWORD

HELP FREE WILLIAM BLAKE FROM SOLITARY
AFTER 32 YEARS

This afterword was originally a preface to the beginning of the book when it was first published. But a few readers complained in reviews that it negatively impacted their reading experience when they read it before they read the story.

I understand their point of view. Yet I was hoping that *all* readers would be more sympathetic to the plight of real people in solitary and understand my desire to put a spotlight on this situation at the beginning of the book.

One of the challenges today is that the people in solitary are hidden from public view and, by tucking this essay in the back of this book, I wonder if I'm guilty of contributing to this problem.

Anyway, I hope *Caged to Kill* has you thinking about solitary confinement as a form of punishment in the United States and elsewhere. I want to tell you a story about one man living in solitary today. His name is Mr. William Blake.

As the epigraph at the beginning of this book suggests, there is much work to be done in the United States on solitary confinement practices. On the one hand, you have a few states that are taking a leadership role in limiting the role of solitary because of its inherent danger to inmates, our neighborhoods, and prison personnel. At the other end of the spectrum, you have states that joke and laugh about solitary like it's no big deal.

Mr. William Blake inspired me to write *Caged to Kill* and his experience in solitary is no laughing matter. It is the embodiment of much of what is wrong with solitary confinement policy today. Mr. Blake has served thirty-two years straight time in solitary confinement after he was convicted of killing a police officer and wounding another in 1987, when he was twenty-three years old. What he did was horrible and he knows it. That's why he's essentially serving a life sentence. The injustice for Mr. Blake is that while he was sentenced to a life in prison, he was not sentenced to a lifetime in solitary confinement. And yet he has not served a single day of his sentence outside of solitary confinement. For over three decades, he has been housed all alone in a closet-sized cage for twenty-three hours per day. The United Nations has cited his treatment as an example of torture. In 2013, the United Nations Special Rapporteur concluded that the rights of Mr. Blake "to be free from torture have been violated, and that the practice of solitary confinement in New York State violates the international obligations of the United States of America."

I crossed paths with Mr. Blake two years ago when he desperately sent out a batch of twenty random letters to attorneys in New York looking for legal help to get him out of solitary confinement. There are about 177,000 lawyers in New York and I haven't practiced a day of criminal law in my life. I knew nothing about Mr. Blake and, because I'm not a famous author, judge, or attorney, and he knew nothing about me. I wrote him back and explained that as a solo practitioner, I was ill-equipped to devote the necessary manpower and resources on his behalf in a protracted legal battle that would last years and would then likely involve years of appeals. Over the course of the next few letters, I told Mr. Blake that I might be able to raise awareness of his plight by writing a work of fiction about a character dealing with the effects of solitary confinement. Mr. Blake agreed to help. We began to correspond, and a story slowly took shape in my head as Mr. Blake detailed his stay in solitary confinement and the challenges faced by people in solitary everywhere. Aided by Mr. Blake's insights, shared with me in over 300 pages of correspondence, and guided by my own research into solitary confinement and other historical events, my imagination created *Caged to Kill* and its characters.

I didn't meet Mr. Blake until nearly two years later, after I had finished the novel. When I first visited him in late January of 2019, I expected to meet someone who would be treated by prison personnel like he was Hannibal Lecter from *Silence of the Lambs.* You see, I had read the trial transcript from Mr. Blake's successful 2005 federal lawsuit against New York

State for unconstitutional solitary confinement in the 1980s and 1990s. I was aware that he acted as his own attorney while handcuffed, with his feet shackled, and surrounded by five members of the New York State Correctional Emergency Response Team. Whether he sat, or stood at the podium in the courtroom, or addressed the jury or a witness, he was shadowed on either shoulder by a member of the team wearing a bullet-proof vest as he moved around the courtroom. So when I arrived at Great Meadow Correctional Facility (a maximum security prison) in Comstock, New York, I expected tight security and a highly monitored visit on the same level as what happened in federal court. I expected that the longest-held prisoner in administrative segregation in New York State would be treated like one of the most dangerous men alive. Was I ever wrong.

I walked into the visitors room unescorted. A corrections officer behind a counter in one corner assigned me a seat about twenty feet away from him and a second corrections officer. These two officers were the only ones in the room and they seemed to be responsible for overseeing the entire visiting area. A third officer may have stopped by to visit here and there. These officers didn't wear bullet proof vests and, if they were armed, they carried a simple wooden nightstick, maybe a canister of mace or pepper spray.

In this facility, inmates from solitary and inmates from the general population have visits in the same large room. It could easily seat over one hundred people. There was only one difference in treatment in the visiting room between inmates from solitary and inmates from the general population. It seemed to be that inmates from solitary were assigned seats closer to the counter where the two corrections officers were stationed. At the time of my first visit, there were about a dozen other inmates and visitors in the room.

When I saw Mr. Blake enter the room from the other end, he was unescorted, free from handcuffs and ankle chains. He walked past prisoners from the general population seated in the room on his way to greet me. Nobody seemed concerned that Mr. Blake would get into an altercation with any other prisoner or visitor in that room.

I stood up and shook his hand over a thigh-high steel counter no wider than three feet, with nothing but air between us. We sat down and talked non-stop for hours like two old friends sharing a meal at a diner. We talked for hours and feasted on food that I bought from the vending machines:

Twix bars, M&M's, potato chips, chicken nuggets, gas station sandwiches, and soda. It was a real treat for him to eat something other than the usual prison fare slipped to him through his cage's meal slot. I bought several glass bottles of Snapple Ice Tea for him from the vending machines. No corrections officer was concerned that he might break one of those bottles and use it as a weapon. I wasn't either.

Our conversation wasn't recorded. I sensed the corrections officer assigned our seats to aid a private conversation. Over the din of several ongoing conversations in the room, the two assigned corrections officers couldn't hear what we said. Nor did they show any particular interest in us.

Over the past few months, I have visited Mr. Blake three times for a total of over fifteen hours. At all times, the corrections officers on duty have acted with total respect toward Mr. Blake and me. They respected our privacy by leaving us alone. I visited the facility not as an author, former judge, or attorney, but as an average citizen. My visits to the prison were totally unannounced. They didn't know I was coming until I showed up at the entrance. Like anyone else on their first visit to a maximum security prison, I had problems passing security because I was unaware of some rules.

Not once during my three visits was I personally treated with anything but professionalism by the staff on duty. I didn't bear witness to unprofessional treatment of anyone else there, either, inmates or visitors alike.

I witnessed friendly first-name conversations between Mr. Blake and the corrections officers on duty in the visiting room. On one occasion, Mr. Blake commented that it was hot in the room. A corrections officer said he'd open the window for Mr. Blake because he never caused him problems while he was assigned to oversee prisoners in solitary. On another occasion, a corrections officer went out of his way to enter the visitor's room to ask Mr. Blake a question. Did he want to give me a calendar addressed to him that was too big for the package office to handle? Another corrections officer came over to our area and politely answered some questions about visitation rules.

At all times during my visits, Mr. Blake behaved well and the corrections officers treated him well. I sensed no friction between the corrections officers and Mr. Blake. The corrections officers were not concerned for my safety any more than they were concerned for the safety of any other visitor in that room. I never felt in danger.

And yet Mr. Blake has been housed in solitary for thirty-two years! At age fifty-five, is he truly one of the most dangerous men in New York State and perhaps in the country? Does he really need to be locked up alone for twenty-three hours per day in a six-foot by eight-foot cage? Why is Son of Sam, the notorious serial killer of seven people, circulating within the general population while Mr. Blake can't seem to get out of solitary? I have to ask myself, how many more prisoners are trapped in solitary confinement in New York State like Mr. Blake?

Actions always speak louder than words in my experience and the summary I've provided about my visits in this preface speaks volumes to me. I think you'll agree that there is something terribly wrong going on here. The good news is that you can do something about it.

As I write this preface, there is currently a bill before the New York State Legislature that will give Mr. Blake his first opportunity to live outside of solitary with the general population. I'm asking you to take a few seconds of your time to sign the petition that I've started on Change.Org at this link: https://smarturl.it/FreeBillyNow. Please tell your family and friends to sign it too. I know you're wondering how Mr. Blake got stuck in solitary. You can read much more about Mr. Blake's story in the petition.

You can always drop me a note through my website at TomSwyers.com.

Tom Swyers
Schenectady, NY
April 2, 2019

September 16, 2019 update. Even though the bill regulating solitary confinement had overwhelming support to pass in the New York Legislature in 2019, it failed to make it to the floor for a vote. Mr. Blake is still in solitary though he's been moved to Attica prison. The bill will be up for consideration again in 2020. Please join support the New York State Campaign for Alternatives to Isolated Confinement at http://smarturl.it/NYCAIC. *The only way to change the system is to change the law.*

ACKNOWLEDGMENTS

When I first started writing *Caged to Kill*, I didn't think that writing about solitary confinement would affect me so deeply. Was I ever wrong! To write this novel, I had to mentally put myself in a cell all alone. For the past two years, I had a taste of solitary confinement because I had to think about it, on average, about five or six hours per day while I sat at my keyboard. If I wasn't writing about solitary, I was researching it. The more and more I wrote about and performed research about the topic, the less and less I was able to, over time, seamlessly reenter my life away from my writing world. The daily transition from my writing and researching life in solitary to my everyday life became increasingly more difficult. Solitary confinement was getting to me and I hadn't even experienced it firsthand.

If *Caged to Kill* was difficult to write, it was certainly difficult to read and edit, not once, but multiple times. If it were not for my editor, Chris Perham, *Caged to Kill* would not exist. Period. Chris stood my side every step of the way, even while she went through major surgery not once, but twice, while the book was in production. She made it a point to get her latest round of edits to me before she went under the surgeon's knife each time over the span of a few months. Much of her post-surgery recovery phase was spent with the manuscript in hand while she painstakingly edited it one more time. She shares a passion for this novel and her support steered me to the finish line. She is one smart, tough lady and I know

Dennis, her husband, and Gayle, their dog, supported her throughout. I am indebted to the entire Perham family.

If it wasn't for Billy Blake, I wouldn't have been inspired to write this story. I talked about Billy earlier in the preface to this book, but I'd like to recount another story about him. I'll never forget the first time I visited him in his maximum-security home at Great Meadow Correctional Facility. It was January 23, 2019 and I had sent the manuscript to him a few weeks earlier. I was afraid it might be confiscated, but it made it to Billy intact. When I first met Billy he apologized profusely for not reading the entire book before my arrival. He said he had a difficult time concentrating because a mental-health inmate in solitary was screaming while banging on his steel walls around the clock. My jaw dropped as I imagined Billy lying on his back, on his mattress, on the floor, while he read my manuscript overhead, as some poor soul had a mental breakdown a few cells away. Billy was in hell, trying to read a novel about the hell he was living, while some poor soul was losing it in this hell a few cells away. And yet here was Billy politely apologizing to me for taking so long to read *Caged to Kill*.

Please take a few seconds of your time to sign the petition I linked to in the preface. It's time for Billy to get the opportunity to live outside of solitary confinement after thirty-two years alone. Here is the link: https://smarturl.it/FreeBillyNow.

I want to express my loving gratitude to my better half, Cher, and my family. Cher has always supported my writing passion and I'm so blessed to have her in my life since high school. My son, Randy, has always been there for me too. The same can be said for my parents, Dick and Betsy, and my mother-in-law, Arden, her best friend, Ellen, and my entire family. Thank you one and all.

I want to thank my wonderful group of early readers for their feedback and support. I've always said that a writer isn't much of anything without readers, and I'm blessed to have so many very loyal ones. Thank you for adopting this author!

Finally, I want to also express my gratitude to Marquina Iliev-Piselli, Sophia Heller, Maggie Graham, and Andrea McCoy for their special contributions. Each one took the time to help me in some phase of the book. Thank you for your kindness.

Made in the USA
Las Vegas, NV
13 September 2021